Praise f

"Williams renders the pass<del>...</del>
civilizations, with <del>...</del>

"Features a busy fa<del>...</del>
ous, memory-dama<del>...</del>
hero; even more my<del>...</del>
ions evincing varyi<del>...</del>
ment; wildly variou<del>...</del>
environments; murky pasts, secret histories, hidden agendas, sudden reversals, murky and shifting alliances; plus the usual amusements of chases, captures, escapes, kidnappings, rescues, befriendings, betrayals, and blowing stuff up."   —*Locus*

"The first in a promising new series from one of the few writers still producing consistently excellent space opera."
          —Don D'Ammassa, author of *Narcissus*

"Sean Williams entertains his readers . . . This is space opera at its very best with its exciting scenes and the descriptions of a puzzle that destroyed the structure of the known universe. Readers will like Imre, a combination of a hard and vulnerable person."   —*Alternative Worlds*

"An intriguing mix of balls-out space opera and head-spinning conspiracies that take in not only the end of civilization but also the nature of the self . . . The action sequences are exciting to read and the book's pace accelerates toward the end, leaving you eager to find out what happens next in this projected three-book series . . . well written, exciting, and surprisingly smart . . . *Saturn Returns* is a great little book, and I honestly look forward to the rest of the series."   —*SF Diplomat*

"Here's a space opera that spans the breadth of the Milky Way galaxy while it focuses on the similarly extant breadth of the internal spaces of humanity that make identity . . . Williams knows how to intrigue and maintains it throughout the novel by answering some questions but opening up bigger questions as the plot unfolds."   —*AntipodeanSF*

"Well written . . . a fast, thrilling, fun read that will give you a few things to think about too."   —*The Bookbag*

continued . . .

Praise for the novels of Sean Williams

"Splendid fun, brimming with heroes, villains, chicanery, neat imaginative details, some seriously cool space battles, and one of the most mind-twisting alien artifacts ever imagined."
—Alastair Reynolds, author of *The Prefect*

"Thoughtful and imaginative . . . superb."   —*Library Journal*

"One of the best writers of future noir thrillers around."
—*Emerald City*

"Full of the sense-of-wonder material that the new space opera wants to generate."   —*Locus*

"Convincingly realized . . . The vigorous narrative whiz[zes] along at hyperspeed."   —*Kirkus Reviews*

"Pure space opera with intriguing speculation."   —*VOYA*

"Expertly twists the familiar into the grotesque . . . deeply spooky."   —*Publishers Weekly*

"A dark and compelling tale."
—Fiona McIntosh, author of *Emissary*

"Compulsively readable, utterly enthralling, seriously disturbing. One of the best fantasy novels I've read in a long, long time."
—Sara Douglass, bestselling author of *The Serpent Bride*

"A master storyteller . . . a celebration of his wild talent."
—Jack Dann, Nebula and World Fantasy Award–winning author

For my beautiful wife, Amanda

I rose again——no matter how——
A woman, and a deeper fall——
I move amongst my people now
The most degraded of them all.
But, if in centuries to come,
I live once more and claim my own,
I'll see my subjects blind and dumb
Before they set me on a throne.

—Henry Lawson, "When I was King"

Contents:

The zodiacal House rising over the horizon at the moment of an individual's birth is said to have a profound effect on not just their developing consciousness but also the environment into which they have been born. To Vedic astrologers, this ascendant House is the defining element in a person's chart.

In other traditions, this ascendant House functions as a shield or mask behind which one's true nature can hide, especially in moments of great public stress.

"Jyotish," the Sanskrit term for Vedic astrology, comes from the words "jyothi," light, and "ish," God, and is occasionally referred to as the "Science of Light."

PROLEGOMENON

The apparition arrived in Dussehra unseen, seeping like argon gas into the cogs of an ancient and delicate timepiece.

First came questing packets along the Line, piggybacking on data streams from the system's closest neighbors in the Carina Arm—systems that had not been infected but which possessed a definite utility as launching grounds for the conquest of the region's most significant power. The Dussehran government maintained powerful defenses against many different sorts of semantic intrusion; a long series of filters, blockers, and choke points all had to be negotiated. The apparition's packets were nothing, however, if not prepared. They performed functions that, independent of each other, posed no threat. Only when they found suitable hosts and reassembled did their real work begin.

Over a million years earlier, Earth astrophysicist Nikolai Kardashev speculated about civilizations significantly more advanced than the one he belonged to. From humanity's fragile Type I beginnings, barely able to hold the entire globe in its grip, the galaxy's sole intelligent species had expanded to a Milky-Way-crossing Type III civilization, guided by self-evolved intelligences that would once have been considered godlike.

Now, the Forts were gone, and isolated pockets of civilization like Dussehra barely clung to Type II status, with habitation across its eight-world system, extensive mining and manufacturing capacities, and a not-inconsiderable space navy.

The apparition's agents had no intention of tackling the indigenous hardware head-on. There was no need for swift or precipitous action. Instead, the vanguard software located and infiltrated suitable processors and redirected material resources to new uses. Economic flows began to shift in numerous subtle and critical ways. Over centuries, phantom companies came and went, each responsible for making a single component in a machine that would enable the next phase of invasion. This was an economic as well as a military exercise. When Dussehra fell, it would do so without a single shot, long before it even realized it was being invaded.

The crucial machine was constructed on the very edge of the system, disguised as an exosperm gene-line prospector. It made subtle changes to the fabric of space, writing a series of zero-dimensional topological frame defects into the quantum foam, forming a self-preserving web of cellular automata. Imbued with structure and process, the web behaved like a string of words written in a complex vacuum code. This code, when complete, formed a software artifact—the true harbinger of war.

The apparition stirred, thinking its first true thoughts in the target system. Linked to the material universe solely through thin streams of leptons, it absorbed data and took stock. From afar it had planned its invasion, acting through dull, material things. Now it was actually present, and its mind was like quicksilver, utterly undetectable by those its master would soon rule.

With insubstantial, multiflavored limbs, it reached out and infiltrated every aspect of the Dussehran economy, using techniques it had employed many times before, in many other systems, as the years Absolute ticked by and the deadline for invasion approached. Already a torrent of vital data was pouring down the Line—data that needed to be stored in vast quantities until it was needed. Under the apparition's command, the unknowing citizens of the target system swarmed like ants in the construction of still more devices, all of them essential to the coming takeover.

Among other things, the Prime Sanctum of the First Church of the Return enjoyed an influx of capital that facilitated a complete rejuvenation of its inner chambers.

When the Prime Sanctum was ready, the apparition brought the Temple to full readiness. Sacred machines sparked into life, prompting a revolution among the faithful and an influx of converts. Rusted cogs began to turn; mired wheels spun at increasing rates. Finally, the Dussehran government began to notice. Investigators chipped at layers of security prepared decades before, but the knot of conspiracy was too densely tied to be undone overnight. Too late, the Dussehrans demanded that the church open its doors, issuing threats when those demands were not met. Legal channels were obfuscated, so troops mobilized. A cordon formed around the Temple and the new converts within. A tense silence fell, waiting for someone to explain what was going on.

The apparition said nothing. Thus far, everything had gone perfectly to plan. All was in place for a smooth, timely arrival. Ordinarily, it would not need to speak, for the one whose way it had prepared would be on the very threshold.

But something strange had happened. Everyone in the First Prime's party had arrived intact—Alphin Freer, Emlee Copas, Chyro Kells, and a retinue numbering in the dozens, all waiting the apparition's word to stir their random atoms into ordered life—but one of the hardcaster bays remained stubbornly empty. The most important one of all.

The apparition scanned the entire datasphere of the system, seeking the missing pieces of the puzzle. There had to be an explanation, and it had to be found before the Dussehrans learned how close their independent civilization was to falling. This, however, was an eventuality it had not been programmed to deal with. It wasn't programmed to act independently in all circumstances; the apparition might be vast and complex, outperforming even its creators' wild expectations, but it was not especially creative. Soon it would reach the limits of its capacity for invention and innovation, and then the invasion would be in trouble.

Even as it searched for the missing piece of the puzzle, the apparition couldn't fight the growing certainty that this was a mystery it could not solve. It began to consider which of the First Prime's companions it would wake, in order to ask them the one question it couldn't answer: *Why?*

Why the ghost of Imre Bergamasc was late.

THIS DISEASE

His ordinary manner had vanished. His ordinary occupations were neglected or forgotten. He roamed from chamber to chamber with hurried, unequal, and objectless step. The pallor of his countenance had assumed, if possible, a more ghastly hue—but the luminousness of his eye had utterly gone out.

—Edgar Allan Poe

"Awake, ruler of the realm," said a sepulchral voice. "I have stilled the ghastly river, and the throng has passed you by. We must speak for a moment, you and I. Evil things assail the monarch's high estate; evil things in robes of sorrow. Awake and smile no more."

Imre stirred, feeling none of the familiar fizz and tingle of life returning to hardcast limbs. His eyes, when he opened them, would not focus. He saw only a blur of shapes and colors no matter how he blinked and strained. The shapes might have composed a phantasmal face, but it wasn't one he recognized.

"Where am I?" he asked, horribly reminded of his awakening at the hands of the Jinc, the gestalt that had rescued his flawed pattern from the edge of the galaxy and rebuilt him incorrectly. His limbs were as indistinct as his sight. Only his mind was sharp, becoming keener by the second. "What's gone wrong?"

"Wanderers unto this unhappy valley have come." The voice was as hollow as an empty tomb. "A dimly remembered story of the old time—do you hear its echoes? Vast forms move fantastically to that distant, discordant melody. Let us mourn the radiant palace—and Thought's dominion, which died with it."

"Who are you?" Imre flailed about him but could feel no solid surfaces, no familiar sensations. Wherever he was, it wasn't a hardcaster sarcophagus. "What happened to the others? Start making sense, man."

"No man am I—nor seraph, nor good angel, nor spirit—nor king. In the olden time, long ago, I thought to sparkle evermore, but each day dawns more desolate than the last. Where once my home did blush and bloom, now all is pale . . . and hideoussssss—"

The voice dissolved into a sigh of such sibilance that it sounded like white noise rushing up to overwhelm the hallucination that had him in its grip. The blurry phantasm shivered and shook; however, Imre was now completely certain that this was no mere fantasy. He had been en route to Dussehra, the last he remembered, and only one kind of being would dare interrupt an encrypted hardcast. That this being moaned of fallen kingdoms and failed dreams only confirmed his guess.

"You're a Fort," he said, forcing him to accept the being's virtual embrace. There was some relief to be had in that acceptance: the world was blurry because it didn't exist, not because he had been revived incomplete. "You're what's left of a Fort, anyway—a partial, a splinter." Wariness turned to excitement. "I've been looking for things like you. Do you know that? Is that why you've brought me here?"

The hiss retreated a degree but didn't quite coalesce into words.

"What was your name?" Imre persisted. "How did you survive the Slow Wave? I've found some partials in the hearts of clusters out on the rim, where stars are so close together the frags never used Q loop technology to connect. I've found them in supersystems and in the hearts of dust clouds. They're fragile, but they're there. It's important for you to know that you're not alone. You're not the only one who made it. There's still hope."

"—ssssuch wit and wisdom!" returned the voice, snapping out of static like a whip. "While your troops dally in this greenest of valleys, who guards *your* fair and stately palace?

Who stands on the ramparts with eyes for the door? Who stands watch by your throne? One comes winged, his glory well befitting, and you, monarch, would best be there to greet him."

Imre had no body in this virtual world, but still he felt as though copper wires had threaded through his veins. "Who's coming? Coming where?"

"Round about your ruby home, your glory, spirits move, pallid but dutiful. Be there, ruler of the realm, to open your red-lit windows and bid him enter. Be there."

"You want me to return to Earth—is that what you're telling me?"

"The message is delivered," breathed the voice. "This maliceful hermit is free at last to expire. Rejoin the river flowing, flowing, flowing past all that is beautiful. Fly your banners, porphyrogene. This—all this ruin—is your dominion."

"No, wait," Imre cried.

It was too late. The blurry artificial world was already fading. All sensation of mouth and lips dissolved, reducing his voice to a series of pitiful vowels. The hiss returned. White mist swallowed the blurry nothingness. A smell like rotting rose petals hit him, and he fell into darkness.

"First Prime?" A hand touched his shoulder and gently rocked him. "First Prime, can you hear me?"

Every cell in his body shuddered at the rude double-awakening. This time, yes, he felt the familiar jolt of hardcast resurrection, of memories and personality assembling themselves from a myriad of dead cells and becoming, strangely, him. It always took a moment for nerves to synchronize and blood to warm. Just hours ago he had been nothing but data, suspended in the Apparatus's vast memory; and before that he had lived in another body, one that had been destroyed in order to turn it into light; and now he was here, reanimated, reborn . . .

"Get out of the way." A woman's voice cut across his drifting thoughts. Shadows moved over his flickering eyelids, and he was shaken more roughly. "Imre, wake up. We know you're conscious; the Apparatus quickened you a minute ago. Answer me, or I'll have you shocked into life."

"Emlee?" His vocal cords were as good as new—they had, in fact, never been used—but still his voice emerged as a croak. "It's all right."

"Don't be so sure about that." People moved about him, fussing, and he didn't have the strength yet to wave them away. "Where have you been? What was it this time—another one of your unscheduled pit stops?"

He frowned. The memory was clear, not fading like a dream—and he had never dreamed during a hardcast before. It was supposed to be impossible.

"Unscheduled for all of us," he said, blinking up into her familiar face. She had had brown eyes on Hyperabad, he remembered, but she had returned them afterward to a brilliant jade green, the way he had remembered her from his former life. A helmet of blond hair framed her oval face. Even when she was angry—as she was at present and seemed so often to be—he could see how many men and women found her beautiful. Her jaw when it clenched gave her a defiant, almost masculine air.

She reached down into the sarcophagus and irresistibly hauled him upright. He braced himself with clumsy hands on the casket's metallic sides while the world turned.

"I hope what you found was worth it," she said. "You've really screwed things up this time."

The message is delivered, the phantom had said. *One comes . . .*

"I have to go back to Earth," he said, feeling the certainty of it in his bones; but Emlee was already gone, replaced by the fussy, antiseptic presence of Chyro Kells. His chief surgeon hadn't changed at all since Hyperabad. Kells's round features remained utterly hairless except for a neatly trimmed black goatee. More than twenty acolytes and aides filled the chamber behind them, making the spacious room feel crowded. He couldn't tell if Emlee had heard what he said or not.

Kells's lips pursed moistly as he examined his subject, using touch as well as instruments extruded from the sleeves of his long, white coat. His stubby but sensitive fingers ran down Imre's back and across his shoulders, then down each arm to his hands. His focused stare saw nothing but processes in front of him rather than flesh. He was good with patterns— their shapes, flows, and flaws—and that made him an excellent posthardcast examiner. Sharp eyes inspected the stump of the missing little finger on Imre's left hand. "You still won't let me fix this, no?"

"No, Chyro. It stays."

"You're definitely you." The surgeon breathed noisily through his nostrils as he continued his meticulous examination. "You feel well, yes?"

Imre nodded, knowing it was better to let the man work uninterrupted. Impatience boiled in him, but Emlee had said something about a screwup. He would at least need to debrief her before leaving the system.

What was its name? He accessed a list chock-full of planets and systems that needed to be annexed on his latest whistle-stop tour of the galaxy. Dussehra?

Kells stepped back, satisfied. "I detect no trace of corruption. The hardcast is sound."

"Good." Imre swung his legs up and out of the sarcophagus. He hadn't lied about feeling well; given a moment or two to catch its wind, his new body had dusted off as good as his old one, nothing now but random atoms hundreds of light-years away. "You said something about a problem, Emlee?"

She talked while he dressed, unembarrassed by the presence of orderlies and acolytes. "You're four weeks late," she said, leaning against a door frame with her arms folded. "The timing's all fouled up because of it. Ordinarily, it wouldn't have been a problem, but the locals got wise earlier than expected, and the spook panicked. It woke Al in your place, to ask for advice."

"And?"

Her expression didn't change. "There have been some complications."

"Fuck. Why didn't it wake you first?" He stepped forward, dressed at last, and flexed his armor-clad limbs. The ceremonial suit was ornate—ivory white with purple-and-gold trim suggestive of military insignia and medals—but perfectly functional underneath the frills. Emlee wore similar garb minus the accoutrements of power. The Henschke Sloan repeater at her side was pure business.

She briskly saluted. "Why would it wake me? I'm just the bodyguard."

He didn't need to respond to that. "Where is Al?"

"Through here." The aides parted, and Emlee led him to a door that remained resolutely shut as they approached. Imre recognized the design: every Prime Sanctum in every occupied system was drawn from a small number of possible plans, broadcast to the faithful down the Line. Any variations were soon smoothed out by the Apparatus when it arrived. The doors were comprehensively blastproof and would resist most determined efforts to open them from the outside. Only three biometric signatures would open a door from within, and the locks required a pair in order to function. Imre and Emlee were two of the signatures; Al Freer was the third. Imre wondered how long Emlee and the acolytes had been locked in before his arrival.

Four weeks, he thought. That was long enough for someone to reassemble his intercepted hardcast, give it a kind of life in a virtual environment, then send it on its way again to Dussehra. Irritating it might be, but it made sense.

The locks hummed audibly, then clicked. With a soft hiss, the blast door slid aside, revealing a corridor lined with gilt-and-silver ornaments, mostly of animals belonging to genera Imre found no more than superficially familiar. A metallic wall hanging on the far side tinkled melodically as air pressures equalized. There was no one waiting for them; Al must be in a chamber nearby, he presumed, with representatives of the local authority, perhaps.

Imre hesitated on the threshold, aware that when he crossed it, he would be out of the familiar and into the unknown. That thought wearied him but not because he had become jaded by novelty. Dussehra was considered a world of strategic importance in this neighborhood of the galaxy. In the context of the wider galaxy, however, it was just a dot. There were hundreds of worlds like it—perhaps thousands. What mattered if it

signed up or not? Why did he have to go through the same ne-
gotiations, time after time, when in the end it might make no
difference at all?

Emlee was watching him. Her scrutiny was like a knife
dragged across his skin, as though at any moment she might
change the angle of her sweep and dig in.

"Are you all right?" he asked her.

"Right as reindeer. Why?"

"There's something you're not telling me."

She glanced at Kells, who stood within earshot, waiting to
follow them through the door. "Our friends were here before
us," she said, leaning microscopically closer. "They killed another Fort revival dead in its tracks. The Apparatus stumbled
on it while trawling through historical records."

"How long ago?" he asked, sharing her interest in the revelation.

"Doesn't matter. I'll fill you in later."

"Tell me this, at least: both groups, or just one?"

"Both."

He nodded. Luminous and Barons, then, here on this world
that might or might not be important. That was unexpected
and confusing.

"I don't know what happened to you on the way here," she
said, "but I want you to remember this: we're twenty thousand
light-years from Sol. If we leave now, there's no guarantee
anything will be left here when we get back. We've got one
shot at this. We have to take it."

He nodded again. So she had heard him—and she was
making sense. But the phantasm had been insistent.

You, monarch, would best be there to greet him.

He was torn.

Imre stepped forward, over the threshold, thinking that
there would be no harm in putting in an appearance before de-
ciding which way to jump.

The explosion ripped through the wall to his right, thrusting
him into Emlee and throwing both of them against the far wall.
The fierce punch of energy deafened him instantly. His suit's
self-protection systems kicked in a microsecond later. Blinded,
agonized, disoriented, he felt darkness creeping over him again.

Resisting it, he upped the tempo of his Prime body—undoubtedly damaged but still retaining some function—and forced himself to remain conscious.

He had fallen over and was lying on what was left of his right arm. The awareness of pain was optional; he could feel it blaring through his nervous system, demanding attention. His suit was responding faster than he could, sending neural patches through his skin in an attempt to restore his senses. Hellish glimpses came and went, of the blackened, smoke-filled corridor and body parts strewn all around. Were any of them his? He couldn't tell.

Armed figures ran in slow motion out of the smoke. He tried to stand but failed. In his ears he heard nothing but a loud shrieking that could have been alarms or tinnitus, or both. Something moved close by: a hand. It took him a moment to realize that it was his, his left hand reaching through the rubble for the figure lying next to him, rolling it over without his conscious intent.

Emlee's face was mostly gone, torn away by the blast. A red mask, jagged and inhuman, took its place, where a wash of blood had rapidly congealed, forming a seal to prevent contaminants entering the wound. She didn't seem to be conscious. A jagged piece of metal ran right through her chest. He was shocked at how badly hurt she was. He had been standing between her and the blast. What did he look like?

He found her pistol before the figures arrived and unevenly brandished it at them, in case their intent was hostile. He couldn't stand for some reason, but he wasn't completely finished. They ignored the warning and formed a cordon around him, presumably guards from the Temple although their uniform was unfamiliar. The tallest, a man, loomed over him, tugging off his helmet with a single, grim movement.

Alphin Freer kneeled down beside Imre, concern and apology in his eyes. No anger yet; Imre knew that would come later, and woe to the person responsible for this attempt on his life. Freer's lips moved. Imre couldn't hear what he said. The suit's sensory integration assigned audio a lower priority than vision.

"I'm all right," Imre tried to say. "Check the others."

If Freer understood, he ignored Imre and barked a series of

orders to the guards. Imre was lifted up and, his protests ignored, carried back into the Prime Sanctum. The guards stepped through a sea of carnage, the remains of the relatively unprotected aides and acolytes in a grisly tangle. Walls were blackened and blood-spattered, but the physical barriers appeared to have held. The shock wave had made mincemeat of flesh, not armor.

Chyro Kells's severed head lay at the base of the hardcast sarcophagus. One of the guards nudged it aside with his foot as Imre was lowered like a discarded doll back into place. He resisted, but there was nothing he could do. He only had one working arm, and it looked as though his legs had been completely severed. The shrieking continued louder than ever. He felt as though a drill bit was spinning behind his eyes.

Freer appeared again, looming over him with thin lips tightened. "Keep him here," said those lips clearly, the words intended to be read by Imre's makeshift senses, "until I say it's safe."

"Wait, Al," he tried to say. "Emlee—"

The big man was already out of his line of sight. Giving up in frustration, Imre let himself fall back into the sarcophagus and close his eyes.

Sensing his repose, the suit and his injured body pressed again for him to sleep. Still he resisted, patching flickering, static-filled channels to senses more robust than sight or hearing and opening a channel direct to the suit. A few minutes' tinkering saw him connected to its comms and seeking a link to the outside world.

"Apparatus," he said over an encrypted line, letting the message flow as simple text rather than spoken words. "Apparatus, can you hear me?"

The shriek ebbed in stages until blessed silence fell. A dozen clicks and buzzes sounded as the suit reactivated the auditory centers of his brain, then the AI said with perfect clarity, as though standing directly beside him, "I hear you, Imre."

"What's going on out there? Specifically, what just happened in the entrance hall to the Prime Sanctum?"

"The explosive device appears to have been secreted between insulating layers—"

"Skip the details. Tell me if there was just the one bomb, or if more have exploded. Is the Temple under attack?"

"There have been no further explosions. This appears to be an isolated act of sabotage."

Imre thought of the acolytes and Kells's head, and wondered if even now, somewhere, Emlee was dying. Sabotage sounded a lot less unpalatable than murder or assassination.

There was nothing he could do about it now. Watching Freer pick through the pieces didn't appeal.

"Fill me in on what's been happening in the system since you arrived," he told the Apparatus. "Emlee was going to, but I doubt she'll be up to that for a while."

"Yes, Imre."

The AI's voice was calm and calming. Imre let it wash through him, cleansing him of his immediate concerns, while he waited for Alphin Freer to return with bad news.

It came as no great surprise that he had forgotten how many times people had tried to kill him—especially after so many military campaigns with the Corps and earlier—but it did surprise him that he had lost count of the assassination attempts since taking control of the galaxy. Including poisonings, shootings, and infections by biological and nanotech agents, he figured the number must be getting close to one hundred. The Apparatus would know, but that was one question he didn't want to ask.

Instead, he let it drone placidly on about Earth-sized, temperate Dussehra and its incumbent government, the Gravamen, who exploited a pervading suspicion of the Returned Continuum to cling to power. They had nothing to offer their billion-odd citizens but xenophobia, retrogressive and isolationist policies, and a skewed vision of galactic history since the Slow Wave; but the poison was proving difficult to dilute. Rumors of massacres elsewhere, of civilizations wiped out for resisting the galactic rule, didn't help. The Apparatus had had little luck so far isolating their source.

Dussehra was little different, then, from the many other worlds Imre had visited on his fourth whistle-stop tour since annexing Earth. There were many more to come. If he had dreamed his encounter with the mysterious phantasm, then no wonder. The thought of returning to Earth was a powerful one—but for what purpose? He couldn't hide there. His responsibilities followed him everywhere, along with the threats. He would be under pressure and endangered no matter where he was, so he might as well be out in the field, doing some good.

He hoped that was what he was doing. Governing a galactic empire was a difficult job for anyone, let alone a single Prime, one of an uncountable horde filling the galaxy from edge to edge. Possessing only the barest modifications to the ancient human form—all designed to increase physical robustness and enable access to external data sources—Primes had once been considered the basic disposable unit of civilization. They came and went in the blink of a cosmic eye, breeding and dying in their billions, on millions of worlds. Only a few lived longer than a thousand years, Absolute, although indefinite life extension was available to all in most civilized regimes. Those who wanted to live longer usually advanced to the singleton caste, in which state many more-evolved options were available.

Imre styled himself as First Prime to make an ideological point—and to send a message to those who opposed him. "I am but one man," he had broadcast once in a speech sent down every Line in the galaxy, "and this man stands at the summit of a pyramid of unimaginable size. Primes have survived when Forts have fallen and thrived where singletons have failed. We are the face of humanity; its heart is our heart. We are the past and the future of the human race. We will never again surrender control of our worlds—even to those we think of as gods, even if they say they have our best interests at heart. The Slow Wave proved the danger of placing too much faith in someone whose goals are not our own. We will never make that mistake again."

Primes, for the most part, responded to his plea for unity. Singletons went along with it because they were relatively few and too scattered to mount a vigorous resistance. Besides, his open acknowledgement of their talents, plus his promotion of two singletons to his intimate staff, assured them that he wasn't deaf to their needs. There was more to it than that, of course, just as there was more to his mission than running the galaxy, but the Returned Continuum didn't need to know that.

Freer sent a message informing him that a local surgeon had been contracted to take the place of Chyro Kells. Emlee was receiving treatment first, since her condition was not yet stable. Also, Imre suspected, to test that the replacement could be trusted. He felt a pang of remorse for those caught in the cross fire and quickly suppressed the emotion. They had known the risks. It wasn't his fault someone had managed to get so close to the Prime Sanctum.

He came to two conclusions while he awaited the surgeon.

First: armor for everyone at their next stop. He was sure Emlee wouldn't argue with that one if she survived.

Second: this attempt was most likely an inside job. Temple security was tight even on borderline worlds—too tight for an outsider to come so close. If that theory proved correct, heads would have to roll—but what effect would that have on Dussehra's already unstable politics?

A dull thud rolled through the sarcophagus's base and through his tangled nerves.

"What was that?"

"There has been a second explosion," the Apparatus informed him.

"Where?"

"In an unoccupied quarter of the Temple. No injuries have been reported."

"What quarter, exactly?"

"F-MAP."

The fermion manipulation and processing plant, he interpreted with a sinking feeling. "Are you telling me the hard-caster has been damaged?"

"That appears to be so, yes."

Imre shut off the link to the Apparatus. If the AI had had ears, they would've blistered.

He was twenty thousand light-years from home, and now he had no way of getting there.

When he felt calmer, he reopened the link.

"Conduct a damage assessment immediately. Let me know how long it will take to fix."

"Yes, Imre."

"And get that local medic here as soon as Emlee is stable. I'm tired of lying around like a slab of meat."

"Yes, Imre."

"Do you have any good news for me? Anything at all?"

"I have located a woman who appears to be Helwise MacPhedron."

That revelation provoked a mixed reaction, one he carefully kept to himself. " 'Appears to be'? She must be hiding, then."

"Yes."

"Good. So tag her and let her go about her business. She has obviously got the message."

His senses crackled and flashed as the suit attempted once again to supplement them with its own data. He endured the distraction until it finished, and black silence descended again. This time he welcomed it. Feeling exhausted but satisfied that he had done everything he could, under the circumstances, he let himself drift on a tide of natural and artificial endorphins, absorbing everything that had happened since he had left the last world on his tour. Oxenbould: a peaceful system, home to an introverted society that had, at first, resisted the advances of the Returned Continuum. A mixture of smooth talk and bribery had greased the way so thoroughly that, when he and his retinue had left, there had been no need to install one of Freer's singletons as a caretaker.

Already Dussehra was proving difficult. Imre felt safe assuming that it was only going to get worse as the day wore on.

When he became naturally weary, he allowed himself to sleep. Immediately, he dreamed a disorienting mixture of the phantasm and a slow drip-feed of Render's reports from Earth. While a large part of his conscious mind rested, isolated corners took note of each detail, integrating it for later appraisal. Thus did he always take stock in each new system on his whistle-stop tours. The secrets Render transmitted were frank, fleeting things that never appeared in official reports. Some details might be obscured when he awoke, but the impression would remain.

Evil things assail the monarch's high estate . . .

The skies of Earth were still blue, from orbit and from the ground. Few people were allowed on the surface; the Returned Continuum's administrative arm operated chiefly from space, with branches in every system of the Round, those astrographically and politically closest to Earth. Imre maintained a court and a retreat on the surface of the home world—both on the island of Paratlantis, connected to Smitherman City in geostationary orbit by a skyline that was almost as old as civilization itself. There, superior aides conducted audiences with diplomats and penitents, strengthening the ties that kept the Returned Continuum together.

That was the theory, anyway.

"Some people disgust me," rasped Render into his dream. A succession of images flowed through his mind, unconnected, disorienting. Faces mainly, with context maps attached. The details flickered by, too staccato to blur, too numerous to sink in. Arguments flared up, died away, flared up anew. It had been several centuries since the last report. Although much of the administration experienced time at a slower tempo than Absolute, Render preferred to live out the years. That made him a thorough, if sometimes madding, observer.

"Is it any wonder?" Render muttered over the endless parade of faces.

Round about your ruby home, your glory, spirits move, pallid but dutiful . . .

During the heady days of the Mad Times, when the Corps had turned on its Fort masters, dragging thousands of systems into the fray, it had been impossible to avoid taking sides. That reflected, possibly, Imre's role in the unfolding drama and the kind of people he associated with—on battlefields, in debriefing sessions, in secret meetings. The same could be said of the Returned Continuum: a certain polarization of opinion came into play long before anyone arrived in Imre's office. The only way, therefore, to learn what the populace was really thinking was to go out among them and take the occasional bullet.

"We generate lies, like you're supposed to. We generate a reason for living." Render's mingled contempt and amusement was unrestrained as delegates gathered for a State of the Continuum muster. Thousands upon thousands of humans in a wide variety of forms crammed under the palace's Astral Dome to hear the Regent's centennial address. The space was modeled after an eighteenth-century French court, with a curving, baby blue ceiling decorated in ivory-and-silver representations of the zodiac and the planets in their traditional, prespace roles. Mars glowered; Mercury flew on feathered wings; Gemini cherubs embraced each other. The slender, robed woman at the focus of the delegates' combined gaze was barely visible, drowned by sheer numbers, but her presence filled the room.

Mother Turin, they still called her, the Regent of the Returned Continuum. Imre knew her better as Helwise MacPhedron. The sight of her veiled form sent a ripple of dread down his spine.

Who guards your fair and stately palace? Who stands on the ramparts with eyes for the door? Who stands watch by your throne?

"This is all just show."

Sometimes Imre agreed, but what choice did he have? Helwise had put him on his throne. Without the First Church of the Return behind him, he would never have whipped up support so quickly on Hyperabad, then in Mandala Supersystem, then ridden that popular wave across the galaxy, gathering momentum as he went. That she had originally invented the religion as a means of snaring other versions of herself in order to kill them was irrelevant.

The end justified the means—but the means remained, long after the end had been achieved. All he could do was be wary of her and warn away other versions of her, lest they fall victim to her as well—or to the same murderous urges she followed. He wasn't the only person enduring the occasional assassination attempt.

Theirs was a tense, finely balanced collaboration that had

lasted far longer than some people had believed—Render among them. And there were contingencies in place, checks and balances he had spoken of to no one and prayed never to need.

Fly your banners, porphyrogene. This—all this ruin—is your dominion.

The phantom's odd word choice puzzled Imre in his state of half-dreaming. It had the ring of something ancient, and he had meant to look up the term immediately on arriving in Dussehra. Circumstances had distracted him, as the dream distracted him now.

"This is the art of survival."

The relentless parade of faces and schemes finally gave way to a catalog of natural disasters: unexpected starbursts, environmental mismanagement, and plagues of novel viruses among them. The galaxy never failed to provide new ways to keep things interesting. Imre let his grip on the information slip in order to sink deeper into unconsciousness. His dreams became darker and more chaotic, lit with flashes of crimson.

Be there, ruler of the realm, to open your red-lit windows and bid him enter. Be there.

The voice of the phantasm pursued him across the killing fields of his psyche, calling a name that no longer sounded familiar, even though it was his own.

"You're not going anywhere without a full escort," Freer said as the two of them left the Prime Sanctum, flanked by guards in faceless armor and with heavy rifles held at the ready. "Not until this is sorted out."

Imre didn't so much walk as glide, held vertically upright by a novel mechanical-assist field prosthetic that healed him at the same time it allowed him to move. He felt like a mobile corpse but was grateful to be out of the sarcophagus.

"Do you have any suspects?"

"That's where I'm taking you now." Freer walked with long, lazy-looking strides; his eyes swept every centimeter of the way ahead, even though Imre assumed bomb squads had scanned it thoroughly. The damaged portion of the corridor had turned from black to a creamy white, bandaided over by quick-setting enamel. "They weren't trying to hide. We caught them on the Temple grounds, claiming to have killed you and spouting propaganda. I think they're members of a suicide squad that couldn't get close enough to do the job properly."

"The usual line, I assume."

"You assume correctly." Freer's cheekbones seemed higher and more severe than ever. "They confessed. I've extracted anything else we're likely to get from them." They came to a locked door, which Freer opened with a gesture. "Basically, I've brought you here to witness their execution."

The words, overheard by the five held at gunpoint as he glided into the room, had the intended effect. One dropped to his knees with a moan; another laughed mockingly; the remaining three just looked frightened and pale.

Fall guy, ringleader, and troopers, Imre thought. All eyes were on his battered, half-skinned face. It was easy to seem impassive, even if on the inside he seethed. In the field, he would have behaved very differently when confronted with people who had tried to kill him. They wouldn't have been talking, for one.

Information on the prisoners came from Freer through Imre's private back door. Singletons, all of them.

"I'm told you belong to something called the Liberation Jihad," he said. "Is that true?"

"Know us by our actions," said the ringleader, his dark-rimmed eyes resentful. His cheeks were sunken, as though he had been hollowed out from the inside. "We won't beg for mercy."

"Good, because it won't make any difference." He held the man's stare, felt the pointless, self-devouring heat of it. "How can you be liberated when you haven't been repressed yet?" Gesturing at one of the armed guards then at the woman on her knees, he said, "Shoot her first, then the others. I want their bodies utterly destroyed."

"No." The threat roused the woman from her despair. "You can't do that."

Imre stayed the guard, who had already raised his rifle and

taken aim. "Of course I can. Shooting you wouldn't be sufficient punishment. You're a singleton. You don't really die. All
I can do is take your memories with you. Where are they
stored? In your brain? In your left breast, near where a
Prime's heart rests? The only way I can punish you—the rest
of you, wherever they are—is by robbing them of the chance
to know what you did and how this body died."

"You are a monster."

"Nonsense. If I were, I'd kill every other version of you
and leave you five alive—alone forever, somewhere dark."

"You'll never stop us," the ringleader said. "We're everywhere, all around you. Once word gets out that we failed,
we'll try again. And we'll keep on trying until one of us finishes the job."

"Do you think you're the first to threaten me this way? Do
you think you'll be the last?" Imre addressed the guards once
more. "Kill the others but let him go. He doesn't frighten
me."

Imre swiveled on the spot and glided for the door. The first
shot rang out behind him, then three more in quick succession. He had no intention of sticking around for the disposal
of the bodies. The ringleader made no attempt to call after
him; he uttered no threats or pleas; and Imre was glad for that.
He hoped the message had sunk in.

I could have killed you, but I didn't. I could have taken
your memories of your friends' deaths along with their lives,
but I didn't. I could at least have lectured you on my grand
plan for Dussehra before letting you go, but I didn't do that
either.

"That's what it's all about," he said to Freer, who had followed him out of the room and resumed guiding him through
the Temple. A feeling of exhaustion plagued him, physical
and mental. "Getting the message across, one way or another."

"You really think he'll spout a different view of things
when he gets out of here?"

"His friends will listen to him differently when they learn
that he's the only one who survived."

"You're kinder than I am." Freer indicated that they should

turn left at a T-junction into an area even more ornately decorated than the last. Gilt edges gleamed everywhere he looked. "You have a faith in human nature that I lack."

"Don't call it a lack, Al. You're probably better off without it. And I'm definitely better off with you just the way you are."

"I am your last resort," the tall soldier intoned in a voice that was either deadpan or just dead. "Over and over again."

"What would I do without you?"

The question was rhetorical; the sentiments were perennial. Such were the woes of someone trying to run the galaxy. Dissidents couldn't be avoided, but they couldn't be allowed to jam the vast machinery of governance either. Best to seem decisive and cold than let his doubts get the better of him.

Freer guided him into an audience chamber and introduced him to three high-ranking priests, his first encounter with the local population, apart from the surgeon who had put him in the field prosthetic. The church was staffed with numerous such prelates, most of whom were abroad at that moment, spreading word of Imre's arrival. They offered no moral codes or creeds, beyond the fact that civilization would one day be restored to its former height if humanity banded together under the banner of the Returned Continuum, in the name of the First Prime. The church had no position of highest authority on Dussehra, reserving that for Imre himself and employing his usual absence as a key assumption of that particular meme. It would hardly have been a Church of the Return unless some kind of return remained to be delivered upon.

Ministers Tilda, Kellow, and Sevaste were bony and sallow-skinned, wearing bright orange robes and tiny bells dangling from their wrists. They too reacted at his appearance in a field prosthetic. He didn't give them time to ask about his well-being.

"Your first priority," he told them, "is to ensure the security of everyone within this compound. I don't want any more deaths—anyone at all. Then I want an audience with Gravaman Zerah. Organize that as soon as possible." The Apparatus had given him the name of the highest-ranking person in the local government. He would speak directly with no one less. "Once that's in train, I want the Temple itself repaired. Every available technician is to overclock until the hardcaster is fully operational. Understood?"

The smallest of the priests, Minister Sevaste, bowed her shaven head. A three-note melodic tinkling accompanied the movement. "We understand, First Prime. Is your presence on our world to remain a secret no longer?"

"No," he said, "unless your leaders would risk something as stupid as a nuclear strike or orbital bombardment . . . ?" He glanced at Freer, who shook his head. "It's not my way to hide in the shadows. Until the Gravamen name themselves as such, I will not call them my enemy. Neither will I allow the actions of a rogue element to determine my course. I have no grievance with the people of Dussehra. We proceed as we would on any world."

The priests nodded. They didn't need to speak their reservations aloud for him to sense them. The Gravamen were powerful. Zerah wouldn't easily be turned. Words alone weren't likely to do the trick, especially when they came from a Prime visibly scarred by the latest attempt on his life.

And there had been conflict already. The Temple had been stormed twice by security arms of the local government. Freer had been on hand to help the priests repel the second invasion, but it hadn't been easy. Several dozen people had died. Security forces remained poised around the Temple, occupying several evacuated city blocks.

The arrival of the Returned Continuum had certainly attracted attention. Fierce gun battles and innocent civilians being shot down, however, wasn't the kind of attention he wanted.

This was a military campaign, he wanted to reassure the priests, but not every military campaign was conducted with weapons and armies. If numbers alone led to victory, he should have given up the Returned Continuum as a lost cause before starting. The Gravamen might think they could win the battle for its people's hearts on Dussehra, but they would never win the war. Imre had the higher ground in more ways than he could count.

"Go about your duties," he told them. "I am available to you should you have any questions."

"Yes, First Prime." All three averted their eyes. Only Minister Sevaste looked up as she backed out of the room. Her irises were a strikingly clear blue. They contained more confidence than she had let show at any other point during the interview. It threw him slightly, this small glimpse into her inner life.

"Is this room secure?" he asked Freer, when the ministers were gone.

"Airtight." Freer gestured to the guards, who stepped outside and took up stations by the door. The portal slid silently shut.

"Good. Now, tell me what you think I should do."

Freer folded his arms across his armored chest. "Well, apart from being holed up in here, we're in a pretty good position. The spook has infiltrated the networks we need to hold the government to ransom. We can shut down the media, health and transport systems, and power supplies, at your word. We can put the military forces in a tailspin by faking orders from the Gravamen and setting them at each other's throats. We can tear Dussehra apart, piece by piece, and put it back together any way we want—all without leaving this room." His grey gaze slid like oil across the ornate walls of the antechamber and returned to Imre's untouched. "That would be your last resort, of course. Messy and not without risks. We're not indestructible, after all. The diplomatic solution, with a bit of leverage, would be better all around, I think."

Imre nodded. The raw, healing skin of his face itched as though ants were burrowing through it. Memetic engineering was long-established science; Dussehra would indeed come around eventually, with the right nudges in the right places, at the right times. But the process was time-consuming and imprecise. Even with the media firmly in their control, it could take decades. There were too many variables in a population this size.

"No wonder Emlee was grouchy because I arrived late," he said.

"Hardly," said Freer with a rare smile. "I think she was worried about you."

"Now that's just crazy." He returned the levity, briefly. "I want to wrap this up quickly, Al, because there's somewhere else I need to be. Apparatus, how long until the hardcaster is fixed?"

"One week," answered the ethereal AI.

"That's not long enough," said Freer. "Mind telling me where you're rushing off to?"

"Earth."

"Why?"

Imre described what he had experienced during the hardcast transmission. *Be there.* "I didn't imagine it. The message was real."

"That doesn't make it worth listening to. How do you know you can trust this supposed partial? How do you know it isn't misdirection—or a trap?"

"Set by whom? Why?"

"By the Barons."

"I don't think they're this kind of threat to us. I was told that if we stayed away from Domgard, we'd be left alone."

"Right enough, assuming they can be trusted. But we're gaining ground out here, Imre. Who knows what we're getting close to? You could be running away from the very thing you've been looking for all this time."

Imre knew what Freer was talking about. He meant the truth about Domgard. Imre took it to mean something more. He was looking for *Himself* as well, the former incarnation of Imre Bergamasc who appeared to be connected to the mysterious Domgard. The Apparatus had yet to find any definite sign of his continued existence.

"Dussehra isn't special," Imre said. "It's a breakaway system no different than many others."

"The Luminous were here."

"I know. Emlee told me. And the Barons were here too. But we've found such intersections before, and they've led nowhere. Why should this one be any different?"

"Why shouldn't it be? If Domgard is hidden, this is just the kind of place you might hide it."

"The purloined letter?"

"Exactly."

"By that argument, it as likely to be anywhere. Earth, even."

"You know it's not."

"I don't know anything at the moment, Al." Imre squirmed in frustration, aching to pace, to stretch his limbs, but held immobile in the tight embrace of the field prosthetic. "How's Emlee doing?"

"She'll be awake in a couple of hours. Don't expect her to be much use to anyone for a while. She's undergoing extensive reconstruction."

Another reason to stay. Imre wouldn't leave without her, and it could be risky to interrupt her treatment to put her in the hardcaster.

"All right," he said. "Let's talk to Gravaman Zerah and see how it goes. But I'm not promising anything. If I see no compelling reason to be here, I'm not going to stay any longer than I have to."

Freer inclined his head in acknowledgment. "That decision is, of course, your own."

There was no trace of mockery in Freer's tone. None at all, and Imre would have been shocked to hear it. Freer was an excellent military adviser, one who wasn't afraid to speak his mind, but he had no desire at all to be the ultimate commander. He worked best when implementing policy, not coming up with his own. If, together, they could work out the best strategy to take with Dussehra, Imre would have no compunctions at all about leaving. He could trust Freer with his life and his life's work both.

"I'll look at the Luminous data now," Imre told him, "and any Line fragments the Apparatus might have collected. Is there somewhere I can go for privacy? I'm not up to meeting anyone else until I'm out of this thing."

"There are quarters prepared for you. I'll take you there in a moment. Should I notify you if we hear from Zerah?"

"Of course, and of any significant changes."

"Will do." Freer moved toward the door. "Just let me say this: I don't for a second believe that we've rooted out everyone involved in the sabotage. There'll be at least one more, buried deep. This isn't over yet."

"I know." And Freer knew that he knew. Saying it aloud was the career soldier's way of making sure that every angle had been covered. "We're ready for it now. I'm not concerned."

Freer nodded once, neither fazed nor reassured by Imre's confidence.

His quarters were luxurious but not embarrassingly so, as they were on some worlds. Wall hangings in red and gold depicted stylized scenes from the system's history, none of which Imre recognized. The bed was square and set into the floor; it rose and fell at his spoken command. An elegant lounge and two chairs occupied an entry foyer opposite the bed, near a desk tucked away in an alcove, fashioned from a pale, fine-grained wood, carved in smooth, elegant curves. There were no windows; instead, the walls could upon request display images of the world outside.

Imre flicked through scenes of snowcapped mountains, blue-green forests, and bright yellow sunsets. Dussehra was a world of wide-ranging but mainly temperate climates, like Earth, with a blend of indigenous and imported life-forms. Views without people or their works held little interest, so he kept flicking until he found cityscapes to look at. The Dussehrans had, for the most part, built up rather than out in order to preserve their environmental assets. Efficient towers crisscrossed with green-topped walkways resembled ice needles connected by mold bridges. Solar-powered helium airships soared over wind farms and wave-generator reefs. Steam rose in long, curling wisps from geothermal sinks. On the surface of the planet, at least, humanity's footprint had been minimized.

Several views of the night sky conveyed a very different impression of the rest of the system. Lights moved constantly, tracking high-energy vehicles as they ferried ore from asteroid mines to habitats and factories near and far. A dense, multicolored ring of orbiting satellites formed an X across the fuzzy line of the Milky Way. The Dussehrans seemed proud of the balance they maintained between reverence of their capital world and exploitation of everywhere else. Hence, Imre knew, they had to be reined in. Expanding empires would not be tolerated, no matter how small they started, because they were philosophically incompatible with the Returned Continuum. Small wanted to become big and big bigger still. Given their head, the galaxy would be swamped by competing empires within a hundred thousand years—and Imre hadn't spent the last hundred millennia bringing everything together in order to watch it fall apart like that.

There were three layers to the Returned Continuum, each with their own natures. Most Primes occupied the first. Planetary cultures rose and fell with all the regularity and impermanence of waves striking the shore. Once one of these cultures reached the stars, they occupied by necessity a longer timescale, and so began thinking beyond one or two thousand years, to interstellar societies with a large percentage of singletons occupying all levels. If left unchecked, such bubbles of pre-Continuum culture wanted inevitably to infect the rest of the galaxy—but to do so brought them into contact with those who didn't want a return to the way things were. Galactic governance needed the extended perspective that the Forts had provided, or something as close to that as Imre could improvise.

Imre stood at the center of the third layer, reaching out through the Apparatus's tenuous webs to find out who had destroyed the Forts and how his former self had been involved.

Clues were difficult but not impossible to find. The chaos following the Slow Wave had severely disrupted the network of communications that had once bound the entire galactic disk in a shimmering web of information. Everything in transit during the death throes of the Forts had become scrambled, and a large amount of data had been lost. Since conquering Earth, Imre had made repairing the Line a priority, not only to reestablish the networks that had been damaged, but also to mop up those truncated fragments. Huge swathes of ancient culture still lurked in that orphaned data, from lost pages of a long-dead Prime's diary to gargantuan leaps in a Fort's ponderings.

Dussehra had its share of such relics, long terabytes of garbled codes that might take months to sift through. Without access to the kind of dedicated AIs he had back on Earth, Imre could do little more than conduct simple searches through the data, looking for specific strings that had occurred in the past. He had found his own name that way in many places, encrypted in numerous different fashions. His former self had been very busy in the years leading up to the Slow Wave, in hundreds of locations. Since embracing the Forts' Q loop technology and becoming something much more than a singleton himself, he had followed an agenda that was difficult to determine almost four thousand centuries later. References such as the fifteenth he found during this search didn't help.

"—ask myself: Is this what Imre Bergamasc really—"

Really what, he asked himself. Wants? Needs? Offered? Meant? There was no way to tell what the author of that tiny fragment had been trying to convey, or for whom the fragment had been intended. It was perhaps nothing more than an idle musing, meant for no one at all.

When the field prosthetic declared him fit enough to crack the seal on his upper body, he gratefully took the opportunity to set the project aside for a while. He breathed deeply as the biofilm retreated from the skin of his face and neck, and his chest and arms emerged from their transparent shell. His skin was flaking and pink with hyperoxygenated blood flow. The joints of his regrown fingers felt creaky with disuse, as though he hadn't moved for days, not just hours. He ran his hands across the former ruin of his face and smiled stiffly. In time, his hair and eyebrows would grow back.

The prosthetic still wouldn't let him walk unaided, but his freedom of movement had significantly improved. He could move his regenerating legs in their protective casings. The prosthetic turned the movements into exaggerated steps of its own lower body rather than gliding as it had before. Experimentally, he walked across the room, feeling as though he were wearing enormous and very heavy plastic trousers. He hoped he wouldn't need to run anytime soon, or attend any serious functions. He felt like a circus clown.

Perversely, or perhaps just because he had regained some

freedom of movement, his mood lightened. Abandoning the fragments—which seemed to contain nothing at all of interest—he shifted his attention to the matter of the Luminous.

Dussehra had changed many times since the Slow Wave, evolving from a net exporter of cultural artifacts before the catastrophe—with a reputation for fine music, poetry, and fiction—through several stages of near technobarbarism. Records were, therefore, fragmentary in places, especially when keeping those records had been left in the hands of Primes. When singletons had been in charge, however, memories had been long and well-laid down. It was in one such time that interest in the lost Forts had been revived.

Imre had first heard about similar experimentation in Mandala Supersystem. The strengths and weaknesses of Forts stemmed from their essential nature. Gestalt intelligences had existed since the twenty-second century, but nothing as widely dispersed as a Fort, through space as well as time, had formed until the middle of the Great Human Expansion, when the galaxy had fallen under the collective eye of its only known sapient species. Forts were no more group minds than humans were big bacteria; they operated on entirely different scales and under entirely different laws. They watched stars evolve and die in real time; they witnessed the birth of humanity's nascent galactic civilization with the only eyes large enough truly to take it in.

Not that they had eyes in the conventional sense, Imre reminded himself. He walked through the Milky Way as someone might view the world through a pinhole camera: one tiny glimpse at a time. Forts had had senses and sensory organs he couldn't even imagine. He had worked with them, negotiated with them, even fought them, but he had never truly understood them.

Everyone in the galaxy had been in the same boat. Perhaps, he admitted, it had been easy to take their positive influence for granted. In the aftermath of their deaths, certainly, so much had fallen apart that it seemed certain now that the Continuum had owed its long existence and relatively stability to their efforts—through such groups as the Corps, or more directly, when they sent individual frags into play. On many worlds, people had come to regard the lost Forts with veneration. On Dussehra, as on Hyperabad, some people took it on themselves to reverse the catastrophe.

Making frags was easy. They were just singletons rewired into a single intelligence and allowed to evolve along protocols conducive to a Fort's way of thinking. There were several stages, just as there were in any childhood. The achievement of a proto-Fort stage, analogous to reaching critical mass, was often called Graduation. Many networks never reached that stage, dissolving into mental chaos before the correct architecture could spontaneously emerge. The art of building a galaxy-spanning mind was subtle and difficult to learn— particularly when the best midwives had all died 431,000 years before.

On Hyperabad, the first proto-Fort had been called Ampersand, a word with an established meaning but also an anagram of "Pam Anders," the name of the woman who had volunteered to be Graduated. Forts had a natural affinity for language and word games; the names they chose often provided an understanding of their relationship with the world around them. Dussehra's proto-Fort styled itself as "Aledaide," from a name meaning "noble" as well as a pun on "alidade," an ancient surveying tool used for measuring angles between distant objects. The distant object, Imre assumed, was the goal of becoming a full-fledged Fort—as noble a goal as anyone in the wake of the Slow Wave could imagine.

The experiment had been a success, at first. Aledaide had coalesced gradually into being, spread across the minds of more than fifty frags, all connected by mundane technology— not a loop shunt between them. It didn't matter how the frags linked up; they could, theoretically, exchange information by handwriting notes to each other on paper. In Dussehra's case, Aledaide's frags enjoyed access to the world's fastest satellite communications. The proto-Fort was thus spread from one side of the planet to the other.

Emlee had experienced the death of Ampersand with an intimacy she hadn't desired. Brought in by the authorities to investigate the gradual assassination of Ampersand's frags, she had fallen in love with the proto-Fort but could do nothing when assassination became open aggression. Two forces fought to annihilate the nascent mind—the Luminous and the Barons—and although their objectives were the same, their methodologies were very different. The Barons had been behind the assassinations and had only come out into the open when the Luminous attacked. They had attacked each other too, Emlee remembered, which only made the situation stranger.

It was no different on Dussehra. Aledaide had seen the threat coming and taken steps to ensure her safety. Where Ampersand had huddled in one place and surrounded herself with guards, Aledaide had spread herself even thinner around the globe—and even off world, taking the first steps in a diaspora that would, if given full freedom, once have embraced the whole galaxy. The Barons were relentless, hunting her down piece by piece, no matter where her frags hid. And then the Luminous had come, springing apparently from nowhere and scouring the system for any trace of her. Manifesting as perfectly reflective silver balls roughly thirty centimeters across, they attacked openly and in great numbers, converging in the hundreds from all directions on the slightest hint of a trail and not stopping until every last piece was destroyed. It had been, for about a month, as though the system had been infected by a macroscale, mercurial virus—plus the black-clad Barons, pursuing their own objectives.

When Aledaide was dead, the strange invaders had disappeared and never returned. The Hyperabadans had tried their best to cover up the experiment's failure. The Dussehrans incorporated it into their national psyche, growing ever more suspicious of outside interference.

Freer called while he was rereading the historical records a second time, hoping to find something new between the familiar lines.

"It's Emlee," Freer said. "She's awake."

"I'll be right there. What about Zerah?"

"No reply."

"Try again, and keep trying until you get a response. Tell him I don't like being snubbed."

"Would you come out to meet him if he grants you an audience?"

"I'd meet him halfway. That would be a more fitting gesture for both sides, I think."

"You're being generous. I'd be inclined to smoke him out if he keeps this up."

"We'll see. Don't do anything, Al, until I tell you."

"I prefer not to."

Imre strode heavily in his clown suit to join the guards outside, who led him through the Temple to where Emlee had been cocooned in a full-body convalescence tube, with numerous drips and patches feeding nutrients into her battered flesh. She looked twisted and bruised and very small: that was his first impression of her when the surgeon stepped aside to allow him through. Naked, she lay with her legs half-curled and her hips tilted onto her right side. Her shoulders and head lay pointing upward. Her undamaged skin, what little of it there was, radiated heat and healing pain.

Both eyes were bloodshot but open in her rebuilt face, staring up at him past swollen cheeks and nose. With a wince, her lips parted.

"You came out of it well," she said.

He leaned closer to hear her cracked voice better. "I was lucky. The bomb was right next to me. It should have cut me to pieces."

She shook her head. "You weren't the target. Al told me the charge was shaped to fit the corridor, so the blast focused right where I was standing. On your left, where I always am, Od damn it." She smiled painfully. Imre could hear echoes of the dressing-down Freer must have given her during her debriefing. Only Freer used that ancient blasphemy to make a point. "Someone's trying to kill your friends, not you."

"Damn near succeeded, too." Imre covered his confusion with bland combat-speak. "You look about ready for the bench."

"No wonder. I feel like it." She shifted minutely in the tank and hissed an indrawn breath through clenched teeth. "I don't know exactly what passes for medicine in these boondocks, but it bloody hurts."

"Take it easy," he said more seriously. "There's no hurry. If you're right about there being a message, I've received it loud and clear."

"But it's not going to change anything, and I don't like being a sitting duck. The sooner I'm up and about, the better for everyone." Her eyelids flickered and shut. "Next door you walk through might have your name on it."

"All right," he said, wanting to reassure her. "I'll be sure to send you through first."

"Don't forget to knock . . ." Then she was asleep, either naturally or under medication. Imre didn't care which so long as she rested.

"I'll stay with her," he told the guards waiting by the door. "And don't worry about what she said about this being the boondocks," he told the surgeon. "You're doing everything you can. I appreciate that."

The tall, slender man bowed his head, relief mostly hidden behind a mask of solemn gratitude.

"I think we've got our response from Zerah," Freer informed him an hour later.

Imre had just stepped free of the field prosthetic and returned to his chambers to dress, leaving Emlee well guarded and still sound asleep. He looked up from securing his ornate body armor with a feeling of certainty in his belly. While sitting with Emlee, he had decided which way events were likely to play out.

"And?"

"The troops around us are moving in."

He half smiled, half grimaced. Spot on. Calling up a map of the Temple surrounds, he said, "Tell me what you're thinking."

"The spook jams the command frequencies and hacks into the operational networks. We cut power and comms to the area and bring down any aircraft in the vicinity. Knocking out satellite coverage and putting any orbital weapons into a spin will make sure we don't have any interruptions from on high. Once it's just us and the troops, we ask Zerah, nicely, to back off and respond to the invitation like a gentleman. Or we start to play rough."

Imre nodded, looking for possible problems in the layout of the city. The Temple occupied a fifty-story tower near one of three central precincts in Dussehra's capital, Veldoen. Neighboring buildings were close enough for physical assaults, while the rooftop and ground floor were obvious points of entry. Temple guards had been stationed at every obvious choke point; automatic security systems watched every door, window, and vent.

Information on movements outside the building came from infrared and vibrational readings of the closest buildings. People and machines were assembling en masse.

"Do it," he told Freer. "Apparatus, comply with Marshal Freer's instructions. The Temple is to be protected at all costs."

"Yes, Imre," said the AI.

It was daylight outside. A black-plumaged bird—genuine, not an uncrewed spy plane in disguise—circled the Temple with wing tips splayed like fingers on an open hand. Imre watched it for a full minute, admiring its magisterial grace. Its beak was wickedly tipped, marking it as a hunter, a killer. Lord of death as well as lord of the air. He wondered what its dark eyes saw far below, what prey scurried innocently about its business, unaware that talons could strike at any moment from above.

When he had finished dressing, he opened the doors and instructed the guards to take him to Freer. They walked briskly along corridors he hadn't visited before, he relishing the full use of his legs but on guard for any further attacks. If Freer was right, and they hadn't completely rooted out the resistance cell within the Temple, another attempted assassination could come at any moment. It didn't matter who was targeted; further internal disruption could only have a detrimental effect on morale at a critical time.

And the hardcaster's damaged F-MAP components were still a long way from being fully operational.

Freer had taken a circular conference room on an upper floor of the building and turned it into a makeshift command center. Numerous wall-screens had been co-opted to serve as visual displays, each flashing a different view of the city blocks around the Temple. Dozens of different colors painted Freer's face where he stood in the middle of the room, limbs hanging in a pose of relaxed readiness, mind linked by more senses than just sight to the data pouring in, his face a mask of concentration.

Imre didn't disturb him. When the room was resecured, he patched into the data flows and quickly brought himself up to date.

The orderly disposition of the Dussehran troops had been thrown into disarray by the Apparatus's interference. Ghostly, insubstantial, pervasive—the AI had slipped tentacles made of electrons, muons, and neutrinos into every information system on the planet and could disrupt anything networked—which was everything, even on backward Dussehra. Imre didn't entirely understand the principles by which the Apparatus existed, but he knew its strengths and limitations well. It was written on space, which meant that it couldn't move independently. Once written "onto" a material anchor, like a planet or a station, each individual part of it retained that reference point forever. It propagated, therefore, by growing new extensions, new tentacles, which reached amorphously across space by leaps and bounds. Its presence could not be inferred by any physical means, which meant that it could breed whole towers of processing power in sensitive locations and go unnoticed. He pictured a vast, ectoplasmic ziggurat rising up over the city, as nebulous as dark matter, smothering the city with its invisible gravity. Devised by ancient minds of Earth for an unknown purpose— or none, simply because they could—the Apparatus now served as the ultimate instrument of state, as it had served another man before him: perfectly loyal, perfectly dependable, perfectly insidious . . .

A rattle of gunfire brought him out of his reflective trance. Numerous external spy-eyes converged their fields of view on a trooper leaning out a window of a nearby building, strafing the side of the Temple with staccato shots.

"What does that idiot think he's doing?" asked Freer.

Imre repressed a smile. One thing the Apparatus could do nothing about was human willfulness. What Freer no doubt thought of as poor discipline could be taken another way, as noble defiance.

Several semi-intelligent weapons systems targeted the lone gunman, planning in exquisite detail the best way to take him out.

"Hold your fire," Imre ordered. "He's not hurting anyone." Indeed, each shot sparked harmlessly off the Temple's bulletproof windows and ricocheted through the empty canyons around them. The gesture was empty, and the trooper certainly knew it. That was retaliation enough.

A second trooper appeared two floors down and also started firing. This one further flaunted safety by having his helmet visor open and shouting abuse across the space between buildings. Imre had no inclination to hear what the man was saying; he could imagine well enough.

When a third emerged, lobbing concussion grenades from a collapsible launcher, his patience began to wear thin.

"Take out the weapons but leave the troopers unharmed."

Freer nodded and relayed the order. Wire-thin laser beams flashed across the short distance, melting critical components and rendering the weapons useless. The troopers retreated and emerged moments later with replacements. A fourth joined them, punctuating his gunfire with taunting gestures.

"Target the window frames this time," said Imre. "Smoke them out."

That worked only as long as it took the soldiers to move to different windows.

"Are you enjoying this?" Freer asked him.

"It's passing the time." Imre feigned dispassion. "Tell Zerah he has five minutes to start talking."

"Or . . . ?"

"I'm working on it."

Imre stood with his arms folded and one hand cupping his chin as more soldiers joined the first, brandishing weapons and daring him to retaliate. Curious, he tapped into audio channels to hear what they were shouting. It turned out to be a song—the Dussehran national anthem, perhaps—loud and stirring from both male and female throats. Gunfire punctuated each phrase like an erratic drumbeat.

A great weariness filled him. These were hearts that couldn't be turned by memes alone, not for generations. They were loyal and bold, and badly out of context. Where once they had served Dussehra's interests well, now they stood in the way of the future.

"Your five minutes are up," said Freer.

"Bring down the building," Imre said. "Level the whole block."

"Yes, sir." There was no trace of dissemblance in Freer's voice as he issued the commands to the Apparatus, which in turn directed the Dussehrans' own weapons systems to target the building. Career soldiers knew the risks they were taking, especially when facing a superior enemy—that, at least, was how Imre imagined Freer's thoughts to be running. Half the views on the room's screens shifted to feeds from above where, high in orbit, subverted satellites responded to new commands.

The soldiers jeered, unknowing, as a chain of events unwound that would inevitably result in their deaths.

"I'm tired of this," Imre said. "We're rooting out cancer one cell at a time. There has to be a better way."

"I guess it depends on your definition of 'better.'"

"I guess it does." He refused to become a singleton and campaign on every front at once. That was the most efficient solution—but efficiency wasn't everything. That was what his former self would have done. He refused to follow that path.

A bright flash of light made him blink and glance away from the screens. That didn't stop the information pouring into him through other channels. Four surgical strikes from above had vaporized the building's internal supports almost as far as the ground. Windows blew out, issuing superhot jets of gas. The structure vanished behind an expanding shell of smoke. Solid debris came a split second later, trailing white streamers as they fell. A thunderous sound resonated through the structure of the Temple. The noise grew louder as the wreckage collapsed in on itself—troops and mortar and glass and all, reduced from order to rubble in little more than a second.

"Open the internal comms of the remaining troops," Imre told Freer. "Let them talk among themselves so they can work out what happened. Then jam everything else in the city. I don't want so much as a squawk on the airwaves, unless it's Zerah calling us to parley. Wires, too. In an hour, we'll release a statement and ram it down the media's throats."

"Saying?"

"That we came here, peacefully, to talk about Dussehra's place in the Returned Continuum. That we have been ambushed, fired at, and mocked. It's up to them what happens next."

"Do you think they'll cave?"

Imre thought of the proto-Fort, Aledaide, and the system's complicated history, so similar in many ways to Hyderabad's, where it all began.

"Whatever they decide, it'll be wholehearted," he said, "or it'll be nothing at all."

An hour after the message was sent—with still no reply from the Gravamen—Imre deferred to a spreading fatigue that started in the bones of his legs, reached up his spine, and manifested as a migraine in the depths of his temples. His body was still repairing itself. He needed to give it time to finish the job. With night falling over the city, he took his cue from the environment and decided to rest.

"Wake me if there are any sudden developments," he told Freer. "Otherwise, let them sleep on it. Maybe Zerah will wake up in a conciliatory mood."

"Not if he's anything like Helwise in the morning."

"Well, that would be an improvement on nothing at all."

With his guards around him, Imre wound his way through the Temple to his rooms, where he collapsed gratefully onto the bed. More than his bones bothered him. He felt flushed and worn-out, as though from a fever, and when he closed his eyes, the world rocked from side to side.

To distract himself, he called up a map of the Milky Way and studied it, apparently suspended in the air above his bed. The illusion was perfect—better than perfect, for his eyes couldn't normally perceive such detail. The data feeding straight into his cortex was unlimited by biological constraints. Individual stars seemed like tiny dust motes, flickering and dancing as the galaxy rotated. It was an unendingly beautiful sight.

Simple commands colored the stars according to political leanings. Blue indicated those already embraced by the Returned Continuum, more than 60 percent of those in or near the major arms; red defined systems inimical to the new order, comprising less than one-twentieth of the total number; the rest were yellow, undecided or uncontacted since the fall of the Forts. If he overlaid the network of Line connections, then the reason for some of the yellows became explicit: whole swathes of the galaxy remained unconnected to the rest, thanks to sabotage or extreme distance. It was difficult sometimes to convince individual systems to invest in the maintenance of their local Line relays, and without constant attention, the links soon snapped. Such holes irked Imre more than the systems marked in red. Hostility was at least a stance; it spoke of a vigorous society, one that took risks and fought for what it thought was important. That was what he wanted the Returned Continuum to be. He knew from long experience that what counted as important could easily be changed.

The right nudge in exactly the right spot; a long enough lever: that, and patience, was all it took.

He fell asleep while tracking the paths his former self had followed across the galaxy—strange trails he found impossible to interpret, from the very edge of the galactic disk to the wild spaces at its heart—and dreamed of the people he had ordered killed that day, four of the five conspirators and the troopers in the demolished building. Some of the latter had undoubtedly been Primes. Through the tortured eye of his imagination, he saw them as faceless figures marching into a furnace, a parade of victims whose memories and thoughts were lost forever. He had no idea how many people had died,

Primes or otherwise, in the destroyed building. His subconscious made a meal of his uncertainty, imagining hundreds of them, if not thousands. They sang as they burned, taking the words from one of the fragments the Apparatus had found in the Line echoes.

> *—music of so strange a sound*
> *And beauty of so wild a birth,—*
> *Farewell! for I have won the Earth.*

The phantasm joined in with words Imre had no memory of ever hearing before:

> *I reach'd my home—my home no more—*
> *For all had flown who made it so.*

Then his own voice called from the shadows:

> *For all we live to know is known*
> *And all we seek to keep hath flown.*

Then everyone, dead or alive, turned to him. It was his turn to sing, but he didn't know the words.

A sliver of noise from the real world intruded and, growing louder, swept the dreamscape away.

"First Prime? I apologize for disturbing you."

He blinked and rolled over on the bed. The sheets had tangled around him like a burial shroud. He was naked apart from a pair of loose hakama pants he must have found somewhere in the room. He didn't remember getting out of his armor, but he felt much better for it, despite the rude awakening.

The room was empty. The voice came from outside, from one of the guards at his door.

"What do you want?" he replied, trying his best to keep the retreating fog in his mind from showing in his voice.

"Minister Sevaste wishes to see you," the guard said. "She says you gave her permission."

He thought for a second, racking his brain as to who she was and why he would have granted her such a license. Then he remembered: the three bald priests Freer had introduced him to, after the bomb. *I am available to you,* he had said.

Sevaste had eyes like the skies of Earth on a cloudless day.

"Let her in," he told the guard, raising himself up in the bed so his back was against the headboard and tidying the sheet across his lap. "Just her."

The door whispered open, and with a tinkling of bells, she stepped two paces into the room. She waited with bald head bowed until the door had closed behind her. Then she raised her chin and looked at him without shyness or humility. Her eyes were as blue as he had remembered and even more direct than before, with the need for dissemblance removed. She didn't say a word until she reached the foot of the bed. By then she was already naked. Her robe shivered away at the touch of one finger to the clasp at her throat, peeling back like folds of plumage to expose the woman beneath. Her bells dropped to the ground in a crystalline chord. Sevaste was slender and gently curved, uncannily echoing the lines of the desk behind her. Her breasts were high, and the space between her legs was furred, as women had once always been.

"You aren't safe here," she said, raising one knee onto the bed, then the other, and approaching like a cat, with her shoulders rising and falling and her eyes swaying like the lights of a boat anchored offshore. "You are in great danger."

The words lit a fuse in his body. Until that moment, he had watched her dispassionately, appreciating her beauty but more interested in the question of why she was there. Now desire filled him. Was she an offering or a double agent? Penitent or political opportunist? Suddenly it didn't matter. The thought that he might be at risk of real physical harm awoke desires he rarely indulged.

"You're the sixth," he said, gripping her shoulders and pulling her onto her back, with him over her, on his knees, hands holding her down so her arms were at her sides. Only her legs could move. They came up and around him, pulling him closer.

"The sixth?" she repeated with her face slightly askew. Her denial was unconvincing.

"We caught five terrorists. We know there are more in the cell. You're one of them."

"Why would I come here now, like this, if my intention was to kill you? Your guards scanned me at the door. I carry no weapons."

"You are the weapon. You think you can change my mind, divert my purpose."

"I'm not so naïve," she said, looking directly at him, as though he had personally affronted her.

"You tell me then. Why are you here?"

She rocked her hips against him. "Need it be more than this?"

"It's always more."

She didn't pout or argue. "Be with me this once. Conduct your interrogation later, if you must."

He reached down with one hand and untied the knots of his hakama, watching her warily as he did so. The skin of her legs was smooth and warm against his back. Her lips were full and slightly parted. The faint perfume of her body was growing stronger.

His pants folded away down the front, freeing him. At last he could feel the heat of her, the wetness pressing against him. He was a considerate lover, when the time was right, but this had nothing to do with love. He entered her smoothly, with one languid motion, and she raised herself to receive him.

"If I could kill you now . . ." she breathed.

"Would you?" he asked, beginning to move.

"Would *you*, if you were I?" Her eyes closed, and she pressed her right cheek against the pillow.

"Kill myself?" He studied the precise line of her jaw, feeling anger as well as fear burning in his gut. That made him move faster. She couldn't possibly know about his other agenda: to find Himself and discover the truth about his own past. In her eyes, he could only be a Prime, with no other versions of himself left in the galaxy. Unless she knew more than she should—

unless that was why she was really there—to blackmail him—
to destroy his reputation—

He reached orgasm quickly and was relieved when it was
over. Her legs remained tight around him as he deflated inside
her. The rise and fall of her breasts was as rapid as if she too
had climaxed, although he was sure she hadn't. He felt her blue
eyes on him, seeking the weak points in his face, and he pulled
out of her, then off her, and rested back on his haunches. The
air felt cold on his moist skin. Gooseflesh rose up his back and
down his arms.

"Tell me why you're here, Minister Sevaste."

She didn't move. With her arms at her side and legs still
splayed, she spoke calmly and with great remove, as though a
negotiating table lay between them.

"I want you to answer my question."

He thought back. "If I were you . . . ?" He shook his head
and rose up onto his knees. "I'd be afraid for my life, right
now. That's for sure. Even if you could kill me, there'd be no
way of leaving the room alive."

"I'm sure your underlings would have me for a toy until
there was nothing left to kill." Her gaze hardened. "I've heard
how you treat other worlds, other systems. I know there's
nothing you cannot overcome, cannot destroy, if it stands in
your way. I'm not frightened of you, or of death. I wonder
only what you are frightened of, and how long it will take for
you to realize that you are the only true obstacle in your path."

Again, that small frisson of fear. "How so?"

"I am a loyal priest," she said. He could see in her clear
blue eyes that she wasn't lying—or thought she wasn't, which
didn't amount to the same thing. "I have served the church
faithfully for over a century. I am a Prime, like you; I would
hardly have attained this rank otherwise. I believe that humanity has lost something great and precious, and that we
must strive across all the galaxy to make it ours again." Now
she moved, sitting up on her folded legs and laying one hand
upon his bare stomach. She placed her left ear against his rib
cage, as though listening for a heartbeat. "The people of
Dussehra are not your enemy."

"If this is the way Zerah treats his allies—"

She surprised him by smacking him hard on his belly, once. "The offense is yours. This may seem like a backward world to you, but Gravaman Zerah is ruler here. He must retain the respect of those beneath him. He would no more meet your emissary than you would his. You insult him by speaking through your senior officers, so he insults you in return."

Comprehension struck him. It should have earlier, and he cursed his stupidity. This wasn't the first such impasse he had been embroiled in, but he had been thrown off-balance by first the phantasm and then the sabotage. He had allowed Freer's preference for a military solution to sway him. Viewed in this new light, the situation might be fixed simply by opening comms and making a call.

"Why didn't you tell me this before?"

"I am a priest, not a soldier."

"You're not on my staff either, yet here you are giving me advice." He tried to look at her face, but she wouldn't let him. "I don't understand. Why are you helping me? If you're part of the cell—"

She smacked him again. "Does it matter what I'm part of? So long as I'm telling the truth, you should listen to me. Listen to everyone. Too long have you fed on your own counsel, like a bird eating its own young. You are starving on the inside—I can see it. What you hunger for, perhaps even you don't realize. But you won't find it here on this world, or in the ashes of its submission. You won't find it on the Line. You might never find it. Don't you think it would be better for the galaxy if you worked that out now, rather than dragged us all after you on some pointless quest?"

"And what? Leave you to squabble and fight for all eternity? I think your fellow Dussehrans deserve better, frankly." He braced himself for another slap. It didn't come. Instead, she kissed him just above the navel.

He laughed, sourly, and pushed her back. "You're more dangerous than I thought. When did they get to you? How did they manifest?"

"Who?"

"The Barons. You don't give a rat's arse about the bigger picture. You're here to keep me focused on Dussehra, nothing else. That's why you targeted F-MAP as well as my friends. To keep me here and to send me a warning. While I'm distracted, I can't be looking for the truth."

"You're paranoid," she said with a new spark in her eyes, "as well as self-obsessed." Was that disgust or genuine fear, for the first time?

"And you're not denying the accusation." He forced her back onto the bed, using his weight to pin her down. Her legs flailed but he placed one hand over her throat and squeezed until she submitted.

"I listen to things," she croaked. "As you do. Whispers on the Line, rumors, subversive talk among the newer recruits. There's truth to be found there—a version of it, at least, if you're willing to see it. But I obey my own will, no one else's." She smiled knowingly. "Part of you wants that to be true."

He was erect again, unintentionally, and he cursed his unpredictable Prime body. "Believing you isn't the same thing as fucking you."

"No. You can easily have one without the other." She shrugged. "I'm not asking you to make a choice. Do both, if you want. Or neither. There's no reason this should change anything, that which passes between us. Let me go, and I'll walk out of here with my head bowed. No one will know except the two of us."

"I still don't know why you came here."

"For no specific reason. To experiment. Does that unnerve you?" Her eyes caught him again. "Kill me, if that makes you feel safer. I couldn't stop you."

He clenched his teeth down hard for a moment—not tempted at all to do as she said but too confused by her to know what else he could do—then rolled off her, onto his back, and stared at the ceiling.

She hesitated, then followed, straddling him so that her pubic hair brushed his thighs and the arc of his penis pressed into her pubic bone. She leaned closer still, breathing deeply of his scent, and put her hands on his upper arms. The touch of her nipples against his abdomen was like Morse code, tapping directly into his primitive nervous system.

She was as aroused as he was. Barely had she begun rubbing against him when her muscles tightened and her breath came in deeper, sharper gasps. With startling strength, she pushed down on him. Her fingers dug deep into his muscles. A red flush spread across her chest. Her lips were open, her eyes closed. She raised herself up higher, blindly, and reached down between her legs for him.

"That's all, Minister Sevaste," he said. "You can leave me now."

She made a low, animal noise in her throat—disappointment? frustration? annoyance?—then she was off him and slipping back into her robes. Without glancing at him, she dressed with efficient, practiced fingers and headed for the door. It didn't open as she approached. She waited there for him to utter the command.

"You wanted to know if I would kill me, were I in your shoes," he said. "The answer is that I would, yes, if I had to."

"I already know that you can kill," she said, still without looking behind her. "I'm just glad that there might be a choice in the matter."

He frowned, wondering what she was driving at. Were the Barons sending him a warning—that they could destroy him anytime they wanted, and would do so if he gave them sufficient reason? Or was she really speaking for herself, of how she had found a reason not to destroy him when the chance—no matter how tenuous—had been in her hands? Was she afraid that he might not be so merciful, on the brink of granting her freedom?

The door opened, and the guards parted to let her through.

When she was gone, Imre sank back onto the mattress and let gravity take him. All desire had fled. Her smell was thick over the bed. He found it hard to think through it. After a brief, cleansing shower, he bundled up the sheets and gave them to the guards to burn. He found her melodious bells abandoned on the floor and disposed of them too.

Then he went to find Freer, the thought of testing her advice utmost in his mind. Whoever had sent her, whatever she wanted, that small piece of information could make all the difference. Or none at all.

Gravaman Zerah was a waxy, heavily tattooed figure of a man standing well over two meters tall, with slumped shoulders that made him look half-melted. His jowls shook as he talked, and his voice was like creeping, cold oil. He wore a black-and-purple suit from which two disproportionately small hands emerged, folded demurely across his midriff. Black lines wound around every digit and created complex intersections across his knuckles. His eyes were heavily bagged and moved with a slowness that might have been taken for boredom but for the dark spark of alertness visible in their black depths. His lips seemed permanently wet.

Imre had to fight the urge to ask why he chose to look like that. There was no practical reason for it; there hadn't been for hundreds of thousands of years. Humans could look any way they wanted—unless it ran against a philosophical ethic to accept the lot that chance had given them. Imre could only suppose that Zerah adhered to such an ethic, or else he liked the effect his appearance had on people.

With a mild feeling of regret that his wounds had completely healed, Imre returned his mind completely to the matter at hand.

"I have come here," he said to Zerah's life-sized hologram, "because your world and its neighbors only recently reconnected completely to the Line. After millennia of isolation, you are part once more of the galactic community. Consider this an introduction rather than an invasion. That's how we regard it."

"You speak of isolation as though it is automatically a bad thing," said Zerah. "Your introduction has already cost us dozens of lives. How many more good people must we lose before you and your opinions move on?"

Imre didn't bother repeating that the provocation lay with terrorists, or that Zerah's unwillingness to talk to anyone but him had resulted in the lethal stalemate.

"My opinions reflect those of the citizens of the galaxy," he said, reiterating the line he had delivered on countless other worlds. "We are the survivors of a dangerous age. It would be a mistake to assume that the danger is passed. While the perpetrators of the Slow Wave remain unknown and presumably at large, we must guard against instability and further devolution. The restoration of the Line brings us together, inevitably, but it will take more than talk to restore that which has been lost. We must put aside our differences and work together— for the sake of humanity and our joint future."

Zerah's fleshy lips peeled back, exposing broad, white teeth and flexing his facial scarification into a forbidding mask. The expression could not remotely be considered a smile. "We must?"

"I ask you as a fellow citizen of the galaxy."

"You are addressing me as First Prime of the Returned Continuum and the savior of the First Church of the Return— the same Imre Bergamasc who once served the Forts, then fought them, and now mourns their passing as one might a hated but wealthy uncle. Forgive me if I mistrust your humility."

"We are the products of our experiences, Gravaman Zerah, and I'm proud to say that I've had a lot of them. I have never claimed to be more than a man. I'm not ashamed for occasionally changing my mind or the side I fought on. You can take this as evidence of my humanity, if you like—and my adaptability. I'm neither hidebound nor close-minded. Every culture welcomed back into the fold brings with it new ideas, new methods. We embrace them as we would our own."

"That is, of course, the purpose behind cultural assimilation. To steal what you find valuable and throw away the rest. I would respect you more if you admitted to empire-building and were done with it."

"Is it empire-building?" Imre asked him. "I don't think so. We're encouraging a phase change from small, disconnected regions to one smoothly continuous whole. This is a return to the way we used to be, so you can't claim it's something we've never enjoyed before. As in a crystal, its strength lies in that continuity, its regularity of connections. Any section that tries to remain apart functions as a defect, ruining the whole.

I'm not trying to rob you of your rights to individuality. I am simply trying to ensure the safety of everyone else—because we all remain under threat, however differently you might like to regard the situation. Humanity as a whole as been targeted. As a whole it must stand in order to prevent another such catastrophe."

"And yet—"

"Let me finish, Zerah. You talk of cultural assimilation and empire-building. That only proves to me how poorly you grasp the situation we're in. Once, yes, I accused the Forts of just these crimes. They had the power, and the patience, and the perspective, to ensure we did what they wanted. Now they're gone, we can see how effective their influence was, covert as well as overt. Without them, the galaxy has fallen to pieces. Some of us are trying to put those pieces back together—but we're not Forts. We're not even close. If we try to rule the galaxy, we're going to fail because we're simply not up to the job. That's the sad but honest fact. I am painfully aware of my limitations, but no less determined to do something to reverse the downward trend. We're not starting from scratch: we have the Line, which is still under repair; we have some continuance of interstellar travel, by ships across short distances or by hardcasting for longer journeys; we have the beginnings of a galactic community, through which we reach out to regions that have closed themselves off to the rest of the galaxy— sometimes out of a very real sense of fear, for the memories of our fall from grace remain strong, and sometimes out of pride, as though they could somehow do better.

"We need everyone to embrace the idea of continuity, even if, behind the mask, it remains an illusion. The Returned Continuum is less an empire than an idea, a principle that has spread almost of its own accord. I am the visible face of that idea, but it would exist without me. People embrace the idea because they know it doesn't threaten them; instead, it binds them with others who share the same loss and hope for rebirth. It reminds us of our origins on Earth and the grand history we're all part of. That history will continue only if we stand up both to our enemies and to the instinct to gather those closest to us and retreat inward. Can you accept that idea,

Gravaman Zerah? Will the people of Dussehra embrace it too? I think so. There is no shame in it, after all, and absolutely nothing to lose."

Zerah's skeptical expression hadn't changed. "Big things come from little ideas. Wasn't that a saying on your precious old Earth? How do I know this meme you spread isn't the vanguard of an invasion that will destroy who we are no less thoroughly than if it rode in on the back of warships?"

"I offer you the rest of the galaxy as evidence." Imre spread his arms as though to cup the entire Milky Way within them. "Were my motives so venal, would I be standing before you now?"

"You very nearly weren't," said Zerah with just a flicker of sly amusement. "Don't tell me that resistance doesn't exist. I have seen it in action."

"Of course you have; I would be a fool to deny it. That only supports my claim that individuality remains intact under the Returned Continuum. Were it the totalitarian regime you seem to imagine, there would be no such resistance."

"I think you underestimate the strength of human character."

"Perhaps I do. You're right to challenge me on it. It's easy, sometimes, to be cocky. To reuse a metaphor: I am no different from any other part of the crystal growing around me. Imagining otherwise is a sure route to disaster. Thank you."

He bowed. That seemed to soften Zerah's stance somewhat.

"You believe that resistance is applied from without, in the form of sabotage and sedition," he said, standing straighter so that he was looking at Imre down his bulbous nose. "I would hear more of that. Our attempts to reconnect the Line were constantly interfered with."

"You're not alone there, I'm afraid. If you are willing to meet in person, we can discuss strategies that may have worked elsewhere—and perhaps some form of material assistance from the Returned Continuum, as well."

"Are you offering me a bribe?"

"I offer Dussehra the means of ensuring its security against those who are enemies of us all."

Zerah laughed. "Sweet words, foul breath—that's what my father would have said."

"You won't know if my breath is fair or foul until we meet."

"This is true. So we will meet. Tomorrow. My Chief Undersecretary will make arrangements." Zerah inclined his head. "Until then."

The hologram winked out and was replaced with an empty service icon.

Imre let himself relax and accepted the flask of water Freer offered him. He looked automatically for Emlee, but she was still recuperating elsewhere in the Temple. He had no doubt she had watched the exchange and would offer her own opinion of how it had gone, later.

"That surely counts as progress," Freer said. "If he withdraws his troops, maybe we'll take him up on his invitation."

"We'll accept," Imre said. "And we'll make the first move. He can't be expected to back down while we have the city in our grip." Imre felt he had a much clearer understanding of Zerah now, and made arrangements with the Apparatus to free up external comms without any reservations. That issue hadn't been raised once during the conversation, even though it had no doubt been constantly on Zerah's mind. "That doesn't mean we're in the clear yet. I won't feel safe until we're off this rock and on our way back home."

"We'll be careful." Freer's long frame occupied the edge of a table with one leg raised at a ninety-degree angle on a chair directly in front of him. His eyes were as sharp as the angles he made with his limbs. "How did you know he'd talk? One minute we're shooting at each other, the next we're arranging tea parties."

Imre thought of Minister Sevaste, who had passed him that morning in the Temple corridors, maintaining a well-defined distance as she went. Her blue eyes had remained determinedly downcast. "A hunch," he said.

Freer shrugged. "Whatever. Do you have any preferences for the venue?"

"No. Surprise me. I'll just be glad to get out of the building." Something was bothering him about the conversation; he couldn't quite pin it down. "I'm going for a walk. Call me if there are any developments."

"Will do."

Imre and his guards left the makeshift control room and explored the far reaches of the Temple. They passed entrances to dormitories and kitchens; they skirted vast engineering sectors, each holding components required for the hardcaster; they briefly stopped in on the reconstruction of F-MAP, examining the blast marks still etched in the walls and watching the automated repairs systems swarming over truncated cables, melted components, and torn metal. They stumbled across a storeroom full of memorabilia, including badges of Imre's face designed to be handed out to the public. They were thickly coated with dust.

He stared at the endlessly reproduced images of his own face—wondering who this stranger was, with his tall, white hair and triangular features, and his eyes that were, in this image at least, a match for Sevaste's. He remained uncomfortable with the portrait, forbidding mirrors in any of his private chambers, for seeing his face reminded him of Himself, the man he had tried briefly to become but whom he had turned his back on long ago, needing to embrace a new version of himself in order to avoid making the same mistakes. The Imre Bergamasc who had entangled himself in something called Domgard and been implicated in the Slow Wave was not he, even though they shared the same face. Yet here was that face, over and over, as though to rub in the fact that they remained entangled.

It suddenly occurred to him what had bothered him about Zerah.

That's what my father would have said . . .

There, in one clause, was evidence of the chasm between him and the ruler of Dussehra. Imre barely remembered his own father, and had no idea if he was alive or dead. It wasn't relevant to him, either way, and neither was anything the man had said, because his personal history had been inherited piecemeal from the Imre Bergamasc he now disavowed. He had no roots at all.

Presumably Zerah's father had died, hence the reference to

him in past tense. Of his own choice, Imre hoped. His memories of being a singleton were so deeply ingrained that he still found the idea of death—permanent, irrevocable, final death—as alien to him as traveling between the stars by rowboat. Even in the face of war, soldiers took precautions.

He thought of Chyro Kells and the others who had died in the bomb blast. They hadn't been soldiers; they should have been well out of harm's way. Accidents happened all the time—but this had been planned, premeditated to hurt those closest to him. That he had trouble forgiving.

Family and mortality. He could afford neither and in truth rarely felt the lack. But he would make amends, later, for those who might.

He instructed the guards to return him to his quarters, where he would resume sifting through the Line echoes for clues to his past activity. Whatever his former self had been up to, its existence couldn't have been completely erased from the galaxy. Nothing disappeared forever; that which had been hidden inevitably came to light.

Sweet words, foul breath . . .

Imre wondered if Gravaman Zerah missed his father. He didn't seem the sort who would, but nothing was impossible. Stranger things lurked in the human heart.

The airship was vast and utterly unlike any Imre had seen before, consisting of more than a dozen lozenge-shaped bags intricately connected by struts and ties that flexed and twisted as wind coursed through the structure. It looked unwieldy to the extreme—and possibly dangerous as well—but Zerah assured Freer that it was safe. That he could be flying with them went some way to reassuring Imre that it wasn't some bizarrely baroque trap.

The craft descended in sections over the Temple, lowering its central airbag like an orchid dipping its stamen. Those bags nearest to it dipped slightly too, and Imre could hear the tension in the stays, humming an ever-changing, atonal chord. The central airbag had windows along each flank and an underside that was at least half transparent. From the opaque section a ramp descended, extruding to taste the platform on which Imre, Freer, and Emlee stood waiting, surrounded by guards and members of the priesthood.

The view over the city was stunning, golden with dawn and crisply chilled after a cloudless night. Crystalline towers crowded close, still scarred with smoke and dust from the destruction of one of their siblings two days before. The city itself was uncannily quiet—not somnolent, Imre thought, but poised like a herd beast wondering when the predator was going to strike again. The whir of the airship's electric motors seemed loud to his ears.

"What did Zerah call this thing, again?" Emlee said in an aside to Freer.

"His Ambassadorial Barque."

"I guess it's an improvement on his bite. But I still don't see why we couldn't take a shuttle like normal people."

"Who wants to be normal?" The three of them were back in their formal armor. Freer raised one gilt-edged white gauntlet to shade his eyes from the brightening sky. In his other hand he balanced on its end a long, silver cylinder, capped at either extremity with a black seal thirty centimeters across. The central airbag was now perfectly still with respect to the Temple landing pad. The rest of the structure swayed and rocked above it, absorbing the momentum of every unexpected gust of wind. "I'll go first, I suppose," he said, as the door at the top of the ramp hissed open.

"No," said Imre, seeing Gravaman Zerah waiting on the far side of the door. "That's my job."

He approached the base of the ramp and walked smoothly upward, grateful for the reassuring rigidity of the slender surface beneath his feet. He had no fear for his safety; the Apparatus had infiltrated the craft hours ago and would act instantly if anyone made a move against any of its passengers. Zerah stepped forward to greet him. Imre forced a smile. The man was even stranger-looking in the flesh. Between the whorled lines of his tattoos, his skin looked entirely too grey to be real.

They didn't shake hands. Zerah waved him into the warm air issuing from the door, maintaining his distance.

Imre considered taking offense but decided to bide his time. Numerous officials waited to be introduced, as Emlee, still moving with a slight limp, and Freer followed. Imre smiled and bowed and made careful note of everyone's name. He hated the rituals that inevitably attached themselves to diplomacy: shake here; nod there; note every gesture, no matter how small and possibly meaningless, for each one was part of a subtle language of compliments and insult. His gaze took in a thousand small details, from the exquisite wood paneling of the surprisingly large space to the discreetly armed guards in every corner. He raised his tempo slightly in order to give himself a faster reaction time.

When everyone was aboard, Zerah made a short speech welcoming them all and asking that they treat the barque as their own. Already the central airbag was rising back into the fold of the others. Imre could barely sense any motion beneath his feet. For such a rickety-looking structure, it possessed an admirable degree of comfort. The space they inhabited was at least three stories high, containing a restaurant, two bars, numerous seats and couches near prime vantage points for the view, and even a dozen small compartments in which the passengers might sleep—or enjoy more active pursuits—throughout the journey.

Zerah addressed Imre and his companions by the long, overblown titles they had been granted by the elaborate bureaucracy of the Round.

Imre was put slightly off guard, as he always was, habituated to thinking of them in less grandiose terms. "Please," he said, raising a gloved hand at the first available pause, "let's not insist on these formalities. We have a long journey ahead of us. I expect we'll be on a first-name basis by the end."

Zerah smiled tightly. "Indeed. That is the purpose of this trip—to get to know each other better and also to show you our beautiful world at close quarters. In a moment we will join the trade winds and begin our great circuit."

When told of Zerah's grand plan, Emlee had initially expressed weary skepticism. *Is he kidding us? I'm not going around the world in some stupid balloon.*

Fine. So stay behind.

And let him push you out over a volcano? If anyone's earned that privilege, it's me—for babysitting you three times around the galaxy and back. Besides, there's Chyro to think of . . .

Her weariness had had a slightly manic edge. He wondered just how many endorphins she was pumping through her veins to keep herself going.

The Ambassadorial Barque rocked ever so slightly as it cleared the tops of the towers and began to move in earnest. Each of the airbag lozenges aligned itself with the wind to minimize drag. Engines running down their centers began to drone, imitating the propulsion systems of giant lungfish Imre had flown with in the atmosphere of a gas giant, long millennia ago. The craft's speed was surprising; within minutes, they were leaving the city behind and heading out over open country, following a pair of perfectly straight rail lines toward the green horizon. The northern horizon bulged with white-capped mountains, a forest creeping over its foothills like mold. To the south lay a gleaming sea, bordered by ivory sand. Clouds painted the sky with illegible hieroglyphs.

Imre went to get himself a drink, resigned to a long journey over landscapes he'd seen many times before, in the company of people in whom he had no particular interest. The crowd—three dozen in all, plus servants and aides— came from the obvious sectors: diplomatic, administrative, military, commercial. Only one represented the planet's education system, a round-faced physicist who was more interested in hearing about exotic wine than some of the Forts' theories that had been rediscovered by Imre's archaeological surveyors. Imre complimented Dussehra on its fine light reds—which were genuinely interesting, with a range of high notes that made the aftertaste linger long after each mouthful was swallowed—and recommended a series of varietals that would become readily available when the planet joined the Returned Continuum.

"Are you telling me you freight this stuff around as a matter of course?" The physicist seemed personally affronted by the suggestion. "The energy expenditure must be unconscionable!"

"Indeed it would be," Imre assured him. "You're absolutely correct on that point. Here we differ from the Forts, for they thought nothing of sending ships all over the galaxy, regarding the expenditure as just part of the cost of business. The Returned Continuum must be more frugal, so we trade patterns, not matter. A fully functional Line allows the exchange of hardcast data so that one world's produce can be replicated elsewhere—perfectly, I might add, or else I wouldn't use the system myself."

"But what about the producer's proprietary methods?" asked a lean, long-jawed economist who had joined the conversation. "Once I have the pattern in my possession, what's to stop me from reproducing it ad nauseam, or selling the pattern elsewhere?"

"Nothing at all. Anyone can drink a bottle of Nettelbeck One Million, for a price, but the secret of making it and wines like it is known only at the source. Information, again, is the key to the galactic economy. Civilizations that nurture creative industries thrive, buoyed up by the novelties they make, while counterfeiters make occasional profits but inevitably stagnate. Remember the economies of scale that apply here. Faked patterns sell to a few dozen worlds, while the original makers have hundreds of millions of other systems at their fingertips. The fraction of a percentage stolen goes unnoticed by older, well-established Continuum members who don't mind waiting a millennium or two to see a profit."

Imre could see that his explanation was having the desired effect. The economist in particular looked as though he had swallowed something sour. Isolated systems weren't used to the kind of numbers that had once seemed everyday to citizens of the Continuum. There were five hundred billion stars in the galaxy, scattered across one hundred thousand light-years. That changed everything.

"A world's only valuable export," he went on, "is the product of its cleverest and most creative minds. There is no long-term profit to be found in imitation. Unlike in ancient times, the Returned Continuum has no need for cheap knockoffs or quick bucks. Hardcasting may not be cheap—no sane regime would use it as a substitute for planetary freight systems, for instance—but it does produce a competitive playing field. You should visit the Round, gentlemen, where the best of the galaxy converges, vying for attention. People have died there—driven mad by sheer variety."

Bowing politely, he left them considering the obvious ramifications of that point. What was unique about Dussehra? Would it sink or swim in the galactic community?

Al Freer was engaged in a serious debate with a trio of dour Gravamen, each as tattooed as their leader. Imre had yet to determine the reason for the scarification. He presumed it was a sign of rank. Swinging by the four of them, he quickly ascertained that the debate wasn't in danger of becoming heated and moved on.

The group lunched on finger food as the sun rode high in the sky. Patchwork fields of yellow undulated below, regularly punctuated by strips of natural foliage. The barque overtook a flock of grey, gooselike birds traveling in the same direction. A bank of ominous black clouds loomed ahead of them. Emlee was assured that the craft had survived much worse weather than a simple thunderstorm.

"It's designed to withstand a full-blown cyclone," boasted the barque's human captain when he came to join them for lunch. "Nothing short of a deliberate act of sabotage would bring us down—and I can assure you that security has never been tighter."

Imre cast Zerah a sober look. The Gravaman inclined his head in acknowledgment of Imre's concern but offered no further reassurance. He didn't need to. If the barque had been targeted by terrorists, they would all go down with it together.

As afternoon drifted toward evening, and the storm fell behind them, they finally reached the coast, which had snaked enigmatically in the distance for the rest of the trip, occasionally bejeweled by city lights. The subliminal thrum of the motors eased once they were over the water. The increasingly rowdy atmosphere of the traveling party ebbed.

Imre took a position at the rear of the barque, near the door through which he had entered. Emlee and Freer flanked him, standing stiffly to attention.

"Every culture has its own way of dealing with death," he

said to the gathering assembled before him. "The Returned Continuum is no different. We live under the shadow of the Forts' passing every day, acutely conscious of what is lost when even one unique being passes from our company. We must take the time to embrace the memories of those who have left us, to mourn them, and to let them go. I am grateful to Gravaman Zerah and all of you with us today for the chance to honor those who died as a result of the terrorist attack two days ago. They will be missed."

Emlee opened the door. Cold wind whipped through the barque, stealing warmth and the perfumes of luxury. Imre watched the crowd closely, noting those who looked most uncomfortable. Was it because of the weather or guilt? He would follow up these leads later.

Freer moved to the door with the cylinder he had brought with him into the barque crooked over his left arm. Within lay the remains of Chyro Kells and the aides who had borne the brunt of the explosion in the Temple, burned to ashes in a Dussehran crematorium. Freer didn't open the canister. At a nod from Imre, he simply lobbed it outside.

The crowd moved to the transparent floor, where the canister was visible tumbling toward the ocean. Before it hit the water, it puffed open, spreading the ashes in a starry cloud.

"Farewell, old friend," Imre said, softly enough to seem reverent but loud enough for everyone in the barque to hear. He was acutely conscious of the natives staring at him, as though he were mad.

Emlee shut the door. The wind stopped instantly, but the cold remained.

When the last of the grey cloud dispersed, servants appeared with drinks and the party resumed.

The moon was sailing high in the night sky by the time they reached the far side of the ocean. Below, an extensive archipelago of odd-shaped islands, some of them linked by slender bridges, segued gradually into an unbroken landmass. Gravaman Zerah offered names of landmarks as they glided by. Imre forgot them all. He was more interested in noting the way

Zerah and the other Gravamen avoided being touched—by anyone. It wasn't just shaking hands; all forms of physical contact seemed to be forbidden.

The two of them were sitting at the front of the barque with the party raging behind them. Audio filters and protocol maintained a relatively clear space around them, but Imre remained very aware that they were the only ones apparently attending to business. Zerah's skin had assumed a more lifelike color, thanks, presumably, to several tumblers of thick red liquor, but his mental faculties seemed unimpaired.

"Without Forts," he said, "how can you possibly maintain your grip on the galaxy? The moment you have it in your grasp, this magnificent, fragile crystal, you will squeeze too tight, and it will crumble to dust."

"You assume, as everyone does," Imre said, "that I have an ordinary grasp." He smiled tightly. "Delegation is the key to the Returned Continuum. Delegation enabled by communication and trust. The Line, obviously, provides the communication. Trust must be earned by everyone to whom responsibility is delegated. The hand I grasp with has millions of fingers. I will not slip."

"Specifically, then, how is control maintained over each system?"

"I would use the word 'coordination' rather than 'control.' In every system there exists a conduit, someone carefully chosen to stand between the Returned Continuum and its members. Juggling the needs of Primes with those of Earth is inevitably a tricky business. The conduit must be exactly the right person, or the network breaks down. We are very careful in choosing the right person for each system."

"'Chosen' was your word this time. This is not a democratic process, I take it."

"No." Imre let the single syllable hang between them for a moment. On that point there would be no negotiation. "You must understand that this role is a highly demanding one. It can only be performed by a singleton, since Primes lack the capacity to synchronize effectively with the tempo of the Returned Continuum. This is one area in which I must acknowledge the effectiveness of others. Were I to govern with a staff composed only of my kind, the Returned Continuum would indeed fall apart. So we work together: the raw vitality of Primes in tandem with the patient flexibility of singletons."

"The people of Dussehra would dislike an outsider dictating policy to them," said Zerah with a sour cast to his lips.

"It doesn't have to be an outsider. We would prefer, in fact, to find someone here to act as the conduit. Local knowledge is a valuable asset."

"I would never ask my people to do something I would not do myself."

"Naturally you would be part of the selection process. I think we can make it clear that this is a bold step for all Dussehrans, not just one of them."

Zerah seemed mollified by that response, for the moment. "Your argument is . . . persuasive. I wish, however, to know what happens to the worlds that refuse your offer. Are there many? Do they survive?"

"There have been a few," he said with great care. "Some are on the edge of the galactic disk and were completely isolated by the Slow Wave; they learned to like it, even though it was doing them harm. Ironically, it's these isolated systems that most need to be reconnected with the rest of humanity, or else they stagnate. Dussehra is, obviously, not in that situation; you are well located here and already have an established relationship with your neighbors. It's a miracle, in fact, that you hadn't reconnected before." A miracle, he added silently to himself, that your isolationist regime has lasted this long.

"Do these renegades always see the light?" pressed Zerah, clearly not willing to be distracted from the full answer he desired.

"Nearly always," said Imre, letting the first word carry the weight of his intended ambiguity. He had no doubt at all that Zerah, like Minister Sevaste and the would-be assassins, had heard the rumors circulating on the Line. If Zerah expected him to confirm them, then he would be disappointed.

"You must understand," said the Gravaman, "that we are not terrorists. We deal openly even with those we count among our enemies. This philosophy is ingrained within us. The attack on your Temple, therefore, did not originate here."

Imre already suspected that. He felt no need to ease Zerah's uncertainties. Feigning nonchalance, Imre leaned forward. "There's one thing I must ask you before the night's out. Your tattoos: what social meaning do they carry? I've not seen their like before." And there had been no information on them anywhere in the system, according to the Apparatus.

Zerah's rubbery expression hardened. "That is not relevant to this conversation."

"On the contrary. They are part of what makes you unique. People will be interested."

"They would not understand."

"How do you know that?" He smiled innocently, hiding his enjoyment at putting him on the spot for a change. "I can understand that you Gravamen—'graven men,' right?—have your secrets. It needn't go any further than here. You can trust me."

Zerah stood and straightened his robe. Without looking at Imre, he walked stiffly off into the crowd.

"Are you determined to make an enemy of him?" asked Emlee, appearing at his side.

"If he isn't already, then he needs to face a few hard truths." Imre stood and slid a finger around his collar, feeling suddenly tired and irritable. "They're only tattoos. What's the big deal?"

Emlee looked as weary as he felt. He wondered if she was still feeling the aftereffects of her recent injuries. "They call them the Veil. If you approach the questions more subtly, you might find your own answers."

"Well, that's just dandy."

"You need to cool down."

"I need to get off this fucking barge." With two swift motions, he opened his ceremonial armor down the front, letting cool in. His undershirt was soaked.

"What do you think you're doing?"

"Letting my hair down a little. Do you have a problem with that?"

"Why would I? The spook is keeping a close eye on things. You don't need me telling you how to behave; that's for sure." She turned and walked away.

"Hey, Emlee—" He made a grab for her arm and missed, wondering if she knew about Minister Sevaste and his blatant defiance of security protocols just two nights earlier. Ignoring him, she moved smoothly between chattering partygoers for the stairs to the upper levels. Snaring a drink from a passing tray, he followed her. "Wait."

"I'm going to get some rest," she said over her shoulder. "Are you going to stop me?"

"Of course not."

"You're not joining me, if that's what you're thinking."

"I wouldn't even suggest it. Let's talk—just for a moment—then I'll leave you alone."

She relented with a weary nod and pushed her way through the crowd to an empty sleeping compartment. The space within was small but well insulated and readily extruded two comfortable chairs for them to ease into. The fixed walls were wood-paneled and smooth to the touch. Through one round porthole, stars gleamed icily.

Imre sipped at his drink—a fizzy cocktail faintly reminiscent of green apples—then offered her a taste. She shook her head.

"You were going to tell me about the proto-Fort experiments here," he said. "I asked the Apparatus for the data while you were out of it. It seems to me that the trail went cold long ago."

Emlee nodded, then changed her mind about the drink. She downed half of it in one gulp, exhibiting no obvious pleasure as she did so.

"I'm sorry," he said.

"You've no need to be. It's my problem, not yours."

"The Luminous and the Barons are both our problems. I wish it were otherwise."

Her green eyes regarded him, half-lidded with fatigue. "Looks like there's no reason to stick around now. You can follow your crazy dream-message all you like. I won't kick up a fuss."

"Maybe I was overreacting," he said. The memory of the phantasm was becoming hazy with time. It was easier to believe that he had dreamed it. "We've made some progress here, yes, but there's still a long way to go. It would be irresponsible to leave Al here on his own."

"You think Zerah will come around?"

"I think he knows he has to, whether he wants to or not. What's one man against the rest of the galaxy?"

"Put that way, it does sound obvious."

She yawned.

"I'll leave you now," he said, standing.

"Take the drink," she said, "and wake me in an hour."

"If I'm still standing."

"Just don't do anything I wouldn't do."

"Coming from you, that doesn't leave me many options."

"If you'd wanted to party, you should've brought Helwise."

He closed the door on her and stood outside for a moment, feeling more alone than ever.

Then a trio of drunken hangers-on in various stages of undress descended upon him and challenged him to a game he'd never heard of. Feigning good-natured bewilderment, he let them sweep him away.

He dreamed of green valleys and red-lit windows, of incorporeal shapes like tattered, black storm clouds, circling him in slow motion. Voices whispered at him.

> *Evil things in robes of sorrow . . .*
> *A bird eating its own young . . .*
> *Sweet words, foul breath . . .*

He resisted the dream, trying to find a way out of its chilling embrace, but its limbs were wrapped tightly about him, and he could no more wriggle away than he could escape fate itself.

> *Wanderers unto this unhappy valley . . .*
> *The only true obstacle in your path . . .*
> *This magnificent, fragile crystal . . .*

A new star burned in the sky above. He clutched at it, sensing a way out of the trap he found himself in. Instead of release, the star unfolded a new wave of memories: the Line echoes and Render's reports from Sol. He squirmed in the dream and was distantly aware of his body doing the same in real life.

This is the art of survival, came Render's insidious, deathly tones—and then another phrase from even further in the past: *persistent luminous archaeoglyphs.*

He woke with a jerk, the final three words writ large in his mind. Freer's hand was on his shoulder, shaking him. Freer wanted to know if he was all right. Imre nodded, brushing him and the nightmare away. Why that memory now?

He blinked and took in his surroundings. He had slumped over in a chair in one dark corner of the barque. Others had done the same, clutching drinks in their lap, alone or in pairs or trios. Music still played, but quieter now, serenading the predawn landscape outside. Imre fought protesting joints and stood, nodding to reassure Freer that all was well. He straightened his armor and walked three steps to a table, where he poured himself a glass of water. He didn't feel dehydrated— even a Prime body was incapable of suffering an unwanted hangover—but his mouth was stale. The water washed away some of the sleep as glands flooded his tongue with a smooth, minty freshness.

"Apparatus," he asked silently, "what's an archaeoglyph?"

"I am not familiar with that word," the AI immediately responded, "but I construe from its construction that it is a specialized term combining 'archaeo-,' meaning 'ancient, primordial,' and 'glyph,' 'carving.'"

"A carving in what?" he wondered. He remembered where he had heard the phrase: not long after his awakening in his new body, the Jinc had probed his subconscious for clues about the Luminous. This was the only phrase that had triggered a reaction. The rest had been technical terms relating to the furthest fringes of high-energy physics. He felt there was a connection to the present, one that eluded him the more he thought about it.

When an explanation came to him, it was disappointingly mundane. He had used the word "graven" with Zerah in the last few hours. Could the connection with "carving" really be so simple?

He had to assume so until another explanation came to him.

Chasing phantoms wasn't on the agenda anymore, if anything he had said to Emlee in the dead of the night had been true. Still, the feeling nagged at him, even as he went about the business of the morning.

The thrumming of the barque's engines began to ease as their starting point appeared on the forward horizon. The city's lights burned brightly against the predawn backdrop. The merest hint of pink blushed in the western sky, pock-marked with fading stars. People began to stir, woken by internal alarms or nudges from companions. The smell of coffee and breakfast snacks filled the luxurious cabin.

Imre wasn't hungry. The sight of Gravaman Zerah descending the stairs didn't help his appetite. The looming man made straight for him and bowed when he arrived.

"I apologize for my rudeness last night," the man said. "You meant no harm. I would be happy to continue our discussion later today, if you remain interested in the subject."

Imre returned both the bow and the sentiments. "Thank you for your trust. I would be honored."

That seemed to end the matter, for Zerah turned to address a series of aides queuing behind him. The sound of his barking voice faded into the rising hubbub as Imre went to stand at the forward viewing area, watching the city grow steadily nearer, his arms tightly folded across his chest. He wondered how the other guests had enjoyed the journey around the world. Few had spent much time admiring the view, being far more interested in the interpersonal politics of the gathering. He wondered how many deals had been made, favors called in, and illicit liaisons enjoyed. The barque could have flown around Veldoen all day and night for all the difference it would have made.

He didn't think any less of them for that. He was no different. Apart from fending off the occasional would-be lover, he had spent most of the night talking shop with anyone who would listen. His mission was to forge bonds between Dussehra and the Returned Continuum, not sightsee—and perhaps if he had slept with an influential partner or two, maybe that would have made a difference. But he hoped not. If Dussehra was the kind of world on which sex substituted for diplomacy, then his mission was going to be harder than ever to see to a satisfactory conclusion.

He thought of Minister Sevaste and wondered if she had come to him like that under express orders from the Barons. Did they know him so well that they could predict what he would respond to? Had he been played in exactly the same way some had tried the previous evening and simply fallen for a more skillful ploy?

It was all too possible. There was a connection between Himself and the Barons—unproved but indubitable. He would much rather think that Sevaste's plan had been entirely her own than accept that he had been seduced by someone who thought they knew him better than anyone else did.

Crystalline towers conspired like giant canine teeth, pointing up at him in gleaming clusters. The sun rose, and shivering reflections danced between the vertical facades, growing brighter and sharper edged with every passing minute. The barque descended until it was at the level of the topmost spires, then descended farther until it hung directly over the top of one particularly ornate building, crenulated and pennanted in the style of a glass castle stretching half a kilometer into the air. Imre turned to find Freer, then remembered Zerah saying something about returning them not to the Temple but to the capital buildings of the Dussehran state. Fair enough, he thought. The sooner the pomp and ceremony was over and the real work of thrashing out the treaty begun, the better.

The ramp extended down to a docking pad that was featureless apart from a single, blocky protuberance with open doors on one side. A line of beefy guards led to the door, leaving no doubt at all which way the guests were supposed to walk. The guards' weapons were sheathed carefully at their sides, for appearance's sake.

"Let's walk down together," said Zerah, appearing at his side, his expression typically dour. How he had ever come to power, Imre couldn't imagine.

"Why not?" He smiled with greater cheer than he felt, although he could see the value in the symbolic gesture—and what it might cost the Gravaman if his fellows disapproved. Side by side, they walked through the crowd to the door. The wind was as brisker than it had been the previous day, for the weather had turned cloudy during the course of the morning. The crystalline docking pad was pimpled with evaporating raindrops.

With slow, ceremonial steps, Gravaman Zerah guided him down the ramp. Emlee followed close behind, with one of Zerah's most senior aides at her side and Freer behind her. The rest of the party, more subdued than it had been the day before, brought up the rear in pairs. There was, to Imre's great relief, no welcoming ceremony to endure and no stopping once they reached level ground. Zerah maintained a steady pace for the open portal, through which Imre could see the inner door of a weather lock.

He stepped inside, looking forward to getting out of the cold air.

A loud bang came from directly behind him and the world went suddenly dark. His reflexes took over, raising his tempo and ramping up all his senses at once. The space inside the weather lock was suddenly cavernous and echoing. His spine groaned in complaint as he twisted to look behind him.

The external door had come down tight, blown faster than was possible by any merely electric motor—explosive charges were behind it, designed to react more quickly than any human could. A molten yellow light, bright to his enhanced eyesight, revealed that the seam had been melted shut. No electronic command from the Apparatus would open this door. The one leading into the building was sealed the same way.

His mind was racing. Long before his protesting Prime muscles had brought him completely about, he knew what he would find.

Zerah's left hand was already coming out from under his robes, moving in ghostly slow motion, a firearm clenched tightly in his fleshy fingers.

A bold step for all Dussehrans, he had said.

We are not terrorists.

And: *I would never ask my people to do something I would not do myself.*

Imre had no doubt that Zerah would pull the trigger once

the pistol had found its target. There wasn't time to dodge and no space to run. The instincts of a soldier gave him one chance of survival only. It all depended on whose tempo was faster: his or Zerah's.

He leapt for the Gravaman with all his strength, heedless of the pain it caused his newly healed legs. His arms came up like leaden weights. The booming of his heart nearly deafened him. He didn't look away from Zerah's eyes. If the trigger was pulled, he would know.

They collided with exaggerated momentum, crashing into the welded door, then falling in a tangle of limbs to the ground. The weapon flashed and dazzled him. A beam laser with a wide dispersal, more effective at close range but handy for blinding at longer distances. Imre closed his eyes and grappled for leverage over Zerah's gun arm. The Gravaman was physically larger than he but didn't know how to fight hand to hand. The laser flashed again; this time his eyelids protected him from the worst of it. Zerah grunted. Imre found an arm and twisted with all his weight.

Zerah was suddenly under him, pinned, and the gun was sliding across the floor. Imre took a split second to breathe. He didn't seem to be injured; the suit had taken most of the damage. He was lucky Zerah had chosen such an outdated weapon and failed to raise it high enough for a lethal head-shot.

And unlucky for Zerah, if being touched ran so contrary to his traditions.

When he was certain Zerah couldn't squirm free, Imre returned his tempo to Absolute.

"That was a mistake," he said.

"It's never a mistake," growled the fallen man, "to stand up for one's people."

"Even when there's no hope of winning? I've been a soldier for seven hundred thousand years; I've survived every possible betrayal." Sounds came through both doors. The Apparatus was calling him. "You're nothing but a fool. Soon you'll be a dead fool, who achieved nothing in the last moments of his life. How does that sit with you?"

"Spare me your speeches. Kill me now and be done with it."

"Oh, I'm not going to kill you." He couldn't help the spite that crept like acid into his voice. "Remember that conversation we had about delegation? You'll find out what I mean by this time tomorrow."

The exterior door split open in a shower of bright red sparks. Daylight swept over them in a rush. Imre looked up into the worried faces of Emlee and Freer, obscured behind their protective visors.

"Don't touch the weapon," he told them, mindful of the guards behind them, frozen in their armor, and the crowd gathered behind them, looking shocked and terrified. The city's lights had gone out. "It bears just one set of prints. Local law enforcement, if it's worth the name, will know what to do with it."

Zerah growled wordlessly as Imre stood, using the man beneath him for leverage. His knees felt like overwound springs, liable to snap at any moment. "Apparatus? We need a ride."

The barque ascended, allowing a smaller airship to take its place on the docking pad. The puzzled crew of four exited and went to join the rest of the onlookers. The people he had met overnight stared at him as though he had grown a new head. Imre didn't waste time explaining what had happened; if they couldn't work it out for themselves, having him do it for them was worse than pointless.

Zerah watched them go with hatred in his eyes, robes in disarray, and his face smudged.

"Are you feeling all right?" Emlee asked him when the airship rose up from the top of the capital building and swooped through the motionless city, heading for the Temple.

Imre didn't know what she meant until he followed the direction of her gaze. Taking off his gloves, he felt the deep burn scored across the throat of his suit. A millimeter or two higher, and Zerah's laser would have beheaded him.

"Never been better," he said, looking down at the gloves in his hands. The fingertips were smudged black, but not by burned carbon. It looked as though he had been rubbing something tarry between them. He thought of Zerah's smudged face and wondered.

"What?" asked Emlee.

"Nothing important," he said, putting the thought aside. "I've made up my mind. You and I are leaving as soon as the hardcaster is functional. Al is staying behind. He and the Apparatus can finish the job."

She frowned. "Are you sure that's the best thing to do?"

"It's the way it's going to be. I can take a hint—and I've got more important things to worry about than some backward world with an attitude problem."

"I think you're making a mistake, drawing a line too soon."

"That's not what you thought last night."

"But last night we weren't talking about the same thing."

"Don't you think Al's up to it?"

"I know exactly what he's capable of."

Freer followed the exchange with cobalt eyes. He didn't question his orders; he never did. "Don't let it be your problem, Emlee," he said. "It doesn't have to be."

"My problem is that we're abandoning everything here in order to chase a fantasy halfway across the galaxy." She looked resigned, pursuing the argument even though she knew she couldn't possibly win it. "What happens if we get there, Imre, and your mystery guest never shows?"

"Or worse," he said. "Depending on who it is, it might be better if he doesn't show."

" 'He'?" Her frown deepened. "Who exactly do you think it's going to be?"

Imre turned away. That was one suspicion he had shared with no one but Render, who had guessed anyway, and nursed the secret like a bruise since the end of the Mad Times—that his former self was still out there, playing games with the galaxy. He had been chasing hints and rumors for so long, the thought that he might finally come face-to-face with Himself was a weird one indeed.

Through the window, he saw a lone bird perched on the summit of the Temple roof, gazing out at the unnaturally silent city. The Apparatus had shut down everything the moment Zerah had sprung his trap. No one had ordered the AI to release its grip. The roads and walkways were still; the power was off. Imre imagined tens of thousands of people trapped in their homes, disconnected from the world outside and wondering what was going on. Unbeknownst to them, everything had changed. Their world would never be the same again.

The bird took fright and flew away as the airship approached. He followed it with his eyes until it was a dot almost too small to identify.

"Let's just see what happens," he said. "Something always seems to."

The airship touched down and they wordlessly disembarked.

THIS SIDE OF HELL

An excited and highly distempered ideality threw a sulphureous lustre over all.

—Edgar Allan Poe

They gathered in the hardcaster room less than a week after Imre had arrived. The blood and black scars left on the walls by the explosion were gone. No evidence at all remained that people had died there. Imre thought of Chyro Kells and felt a twinge of something that wasn't quite guilt, unless it were possible to feel that emotion in advance.

Two sarcophagi were active, gaping like open mouths at the three people in the room.

"That little priest of yours hasn't come to say good-bye," Emlee said.

Imre looked up at her and said nothing. So, she had found out about him and Minister Sevaste. Not that there was anything to know. Sevaste hadn't been seen in the Temple since Zerah's betrayal. Her disappearance had barely registered during the events of the previous days.

"Jealous, Emlee?" asked Freer.

"Stupidity," she scoffed, "is nothing to be proud of."

Imre didn't rise to the bait, concentrating instead on disrobing. The smooth interior of the sarcophagus was cool against his backside when he lowered himself inside it. He sat there for a moment, searching his mind for any last-minute messages he wanted to convey. Freer clearly had none; he watched dispassionately as his last personal links with the Returned Continuum prepared to leave him for good. Even if all went well, it would be centuries or more before Dussehra was stable and reconnected. Freer would set himself up as conduit between the world and the galaxy surrounding it, and so it would stay until the locals could be completely trusted and a local replacement found.

Imre left in complete confidence that, whatever it took and however Dussehra would look afterward, Freer always got the job done.

"Thanks, Al," was all Imre said in the end.

Freer just nodded.

Emlee settled back into her sarcophagus. Her lid began to lower immediately. She wasn't ordinarily one to waste time on good-byes and good lucks.

Imre lay down and let the sarcophagus close over him. He had done this thousands of times and never quite got over the feeling of being buried alive. The interior of the casket was utterly dark and silent apart from his own breathing. He counted the seconds until the process began, knowing that on the far side he wouldn't remember how it felt. Did it hurt? Did it come as a flash of bright light, blindingly euphoric? Or was it nothing at all, as anticlimactic as falling asleep?

Hardcasting was routine; the questions it inspired were anything but.

A comms channel opened up between Emlee and him. She said only two words before the channel closed again.

"Sweet dreams."

He had enough time to wonder if it was a throwaway comment, or if she was referring to the visions he had received last time—

—and then his eyes were opening in a new body, a new place, and this time there was no sense of disorientation. He could see nothing at all, but at least the darkness was untainted by phantoms. The air smelled sharp-edged and metallic. His mind was clear. He hadn't dreamed at all.

On the other side of the sarcophagus lid, Earth awaited him. Earth and an entirely new set of circumstances. Between one instant and the next, while the thin thread of his hardcast had wound through the complex tangle of the Line, twenty thousand years Absolute had passed. Dussehra was far behind him now. For better or for worse, whatever had happened there was long over. He hoped the situation he was walking into would be less rather than more complicated—although given Earth, and given the person who would no doubt be waiting for him, he was prepared for disappointment.

The seal of the lid hissed. The hinges behind his head creaked. He steeled himself for the shock of light on his unprepared irises. The effort didn't go to waste. The room outside was blindingly white. For a moment he could barely make out the figure standing at the foot of the opening sarcophagus.

"You're early," said a voice that was as familiar to him as his own.

"Hello, Helwise." He sat up as soon as there was room and flexed his new tissues under the welcome one gravity of Earth. "You don't sound very pleased to see me."

"I hate surprises." She stood with her arms folded over a tight-fitting, deep red outfit with pointed shoulders. Her black hair lay flat against her head and curled under her ears like snakes. One long fingernail tapped restlessly against the muscle on her upper arm. "Where's Chyro? It's not like you to travel without that creepy little fuck in tow."

"Between you and me, he's dead." He studied her for any kind of emotional reaction and found none. "We only got as far as Dussehra. There was some trouble."

"More of the same?"

He thought of Sevaste, Zerah, and the four dissidents he had had shot for nearly killing Emlee. "It doesn't really matter what it was. What brought me back is the partial Fort that intercepted me on the way there." The room contained only his sarcophagus and a small table next to it, and Helwise, alone. Folded neatly on the table was a white cotton robe, which he slipped over his stubbled head once he was on his feet. "Have there been any unexpected arrivals?"

"Apart from yours?" She rolled her gold-flecked eyes. "Of course there have been."

"Anyone significant, I mean. Out of the ordinary. Unique."

"Look through the registers yourself, if you like."

He studied her, wanting to diffuse the sublimated hostility that issued from her like hard radiation. They needed each other. That was his motto, repeated every moment he was on Earth with the same determined circularity as a Tibetan mantra. But the indicators he might have employed to find a path through her emotional minefield were as unreadable to him now as ancient Chinese pictograms. It was like playing chess in the dark with a mad grand master.

"I haven't come back to check on you," he said.

"You don't do anything without a reason."

"That's true, Helwise, but you've got the reason wrong. This could be the break I've been waiting for. It's nothing to do with you."

Her guard cracked for a moment, and he wondered what he saw beneath. He couldn't tell if she was relieved or disappointed, or simply shifting to a new strategy.

"So what is it?" she asked. "Barons? Domgard? The Luminous?"

"I don't know for sure," he said. "The message was cryptic on every point but this one: that I had to come here as soon as possible." *Be there, ruler of the realm, to open your red-lit windows and bid him enter.* "I'm telling myself to be patient."

"Never a strong suit for you." She gave him half a smile in return; it had an edge to it that he still couldn't interpret. "Emlee's two rooms down the hall, being checked over. You're next in the queue. We don't have anything scheduled—"

"That's fine," he said. "I don't want to get in the way of your plans. Pretend I'm not here. If I find what I'm looking for sooner rather than later, I might not stay very long."

"Back out on the road," she drawled, "meeting and greeting. These whistle-stop tours of yours sound like one endless barbecue."

"Believe me," he said, raising one hand to touch his throat. "It's harder than it sounds."

"Oh, you're completely welcome to it. I hate barbecues." She moved for the door. "You'll find some things have changed around here."

"Anything important?"

"That depends on your definition, I guess." She pulled a veil across the lower half of her face and exited the room, more a stranger to him than ever. A retinue of identical, cream-clad acolytes enfolded her and escorted her up the hallway, matching their steps perfectly to hers. Four armored guards filled the vacancy at his door, all sweeping curves and faceless metal. Their reflective armor gleamed like polished silver. Mirror images of him, twisted and warped from true, stared back at him in puzzlement.

Since when had he needed guards on Earth?

Taking a deep, preparatory breath, he closed the sarcophagus lid and went to find Emlee.

The physician, a bland, sexless blonde Imre had never seen before, was just finishing up with her when he entered. He thought of the phantasm's words, *Round about your ruby home, your glory, spirits move, pallid but dutiful,* and was momentarily taken off guard.

"All clear," Emlee said, turning her back and slipping a matching white tunic over her head. Imre watched her, distracted. Her skin was pale and unblemished. There was no sign at all of the injuries she had received on Dussehra beyond a slight bleaching of her short, straw-colored hair.

"Any new messages?" she asked.

"None," he said as he submitted to his own examination. Apart from a minor infection with an unknown biological agent, treatable by a simple course of antibiotics, the biosphere of Dussehra had left no mark on him. "Whatever caught me on the way in to Dussehra didn't bother repeating the trick on the way out."

"Nothing else to say, I guess. You either listened, or you didn't."

"And now it comes to the crunch."

"You look nervous," she said. "You're never nervous. What's going on, Imre?"

"Nothing." He waved away her concern in a way he hoped was more in character.

"Whatever you say." She waited patiently until the physician was finished, her green eyes never leaving him. "I thought Render would've come to say hello."

"No sign of him yet." That didn't worry him. He could feel the usual drip-feed of data pressing for his subconscious appraisal, so the oldest member of his retinue was still hard at work. Imre wondered what surprises might appear within his dreams the next time he found the chance to sleep.

The physician pronounced his satisfaction, bowed, and left. Imre didn't ask the guards where they might find new clothes. Unless the layout of the hardcasting facility had changed, he knew where to go.

Imre and Emlee keyed a selection of new outfits from a fabricator near the main entrance of the facility. Fashions had definitely changed while he was gone and currently favored impractical ballooning forms originating in zero gee. He chose a bodysuit in black with a matching cloak and no insignia. Emlee opted for a white security uniform that was as sleek as it was functional. Both garments arrived within seconds, warm and slightly furry to the touch after the fabrication process. They slipped into separate cubicles to change.

Dressed, Imre felt the mantle of responsibility for the Returned Continuum settling over him. He resisted it. Just because he was home, that didn't mean he had to assume his official role. He knew from experience just how overwhelming the duty was. The moment he announced his return, he would be overrun by appointments and forced to work without pause, no matter how he overclocked. He could completely forget about searching for mysterious arrivals and making sure they too weren't swamped by the system, whoever they might be.

The warren of rooms and corridors was much smaller than the equivalent complex in Smitherman City, far above. No one came directly to Earth's surface without special permission. The Apparatus made certain of that. There were two ways to leave the hardcast facility—three, counting being sent as a hardcast itself. Imre chose the smaller, secure exit that opened only for inner-circle biometrics. It led to a little-used corridor winding around the public spaces of Citadel Terra, the largest single structure on Earth and the "jewel of the empire," as media commentators occasionally called it. Containing opulent residences for official visitors, expansive conference rooms, and glittering reception halls—the most magnificent and ostentatious being the Throne Room occupying most of the ground floor—the building functioned as a focal point for both the First Church of the Return and the Returned Continuum. Indeed, the two ideological entities became functionally identical on the surface of the Earth, where Imre Bergamasc's secular godhead was realized. The Citadel was large enough to house many thousands of people at a time, offering them places both to work and to play. Most of them were visitors, supplicants and diplomats from the many millions of systems comprising the Returned Continuum, bringing with them all the issues and artistry of far-off lands. A steady flow came down the skyline from Smitherman City; an equal amount returned every day, after their moment in the spotlight. Much of the city's management was automatic, overseen by the Apparatus and other smaller AIs. There were servants and guards, mostly for show—recruited by lottery from the trillions of volunteers all wanting to spend some time on the home planet. Protected by the nearby systems of the Round and layer upon layer of security, there were few physical threats to be found in the Citadel's glittering corridors. Normally.

At the smaller exit, Imre stopped and dismissed the guards.

"Thank you," he told them, "but I'm sure you have more important duties."

"We have been ordered by the Regent to remain with you at all times," protested the burliest.

"And I'm countermanding her orders. We can look after ourselves."

"Yes, First Prime." The guards reluctantly bowed and tramped back the way they had come.

Emlee watched them go. "Are you sure that's a good idea?" she asked him, when they were out of earshot.

"To ditch Helwise's goons? I'm sure it won't hurt us. Besides, we have the Apparatus to watch over us. Is that right, Apparatus? Are you listening?"

"I am, Imre," said the impersonal voice in his ear.

"Then we have nothing to worry about. Keep our location off the radar," he told the AI. "I want to look around before too many people know I'm here."

He keyed the biometric lock, and the exit slid open. A feeling of mild euphoria hit him as he stepped through. The air smelled different in the Citadel than it had on Dussehra. It tasted more vital, more charged with potential, as though the sheer concentration of power physically altered the atoms comprising it.

"Where to first?" asked Emlee, walking a pace ahead of him on his right side, pointedly not his left. The corridor curved gently away from them, toward an unseen destination. All he could hear was the faint whir of air-conditioning.

"Somewhere quiet," he said. "I want you and me to look through the transit records and see who exactly has been through here and who's expected to come. System traffic logs might be worth a scan too. If we don't find anything right away, transcripts of Helwise's audience requests could give us a clue. Whatever that partial Fort knew, it has to show up somewhere."

"Unless it was lying."

"Again with that theory. What would a Fort have to gain by making my life more difficult? We're on their side."

"There are no sides," called a voice from farther up the corridor. "Haven't you heard?"

Emlee was instantly on guard, putting herself between Imre and anything that might suddenly come at them. "Who's there?"

Laughter, braying and brash, preceded the padding of unshod feet as someone ran toward them.

Imre pushed Emlee out of the way, determined to meet whoever it was without cowering behind her. But the figure that appeared was at first glance anything but a threat. A slender man with wild, streaked hair, he ran with an uncoordinated but highly energized gait. He didn't seem to be armed. His clothes looked as though they had spent a year in the back of an asteroid freighter before being run over by a drove of pigs.

He skidded to a halt in front of them and braced himself in

readiness to run away. A powerful stink of urine and sweat roiled from him. His teeth were yellow.

"Are you who I think you are?" he asked Imre, tilting his head. "Or do I think you are because I think you want to be?"

"Don't come any closer," Emlee warned him. "I won't tell you again."

The manifestation straightened and executed an elaborate curtsy. "My hearing is excellent," he said, "my willingness to obey sporadic. I won't expect you to forgive me if I make you do something you'll regret later."

He was rattling Emlee. Her unease took the form of an unnatural stillness in every muscle of her body as she tensed, ready to lash out.

"Be calm," Imre told the man. "Don't make any sudden moves. Just tell me your name and there will be no trouble."

"You should know it." He grinned as though glad to be distracted. "I am Ra, the child of the Citadel."

"A child?" Emlee snorted in disbelief. "Who'd be so stupid as to bring a kid here?"

"Oh, I'm not a guest. I live here." Ra's head tilted again, and his grin widened to expose the stumps of his teeth. "Who are you to say my parents are anything other than exemplary?"

"Just back off," she said. "Go play with someone else. We're not your babysitters."

"I came to meet you," he said. "I heard you were here, and I ran as fast as I could. Should I be disappointed at my reception? Should I throw a tantrum and stamp my feet?" Again, he laughed; it shook him like a convulsion, painful for its lack of hilarity as well as its volume. "There are things a child is allowed to do. There's a certain madness that's expected—even demanded—"

He lunged for Imre with a look in his eyes that wasn't entirely playful. Before he could get close, Emlee reached out and took his right arm in both of hers and swung him down and around so her knee was in his back. With a grunt she put all her weight into keeping him flat against the floor.

"Prime or singleton," she asked him. "Your life depends on it."

"Singleton," he gasped.

"If that's a lie, it's the last you'll ever utter." She wrenched him like a shearer throwing a sheep and got him into a choke-hold.

"It's not a lie!" he managed to say. "Don't hurt me!"

She held him still, and Imre knew what she was thinking: if everything they had heard was true, then the child she had pinned would possess many such bodies, elsewhere, and killing this one would do him little harm. Until his personality solidified, dramatic change was the norm for any young singleton.

But the fact remained that he was a child. Whatever he was doing here and whoever his parents were, what right did she have to discipline him? At any other time, his antics would be tolerated as the outbursts of a developing mind. It wasn't his fault that he had strayed across their path.

She looked up at Imre for guidance, a look of upset worn deeply into the lines of her face.

"Apparatus," Imre asked aloud, so she would know that he was seeking answers from elsewhere, "do you know this person? Is he really a permanent citizen of Earth?"

"He is. The name he has chosen is 'Ra.' "

"That was the name he used." Emlee watched him closely as he spoke. "Why didn't you warn us he was there?"

"He is not rated as a threat."

"By whom?"

"The Regent."

"What does Helwise have to do with him?"

"She is his mother."

The matter-of-fact sentence exploded in Imre's chest like a depth charge. "His what?"

"What's the ghost telling you?" Emlee asked him. "Who is this brat?"

"I—" gasped the child. "—sorry I—didn't mean—"

"Let him go," Imre told her. A rising dizziness made the world feel distant and strange. "He won't hurt us."

"But—" She swallowed her protest. "All right. Then will you tell me what's going on?"

"Yes."

She eased her grip on the child and stepped away. Ra

rolled over, rubbing his throat, and looked at them with renewed playfulness. Imre saw gold flecks in his dark blue eyes and knew that he had inherited them with his maternal genes.

"No sides, like a circle!" The child sprang to his feet. Emlee tensed, but his attention wasn't focused on them anymore. Shouting his name like a bird, he spun in a circle and ran headlong up the corridor, away from them. "Ra! Ra! Ra!"

They let him go. Instead of answering Emlee's questions, Imre turned his attention back to the Apparatus and asked in urgent tones, "Is Helwise the sole parent?"

"No other is registered."

"How did she have it? I mean, is he adopted, biological—what?"

"The child was partured normally, according to medical records."

"When was he born?"

"Eight sidereal years ago, Absolute."

Not even a child, then. Ra was barely more than a baby; in singleton terms, he hardly counted as a *person*.

Imre gripped his temples with the thumb and forefingers of his right hand. This was a mess. Helwise had warned him in a halfhearted way, but it still came as a shock. Helwise, a mother? The chess game they were playing had suddenly become very serious indeed.

"Could you be—?" Emlee began, her voice hushed.

"Don't ask it," he said. "Don't even think it." Suddenly his legs were moving, propelling him in Ra's wake like a clockwork robot and gaining momentum with every pace. He wasn't sure where he was going at first; the revelation had thrown him more than it should have. All he knew was that he had to move before something else blindsided him. Or, heaven help him, the boy returned.

Emlee trailed him, fists clenched at her side. "I don't understand," she said. "Why does this make such a difference?"

Imre ignored her. "Where's Render?" he asked the AI through the privacy of his implants.

"Render is in the Adytum."

"Tell him I'm on my way." An intersection appeared around

the bend of the corridor. He stopped so suddenly, Emlee collided with his shoulder. They bounced apart. He couldn't meet her gaze. "I'm sorry, Emlee. You'll have to chase those records without me."

"But—"

"Don't argue. We'll talk later."

"I don't know what I'm looking for," she yelled after him as he ran ahead and took the turn.

"Just use your instincts," he called back over his shoulder.

Then he was running with all his strength, pounding the floor and feeling the charged air streaming past his face and scalp, toward the only place on Earth he knew he could feel completely safe.

Humanity's home world had changed many times since its dominant species had reached the stars. Oceans had risen and fallen; rivers of ice and had encroached from and retreated to the poles; forests had turned to deserts and deserts to forests; rivers had changed course; lakes had formed and dried up; and coastlines had shifted.

Paratlantis was no different, although it had been spared major disruption by virtue of its location at the base of the world's oldest skyline, thereby linking the birthplace of a species with the galactic vistas it would one day conquer. The mid-Atlantic ridge beneath it might wander and buckle; the seas might lap higher or lower at its sides. The island itself would remain, fixed like the imaginary line connecting the moon's Earthward face and the center of the planet.

When Imre had conquered the Earth, Paratlantis had been little more than a ruin overtaken by tropical jungle. The first official project he had enacted on assuming control of the Apparatus was to create on the ancient island a refuge for those wishing to visit Earth. Little more than a dozen buildings at first, the refuge had spread to occupy the entire island and soon extended over the ocean surrounding it. Realizing that such growth could not be supported indefinitely—not without allowing a return of the depredations the planet had suffered in the past—Imre had introduced strict caps on the number of people allowed on the surface, moved the administration into upper orbit, and commissioned the palace that remained the most visible sign of the Returned Continuum's occupation of Earth. Citadel Terra was a vast, terraced pyramid embracing the base of the skyline, one kilometer across and half that high. The jungle was allowed to reclaim the remaining land, providing a wealth of natural life for visitors to goggle at: graceful, swaying palms; brightly colored parrots; even a colony of macaque monkeys, restored to their natural state by geneticists determined to undo the damage of their forebears. Twice a year, the equinox was celebrated by opening the roof of the Throne Room at noon and flying kites painted the colors of the Round. Only those closest to Earth could expect to come, although special guests from farther afield were invited every year, to strengthen political ties. Imre had attended so many such celebrations in the past that his memories of them had blurred into one.

Unknown to everyone who visited the planet, there existed a second structure on Paratlantis that was linked to the first by an underground tunnel slicing deep through the bedrock, far below the network of ancient basements and subways left behind by the waves of former colonization, now maintained by persistent automated repair systems or slowly filling up with dust and tree roots. The entrance to this particular tunnel changed regularly, moved by the Apparatus under the guise of regular maintenance. The AI patiently guided him through a maze of service corridors to where the current entrance resided. It looked like an ordinary maintenance closet, with no security measures in evidence. Imre was certain, however, that it was carefully protected from accidental discovery.

He pushed the grey metal panel, and it swung silently open. Musty air greeted him, and he screwed up his nose. No matter how airtight the secret tunnel was supposed to be, it always stank of old earth and civilization's decay.

Some of his frantic urgency vanished, then. What, exactly, was he running from? So Helwise had a child. So what? It had nothing to do with him.

That she hadn't told him in advance suggested that this wasn't true. And there was an issue of timing, too, that he wanted to check with Render before he made a response of any kind, to anyone. He was afraid of thinking about it too much, lest he tied himself in knots he couldn't undo.

He passed through the door and closed it carefully behind him. Dim white lights shone on a concrete staircase that wound down into the bowels of the island. He descended quickly, listening to the echoes his feet made down the sterile shaft. It sounded like an army was following when in fact he and Render were, most likely, the only people who would ever come that way.

At the bottom was a thin, gleaming maglev track that led along a cylindrical pipe. A two-seat car waited for him there, humming. He mounted it and clung tight to handlebar grips as it rapidly picked up speed. The track curved and tilted along several complex trajectories before finally joining the tunnel he remembered: a broad, well-lit tube almost identical to the subways of old. The maglev track hugged the left-hand wall. His car picked up speed until it was almost too painful to keep his eyes open. His cloak flapped and snapped behind him like a flag in a hurricane.

Fly your banners, porphyrogene, the phantasm had told him. He had eventually looked up the unusual word on Dussehra. It had puzzled him then, and it positively irked him now. Redolent with literary allusions, the word had no clear-cut meaning. It was most frequently linked to royalty and the progeny of kings. He had thought that maybe the phantasm was referring to himself, being a strange offshoot of his former life, but now . . .

This—all this ruin—is your dominion.

It was impossible, he told himself. Utterly impossible that the phantasm could have known about Ra before Imre had arrived at Dussehra. It felt like only days ago to Imre, but on Earth twenty thousand years had passed while he had hardcast his way along the Line. Although Forts—even partial Forts—had prodigious mental capacities, supernatural foresight wasn't one of them. Ra hadn't been a thought in his mother's mind when the phantasm had uttered that word.

Unless the zygote had already existed and had not yet been brought to term . . . ?

Again Imre quashed all thought along that line. It brought with it too much emotional baggage and far too many complex ramifications.

He almost groaned aloud at the thought that he had asked Helwise about any unexpected arrivals—without knowing how appropriate the question really was.

Deceleration came all too quickly, and he was soon stepping off the car onto the platform at the far end, feeling chilled from the rapid transit. There was nothing to suggest that he had arrived anywhere special. Just a grey door set into naked stone. The air was even denser there, if that were possible, and Imre didn't waste any time getting out of it.

Now that he was back on familiar territory, he felt more confident. The grey door led to a spiral staircase that wound five complete circuits steeply upward through a shaft six meters wide. He took his time, knowing Render would register his presence long before he actually arrived. The air in the shaft became less chilly the higher he ascended. He began to feel naturally warm again. When his nostrils caught the scent of chocolate on the final circuit, he knew he was almost home.

Crimson light spilled from a triangular door at the top of the stairs. He walked through unhesitatingly, into a haven of red glass and sharp angles. The underground space was modeled on a Latin Cross cathedral. He had entered by the northern transept. Steep walls rose above him to meet in a vaulted ceiling dozens of meters high. There were no windows; natural light filtered down from the surface by thousands of fiberoptic channels, each illuminating a different section of the glass walls from behind. The walls themselves were composed of fragments of stained glass, all in various shades of red.

To some people's eyes, Imre was sure, it might look like an anachronistic version of hell. To his, it was the culmination of an obsession he had glimpsed in the Corps' secret habitat, long ago—an obsession his former self had explored in secret and which he had continued upon the original collection's destruction. Why stained glass? The answer to that question no longer remained in his memory. He continued it out of momentum and out of tribute to his triumphant return to public life in Mandala Supersystem. The only memento he had retained of his former life was a single shard of precious red glass, which lay even now in a padded box in the cathedral's apse.

There were other secrets, too, in the dark corners of his sanctuary—his Adytum, where no one but he and Render were allowed to go—and they would stay there forever, if he had his way.

A single column of yellow light descended vertically to where the crossing would have been, illuminating a bed, two couches, and a desk, none of them occupied. They were the room's sole gesture to human habitation, apart from a small bathroom he rarely used. The nave contained a labyrinth of files, drawers, and bookcases in which was assembled the largest collection of ancient human relics in the galaxy. Earth's graves and rubbish tips were deep. Layer upon layer of habitation, some erased from or never recorded in the electronic archives, had succumbed to Imre's surveys of the planet. In the early days of the Returned Continuum, it had been an all-pervading obsession—sifting through the past while putting the present in order. Both tasks, he feared, were perpetual.

He strode to the nave and looked around. No sign of Render apart from a steaming mug of chocolate and an open book lying flat upon the desk. He recognized it on sight: *Zaknythos*, by Henre Le Rennet and Edgar A. Perry. Imre had found the book in a subterranean cache protected by layers upon layers of security measures. Its extreme rarity—a genuine paper book, one of the few remaining from the twenty-first century—ensured it a prized position in his collection.

He picked up the book, winced at the sight of the newly cracked spine, closed it, and laid it carefully on its back in the center of the desk.

"Hello," said a voice from behind him.

Imre looked around. Render was strolling out of a corridor between two tall bookcases with half a green apple in one hand and a second book in the other, the pitted skin of his face twisted into something that might have been a smile. He was close-shaven across his entire head, as always, and he wore the same functional grey uniform that Imre had rarely seen him out of. His frame was extraordinarily solid, containing nothing but muscle upon muscle, from the slopes of his massive shoulders down to his sturdy ankles, and he walked with a slight stoop, as though carrying a small mountain on his back. Imre had seen him move like a whippet when he needed to, however, and would trust his life to the dexterity of those deceptively blunt fingers.

"Hello to you," he said in return, unable to tell just yet what frame of mind his oldest friend was in.

"Seen the man?" Before Imre could reply, he answered his own question with a sharp nod. "The son of God."

"He was something of a surprise, I'll admit." They sat on different couches, facing each other. Render crossed his legs, looking perfectly at ease. Imre leaned forward with his elbows on his knees. "Is Helwise the only parent, do you think?"

"I can't be sure." Render shrugged. "It could be yours."

"But why?"

"He is a puppet."

"Do you think so?"

Render winked his green eye, leaving the stare of his mismatched blue eye unbroken. "I don't want to think about it."

Behind Render's barbed flippancy, Imre sensed a keen awareness of the situation. Helwise had created a child that might in part be Imre's, without telling him, let alone asking his permission. She had done it while he was away. With anyone else he might have assumed that his timing had been fortuitous, to catch the act so soon after its accomplishment. But with Helwise . . .

"Ra is eight sidereal years old," he said, thinking aloud. "Hardcast packets can take that long to recombine, if they've traveled a great distance—which we certainly did. Can you tell me how long it was between the first packets arriving and Helwise bringing this child into being?"

"Hours."

"So while it might not have been something she had planned to do right now, it certainly wasn't something she did on a whim. My coming back early forced her hand." He returned to his metaphor of a chess game. If she took his early return as an aggressive move, then this was her response. Even now, she would be waiting to see what he did next. "Has she said anything to you?"

"She's still waiting, searching for the truth."

"Well, I already told her the truth. I don't think she believed me."

"She won't. She has the problem. She's like the heart of the world. But you—you have the face, the kindness of God to man, here to pick up the pieces. She don't like God."

Imre sighed and rubbed the space between his eyes, where an ache was beginning to develop. Render was as vague as he was perceptive. In his extraordinarily long life, he had learned to see through the walls most people threw around themselves, but he found it increasingly difficult to scale the walls around himself. Having a conversation with Render was like trying to decode Sanskrit.

"So here we are," Render said, perhaps sensing the mental roadblock Imre had found himself confronting.

"Where is that, exactly?"

Render took a swig from the mug of hot chocolate and grinned with dark-stained teeth. The effect was gruesome. "I was young, once. You too, I suppose. Young things fed on garbage and lies. 'Welcome, boys. Welcome to the real world!' Prepare to fight; turn off the pain; grow old. Just wrong. Young things never stay young for long. It's better that way. Young boys just make me laugh." And he did laugh, like an ancient panther growling, all rheum and no joy at all.

"I hope it'll be that simple, Render." Imre told himself that he didn't have to play Helwise's game if he didn't want to. "I'm here to find someone. That's my first priority. That doesn't mean, though, that I'll abandon everything else. There's work to be done, and I'm capable of doing it."

"Amen." Render put down the mug, picked up what remained of his apple, and stood.

Imre thought about letting him go. He glanced involuntarily at an opaque black box tucked into a niche down the southern transept of the Adytum. The box was made from polished obsidian with no external markings at all. Once his eye was drawn to it, he found it hard to look away.

Tempting, but he wasn't that desperate yet.

"No, stay. Finish the book." Imre indicated *Zaknythos* with calculated nonchalance. "Then you can tell me what it was about."

"Just another old story." Render sat back down with a shrug. He picked up the book, flicked to the page it had been open to before, and folded the spine back on itself so he could hold it in one hand. He closed his green left eye while reading, giving himself a lopsided look.

Imre had had enough. He went to the bed and lay prostrate upon it, willing himself to sleep. As consciousness fled, data trickled into his mind—all the reports that Render had sent in the last twenty thousand years, which should have reached him at his intended destinations, with his running commentary erratically attached. And into those words some of the present Render seemed to bleed, as though the waking man was nudging his sleeping friend, leaving Imre's unconscious mind utterly unsure what was dream, what was real, and how to take any of it.

"Welcome home," Render said. "Welcome to shadows and pain."

The administration of the Returned Continuum existed as an independent organ of state, much like the Apparatus itself. A significant percentage of the people comprising it were Primes and therefore less long-lived than singletons like Helwise or Freer. Some skipped down the ages by taking periods of voluntary hibernation or hard storage; others lost centuries at a stretch by hardcasting to and from secondary administration centers in the Round; most, however, were born in orbit around the Earth, lived their entire lives there, then returned to the soil of the home world when they died.

A vanishingly small percentage had been citizens of Earth during his takeover. Entirely consisting of frags left in the wake of the Slow Wave, when the contemplative minds of Earth had been destroyed along with every other Fort in the galaxy, this remnant indigenous population had been integrated into key points of the administration, where their particular skills, pursued with autistic single-mindedness, proved endlessly useful.

One such was Alice-Angeles, Imre's Secretary of Affairs, who showed no surprise at all when he contacted her to say that he had returned unexpectedly. A very beautiful woman, with high cheekbones and full lips, she carried herself efficiently and without any apparent awareness of her physical appearance. She was naturally bald, as many frags were, and when she met him at the base of the Citadel to take him to his office, he thought for one alarmed moment that she was Minister Sevaste.

"First Prime." She inclined her head and upper body in the quarter bow that was the most he would allow of his personal staff. "Your office is prepared. Shall I take you there?"

"In a moment," he replied. "Emlee Copas is on her way. We'll go with her."

Leaving Render with one simple assignment, he had sneaked into the basements earlier that morning and sent out his first official feelers into the Citadel. Alice-Angeles had already known of his return, alerted, Imre presumed, by Render. Emlee had been deeply immersed in the transient population archives, pursuing any information about unusual visitors to the system. She was well used to such demanding tasks, having been the Corps' information specialist in ages past. He could tell from her response that she had been overclocking all night and would take a while to rejoin normality. What passed for normality in the Citadel, anyway.

She arrived within five minutes, looking clear-eyed and refreshed but dressed in the same uniform she had changed into on their arrival. Her short blond hair stood up like a static-electricity halo.

"Any discoveries?" he asked her.

"Only that it's busier here than ever," she said. There was a slight burr to her words from immersion fatigue. "They had seventy thousand people down here for the last Equinox. Can you imagine that?"

Imre didn't want to. He could picture the crowds overflowing from the Citadel, damaging the natural surrounds. On the issue of preserving the natural environment, he and the Gravamen of Dussehra were in complete agreement. He would take any sign of that policy unraveling as a step backward for the Returned Continuum.

Imre led the three of them to an elevator and requested the upper administration levels. Once the carriage was moving, he instructed the Apparatus to remove the veil of secrecy over his presence in the Citadel. Within moments of the communications ban lifting, messages began to pour in. Imre didn't read them. He left that to Alice-Angeles. He just noted the numbers. They were approaching a vertical asymptote by the time the elevator came to a halt.

The doors slid open, revealing a mercifully empty hallway. Imre looked neither right nor left as he followed the familiar route through the executive suites and offices. People were visible through glass walls, moving at a wide variety of tempos. Some blurred like ghosts, visible for an instant then absent, as though they had never been there. Others stood like statues, engaged in conversations that might take years to finish. The walls, transparent and opaque alike, were hung with art from all over the galaxy, ranging from the insistently discordant to the barely visible. The outermost offices had windows. Imre looked forward to seeing the view from his, even if he had never found the room itself particularly comfortable.

Helwise and a local version of Al Freer were waiting for him outside when he took the corner. Standing together, glancing up as though interrupted in the middle of a conversation, they looked for an instant like alien beings: one tall and geometrically defined, wearing his singleton status as a soldier wore a firearm; the other small but striking, with a spine that curved just a little bit too far and gold-black eyes that seemed all pupil peering over the top of her veil.

"So much for pretending you're not here," Helwise said. "I knew that wouldn't last long."

"Well, I didn't ask for a welcoming committee," he said lightly, as though he'd only stepped out for an afternoon stroll.

Freer smiled and nodded. "I would've contacted you earlier, but the spook was insistent."

"Thanks for trying, Al. Don't take it personally. Either of you." He glided past them through the automatically opening doors. The room was triangular; he entered via the apex. Directly ahead of him, through one unbroken window five meters across, was the view of the jungle, the ocean, and the sky, a wash of juxtaposed greens and blues that human eyes had regarded as natural for millions of years. On seeing it, he chided himself for feeling bored on Dussehra: that world had been similar to Earth but different in all the important ways. There was something in Sol's light freckling on waves and the feathery paw strokes of the clouds that had never been repeated elsewhere. The horizon, that barely visible but fundamental crack in the fundament, tempted his eye to stare into infinity.

He forced himself to drop his gaze. A wide, low desk cut from naturally fallen timber occupied the view's foreground. The polished surface of the desk was empty. He rarely used it, except to lean against, as he did now to face the four of them.

"I presume Helwise told you what I told her," he said. Freer nodded; he looked and behaved exactly as he had on Dussehra; he always did. "I don't know why I'm supposed to be here. I'm not afraid to tell you that, and I don't think it in any way invalidates my reason for coming back early. The galaxy's a mysterious place; we're a long way from knowing everything that's going on. Everyone in this room understands how important it is not to let anything that might be significant slip by us."

Helwise tugged the veil away from the lower half of her face. "We stand by your decision, of course."

He couldn't tell if she was being sarcastic or not. "Congratulations, by the way," he said. "It's a good sign, when the people in charge start having kids. Shows confidence, and that's exactly what we need right now."

She registered his approval with barely a flicker of surprise. "Sabotage is up," she said, bypassing the issue of her anomalous child. "Unrest, too. There's a relationship between the two, of course. I hesitate to assume they have the same cause."

"People want what we lost sooner than we can give it to them," said Freer. "Those who weren't there have access to records. Anyone can see that we have a long way to go, and that's dispiriting, sometimes. People wonder if they can do better. They don't like to be told that they can't."

"Maybe they're right," said Emlee.

"We listen," said Helwise without looking away from Imre. "We make a show of listening to everyone, even the fucking fruit-loops, and we do hear the sane ones out. We haven't forgotten how this works. We need local cooperation, or else it'll all fall apart. Goodwill or good-bye—that's the motto."

She folded her arms as though closing the book on that subject.

Imre wasn't finished. "The Barons' sabotage doesn't stop with damaging the Line," he said. "They know how we work. I wouldn't be surprised if they're at least partly behind the unrest."

"Keeping us preoccupied," Freer said. "Keeping us small."

"Why wouldn't they want us to function properly?" said Emlee. "That's what I don't get. What have we done to them?"

"I don't know," said Imre, "but we should avoid jumping to conclusions. We need data. We need to know if the citizens of the Returned Continuum are as dissatisfied as everyone seems to fear."

"You've been out there," said Freer. "It's no picnic."

"Neither is it a barbecue," he said, referencing Helwise's earlier comment. "It's a very complex situation, with a lot of players all vying for their particular bit of turf—be it territorial, ideological, whatever. Some of them are happy enough; others still don't know we exist." He studied all of them, one by one. "That's why we're rebuilding, not empire-building."

"Thanks for the pep talk," Helwise said, "but you didn't come all this way for that."

Alice-Angeles watched the exchange with keen neutrality, taking it all in but making no judgments of her own.

"The fronts I'm fighting on aren't the same as yours," Imre said. "That doesn't mean we aren't fighting the same battles."

Freer nodded, responding to both the sentiment and the metaphor, as Imre had known he would. "It's good to have you back down here in the trenches again."

Imre smiled and mimed a knife at his throat. "A week ago, from my point of view, someone almost cut my head clean off. I think I'm safer here than I've been in years."

"Not from paperwork," said Helwise with a satisfied tone. "Although we can manage perfectly well without you, as you know, it is good to have you here. There's always someone who won't take my word for anything—because I'm not a Prime, because I'm not you, sometimes even because I'm a woman, from particularly backward types. If I can handball some of these dickheads to you, that would be a relief."

"By all means." If she thought that burying him under ad-ministrivia would keep him from getting in her way, Imre was all for letting her believe it. He nodded to Emlee. "You'll keep working the files?" She agreed without emoting in any de-tectable way. "Good. Alice-Angeles, Helwise, Al—I'm all yours."

He walked around the desk, sat in his chair with his back to the view, and waited for life to surprise him, rather than the other way around.

Emlee found nothing that day, or the day after that, despite conducting thorough searches of everyone who had visited Earth in the last century, or applied for a visitation permit for the century to come. He ordered her to expand the search.

In the meantime, he waded through delegation after dele-gation, slipping smoothly into the role of First Prime even if the whole of his attention wasn't on the performance. The job wasn't especially challenging. Those who came to Earth were among the converted, for the most part. His function was mostly to flatter, soothe, and caution those with grievances against their neighbors. There were none of the life-and-death decisions he was forced to make sometimes on tour. How many people had died in Dussehra since he had left? He didn't know, and it wasn't especially relevant. It simply served as a contrast to issues that he couldn't help but regard as trivial, sometimes.

A group mind seeking the support of the Returned Continuum to explore a new branch of extreme mathematics . . . Three delegates from the Endless Stair wanting legal recognition for their particular branch of Eschertology . . . A conspiracy theorist called Reynolds from Tau Ceti who thought the failure of three extragalactic probes to be evidence of alien life . . . The conduit from a colony called Al-A'raaf who had been sent into exile for cloning Prime children and murdering them, and who failed to see that he had committed a crime at all . . . A dozen prelates, one after the other, trying to regain their faith simply by being in his presence . . .

His mind drifted, scanning through the information Alice-Angeles had given him that hadn't been covered in Render's subliminal infodumps, Fort-related technologies among them. The Q loop shunts that had provided the nervous system of the galactic overminds was considered verboten by both the Barons and the Luminous, but that didn't mean the search for alternatives had been abandoned. Acting on the assumption that the Earth was closely monitored, no radical experiments were conducted there. Secret experiments in no less than fifteen locations in the nearby Crux Arm had yielded some results. One proto-Fort, a merger between a partial and a singleton volunteer, had flourished for seven thousand years deep in the Metzengerstein Nebula before being destroyed by the Luminous. What had given it away remained a mystery, and that it hadn't drawn the attention of the Barons as well was also noteworthy. A pattern was emerging—of Barons working to destroy Forts in densely inhabited areas, such as planets or systems, whereas the Luminous operated in the sparser regions of space. Why that should be so, again, remained a mystery.

So much information. So little understanding. No wonder his frustration built so quickly into a thunderhead. Imre worked around the clock, stopping only to change his outfit at sunset every day. He began to feel like a prisoner in his own office, tormented by an endless series of jailers. A slightly manic edge crept into his diplomatic repartee, one he recognized from past experience. He wasn't a statesman; he was a soldier, like Freer and Render. How had he managed to end up here, in an office with a retinue of underlings larger than any army he had ever commanded? And beyond them, thousands of billions of ordinary people, going about their lives completely unaware of any bigger picture, of politics and grand schemes, of their places in humanity's great journey through time.

Sometimes he wished he could be one of them.

Emlee continued to look and continued to find nothing. "My instincts are getting me nowhere," she complained.

He insisted she keep at it. "If it's there, you'll find it."

"And if it's not there?"

"Then you're going to be busy for a long, long time."

That answer pleased her no more than the lack of answers pleased him.

A week Absolute after his arrival, he received a message from Render, saying simply, "He's alive."

Imre stared at the two words for a full minute before he was able to connect them to the task he had given Render so many relative days before. It was his cue to take a break, finally—to step away from the imaginary chessboard and do something real.

"Clear my diary," he told Alice-Angeles through the office's video link. "I'm going AWOL for a bit."

"The delegation from Ulalune—"

"Can either wait or meet with Helwise instead. Take your pick."

"Yes, sir. But there's someone else," she added before he could break the connection. She looked uncharacteristically awkward. "I told him you're too busy. He's insisted on waiting outside your office. I'll have him forcibly removed if you want to leave unseen."

That seemed extreme, even in the face of Imre's urgency to be elsewhere. Perhaps he could squeeze one last meeting in before slipping away. "Who is it?"

"Ra MacPhedron."

His stomach sank. "What does he want?"

"He won't say."

"And how long exactly has he been waiting?"

"Four days, three hours, and seventeen minutes," she answered with the precision Imre should have expected. "Absolute."

He cursed under his breath. Did the kid suspect the same thing he did? Was that why he had come to meet them by the hardcaster facility and persisted again now?

He didn't want anyone following him out of the Citadel when he had a particularly sensitive appointment to keep, especially not someone as volatile as Ra MacPhedron.

"All right," he told his loyal gatekeeper, who would happily have called Citadel security if Imre had wanted her to, and to hell with Helwise.

Her image slid to one corner of his field of view as the doors opened and no less than nine people entered.

He tensed, thinking for a moment that Ra had somehow tricked Alice-Angeles into letting in an execution squad. The desk housed several small but potent weapons, all within easy reach. Nine against one, though, was long odds.

Was this, he wondered, Helwise's next move?

Taking the measure of them—noting their weight, their build, their clothing, the way they carried themselves—he came to a very different conclusion.

Alice-Angeles hadn't been fooled. Nine people hadn't entered his office, but one person repeated nine times, in nine different stages of development, expressing nine different aspects of one personality. One had grey hair and wrinkles; another was physically immature, almost half a meter shorter than the others and slight with it. Three were female. Some looked pleased to see him; others scowled or avoided his gaze. Two walked arm in arm, as though they were lovers.

Every one of them had the same eyes—dark blue with gold flecks—that looked all too much like the combination of Imre's and Helwise's might.

They stopped in a line along the front of the desk, uncomfortably close.

He rose unhurriedly to his feet and looked at all of them in turn. "Hello, Ra."

"Thank you for seeing me, First Prime," said the middle

one, perhaps the same one Imre had met before but with tidier hair and a beardless chin. "I want to apologize for the scene I made the other day. It was undignified."

"It came as a shock," said another, the youngest-looking one. "You weren't expected. I wasn't ready."

"Your mother didn't tell you?"

"Tell me what?" growled the version of Ra on Imre's far left.

"That I was on my way. She must have known—in fact, I assume she did know. It would be very strange otherwise." Imre didn't say any more than that. Let the kid work out the timing himself if he hadn't already.

"Helwise has her secrets," said the first of Ra's singleton bodies. "She's a circle too, but in a different way from you. She just has one side: her own."

"What about you?" Imre asked him. "Do you have a shape?"

"I'm still figuring that out," said the one on the far left, his aggressive tone undiminished.

"Well, when you do, let me know." Imre looked down at the desk, miming piles of invisible paperwork. "Unless you have something else you want to say . . . ?"

Five shook their heads. Four looked uncertain. One, a female with haunted eyes said, "What does it mean if you're my father?"

"Mean?" He took a deep breath. "It doesn't have to mean anything if we don't want it to."

"It's just genes," Ra said, provoking an argument within himself.

"It's not just genes. They were lovers once."

"She's not a romantic, clinging to the past."

"But there's more to it than romance. There's politics too."

"Helwise doesn't do anything without a reason."

Imre smiled, hearing the clear echo of Helwise's same comment about himself and agreeing with it completely. They were alike in more ways than he preferred to consider. "If it makes you feel any better, Ra, she didn't tell me either. The first I knew about it was when you confronted Emlee and me in the corridor. I'm still getting my head around it too."

"Why wouldn't she want you to know?"

"I think she does. I also think she wanted it to come as a shock. Surprising me was part of the deal. She usually has several reasons running at once, whenever she does something dramatic."

"People are nervous," Ra confessed. "They don't know how to talk to me. I'm not one of them, but they can't avoid me. There are no other children here. I find it very confusing."

Imre began to feel uncomfortable. Behind his back, the fingers of his right hand tapped against the stump of his left little finger. Whether the kid had his genes or not, he wasn't interested in playing any kind of parental role, confessor included. "Growing up is supposed to be confusing. That's how we learn to be who we are."

"Who am I?" Ra asked through seven mouths. "Why am I here?"

"You'll have to find the answer to those questions yourself," Imre told him, "and I fear it'll be a long time coming." Sensing the kid needed more than that, he went on to explain: "Things are tense between me and Helwise; they have been for a long time. I won't lie to you about that. But I won't hold you responsible for anything she's got planned. Not until you can decide for yourself what kind of person you are—what shape you've taken in your mind. Then it'll be your call, and we can take it from there. Until that happens, though, you're caught in the middle. I won't use you as a pawn or blame you for existing. I won't avoid you either. You can ask me anything, and I'll be as honest as I can."

That seemed to settle the kid down a little. Eight of the nine looked relieved, as though he had given them something they hadn't dared think they might deserve. The ninth, the same one who had spoken aggressively earlier, was the only one who seemed disappointed.

"Who do you think Helwise hates more?" that version of Ra asked. "You or herself?"

"I don't think she hates either of us," he said, keeping his word to be as honest as he could. "I think it's a case of two emotions that have become mutually exclusive. Hate, love, whatever—in her mind, they're like matter and antimatter. Put them together, and things get very interesting very quickly."

"Is that what I am? A manifestation of her inner turmoil?"

"Remember what I said, Ra. There's always more than one reason."

With that, he insisted that he had work to do but that Ra should feel free to approach him another time. "Tell Alice-Angeles what you want. We'll make an appointment. Don't lurk around my office waiting for me to walk out of it. I've been here months on end, sometimes."

"I'm still working on the slower tempos," Ra said, moving en masse to the door. "It's a good excuse to practice."

"Well, do it somewhere else, if you wouldn't mind. We can talk anywhere in the Citadel. It doesn't have to be here. You must have favorite spaces. Perhaps next time we could go to one of those."

That prospect pleased Ra to the point that even his angry incarnation seemed mollified. They said good-bye to each other at the door; handshakes were exchanged but no hugs.

Imre closed the door behind Ra and leaned against it, mentally drained. He had next to no experience with children, and he found the doublethink required ten times more exhausting than diplomacy. Already dreading the thought of their next encounter, he prayed that it became easier with time. Whether Ra was his or not, he didn't need another reason to stress about the child's existence.

It was messy. That was what bothered him most of all. All the loose ends, all the ambiguities—he found the need to tidy them up almost unbearable. But this wasn't something that could be easily tucked away. Children, like Helwise herself, were inherently unpredictable. That Ra's visit hadn't been a play from Helwise, then, didn't make it any easier to live with.

Parceling up his own feelings and uncertainties as best he could, he watched through security until was Ra well out of the way. Then he called Emlee—something he wasn't looking forward to but knew he couldn't avoid.

"Have you found anything?" he asked her.

"Only the limits of my patience."

"Take a break. Meet me down in the basements again. Same place, ten minutes. There's something I want to show you."

She was early, leaning against a wall and tapping one foot. When Imre arrived, trailing a trio of guards he'd let come this far, she looked up from whatever internal thought she had been pursuing and said, "What happened to Render? He's not answering my calls."

"Don't worry. He's where we're going. I've been keeping him busy." Imre dismissed the guards and waited until they had crisply saluted and marched off before turning back to her. "I've taken us off the grid again. If anyone looks, they'll think we're somewhere else."

"By 'anyone,' you mean Helwise."

"Most likely, but not only," he said. "Let's not limit our paranoia unnecessarily."

She half smiled. That was something he'd often said in the field. "Everyone's still out to get you, huh?"

"Not everyone. Not all the time. But near enough to keep life busy."

"Is that why we're down here? Are you going to cap me for stalling?"

"Is that what you've been doing?"

"No." She shook her head. "But I did give up on the skyline transit logs three days ago. I've been exploring other avenues since then."

"Which avenues, exactly?"

"Transmissions, in and out. I thought someone might have hardcasted in through the back door, or be in the middle of trying. Turns out there's nothing weird going on in that regard—but I did find something else odd."

She waited for him to ask, and he gave her the satisfaction. He was, in fact, surprised by her audacity. For every person coming to and leaving the Citadel, there were terabytes of information doing the same. Searching through all those packets was a truly formidable task, one he would have hesitated giving a team of experts, yet she raised the subject as casually as though she had spent the day flipping through an old novel or two.

That was why she had been the Corps' information officer and why he had encouraged her to follow her instincts.

"What did you find?"

"A series of deeply encrypted transmissions," she said, "flowing to and from the highest levels of Citadel security. They're disguised, buried in innocuous files that have no apparent connection with each other, so someone's gone to some effort to keep the transmissions hidden. But whoever they are, they're not as smart as they think they are. Deep encryption is dense; it stands out like spikes of white noise in a recording of a symphony. Once you have the signature, you can spot it a mile off—especially if there are a lot of them, which there are."

"What's in the files?"

"I don't know. Spotting them is one thing, unpacking them another. And before you ask—no, I don't know who sent them. That'll take a while longer to find out. But I'm confident I can do it. The packets come down the Line from out-system. If I can spot one in transit, I should be able to trace it to the source here."

Imre nodded, taking it in. "This is the Citadel," he said, playing the devil's advocate. "You'd expect secret transmissions. It goes with the territory."

"Of course. But these aren't coming from some petty delegate reporting home to their constituents. These have been going for years. Centuries, or even longer. As far back as I go, I find evidence of them—and that makes a whole lot of data to sift through, too much for one person in a hurry. Give me a month, and I might be able to find out when they started."

"If I can give you that month," he said, "you'll have it."

"Is that supposed to be my reward? More work?"

The question wasn't intended seriously. It was about as close to a joke as Emlee got—and he knew how much she liked a mystery. "You confess to disobeying orders, and then you tell me someone in the Citadel's inner circle is engaged in a secret conversation with someone outside the system. A lesser tyrant would have you capped immediately."

"I'll count myself lucky."

"Later," he said. "We're going for a ride first."

"To your secret hideout?"

He stopped in the process of opening the maintenance hatch and turned to her, crooking a regrown eyebrow.

"What?" she said. "You go off the grid sometimes. I can't help but jump to conclusions. If it makes you feel any better, I've no idea where it is. And I haven't told anyone else, of course."

"I hope not. You and Render are the only people I can trust with this."

"Because we're Primes like you?"

He nodded. "Because you know I really will kill you dead if you betray me."

"I'd expect nothing less." That wasn't a joke, but neither was it said with rancor. It was a statement of fact.

"Good. Now that we've laid that on the table, let's go. I want to get back before someone misses us."

She followed him down into the subbasement level, through a series of new switchbacks and apparent dead ends to where the transit tunnel waited. The stink of old things didn't quite smother a hint of ozone from the last time he had used the maglev track. The two-seater car still waited where he had left it, humming patiently to itself.

"Get on," he told her, then took the space behind her. They rocked together as the car began moving, then leaned into the acceleration as one.

"Classy," she said over the wind.

"No luxury down here," he called back. "Who would it impress?"

She didn't say anything else until the car began to decelerate. "Why now?"

"What do you mean, why now?"

"This place has been around a while. You could've brought me here anytime. What's changed?"

"I told you. There's something you need to see."

She dismounted after him. "So this isn't it?"

"No. It's waiting for us. We're almost there."

"Okay. I'll let you be mysterious."

"Just promise me one thing," he said at the base of the stairs leading up into the Adytum. "Hear me out. I'm not doing this on a whim."

"Since when do you anything on a whim?"

That reminded him a little too much of the conversation he had had with Ra earlier that day. "There are two ways to endure a long life," he said. "One's to avoid things you might regret later; the other is to learn not to care."

"What type are you?"

"Both," he said, waving her ahead of him.

Two minutes later, in the Adytum's northern transept, she was staring down into a glass-covered crypt—one of two set into the ground so their lids were at floor level—at the body of Chyro Kells. An expression of horror spread inevitably across her face.

"What is this—some kind of joke?"

"No joke, Emlee. He's alive," he said, borrowing Render's words from earlier. The old soldier stood to one side with his arms folded, watching silently. "Or will be, once we kick-start him."

"He was blown to bits on Dussehra," she said, staring at him now, not the body. "You can't have put him back together like this. It's impossible."

"We did put him back together," he explained, "but not from what remained after the explosion. This is the version of him that left Oxenbould, the planet before Dussehra. We rebuilt him from scratch." Her puzzlement deepened, so he explained further. "Before we returned here, I asked the Apparatus to exhume his previous hardcast pattern and send it along too. It's as easy as restoring a deleted file. This version of him never arrived on Dussehra and therefore never died there. To him it never happened at all."

"But," she said, then stopped. "You resurrected him." Her voice was as cold as a snowstorm on Neptune.

"That's right."

"He was a Prime, and he died, and you brought him back." She stepped away from the crypt where Imre's chief surgeon lay sleeping, awaiting the electrical pulse that would return him to full health and his duties.

"I've done nothing that hasn't already happened to him dozens of times, with every hardcast we've been through. At the end of the day, there's still just one of him. It's not as if I'm making him into a singleton or anything."

"Semantics. There's a principle at stake. What you've done isn't right."

"We've done lots of things in wartime that, by other standards, aren't right."

"Are we at war, Imre?" she snapped. "I don't see any invading hordes. I don't see a gun to your head." Her green eyes were blazing at him. "You became a Prime for a reason—because you didn't like what singletons could do. Because the person at the top needed to understand what it meant when decisions cost lives. That's what you told us, anyway. Shouldn't we have believed you?"

"I still believe it," he said, even though it wasn't close to the whole truth. He had become a Prime to create some ideological distance between himself and Himself, the strange half singleton, half Fort who had addressed him on his escape from Kismet. The kind of body people chose—when they had the choice—reflected their state of mind as well as their physical circumstances. His former self was pursuing a philosophy he didn't want to follow, no matter the temptation. "We *are* besieged, whether you can see the battle lines or not. I don't believe you'd be so naïve as to think otherwise. Saboteurs, spies, traitors—for God's sake, the bomb that killed Chyro almost killed you too. And all this lies under the shadow of the Slow Wave. That was the first shot in a war that hasn't ended yet. Until it's over, I'm reluctant to regard peace as anything other than temporary."

"All right," she said. "We're at war. But what does Chyro have to do with it? How's resurrection going to solve anything?"

"I need him," Imre confessed. "He's been with me from the start, and I trust him. He made me back into myself, remember?" He felt awkward explaining this aloud, but he knew he had to try in order to win her over. "He put me back together from the mess the Jinc made of me. And he took out the loop shunt they put inside me, so we couldn't be tracked. I owe him."

Her gaze didn't flicker at the mention of the loop shunt. That was good, he thought. There were some secrets she still hadn't unraveled.

"You owe him a death," she said. "If he'd wanted to be immortal, he wouldn't have been a Prime."

"Why don't we ask him ourselves?" he suggested. "Maybe he changed his mind. People usually do when they're confronted by the reality of no longer existing."

He turned to give Render the order.

Emlee took his arm. "Don't," she said. "This is a slippery slope. You know it's dangerous."

"Don't worry," Imre said. "I'm not going to start building clone armies or filling the Citadel with copies of myself. Resurrecting from a hardcast is time-consuming and expensive. I'd only do it for the right people."

"People you can't afford to let go of."

"That's right. And yes, I'm being selfish."

"What about you, Render?" she asked suddenly. "Do you buy this?"

"This is survival," said the old soldier. "Life is cruel. I won't quit."

"I'm not saying you're a quitter. I just don't understand why you'd go along with this."

"Die if you want to. I want to be, to overdose on time. If only we could *all* live forever."

Render's sentiments were inflexible. Imre could see how it hurt Emlee to hear her old friend disagreeing with her. "Render is well out of danger here," he broke in. "That's why he doesn't come with us on the whistle-stop tours. He's an Old-Timer. I don't want his death on my conscience—or the decision to bring him back either."

"But Chyro is different. That's what you're saying."

"Yes. I think he deserves a choice, either way. I dragged him into this, after all. If it wasn't for me, he'd still be alive."

"Or he'd be dead back on Hyperabad, or a thousand other fates might have befallen him."

"The same goes for you. Are you telling me you'd rather be living—or dead—in that shitty dust bowl than here?"

She shot him a shrewd and unforgiving look. "I almost died on Dussehra. Al told me how angry you were. But you didn't worry about Chyro. You barely spared him a second thought, apart from that sham funeral you threw to make the locals feel guilty. Now I know why. You knew you could bring him back anytime you wanted." Her lips tightened. "If I'd died instead of him, would it be me down there?"

"I don't know," said Imre, with all honesty. "We've never been hit so close before—on the edge of the Inner Sanctum, right where we're most vulnerable. Someone sent us a message. I received it. That's why I'm changing the rules. I'm not going to be governed by fear. I want you with me, risking your life every time we arrive somewhere new, not dead because something went wrong. This is all I can offer in return."

"Well, I don't want it."

"That's your decision. I'll honor it."

"But you'll expect me to keep your secret, no doubt. How would the masses feel if they knew you were bringing your favorites back from the dead while everyday plebs dropped like flies? It wouldn't go down well at all."

"You won't tell anyone because you know it would cause civil war. You're not that principled."

She looked for a second as though she might argue the point. In the end, she nodded. "True enough, I guess. But I don't have to like it."

"I don't like it either, Emlee, but that's the way it's going to be. I'm going to ask Chyro what he wants, then I'll abide by his decision. If he stays, I'll alter the report on Dussehra to show that he didn't die. I'll have him recorded as a late arrival. The Apparatus can make it look plausible, should anyone become suspicious."

"I bet it can." Her brows were bunched like a fist. "You, the spook, and I are the only eyewitnesses—apart from Al and a bunch of other people on Dussehra, and they're safely out of the way. You've got it all wrapped up." She walked away from them, head tipped back to take in the expanse of red stained glass above them. "And here you sit, you two old boys, concocting your schemes and playing with people's lives as though they mean nothing."

"Not nothing," said Imre. "The exact opposite. That's the point."

Her emerald gaze dropped to meet his. "There's more to life than just not dying, just as there's more to running an empire than declaring yourself emperor. You should know that better than anyone."

She left with a cloud of anger and disapproval trailing in her wake. Imre chided himself for thinking that she might have approved of what he had done. She understood well enough; of that he was completely certain. Acceptance was too much to hope for—but still, he had felt the need to tell her, and not just because she was a witness to Kells's death and would naturally wonder about his reappearance. They had spent many years together on tour; he trusted her with his life, just as he trusted Kells, and he wanted her to know that he valued hers in return.

"Wake him up," he told Render, knowing that he wouldn't be able to shake the grim mood Emlee had left him in by stewing over it.

Render did as he was told without questioning. And when Kells woke, blinking, to be told of the situation, the surgeon thought hard for a moment with the skin between his black eyebrows deeply furrowed, then said, "Yes. I would rather be alive than dead. Who wouldn't?"

"You'd be surprised," Imre said, feeling a rush of relief spread through him.

"People always surprise me. Life wouldn't be worth living otherwise, no?"

Imre helped him out of the sarcophagus and closed the crypt behind him. "Take him back to the Citadel," he told Render. "Give Helwise the story. The Apparatus will have the cover in place by then. I have work to do, and I'd like to be alone for a while."

The two men left via the spiral staircase. Imre waited at the top until he heard the maglev car whir off into the distance. He stood there silently for five minutes, listening for any sign of someone creeping up the stairs. Render could be as silent as a cat, but Imre knew the way he moved. Eventually, he was satisfied that no one had stayed behind.

He went back into the Adytum and stood in front of the obsidian case. Emlee had found nothing. The Apparatus had found nothing. Whoever he was supposed to be on Earth to meet, they hadn't shown up.

One comes winged, his glory well befitting, and you, monarch, would best be there to greet him.

Some monarch he had turned out to be. Distracted by ghostly messages. Haunted by phantoms from the past. Plagued by doubts. Harangued by the people who were supposed to be his closest allies. The way things were going, he would be lucky to hold things together, let alone achieve everything else he had set out to do.

Find Himself. Avenge the Forts. It was simple in principle but fiendishly difficult in practice. The Luminous and the Barons could be hiding anywhere in a galaxy of 100,000 million stars, not to mention the vast gulfs of space between them. Finding them was only the beginning.

There's more to running an empire than declaring yourself emperor, Emlee had said.

Yes indeed, he thought to himself. You're not telling me anything I don't already know.

Reaching out with his right hand, he pressed all five fingertips to the surface of the case. The obsidian was smooth and cool to the touch. A mechanism within the case clicked in recognition, and a perfectly straight line appeared around the case's midsection. The line became a seam, through which air hissed as the near vacuum within equalized with the exterior. The lid of the case lifted up and tipped to one side, then slid down so it lay flush against the case's left-hand side. The case became quiet, then, its contents exposed.

Imre stepped so close to the case that the front of his shirt brushed against the black surface. Looking down, he saw the familiar containment fields stacked like layers of smoked glass. He deactivated them, one after the other, until just one remained between him and the object at its heart. He contemplated changing his mind at that moment and sealing the case back up. It wasn't too late. And maybe this time, finally, he would take it off Earth and drop it into the roiling, fiery surf of the sun, as he should have done right from the beginning.

He switched off the last field, as he had known he would, and stared into the eye of the loop shunt.

It was an unremarkable thing, not much larger than an ordinary human eye. A mottled grey sphere with two dark, roughly circular patches at opposite poles, it seemed to be staring in two directions at once, like Janus, the ancient Roman god of gateways. Neither entirely biological nor entirely mechanical, it was a complex hybrid of technologies, as many Fort devices were, designed to integrate with both the bodies of frags and the complex physics of the universe around them. The principles of Q loop technology were not well understood by the reverse engineers of the Returned Continuum. All anyone knew for certain was that the shunts had enabled cheap and reliable communications across interstellar distances, and that the Slow Wave had cut the link for good by fusing active shunts as it passed through them. Severed from their larger minds, individual frags had gone mad, or died, or found some other way to survive until the next attack had come. What the Slow Wave hadn't killed, the Luminous and the Barons had been certain to finish off.

Yet, in Mandala Supersystem, over four hundred thousand years earlier, someone working with the Barons had admitted that they were following Imre by virtue of a loop shunt inside his body—one given to him by the Jinc, which had found his pattern in pieces on the edge of the galaxy and rebuilt him from scratch. The loop shunt had been part of that pattern, suggesting that sometime after his last memory and the recording of that pattern, he had become part of a group mind very much like one of his ancient enemies. A Fort.

Swearing to turn his back on the actions and decisions of his former self, he had instructed Chyro Kells to remove the shunt, fully intending to destroy it and any connection it might have to his former self—or to Himself in the present, wherever he was. But Imre had not been able to take that step.

He had hunted too long for just such a connection. He couldn't throw it away.

So it remained hidden in his sanctuary, the darkest of his secrets, completely hidden from the rest of the universe. He had opened the case only once before, on assuming control of the Earth and declaring himself First Prime. He hadn't known what to expect. Kells had warned him on extraction that the device was still active and linked to him in some subtle way, whether it was inside him or not. Hence the shielding, just in case. But the shunt might have been utterly inert that night, an ugly glass bauble with no function or purpose but to remind him of sins he couldn't remember committing.

He stared down at the shunt and, when nothing happened, asked, "Is it you?"

Silence.

"I was told to come back here. I was told that someone was coming and that I should be here when they arrived. I did as instructed, but no one's here. Is it you? Are you trying to tell me something?"

Silence.

He kept talking: "I was on Dussehra. Your agent there gave me your message. I presume it was your message: give up my quest; focus on the here and now. You expect me to believe that you and I want the same thing: humanity to be great again and the Continuum restored. I can't believe that this is true, for why would you work against us at every turn? Why would you destroy our Forts? Why do you sabotage the Line? Why do you try to kill *me*?"

Silence.

He tried a different tack: "At Kismet, you warned me never to use this loop shunt. It would put me in danger, you said. But you never told me who from. You? The Luminous? Someone else entirely? You told me you weren't with the Barons, that you were on your own side, but what does *that* mean? You said you monitor the Line, but you didn't tell me what you were listening for. I'm listening too, and I'm as much in the dark as ever. You told me not to assume who you are, but who else could you possibly be? The shunt came *out of my body*. It has to connect to you. If you're not the one who's coming here, to finally give me some answers, then *what the hell is going on*?"

He was shouting now. The echoes of his own voice were the only reply.

—connect to you—give me some answers—could you possibly be—

Imre took a deep breath and waited for the echoes to die away.

In desperation, he said, "Helwise is turning against me." He continued in wearier, more restrained tones. "That's not entirely unexpected. I have contingencies in place against a direct takeover bid, but her tactics have taken me by surprise. She's partured a son—our son, I think—and is raising him in the Citadel. I think she's trying to create a line of succession. The people link the Returned Continuum to me, so she can't easily oust me and put herself in charge—but my son might be acceptable. It might even be a good idea. I'm a soldier, not a governor. I know how to give orders and shoot people. Peacetime is not my specialty. The Forts knew that all along—that's why they asked me to do their dirty work—and I guess I know it too. That's why I surround myself with people who do know what they're doing. But now it's starting to unravel, and I don't think I have the heart to do what needs to be done. I should force Helwise's hand; I should kill the kid, or have him killed; I should end that little experiment right now. Would that do the trick? Is that what the Returned Continuum needs—a firm hand and no quarter given?"

He placed both hands on the side of the obsidian box and leaned forward with his eyes shut. A bitter laugh escaped his lips.

"The Jinc thought you were a hotline to God; it called you a prophet and an angel. But I won't pray to you. I'm the figurehead of a church stretching from one side of the galaxy to the other; I've given myself the power of life over death. We should talk, yes, but not like this. Never like this. As equals, if not as allies. Unless I'm very much mistaken, our enemies are the same. You and I are the same. We should work together, not—"

He stopped. A bright ultraviolet light was shining up into his face. He opened his eyes and saw that the shunt was glowing brightly and twitching from side to side as though looking around the cavernous room. He straightened, not sure what he should do next. Was this the answer he had hoped for, or had he inadvertently triggered something much more deadly, like a self-destruct sequence?

He raised one hand, ready to reactivate the containment fields.

Before the signals could complete the journey down the superfast nerves of his arm, the shunt had locked on him, and all his perceptions were swept away.

Blackness, vast and endless, freckled with a scattering of tiny, fiery dots. The dots swirled and turned like motes of dust in a hurricane, like the millions of microsatellites orbiting the ancient Earth, like the stars in a spiral galaxy—which in fact they seemed to be, fragile, fleeting things when viewed on a timescale that regarded the life span of a hot sun as but a moment or two. They turned and turned, ebbing and flowing about the galaxy's bright center of gravity—and as they turned, a darkness swept over them, dimming their light and turning them to dust. The shadow spread like ink in water, starting off at a point near the center and spreading outward in a wave until only a few flickering sparks remained, surrounded on all sides by darkness. Individually, each of those sparks succumbed too. When the last was gone, all the galaxy was dark.

The Slow Wave, he thought. Those three words echoed in the void like the tolling of a gigantic bell. The stars in the vision weren't actually stars, but minds, the minds of the Forts. Four more words followed: I already know this.

A pressure bore down on his mind, a weight of cognition he fought but couldn't resist. As though a huge mental mass had collapsed on him, he felt himself being subsumed, drowning in thoughts with the momentum of mountains. One pebble in an avalanche, he could no more fight than he could turn the world on its head.

Light—a light so powerful it would have torn his atoms apart. And sound—a roar throbbing so deeply through him

*that it shook his mind apart. In his previous life, he had floated
once on the surface of a star and exposed himself to the stel-
lar atmosphere. Its song had deafened him, left him mentally
numb for a week afterward. This was a thousand times worse.
A million times. Unable to escape neither the sound nor the
light, he struggled to hold on to himself. If he let himself dissolve, this time he might never return.*

*A structure loomed at him out of the fiery chaos. Not a
thing; no solid could exist in this high-energy cauldron. A process, an order arising out of the chaos; an imprint. It was huge
and yet fleeting, existing barely for nanoseconds before the
sound and light tore it apart again. But in those nanoseconds
the process had spawned other, similar processes that mingled
and danced around him like candle flames in a nuclear furnace. Again, he thought of his sojourn on that faraway sun,
where gaseous life-forms had been found living in the chro-
mosphere: nonsentient creatures more like plants or molds
than animals that fueled their fleeting existences along field
lines crackling and snapping over sunspot oases. And again
he understood that the furious plasma he saw now made a sun
look like an ice cube in comparison. A sun-mold would have
as much chance as he of surviving longer than an instant.*

The mysterious phrase used by the Jinc passed briefly
through his drowning mind, as it had on Dussehra an age ago:
persistent luminous archaeoglyphs.

The vast presence lifted. The fire faded away. He could
think again.

You're testing me, he said. You want to know what I know.
Or are you giving me hints? Is this your way of telling me the
truth at last?

The great mind that had invaded his said nothing.

Then another thought occurred to him. Maybe you're dis-
tracting me, too. Maybe these images you're giving me don't
mean anything. They just keep me looking the other way
while you poke around inside my head. Is that it?

*More glowing dots appeared before him. This time they
weren't moving. He was hanging under a black curtain that
surrounded him on all sides. On the curtain were tiny smudges
of light—not dots at all, he realized as he looked more closely,*

but fuzzy patches that made his eyes skid and slide, unable to find a solid anchor. There were as many of these fuzzy patches as there were stars in the night sky, hanging in tendrils and threads with black gulfs between them. And as he watched, he could see that they were in fact moving, only so slowly that he could barely measure it with his eyes. Ponderously, gracefully, they drifted across the black curtain of infinity, dancing at the whim of invisible forces.

Galaxies, he realized. This cosmic tour is getting repetitive.

The mind probing him said nothing and didn't change the view. He felt as though he had missed the point this time. The point of the vision might not be the galaxies—but if it wasn't, what was? That was all the vision contained.

The fuzzy specks faded and went out. Some collided and flared up briefly, but they too died eventually. Everything died and only blackness remained.

Very grim, he thought.

The blackness suddenly flared into colors, as though he was seeing the night through infrared specs, painted garishly in blue, green, and yellow. Shapes appeared, spanning the heavens. Structures had formed in the wake of the galaxies, structures that couldn't be seen by ordinary eyes—weblike strands connecting far-flung blobs and radiant stars with triangular tips, waving in an unseen wind. When the view changed again, as though yet another frequency filter had dropped down in front of his eyes, he saw that the structure was partly itself a living thing, flexing and shifting like an elephant trying to find a comfortable position on its side.

Ah, that's better.

A new shape slashed across the sky, something angular and sharp and much faster than anything that big should ever move. The strands parted, issuing bright red energy that painted the sky crimson in vast, vivid splashes, and the rest of the injured creature reacted, stretching and bunching and flailing like a wounded sea anemone.

Tooth and claw. Next you're going to raise the scale and reveal that we're inside one of my cells, right? Not watching giant amoeba fighting at the cold end of time.

Even as he said those words, he thought of the fiery angels dancing in a heat haze denser and hotter than the inside of any star, and he wondered.

The vast mind pulled away. He felt both loss and relief at the absence of its unbearable weight. He wondered if he really had its attention, or if he was just tapping into cosmic thoughts that happened to be flowing his way. He had watched baby red crabs being swept out to sea, once, on an isolated beach in the Earth's southern hemisphere. They had run like frantic clockwork toys, each leg a blur in their effort to outrace each encroaching wave. The waves were nothing at all compared to the mass of the sea, but even tiny surges dragged the crabs off the beach. Subsumed, they could no more fight the sea than a Prime could withstand the mental momentum of a Fort.

If that was what he had tapped into. And it couldn't be, surely, or else the Luminous would descend upon him and wipe out the source of the Q loop transmission. Except he had had the shunt inside him for years Absolute before realizing it, and it had been patiently revealing his location to the Barons without calling down destruction. Perhaps it took time for the Luminous to notice such anomalies. Maybe one or two transmissions were nothing to worry about.

He hoped so. The Earth had suffered enough. And he needed answers that made sense, not these suggestive images that told him nothing.

What do the Luminous want, he asked the vast, dark mind, and how do you fit into it?

The pressure returned, redoubled, and Imre feared he might immediately black out. His sense of self eroded to a mere speck, to which he clung with desperation. Fragments of thoughts struck him like icebergs; phrases tens of thousands of syllables long coiled around and smothered him; the discharge of ideas too large for his mind to contain roared through him with the force of a lightning bolt.

The Slow Wave.

Those three words were the only ones he could discern from the maelstrom.

The Slow Wave.

The mind roared and flailed at itself, a tentacled behemoth dragging itself down into oblivion.

The Slow Wave!

Imre protected himself as best he could, adopting the psychic equivalent of a fetal position and riding it out. The storm had raged for millennia, and might rage for millennia more, but he would hold on to himself, he swore. He would survive.

But even he couldn't do the impossible. He had as much chance as a candle in an Antarctic winter. The flame of his consciousness guttered under the onslaught. Darkness pressed in on all sides. He couldn't tell if he was being subsumed or extinguished, so he fought both equally. He had to survive unscathed, for the sake of himself and the Returned Continuum—and perhaps Himself too, if his former self was part of this violent expurgation of guilt. Was that really what he felt swirling through this insurmountable storm? *Guilt?*

Could such guilt ever be atoned?

Anger like the bootheel of a god came down on him then, crushing him utterly out of existence.

When he woke, it was to blinding agony in his occipital lobe. Or so it felt to him, even though the brain of a Prime contained no pain receptors. The pain was an echo of his visions—which, even as he tried to remember them, began to dissolve away like sand under a storm surge.

Then a foot came down on his throat, and he struggled to open his eyes.

Red light. Still in the Adytum, then. He was lying on the floor with his right arm outstretched beside him. Something pulsed in the palm of that hand, beating like an electric heart, then fell still.

The foot came down harder. He peered up at the figure looming over him, wondering how an assassin could possibly have got so close to him.

"I've seen enough dead frags," Emlee said, "to be able to guess what that is."

She pointed at the object in his hand. The loop shunt, now inactive.

Emlee pointed with the barrel of her Henschke Sloan repeater in order to get his attention, then swung the gun across to aim at his aching temples.

"I came here to tell you something," she said, "and to ask you a question. I figure they're both irrelevant now."

Her foot had closed his windpipe, but he could still talk to her via electronic means. He had no idea how long he had been lying unconscious on the floor.

"What exactly do you think I'm up to?" he asked her.

"Talking to the Barons," she said. "Reporting in like the good little spy you are."

"Why would I do that?"

"Because you're on their side. You don't want the Forts back, and you never have."

"If that's the case, then I'm a better liar than even I would give myself credit for."

"Your capacity for deception has never surprised me."

"Here." He offered her the loop shunt. "Take it. Destroy it. That's how little it means to me. Yes, I kept it when I should've destroyed it, but it's part of this problem, it's evidence, and I couldn't bring myself to do it." She brushed his hand away. "This is the first time I've tried consciously to use it and—" He rubbed his forehead. "Well, let's say I'm not in a hurry to try that again."

The business end of the pistol didn't shift a micrometer. "Tell that to Al."

"So he's the one you'll run to—not Render or Helwise?" He almost smiled. The emotion behind it was more weary than amused. "You think Render already knows, that he's my lapdog, and you think Helwise and I still have something going on between us, in some fucked-up way. Al will shoot me right here if he thinks I've betrayed the cause. You know that, too."

"Isn't that what you deserve?"

"No, because you're wrong. Completely wrong, as it happens."

"Can you prove it?"

"Would you change your mind if I could?"

She hesitated. "You're wrong about Helwise," she said. "I wouldn't go to her because I don't trust her either."

"You can trust her to look after her best interests. Executing me as a traitor would sit well with her right now, I think."

"She's the source of the transmissions."

"What transmissions?" Then he remembered. "The coded messages you've been tracing?"

"Into and out of the Citadel. She's leaking information to someone, and I don't know who it is."

"So now you think both she and I are traitors? That's absurd. Why not Al as well? Or Render? Maybe you feel angry because we left you out. Is that the problem, Emlee? Are you wishing we trusted your enough to let you in on our big conspiracy?"

His mocking tone had the desired effect. Her lips tightened. "Don't be an idiot, Imre."

"You'd be an idiot to shoot me now." He tipped his chin to one side, as though easing the pressure on his windpipe. His right hand gripped the loop shunt tightly between thumb and forefinger. "Was that what you came to tell me—about Helwise?"

"Yes, I—"

He threw the shunt up into her face. Her automatic recoil shifted her center of gravity backward just enough for him to wrench his neck out from under her boot. Her aim drifted. When the pistol discharged, he was out of harm's way, just. A flash of energy and heat scored down one side of his head. He ignored it.

Emlee had been in more combat situations than he could count, but she had never equaled him at hand-to-hand combat. Even though a pistol was worse than useless at close range, she insisted on trying to right her aim rather than free up her hands. He kicked her legs out from under her before she could manage it. The gun fired again, this time up into the air. A rain of red glass fragments fell on them.

A second later, the situation was completely reversed. She was down with his knee and shin pinning her chest and left arm and the pistol jammed into her right ear. Her breathing was hard and angry. She wouldn't look at him.

Imre's pulse had risen, but not because of the exertion. The pain in his head was completely forgotten in the wild dance of power play and danger. "We're both idiots. That's the more likely scenario."

"If you kill me," she said in a tight voice, "you'll only bring me back."

"I said I wouldn't."

"What do you care about my feelings? You could blow my head off and re-create me as I was when I left Dussehra. I trusted you then."

"And you should trust me now. Nothing's changed."

"Everything's changed." Her green eyes skated over his face, then away. "Have you done it before?"

"Done what?"

"Resurrected me. You could have done it a dozen times, and I'd never know. It struck me an hour ago. You're only telling me now so I'll keep quiet about Chyro. You have no choice but to tell me the truth, because this time the attack spared me. How many times have we both died and the Apparatus has brought us back? How many times have *you* died, for that matter? Dozens? Hundreds?"

"And that's what you came to ask me. Great. No matter what I say, you won't be happy. I could swear black-and-blue that I'd never done it before, and you wouldn't believe me."

"Do you swear it?"

"I have no reason to lie. If you're right, I could just shoot you now and start again. That I'm making the effort to convince you of my innocence should tell you something."

He felt some of the tension drain from her. "I thought about killing you," she said. "It was the only way to test the theory. Kill you here, in secret, and see if you came back."

"Boy, am I ever glad I told you about this place."

"Well, do you blame me for considering it? And look how I found you."

He glanced to his left, where the shunt lay like a forgotten marble, staring blankly at the glass ceiling. "Pretty incriminating, I'll admit."

She shifted underneath him. "Are you going to let me go now?"

"Are you going to try to shoot me again?"

"Not if you tell me what you saw through the shunt."

He frowned. "I don't know. Jumbled images. Nothing coherent. It was like plugging my mind directly into the Line and drowning in raw data. And I guess that's what I might have been doing if there's a Fort on the other end of that shunt."

"A Fort that survived the Slow Wave?"

He remembered the strange sense of guilt and anger at the climax of his vision. "Maybe the Fort that *caused* the Slow Wave."

The thought was supremely sobering. They had been working on the assumption that the Slow Wave was either an accident—the backfiring of an experiment, perhaps, related to the mysterious Domgard—or the discharge of a weapon beyond anything ever developed before. Imre's former self had been entangled with either scenario, which was bad enough. This new possibility was even worse. The Forts had rarely exhibited internecine violence before. Was it conceivable that one Fort could have attempted to kill all the others? Could Imre have been part of that murderous entity?

He put the gun down beside her head and lifted his weight off. Standing over her, he reached down to help her up.

She stood under her own steam. "I'm sorry," she said. Two bright spots burned in her cheeks.

"You're not really; otherwise, you wouldn't keep thinking the worst of me."

"Well, this time I jumped to the wrong conclusion."

"I would have too, under the circumstances. You're my bodyguard, and part of that job is to keep me in line. If you hadn't reacted the way you did, I'd worry that you were getting slack."

Emlee didn't smile. She bent down and picked up the sidearm, then slid it smoothly into the holster at her side. Slivers of glass crunched under her feet. "Now what?"

He thought of Helwise with a kind of flat emptiness. There was no thrill left in the contemplation of confronting her. Whatever spark had once driven their relationship, it was completely extinguished. Now it was all preemptive strikes and gameplay. He was heartily tired of playing. "We've got a real knot to untangle, here. Why would Helwise be feeding information to someone outside the Citadel?"

"To let assassins know where you'll be, so they can lay traps for you, like on Dussehra?"

"The whistle-stop locations are decided en route. She doesn't know where I'll be from one trip to the next."

"And she wouldn't be working with the Barons," Emlee said, "because that doesn't make sense either."

"Could it be something completely innocent?"

"Highly unlikely." A thought struck her. "Maybe she's still trying to wipe out her other selves. Paying bounty hunters and trying to keep it out of your sight."

He considered it. That made a bizarre kind of sense. He could almost accept it.

"What time is it?" he asked her.

"Six in the evening."

He was startled. That meant he had been out cold for over twelve hours, Absolute. "Tell Render what you've found. He needs to know about it, if only because Helwise managed to get away with it on his watch."

"Not his field," Emlee said, dismissing any possibility that the old soldier could be to blame. "He sees with different eyes."

He let her concentrate on calling Render while he went to sweep up the mess of broken glass. Machines could have done it, but they would have intruded on the emptiness of his retreat. The untidiness reflected the complicated mess of his thoughts. Whatever Helwise was up to, it had just become a whole lot more serious. The menial task gave him time to collect himself.

When Emlee returned, her expression was very strange. "Render's been looking for us," she said. "The spook picked up an anomalous transmission an hour ago. It's from a Fort who says you've been expecting him."

His blood slowed in his veins. The pain in his head vanished. *Be there, ruler of the realm . . .* "Anomalous how?"

"It's coming from inside the Throne Room."

"What? Why didn't the Apparatus tell me itself?"

"Render says that you should ask it for him. If it talks to you, we'll be one step closer to getting some answers. It's said nothing since making that last report."

Beyond slow, his heartbeat seemed to stop entirely . . . *open your red-lit windows* . . . "Apparatus? Answer me. What's going on?"

Silence.

Tired of that game, he threw the broom aside, grabbed Emlee by the arm, and pulled her with him to the exit.

. . . and bid him enter.

THIS INFECTION
OF TIME

●

*It was, indeed, a tempestuous yet sternly beautiful night, and
one wildly singular in its terror and its beauty.*

—Edgar Allan Poe

The Citadel was in a state of extreme lockdown. Jumpy
guards challenged Imre and Emlee at every turn. Without the
Apparatus whispering regular assurances in his ear, Imre was
loath to take any chances. Every guard he encountered was
co-opted into the growing phalanx marching with him into the
center of the Citadel. Security be damned, he thought. If
something was already in the Throne Room, what did it matter who got in from outside?

By the time he reached the feeder corridors for the massive
hall, a crowd of forty armed guards surrounded him, larger
than the number protecting Helwise. She was waiting for him
by the entrance, looking entirely too composed while overclocking blurs swirled around her, watching every possible
angle at speeds too fast to follow. Freer was there too.

"You have a visitor," she said.

She hates this, Imre knew. She's lost control, just for a
moment, and she hates it. The chessboard had just been
tipped over, and there were pieces everywhere. "Is it really a
Fort?"

"It doesn't seem to be much at all," she said with a cryptic
look. She turned and gestured for the door to be opened. The
massive, titanium panels swung aside on silent gimbals, exposing the vast space beyond. Imre hadn't seen it empty since its
construction, many centuries ago. Rows of seats stepped up
into darkness under a ceiling dotted with powerful lights and
discreet gun emplacements, all facing inward at the circular

stage. The ostentation of the throne itself appalled him: an enormous, iron edifice surrounded by holographic projectors that, although currently inactive, normally painted the air with ghostly images of the First Prime, the Regent, and those they had granted an audience. Imre hated official receptions, with their processions and their pomp, and he had come to hate sitting in the center of such a large crowd. The Throne Room was nothing more than theater and like all theater invited detractors.

Now it was echoing and hollow, containing only the blurs of overclocking guards, picked out when they crossed spotlights as brief, strobing still lifes.

Render was suddenly at his side, his uniform literally smoking from friction and a lightweight Balzac beamer in one hand. His mismatched eyes were an added discordant note to the scene.

"Where is it?" Imre asked.

"Take a look."

"I don't see anything."

Render nodded. "Come closer." He led the way across the open expanse between the first raised row of chairs and the base of the throne. The floor was lined with hairline seams, defining panels that hid retractable seats safely out of sight. The width of the open inner ring exceeded thirty meters and seemed to be completely empty.

Imre had listened to the original message a dozen times on the way from the Adytum into the Citadel. It was brief and to the point, as though scripted many times over and edited almost out of existence.

"MZ has arrived. Tell Imre Bergamasc. He is waiting for me."

Something about the method of transmission, something so strange that Render had insisted on showing him in person, plus the meaning embedded in the unusual name—"MZ" was a pun on the ancient word "emzee," *old person*—convinced Render that they were dealing with a full-fledged Fort. Imre trusted Render's instincts where Forts were concerned. They had hunted enough together, back in the Mad Times.

Imre and his untidy entourage padded warily across the open space. He felt exposed, unsure what to expect. He had never heard of anyone called "MZ," so there was no reason to assume it was psychotic or murderous—but until he knew how it had survived the Slow Wave intact and why it had come to him now, he wasn't taking any chances.

"Stop." Render raised a hand, and they all came to a halt. "Here."

Imre could see nothing distinctive about the patch on which they were standing. "Want to be more specific, Render?"

"Look down."

At Imre's feet was a simple LED mounted flush to the floor. Something to do with an automated ushering system, he assumed, or for emergency situations, one of a line leading to the nearest exit.

"It's in the wiring," Emlee said, breaking the silence. "A short circuit, sparking in code."

"How could you possibly have known that?" asked Helwise.

"Because that's the way the Apparatus talks to me." Imre squatted down beside the LED, then looked past the heads of those staring at him, to the cavernous reaches of the hall. He spoke over an extremely private channel, so only those in his inner circle could hear. "The communications we receive from it come over normal channels—through the Line, out of our implants, along ordinary fiber optics—because that's the only way it can communicate. It can't have any physical interaction with a medium like air, as we do. But how does it intersect with those devices? Emlee and I traced the path it followed and found the source, except it wasn't a source at all, really, just glitches like this one, sparking when they shouldn't. Relays, circuits, RAM, gates, deep down in the guts of any machine that connects to us—small things that don't take much energy to influence, because even energy is a hard thing for something written in the vacuum to come by. Once it's got that tiny material toehold, it can infiltrate anywhere."

"Like this thing has?" asked Freer, looking shaken. "One spook is bad enough. I'm not sure how I feel about two."

"The original ghost still isn't talking," Imre said in a worried tone, "so maybe it's one after all."

"The Apparatus clammed up right after we decoded the message from MZ," said Helwise. "I don't think that's a coincidence."

"Neither do I." Imre stood up. The hall echoed with the sound of security personnel and a high-pitched susurrus of encrypted communications. "Is it still transmitting?"

"Once every ninety seconds."

"Well, let's talk back and see what happens. Emlee, inspect what's been done here and take over."

"Already on it," she said.

"Run some current through the circuit, using the same code. Tell this thing we got its message. I'm here and ready to talk."

She nodded again. A second later, the LED began to flicker as high-frequency currents danced through it. Emlee's head tilted to one side as though listening to something.

Why not, he thought.

"Let's all hear it," he said.

A sequence of rapid staccato blips filled the secure channel connecting them, seeming to emanate from the air of the Throne Room itself. It wasn't a rhythm Imre recognized. That meant little. He wasn't an expert code breaker, although he'd tackled a few in his time, and humanity's ability to hide secrets had never been fully exhausted.

They didn't have to wait long for a response. A stronger sequence of pulses, more measured than Emlee's, overlaid the initial sequence.

"What's it saying?" Helwise asked.

Emlee waved her silent, then said, "It wants to open a digital channel into the Citadel infrastructure, but apparently the Apparatus is blocking it. It needs you, Imre, to issue the order."

"The order to open our firewalls?" Imre shook his head. "I'm going to need a very good reason to do that."

Emlee sent a series of new coded pulses through the LED. A reply came almost immediately. "It wants you to know the truth about yourself," she translated.

He kept his expression carefully wooden. "It doesn't need a high bandwidth to tell me that."

Another brief exchange followed, sounding like two antique computer games at war. "It says it can't tell you. It has to show you."

"I want to know more about it, first. Where does it come from? Why has it come out of hiding just to talk to me?"

Imre noticed the coded translation beginning before he had finished speaking. Emlee had obviously rigged up some kind of automatic translation.

On the heels of that thought came a smooth, artificial voice over the secure channel.

"I come from Earth," it said. "Originally, not recently. I took leave of my fellow architects before the Slow Wave, when the experiments were well advanced. My part in the project was done; I had achieved everything I set out to do. I was as you see me now, liberated from the strictures of matter and energy, free to wander as I willed."

"You're like the Apparatus," Imre said. "We guessed that."

"I helped build the Apparatus. Without me it wouldn't exist, and neither would your pale imitation of the Continuum."

Even down through such strange means, Imre heard an unmistakable flash of pride and indignation. "So why won't it talk to you?"

"I left on uncertain terms with my colleagues. The Apparatus has been instructed never to let me approach the Earth again. You have authority over it now. Only you can countermand that order."

"But you are here. At least I presume you are."

"Only a fraction of myself and only at the expense of my creation. I can't control it. I can only interfere with its workings. I know it better than it knows itself, you see; I know its weakness and its back doors. It will return to full functionality once you have issued the command, and it has removed the ban on my presence."

An image of two ectoplasmic jellyfish grappling over control of that tiny circuit flashed through Imre's mind. "Was it part of you that intercepted my hardcast near Dussehra?"

"That must certainly be the case. Did it not explain that to you?"

"No. It only told me to be here."

"Parts of me are stranger than others now, since the Slow Wave tore me limb from limb, mind from mind. I could only propagate a message and hope that your path would cross mine somewhere."

Imre thought of the phantasm, the *maliceful hermit* that had threatened to expire the moment he was back on his way to Dussehra. The description matched.

"What happens if I don't give you what you want?" he asked it. "What if I refuse to tell the Apparatus to let you in?"

"Then our conversation is over, and I will have no choice but to leave you—although I suspect it won't be remotely in peace."

"Why can't you just tell me what you need to say right now and be done with it?"

"You won't believe me unless I show you, unless I take you there myself."

"Take me where?"

"To where it started. To Domgard."

Imre felt the eyes of his oldest associates on him.

"You can move independently?" he asked to gain a second in which to think.

"Yes. I am like the Apparatus, but not identical."

That was intriguing enough to make the decision easier.

"All right. You've got something to tell me, and I want to hear it." Helwise shook her head as though unable to believe what she was hearing. "Let's meet halfway. I'm not going to give you the Citadel, because that would mean effectively giving you the Earth. If the Forts you used to work with didn't want you back here, I'm sure it was for a reason. Unless you're willing to tell me what that reason was, of course . . . ?" He waited long enough for Emlee's translator to catch up, then another minute for MZ to offer a response. Nothing came. "All right. So here's what we'll do. I presume the ban doesn't extend as far as the moon's orbit, so we'll talk on the dark side somewhere. Your choice where, if you like. How would that be?"

The Fort took a long time to reply. Imre waited it out, tapping the index finger of his left hand against his thigh.

He would have liked to pace off some of the energy building up inside him, but that would have made him look inde-
cisive. He was playing fast and loose with people's opinions
as it was.

The silence on the circuit broke with a series of firm
pulses. "Hansfaall Base," the Fort said, with some of its original curtness. "I will await you there."

"Done," Imre responded.

That appeared to be the end of the exchange. Emlee kept
her translator running, but there was nothing incoming to interpret.

"The Apparatus isn't back online," said Helwise irritably.

"So we move fast," Imre told her. "Ready a high-speed
cage to Smitherman and a shuttle for the rest of the way. I
want us breathing moondust within twenty-four hours."

"I hope you don't expect me to go on this lunatic mission,"
she said.

"No. Stay here. Emlee, Render, Al—you're coming with
me, with as much backup as we can squeeze into a shuttle."

"Do you think it'll help?" Emlee asked.

"Against a ghost? I doubt it. But I'll feel better for having
someone at my back." He turned back to Helwise, and added,
"Right?"

"Fucking A." If she read his comment as a criticism of her
loyalty, it didn't show.

At the base of the skyline, Imre was met by Ra MacPhedron.
The child was present in only two of his singleton bodies, representing two extremes of his developing personality: youth-
ful exuberance and hostile forthrightness.

"I know where you're going," said the second.

"Take me with you," added the first. "I want to come."

"You're not going anywhere," Imre told him without
breaking stride. He could see the entrance to the cage waiting
for him, just a dozen meters away. "How the hell does he
know about this?" he asked Freer, not keeping his annoyance
private. He would have asked Helwise, had she not peeled off
minutes earlier to attend to other business.

"He's permanently patched into Regent's Citadel feed," Freer said.

"What the hell for?"

Freer just shrugged. Imre could think of only one answer: training.

Ra wasn't going to take no for an answer. "I won't interfere," he persisted. "I just want to observe."

"You can do that through your mother's feed."

"But it's not the same thing as being there."

"I'm not going to put you in any unnecessary danger."

"Do you think I can't handle it? Is that your problem with me?"

Imre stopped and turned to face both of them. "My problem with you has nothing to do with your abilities, real or imagined. My problem is that you're unpredictable. Whatever happens at Hansfaall Base, I don't want any surprises coming from my side."

"You don't trust me, then."

It wasn't a question. Imre didn't have to answer it, but he responded anyway. Better to leave the kid with no misunderstandings. "I don't trust you because I don't know you. It's that simple. When you're older, trained—"

"You don't mean that." Ra's quieter form looked stricken and on the verge of weeping. The other's face flushed, and his fists clenched.

"Don't you dare," said Emlee said to the other. "You know where you stand. If you take one step forward, I'll drop you, hard. I don't care whose kid you are."

Ra looked on the verge of testing her determination. Imre could almost read the thoughts running through his mind. Two against one, and his mother's influence over the others. But reason prevailed. Imre wasn't going to be swayed by Helwise. Render was glowering at him from under heavy brows.

"You said I could come to you at any time," Ra tried, one last time, in a plaintive voice.

"To talk," Imre told him. "That's all."

Ra turned tail and ran, silently, into the warren of the Citadel.

"Christ," Emlee breathed. "Isn't there any way to keep a lid on him?"

"He has the run of the place," said Freer, revealing nothing about his opinion on the matter.

"New young thing," Render added, with a similar lack of commitment.

Imre suppressed his annoyance. "Let's not waste any more time." The cage door hung open, waiting for him. "Is the transport organized topside?"

"Almost," said Freer. "We have a priority ascent. It'll be ready by the time we arrive."

They filed into the cage, an opulent space containing seats, cushions, and work spaces for more than fifty people. Imre and his contingent would barely half fill it. That was all right; a priority ascent wasn't about company or comfort. They would be pulling several gees along the way. All other traffic had been hustled ahead of them, or canceled outright.

A blow for diplomacy, Imre thought. Deadlines wouldn't be met; numerous egos would be bruised.

Fuck it.

The cage ascended almost silently. His Prime body adjusted to the increased strain within seconds and moved about as easily as if he were standing motionless on the Earth. The discomfort lay in the way other things moved: a dropped apple; the clothes on his shoulders; the air itself. He couldn't completely suppress the thought that he was heading under high acceleration out of the gravity well he called home. It had been a long time since he had physically left Earth, as opposed to hardcaster.

He kept his thoughts carefully on the present concern: MZ and his mysterious message. The Apparatus remained steadfastly silent. Gagged? Speechless? Dead? There was no way of telling. Since inheriting the AI from the home world's previous ruler, he had become complacent about the Apparatus's abilities and his reliance upon it. Without the ghost—the glue knitting the disparate parts of the Returned Continuum together—everything he had worked for might come instantly apart.

Imre paced the entire way to geocentric orbit while Emlee searched files in a vain quest to identify the mysterious Fort.

There was no record anywhere of MZ's existence, but that came as no great surprise: perhaps two hundred Forts had ruled the galaxy before the Slow Wave, and only fifty or so had been acquainted with the rest of humanity. Most had worked at a self-imposed remove, finding company only among those who shared their rhythms, needs, and objectives. What did a Prime have in common with a being whose life span was measured in thousands of centuries and whose physical existence spanned vast swathes of the galaxy? The minds of Earth had been an even more isolated breed. Protected—or kept deliberately apart, as some would have it—by the civilizations of the Round, they had pursued their own ends with patient deliberation.

But one of them had left, and now that one was back bearing revelations—or at least the promise of them. Imre felt like a pawn, and that wasn't a feeling he liked at all. He had gone to war with the Forts once before over just such a feeling; he wasn't afraid of taking on another, if that was how it turned out. He could only follow MZ's play as far as it led, then see what happened.

Smitherman City was vast and tangled, an unruly outgrowth of Earth that had been accruing and disintegrating in waves for over a million years. As large as a small moon and containing a permanent population of over nine hundred thousand, it served as a major stepping-stone from Earth and the rest of the system. No one entered the home planet's airspace except through the City. The penalty for testing that rule was severe. Trespassers were routinely shot down from low orbit every year, well before they could set foot on the pristine surface below—a policy enforced by Smitherman itself, since that only tightened its chokehold on the skyline.

Imre paused briefly at the top of the magnificent structure, looking down along the precipitous line to the surface far below. On all sides unfolded the vast flower that was Earth's first city in outer space: baroque, ugly, dirty, and magnificent all at once. He could feel the distant susurrus of human occupation as much through his feet as through his ears. The air smelled lived-in and vital. He knew from experience that if he stayed there for long, the stink would get into his skin and take weeks to get out.

A Vespula was waiting for them at a secure dock, along with a dozen soldiers in a high state of readiness. No voluntary guards these; clad in the latest wasp-waisted armor and standing three meters high, they looked barely human and moved with the protracted caution of beings thinking much faster than those in their care. Every angle was calculated and weighed against every other angle. No contingency was left unconsidered. Imre remembered that state well from his days as a singleton mercenary. He had felt capable of sidestepping individual atoms.

The hopper was crowded. The company of ordinary troops was faintly soothing, so the inability to pace didn't chafe him as it might have. He ran through the specs of Hansfaall Base as they powered their way there, pulling even higher levels of acceleration than they had during their ascent. The roar of engines filled his head.

The base was a small facility, home to less than fifty people—visiting historians and archaeologists mostly, with a small support staff. They had all been evacuated under the pretext of a military exercise. Some lies never changed. No doubt Helwise was fielding complaints already, but Imre didn't care. He would happily bury her under an avalanche of details if it left him free to explore the big picture. And if MZ was to be even partly believed, this could be the biggest picture of all.

Domgard. *Where it started.*

He had first learned the name through Al Freer, who had heard Himself referred to as *the architect of Domgard.* Later, a Baron had threatened them all, saying, *Your immediate future, and the future of the human race, depend on your never saying that name again.* Imre's former self had called it *the greatest experiment ever undertaken,* or so Emlee had reported, and Emlee's Fort friend Ampersand had deduced the existence of it on Hyperabad, before being killed by the Luminous and the Barons. Imre's former self had issued a stern warning to stay away from it—and he still had no idea what it was.

Imre already suspected that he would go anywhere MZ

suggested—assuming only that the Fort seemed halfway reliable. If hard answers waited at the end of the journey, how could he do otherwise? It didn't feel like a trap; he was much more vulnerable in the middle of a whistle-stop tour, so why target him in his stronghold? It wouldn't even work as a feint, allowing him a false sense of security while some subtle trap sprang into play elsewhere. There were too many people around him, too many capable warriors like Freer, Render, and Emlee Copas, who would be watchful if he allowed his guard to drop. Besides, MZ had already proved himself quite capable of stopping the Apparatus in its tracks, so what need had he of complicated ruses?

Hansfaall Base grew from a speck to a cluster of shining silver habitats. The hopper furiously decelerated, casting harsh purple light across the moonscape and kicking up thousands of years' worth of dust. The face of the Earth, hanging over them quarter-full, disappeared for a minute and only reappeared when they had touched down. No umbilical snaked out to meet them. They would walk out to the nearest habitat protected from the vacuum by their armor and the skin suits beneath.

It had been a very long time since Imre had walked on the moon. The one-sixth gravity took a second to get used to. His usual sure-footedness returned only after he had taken a dozen steps. Getting old, he thought with a grimace.

MZ wasn't visible either outside or within the habitat. Imre stationed a mix of soldiers and Citadel guards outside and took a dozen inside with him. Emlee stayed close, as Render and Freer paced out the interior of the small structure. It contained five pentagonal rooms, not significantly more area in total than the hopper itself. All were empty.

"Patch into the electricals," Imre told Emlee. "Our friend will be here somewhere."

"No need," spoke a voice from the main chamber's entertainment system. Imre recognized it immediately: the voice of the phantasm that had ambushed him on the way to Dussehra. "I have been watching you ever since you landed."

Imre resisted the impulse to address the ceiling. Forts were no more gods than he was, for all that they sometimes behaved as though they thought they were. "Does that mean you're actually here with us, or patched into the network?"

"Define 'actually,' and I will attempt to answer your question."

"I didn't come here to play word games."

"Isn't that all we have, Imre Bergamasc? The history of humanity is an edifice built of words. All our stories, our arguments, our dreams, our declarations. That's all we've really added to the universe. The rest is just physics, in one form or another."

"Physics made you what you are," he said, "if your word is to be believed."

"I made myself. This form is just one of many I have inhabited."

There was too much flippancy in the reply. Imre could tell that MZ was hiding something. "What was your name before you Graduated?"

"Misha Zuccolo. Don't bother looking for it in any of the archives. I was no one famous: not an Old-Timer, not a combatant in the war you fought with my fellows, not even a fatality during the Slow Wave. Events in the galaxy have passed me by. That is only mostly by design. Sometimes I want to connect but fail. Sometimes I have no choice but to try."

"This is one of those times, I presume?"

"Actually, I'm here by choice. I have been waiting for you beyond the orbit of Neptune, where the sky is empty of traffic and I was unlikely to be disturbed. As soon as I detected your return, I came to talk with you. I might be the last of my kind, and the knowledge I possess is important to you. It would be wrong to stand apart and watch. When you know what I know, I think you will agree."

"I've traced the source of his voice," said Emlee over the private channel. "He's coming in through seven separate channels and linking up in the base's life-support and infrastructure AI."

"What are the risks, being in here?" he asked her.

"If he can patch into any system off-Earth," she said in a serious voice, "then we'd be at risk anywhere."

Imre nodded, remembering Forts worming through skin-suit software and melting the people within, filling whole warships with hard radiation by dropping shields in transit, and interfacing directly with neurons to drive susceptible victims mad. They were insidious and, in the right frame of mind, utterly ruthless.

Imre could only guess at MZ's mood. The Fort must have known that they would trace the source of his infiltrations. He would know that they would consider the question of his threat to their well-being. His silence on the subject wasn't hiding the truth but implying another: he could try to kill them at any moment. He was both threatening them and reassuring them at the same time, as Imre had the dissidents on Dussehra.

The irony wasn't lost on him.

"Knowledge," Imre said, "is the only tradable commodity in the galaxy. Are you here to trade? Is that what you're playing at?"

"Don't paint me with your colors, Prime," the voice snapped. "I am not so easily reducible."

"Neither am I, Fort. And you should know that well—if you know anything at all about Domgard, as you claim to."

There was a small silence. Imre counted to five inside his head, hoping his gamble would pay off. He presumed that MZ had no idea how much he knew about Domgard. MZ couldn't know either how Imre felt about that knowledge. Was Imre part of that mysterious project or opposed to it? Was he trawling the galaxy in search of knowledge he himself had lost, or for those who still retained such forbidden knowledge in order to destroy them? Both of them were playing weak hands as strongly as possible.

Finally, the Fort spoke. "We are much reduced, you and I, from the heights of our power. Surviving at what cost? I bow under the weight of my memories. Everything I designed, everything I claimed as my own, everything of value to me has come to nothing. All that's left to me is this gift I offer you—the gift of knowledge, which, as you rightly say, is all that matters anymore."

"You might not be trading," said Freer, with eyes gleaming sharply, "but I bet there's going to be a price anyway."

"All you have to do is leave here with me. I will show you everything that remains of Domgard—everything that remains to be seen—and you will see where the Slow Wave started. Perhaps you will understand better, then, how you figure in this terrible dance of shadows."

MZ was answering Freer's question but addressing only Imre. "Leave Earth? I'm going to need a little more information before I'll agree to that."

"This distance is great, but the journey won't be arduous."

"How great, precisely?"

"Twenty three thousand, three hundred and ninety-one light-years, based on the Earth's current location."

"Is that one way," Emlee asked, "or there and back?"

"One way."

Fifty thousand years Absolute, Imre thought, assuming MZ traveled at anything remotely like light-speed. A lot could happen in that time.

"Too long," said Render in his flattest, no-nonsense voice.

"What's at the other end?" Imre asked the Fort.

"I've told you. All that remains of Domgard."

"And that is?"

"Ruins and ashes, the aftermath of dreams."

Imre waited for MZ to say more and was once again frustrated by the obliqueness of Forts.

"You must know some of what happened here on Earth," MZ said. There was a new edge to his voice: guilt, perhaps. "You must know about the attempt to create a god, a being that would lift humanity out of the rut it had dug itself into. A rut, admittedly, that was as broad as the galaxy and as long as all of history itself—but a rut nonetheless. The view from this ancient vantage point was no more or less magnificent than it is now: the stars don't care what happens to us; the galactic wheel still turns. Nothing but hubris convinces us that we are important, that we are anything other than a glitch in the universe's usual operations. We were as proud as the kings of ancient Earth, who conquered whole continents and thought themselves the rulers of all. Humanity has indulged many delusions. That one was as relevant then as it is today."

"I know about the god," Imre said, ignoring the barb aimed at his own regime. "The experiment failed. The Slow Wave killed it before it could finish. The Apparatus was the only component left working when the minds of Earth died. That was all."

"Yes. But it came so close. A century or two, and they might have succeeded. Who knows what the galaxy might look like now if they had? The experiment was audacious in its inception—to take a Type III galactic civilization and elevate it to something even higher, to a level of existence barely dreamed of by our ancestors. A Type IV civilization, with footholds in more than one galaxy, or even beyond. Type IV, Type V . . . Our minds cannot hold such thoughts intact. We must break them down and examine their component parts. We must regard the grand work one facet at a time and never apprehend the entire jewel. Were it to come into being, it would be as far above its makers as they were above you."

Imre took to pacing again, made restless not by that particular point, since it was likely a statement of fact, but by the length of the Fort's digression. "Tell me what Earth has to do with Domgard."

"The experiments were different," MZ said, "but the intent was the same."

"To take a Type III civilization and raise it to Type IV?"

"Or beyond."

His pulse quickened. "A faster-than-light drive. Domgard was all about FTL."

"No. Some laws are unbreakable."

Again that strange hint of emotion in MZ's voice. "What, then? What else could the Forts have needed so badly?"

"Transformation of a fundamental kind. That is my belief, anyway. Only you might ever know for certain. And that is why you must go to Domgard—to unpick the knot you tied around both past and future, and to set free humanity's potential. My dead brethren couldn't do that; I can't do that; our only hope now is you."

Imre stopped pacing. "I'm not thinking about the future," he said. "I'm just trying to survive the present."

"One leads to the other, of course. The manner of your survival determines how well you enjoy the days ahead—a fact I ignored to my own detriment, long ago."

Yes, Imre thought. Definitely guilt.

He raised his eyes. "What did you do, MZ?"

"My past is irrelevant."

"Not if I'm to trust you. I need to know all of it."

"I cannot tell you." MZ sounded stricken. "But the being you call the Apparatus will. You can ask it when I restore it to full functionality. I offer you this in good faith, even though I suspect you will trust me less for it."

"We'll just have to see. When do you think that will be?"

"Now, if you like. There's no reason to delay."

"Do it, then."

Nothing changed; there was no half-felt stirring in the air, no subtle shift in the ambience of his many data feeds; but Imre knew, somehow, when the Apparatus returned. That supposition was confirmed almost instantly when the AI's smooth voice spoke directly into his ears.

"Imre, I have detected an intrusion."

"We're aware of it," he said, hearing relief naked in his voice. "Tell me everything you can about the source."

"MZ is an exile, forbidden ever to return to Earth."

"We know that too. What did he do?"

"He stole the secret of my existence. He used it to encode himself into the vacuum in an attempt to become immortal. Then he fled, abandoning the experiment. His absence set the project back ten thousand years. His actions were unforgivable."

My part in the project was done, MZ had said. *I had achieved everything I set out to do.*

And then what, Imre wondered. If MZ knew how to write information directly onto the vacuum, why wasn't he omnipresent, like the Apparatus was quickly becoming? Why did he exist in isolated fragments, twisted and miserable?

"The secrets he stole," Imre said, guessing, "weren't complete. They were a prototype. He couldn't grow or spread; he could only stay pretty much as he was. The exile imposed on him was to stop him ever finding out how to finish the job. So instead of stealing immortality, all he stole was a lingering, lonely death."

His words were provocative. He was hoping for a reaction from the Fort. MZ, however, stayed silent.

Then another thought occurred to him. Ten thousand years, the Apparatus had said. That was how long MZ's actions had set the experiment back. But they had recovered. The minds of Earth had found a way to move on without whatever skills MZ had originally brought to the mix. They had made up the lost time, but not quickly enough.

A century or two, MZ had said, *and they might have succeeded.*

The Fort blamed himself for the failure of the experiment. Deservedly so, Imre thought, and for two very good reasons. Not only would the new god the minds of Earth had promised never be born, but now MZ couldn't be forgiven. Humanity had slipped even deeper into its rut thanks to one person's selfish desire to preserve his own life.

And now he was back, trying to make amends. Or trying to warn Imre of the dangers of such experiments and the way they affect people involved . . .

Ruins and ashes, the aftermath of dreams.

"I'm going with him," he said, speaking not to the Apparatus but to the room in general. "I need to know what Domgard was. We all do. But I'm not taking anyone else with me. The risk is mine and mine alone."

"You're wrong there," said Emlee, "and you know it. What was it you said earlier about my being your bodyguard? If you don't believe it, you might as well sack me now."

Part of that job is to keep me in line. True, Imre thought, now more than ever.

"All right. But just you. Al has work to do, and I need Render here to keep an eye on things."

"And what about Chyro?" she said with a sharp look that said as clearly as words: *You needed him before, but you're dumping him now?*

"Okay, okay." Then he considered it a second longer. "Actually, yes, you're absolutely right. We're both going to need him, where we're going." In more ways than one, he thought.

She frowned. "Why? What do you know about it?"

"Think it through. How's MZ going to get us anywhere? Not by ship, that's for sure. He barely exists, as far as matter is concerned, so he's not going to be giving us a lift in any conventional way."

"I'm not hardcasting to an unknown destination."

"That's only part of the story, I think."

Her frown deepened until it seemed permanently etched in the ageless skin of her face.

"Al, will you bring Helwise up to date for me?"

Freer nodded, and Imre felt relief. I'm not playing anymore, he wanted to tell her. I've got better things to do.

He woke to a blur of primary colors and thought, Oh hell, here we go again. He was inside the world of the phantasm and finding it no less uncomfortable than the first time.

Then, however, the blur shifted. Fuzzy boundaries sharpened, came closer to proper focus. More intricate shades emerged from the initial, primary palette. Flat surfaces took on three-dimensional textures. Other senses woke, giving him taste, smell, touch. A well-defined image took shape before him—a familiar face.

"There," said Chyro Kells, leaning into shot with near-perfect realism. A slight graininess faded, and the illusion was indistinguishable from reality.

Imre looked around. He was lying on a day bed under a natural arbor formed by two rows of plane trees, ten to a side. Dappled sunlight with no obvious source gave the mossy ground beneath them a restless appearance, as though it might at any moment turn to liquid; but that was a very different sort of illusion from the one he was testing out. What lay beyond the trunks of the trees was sketchily defined: a green surface much like a lawn; a band of deeper green that might have been a hedge; a suggestion of more trees; the hint of clouds in a blue sky.

He turned his eye to either end of the arbor, where the detail was most impressive.

Ahead of him lay the entrance to a white, Georgian town house standing on its own, austere and opulent at the same time, with green marble steps and matching pillars under a starkly geometrical portico. The door was open. Imre could see polished wooden floorboards beyond it, paintings on the walls, and a flight of stairs curving clockwise to an upper floor. The windows reflected blue sky like mirrors. A curl of smoke rose up into the firmament like the sweep of an artist's thumb across wet paint.

"Very nice," he told Kells, turning back to face his physician. They were both dressed in simple white smocks, similar to the ones he wore on Earth after stepping out of a hardcaster. "How long did it take MZ to put it together?"

"Six days."

Less than half the time it took to deconstruct a full-sized human in a hardcaster and rebuild them again from scratch. Imre supposed that the second half of the equation wasn't necessary.

"No complications?"

"None that couldn't easily be fixed. Our host has forgotten how to be human in more than name. I reminded him."

Imre didn't want the details. As long as the virtual environment was safe and comfortable, he had no pressing complaints.

"Emlee?"

"She awaits you in the map room."

"Where's that?"

"First floor, second door on the right."

"Thanks." Imre stood. The movement flowed as naturally as any he would have made in his actual body. Muscles flexed with perfect verisimilitude between skin and bone. He could feel the roughness of the path beneath his bare feet. The air moved against his face. When he blinked, the view came and went.

Seamless and completely fake. They were inside the belly of the beast, as Emlee had described it—hardcast into a virtual space maintained by MZ and possessing no physical reality. The data and algorithms that encoded their beings were written onto space as MZ himself was. They owed their existence, temporarily, to the superior, long-lost technologies of the minds of Earth.

If the reality underlying the illusion troubled Emlee, he knew that she would keep her reservations to herself. There would be no privacy in MZ's world.

Are you sure we can trust him? Emlee had asked before stepping into her sarcophagus.

Trust and reliability are two completely different things, he had told her. *We can rely on him to keep us safe if he ever wants to me to rescind the ban on Earth.*

What about the rest?

No way to tell until he's shown us his little secret. At the worst, we'll have wasted a little time.

Fifty thousand years is hardly little, she told him, echoing his earlier thought.

To us, it won't be any time at all.

The interior of the town house was cool and quiet. He could smell the carpets, polished wood, and a faint hint of cigar smoke in the air. The paintings were of the right period, the work of masters who had died an eternity ago, preserved down the countless generations since. Exact copies of these paintings existed on worlds all across the galaxy, a more permanent fixture of humanity's culture than the people who gazed upon them. Including himself, he supposed.

Emlee was in a room lined with floor-to-ceiling bookcases stuffed to capacity with leather-bound tomes. She was leaning over an oak table, studying an unfurled sheet of vellum wider across than her outstretched arms, wearing a white smock identical to his and belted around the waist. Lines and marks in browning ink on the vellum occupied her attention so completely that she didn't look up until he was standing right next to her.

"Where are we headed?" he asked.

"Heading, you mean. We're already on our way." She anchored the corners of the map with loose books and pointed one pragmatically nailed finger at the map. "This is the Local Arm. There's Sol. That's us."

The dot marking MZ's location was moving with considerable speed across the page. There was no distance scale that he could see, so he could only estimate. According to the map, they were traveling at over a million times the speed of light. Of course, that was impossible, even for a being made entirely of encoded space-time, so the explanation had to lie in the way they were perceiving time.

"We're operating way below Absolute," he said. "At tempo Fort."

She nodded. "You should see the view. It's unforgettable."

Imre looked around. "How do I do that?"

"Go back out into the hallway. There's a picture leaning against the far wall with a curtain over it. That's the view."

"What's it doing there?"

"I could only take so much."

He followed her directions, out of the map room and into the wide corridor framing the stairwell. One of the thick drapes had been pulled down and arranged unceremoniously over a broad, gilt-framed painting. He tugged the drapes aside and stared.

A star was coming right for him, out of the frame: blue and fat, with enormous promontories reaching out like the tentacles of an octopus. He could almost feel the high-energy heat blazing from it and raised a hand to steady himself, even though no sensation of motion came through the floor beneath him.

Imre expected his point of view to change course and swoop by the celestial behemoth. It didn't. MZ flew them right into the sun, through bubbling plasma and roiling gas deep into the fiery heart, then out the far side unscathed. By the time stars appeared again, after barely a second, Imre's face had broken out in a thick, cold sweat.

MZ flew on into interstellar space, ignoring the system's baked and sterile worlds. It took less than a minute to approach the next sun, a G-type star on the Main Sequence. It slid by like a droplet of water down a windscreen, glowing welcomingly. Imre saw more planets and wondered if they were inhabited, wondered if the system had a name, wondered once again where, exactly, they were heading.

Emlee was waiting for him when he returned to the map room. "By the look on you face," she said, "you saw MZ's trick with the blue giants."

"That's deliberate? I assumed he just couldn't be bothered changing course."

"Something to do with refueling, he tells me. I don't have the science to understand it. When we get somewhere interesting, I'll bring the picture frame back in."

"So he is talking," Imre said, rejoining her at the table and trying to decipher the deliberately antiquated, two-dimensional chart in front of her.

"If you're persistent, he'll say something. Otherwise, he'd rather concentrate on getting us from A to B. It's not a matter of switching on an engine or two and settling in for the ride, I gather. He's part of the package. He's the ship, even though he calls it by a separate name: the *Wickthing*."

"Another old word," Imre said, finding its meaning buried deep in his built-in archives. A "creeping animal"; not particularly flattering. "The Ghost of Christmas Past."

She half smiled. "At least he doesn't manifest as a transparent sheet with chains."

"How does he manifest in here?"

"He doesn't. This is him. There's no homunculus inside his head to make life easier for us."

Imre glanced down at the map. The dot—MZ, or the *Wickthing*, or whatever he should call it—had reached the inner boundary of the Local Arm and was moving into relatively clear space.

"We're going in," he said. "To the core."

"I certainly hope not." Turning the map around changed the angle. Instead of seeing the galaxy from above, with the vortex of its arms laid out neatly and symmetrically, he now saw it as a cross section. The arms were fat ovals full of stars radiating in step from the much larger central bulge. There were three ovals between the Local Arm, where Sol lay, and the fringes of the galaxy's heart. At the rate they were moving, relatively speaking, they would reach the latter in a matter of hours. Like Emlee, he hoped their journey wouldn't go much farther than that; the core had been a dangerous place even during the glory days of the Continuum. Without the benefit of the Forts' navigational aids and governance, he doubted it would be any safer now.

"No clues as to what's waiting for us at the end of this little jaunt?"

"He hasn't said anything to me, if that's what you mean. Why would he? He's too much of a drama queen to spill anything until we arrive."

She was watching him while he studied the map. He could feel the pressure of her gaze on the left side of his face and resisted the urge to look up at her.

"I think we're doing the right thing," he said. "If that's what you're wondering."

"I already know you think that," she said. "I'm wondering why."

He opened his mouth to tell her—to reveal that his former self might still be out there, alive and active behind the scenes, and that was why he needed to follow any trail he could that might lead to Domgard—but he shut it again, having said nothing. The truth about the loop shunt in his sanctuary was only part of a much larger picture. He would have to explain about the Mad Times, when he had surrendered to the Forts in order to join their secret cause. He would have to tell her that he didn't know what that cause was, that his memory was frustratingly incomplete on that point, containing only isolated pieces of those final years. He would have to describe the secret meetings he had had with their ancient enemy, and one particular conversation when a Fort called Factotem, now long dead, had told him, *We are thinking in the long term, Imre Bergamasc. You must remember that. The juncture we have reached today will seal the destiny of all humanity, not just the Forts. You are invited to join us in that great venture. Are you interested?*

Imre must have been, or else why would he have betrayed his principles and his friends so completely?

"Maybe Domgard is the real ghost here," she said, taking his silence correctly, as an unwillingness to talk, but for the wrong reasons. "You're clinging to it like understanding it will solve all your problems. But what if it can't? What if it's dead and gone and should have been forgotten long ago? Maybe you're tying yourself to something that will ultimately bring you down. Maybe that's the real problem."

"We're soldiers at heart, Emlee. We're trained to see the things that will bring us down. It's the things we don't see that are the problem."

"Like Ra MacPhedron. Like some pissy little star system with a grievance."

"We've seen them. We're still here."

"Well, we're here, actually," she said, pointing at the creeping dot on the map. Her finger slid back to where Sol lay. "Who knows what's going on back there?"

"I can't do everything, Emlee," he said with the beginnings of annoyance showing in his voice. "I couldn't send anyone else to do this. It has to be me. But I can't wait either, while we sort out the mess on Earth. What if we never sorted it out and the answer to our problems stayed just out of our grasp? The things we don't see, remember. We need to see it all. It's the only way."

"And if there's nothing there?"

"Then you tell me 'I told you so,' and we go home to face the music."

"Promise?"

"I've no reason to lie to you about that," he said, "and every reason to suspect you'd see through me if I tried."

She brushed a strand of hair out of her eyes. "I don't know you that well."

You don't trust me, he thought. "You know me better than you think."

"I guess I'll know more when we find out what Domgard is all about."

The dot crept onward across the gulf between galactic arms, and Imre didn't reply.

When it became clear that MZ wasn't taking them on a fatal plunge into the very heart of the galaxy, Imre brought the magic picture frame back into the map room and hung it up where it had been, on the one patch of clear wall between the expansive bookcases. While doing so, he happened to glance at one of the books more closely and noticed that the text on its spine identified it not as a classic work of literature but as something much more relevant to their present situation.

When the painting was fixed in place—showing a loose-linked triple system growing steadily closer—Imre slipped the book down and held it flat before him. It was a substantial volume bound in red cloth with titles printed in gold leaf. Where a publishing imprint would have rested were only the letters *MZ*. The title read *Dubito 675,101*. He recognized the word from the Latin translation of René Descartes' statement, "I doubt, therefore I think, therefore I am." The numbers he assumed defined a date—a year in the life of a Fort.

He tried to open the book. The cover wouldn't budge.

"There are limits, obviously," Emlee said from the other side of the room. "I tried opening one earlier."

Imre slid the volume back into its slot and unsuccessfully suppressed his curiosity. "Do you think we'd be able to read the writing?"

"I think if we could, it'd drive us mad." She didn't seem to be joking. "Or turn us into one of them."

He came back to the table. The room contained just the two of them. Kells's interest in their situation extended no further than the verisimilitude of their environment. Having ascertained that they were in perfect physical health, he had moved on to testing the boundaries of the garden outside and was occasionally visible through the map-room window, poking into indistinct corners and running his hands across leafy textures. MZ had said nothing during their journey so far. Imre had given up trying to attract his attention. The Fort had what he wanted; until they arrived, Imre assumed he would have nothing to add.

Earth was an invisible speck far from their present location. Raising the map off the table activated a zoom function, enabling him to examine their vicinity at various scales. By focusing on the speck representing them, Imre and Emlee had discovered that the *Wickthing* was more than just a dimensionless dot. When viewed up close, it looked more like a flower, an unfolding mathematical function plotted on vertical axes almost ten kilometers long. He imagined it hovering over

Hansfaall Base on the moon or filling the cavernous space of the Throne Room, and shuddered. Humanity had built larger structures but never out of such a strange material, one able to pass through matter as though it were smoke, one even less substantial than neutrinos. He wondered what the Apparatus would look like if it appeared on such a map. He decided he didn't want to know.

Stars rushed by them. The constellations changed visibly, becoming denser and more complex the closer the *Wickthing* and its virtual contents came to the edge of the core. They were headed for the Solward side of the Milky Way's central bar, the line of tightly packed gas and stars that crossed the central bulge from one side to the other. Thousands of suns packed into volumes no larger than a few dozen cubic light-years, with planets and brown dwarfs wandering between them, following unpredictable orbits. Humans had settled there hundreds of thousands of years ago, but their connection to the Continuum had always been tenuous. Life in a high-energy, high-risk environment encouraged overclocking, and many of these offshoot civilizations had burned out in the time it took signals to travel to and from the outer regions. Continuum astronomers had observed furious changes from a distance, some comprehensible, most utterly mysterious. Explorers had frequently claimed to have discovered vast and unlikely treasures deep in the tangle of stars, from alien ruins to technological impossibilities abandoned by humanity's advanced offshoots; not one of them had ever been verified.

Imre himself had been to the region only once before, while on a diplomatic mission for the Forts to a gestalt calling itself the Paradoxolog. He had found the core intellectually challenging but culturally barren, so hostile to civilization that there was little of interest to him. He preferred people to ruins, and people he could communicate with to beings so evolved that they might as well have been a completely different species.

His mission had been a failure; the Paradoxolog had destroyed itself long before his arrival, apparently by writing itself out of reality in an attempt to create a time machine. Its backstory had been difficult to put together from the testimony of the survivors, but he had done what he could for his masters in the outer regions of the galaxy. They had seemed happy enough with his report.

The *Wickthing* swept around the core like a shuttle orbiting the Earth. Stars rushed at them in the picture's forward view, bright and all too numerous, bound by gravity and tides in an endlessly complex dance. A red speck, the only one out of thousands of black specks in their vicinity, hove into view on the map. The *Wickthing* began to shed some of its headlong velocity, if that term could apply to a body without any measurable mass. Something about the area they were heading into rang a faint bell, although Imre couldn't immediately work out why.

"I think we have a destination," he said aloud. His stomach felt lighter in his chest cavity, as though it was trying to come out his mouth. Was that bloodred dot Domgard, at last?

"Are you okay?" She was watching him, not the map.

He started to tell her that of course he was, but the feeling intensified, leaving him giddy. "I'll be fine," he said, turning away. "Just give me a moment."

He walked out into the hallway and squatted with his back against the wall.

Domgard.

You are invited to join us in that great venture.

The greatest experiment ever undertaken.

Stay away.

All he had were hints and inferences. His former self had allied himself more closely than ever with the Forts after the Mad Times. They had offered him a role in an experiment designed to make humanity even greater than it already was. Then the Slow Wave had happened, and it seemed to have taken everyone—Himself included—by surprise. His former self had trawled the galaxy looking for clues, contacting Old-Timers like the infamous Line-trawler Bianca Biancotti and other versions of Himself. Then he had disappeared, except to issue dire warnings to the only remaining part of him not involved in the conspiracy, whatever it was.

You'll know how to contact us when you work out what you want. I can't promise we'll take you in, but that is an option.

Imre had turned his back on that possibility, becoming a Prime and doing everything in his power to solve the problem his way.

But here he was, tracing his former self's footsteps with the galaxy's last-known Fort, slipping like a ghost in search of a cenotaph with his name on it . . .

He breathed evenly and deeply, surprised to find that he cared what Emlee must be thinking of him at that moment. Did it matter if she thought him weak? He knew he was flawed, and she knew it as well as he did.

Perhaps she was reading even more than he realized. She was a signals specialist, used to decoding information that had been deeply buried. What was she seeing that even he wasn't aware of? What would this moment of frailty reveal to her?

Whatever she had learned, she was bound to discover a whole lot more in the coming days—and that worried him more than he had previously admitted to himself.

The dizziness passed. He stood up and smoothed down his smock. Worried or not, the time had come to confront his past—or the past of a man he had once been, at least.

A moon-sized world hung in the magic picture frame when he entered the room, its face as dark and scarred as a beaten man's. A ring of moonlets orbited it, dense and narrow, like a pencil line drawn about its equator. Emlee stared at the image, not at him, and he silently thanked her for not drawing attention to his departure. He joined her at the table and glanced down at the map. The dot was as stationary as though it had been dabbed there with thick, red ink.

Through the window, the sky was still incongruously blue. He crossed the room and pulled the embroidered curtains closed. The light dimmed, wrapping them in dense shadows.

"We're not in orbit," she said. "We're just hanging here, a couple of klicks up. I keep thinking that we should fall, but of course we're invisible to gravity—or at least not visible in the usual way. Gravity warps space-time. MZ is made out of lots of little warps, so it would make sense that one influences the other. How, though, is beyond me."

Imre was no better off. He pictured MZ as the hole left behind in a rubber mold when the original was removed. An empty space, albeit one defined in a very real way. That MZ was viewing the world "outside" by direct means rather than through a scanner suggested that he interacted with the universe via a different means from the one used by the Apparatus; perhaps via gauge bosons instead, he thought. Being able to detect photons directly by some subtle science of light would make it easier when it came to absorbing information, but it could make communication the other way more difficult. Photons packed a lot less punch than electrons.

He turned his attention back to the view. Behind the world was a mess of stars. The backdrop was much brighter than the night skies of Earth. No particular star stood out as the small world's primary. Perhaps it didn't have one at all and wandered the interstellar lanes at the whim of distant gravitational nudges. It might follow a path around more than one star, taking thousands, maybe millions, of years to complete a single circuit. It might not be moving at all. The only way to tell would be to take a long, careful measurement.

He shook his head. What did he care about the world's movements? That wasn't what he had come so far to find out.

The world turned beneath them. Its muddy features showed evidence of thick hydrocarbon deposition, perhaps from when a former atmosphere had frozen over, forming a thick scum of ice. Several sharp-ridged mountain chains poked through. They looked cold too. The core might once have been molten, but it was now frozen right through. Several long cracks scarred the world's equator, their bottoms hidden in blackness.

A sprawling grey shape came into view from around the planet's far side, its leading edge a mass of tangled straight lines that gradually gave way to a solid, clearly artificial structure. Filling a basin several hundred kilometers across, it looked like a city built by people who had never heard of either right angles or curves. Every line was rigid and unbending, every angle oblique. The planes defining the heart of the structure were tilted without reference to either vertical or horizontal. It hurt Imre's sensibilities to look at it.

"I had nothing to do with that thing," he said, fighting the rising dread that filled him.

"You built it," said MZ, speaking to Imre for the first time since they had left the Earth.

"Impossible."

"There's no doubt."

"There has to be. I know how my mind works. It would no more allow such a thing to exist than it would—"

"—become a Fort?" MZ paused significantly. Emlee's expression didn't change; perhaps she assumed the comment nothing more than a provocative hypothetical. "We are here now. This is Domgard. There is no point dissembling any longer, or quibbling over details."

Imre wanted to ask how MZ knew, but didn't. Every Fort in the galaxy might have known. "This isn't a detail," he said. "I saw the habitat my former self built at the Cat's Arse; it was perfect, exactly to my tastes. I couldn't have changed that much since then. This thing, whatever it is, is ugly three times over, and it wouldn't have been if I had designed it."

"Then it's changed since you designed it," Emlee said. "What's the problem? If this was built before the Slow Wave, it's been out here a long time. You can both be right."

"True." Imre forced himself to breathe more slowly. The creeping anxiety settling over him came from confronting new details of his former life, as it always did. He never knew exactly what he would find, or what it might tell him about Himself. Sometimes, he thought, it might be easier never to know. "Can you take us closer?"

"That is my intention," MZ said in a stiff voice.

Their point of view shifted as the *Wickthing* adjusted its location. Imre still felt no acceleration, but he wondered idly if the ectoplasmic *Wickthing* did. Emlee's image of spikes in space-time was provocative. He imagined a rubber sheet with a stick poking up into it from below. The deformation of the rubber could appear to move as the stick slid backward and forward, even though the actual rubber remained unchanged. Without stretching his brain too far, he could imagine MZ moving around as a series of peaks in the rubber of space-time, but he had no idea what physical principles could supply the stick.

The structure grew larger in the picture frame. Light

gleamed from it in sickly rainbows. He knew that look: a frozen atmosphere, vented and left to settle. The world was old and cold and hadn't been disturbed for a long time. He dismissed his earlier thought that it might come anywhere near neighboring stars. This was an interstellar loner, drifting a long way from anyone, forever.

"Is this structure called Domgard," Emlee asked, "or the world?"

Again he was glad for her comment. She seemed to be the only one of the two of them actively thinking of the right thing to say.

"The world is called Spargamos," MZ answered, "although its name was soon forgotten."

"By whom?"

"By the people who worked here."

"Were you one of them?"

"No. Everything I know about this place, I deduced long afterward."

"How?"

"By following your own methods: interrogating partials; studying the Line; putting the pieces of the puzzle back together, one at a time. You might have eventually reached the same conclusions as I, were you not handicapped in a way that I am not."

"How's that?"

"You are not a Fort."

Emlee looked like she was going to react huffily to that statement. Imre cut her off. No use arguing about the obvious.

"Take us to where that spur is sticking up on the left. I want to see what's under it."

The view shifted with the same ease that Imre might adjust a video monitor. The spar was long and fluted, its white exterior surface waxy underneath the frozen air, like polished ivory. The scale had defeated for him a moment, but he could see as they drew nearer that it was approximately fifteen meters across and more than a hundred long. Human-sized decks were visible through the narrow end, which was open to the vacuum. Beneath that end lay the specks that he had noticed from a distance.

They were corpses.

"Now I know why it doesn't look like something I designed," he said grimly. "It's broken."

The evidence lay everywhere they looked: shattered structures, fallen bodies, and no attempt to tidy up any of the mess. A single sheer line ran right through the entire structure, as though it had been cracked in two by a mighty blow. Dusted by starlight and ice, the dead stared grimly into the void, unmourned.

He shook his head. That was a melodramatic thought. Of course they were mourned.

"They're frags," he said. "We're seeing the remains of a dead Fort."

"Or more than one," said Emlee, her jaw tight. "What killed them?"

"The Slow Wave," said MZ.

"But you said this place was the source of the Slow Wave."

"No. I told you that you would see the place the Slow Wave started."

Something came to Imre then that should have occurred to him earlier. "This area," he said. "I knew I recognized it. Things have moved a bit in all the years since, given the rotation of the core, but it hasn't changed that much. This is Volume Zero."

Emlee looked at him with understanding in her eyes. Volume Zero: a name for something that had once seemed absolutely critical in the post-Fort galaxy but which had faded in significance for lack of further information. The Slow Wave had traveled through the galaxy's arms and clusters at the speed of light, breaking every active Q loop link in its path. By tracing the exact moments at which the Forts had died, one after the other, like dominos flicked by an invisible finger, a pattern emerged. The Slow Wave hadn't moved across the galaxy from one side to the other. It had spread outward in a sphere, like the burst of high-energy photons from a supernova, and when the scientists autopsying the catastrophe had plotted the expansion of that sphere, they had pinpointed one particular location close to the core, one that seemed no different from any of the places nearby except that something inside it had changed the course of human history.

"People searched," Emlee said. "They didn't find anything."

"They found many things," MZ disagreed, "this place among them. But what was it to them? They didn't know what they were seeing. They were looking for a weapon capable of destroying the Forts. This was just another planet on which a number of Forts died."

Imre nodded. He could see how the evidence might be misinterpreted and didn't feel bad for missing the connection himself. Systems had drifted a long way since the death of the Forts. "The Slow Wave doesn't leave wreckage like this behind."

"Exactly. Which makes this site unique."

"If everything you're telling us is true," Emlee added.

MZ sounded affronted. "I have no reason to lie."

"You might have a dozen reasons. You keep telling us that you're a Fort. The minute we think we understand you, that's when we can be sure we really don't."

"The facts will speak for themselves," Imre said. "That's one thing we can be sure of."

"As you say." MZ's huffiness had multiplied. In Imre's experience, Forts hated being direct. They liked it even less when the opportunity to be indirect was taken from them. "I will let you come to your own conclusions, no matter how long it takes."

Imre didn't rise to the bait. "What tempo are we operating on here, by the way?"

"Absolute."

"Then we're not eating up centuries by looking around. I can live with taking it slow."

Their point of view swung into the shadow under the spar. Light-enhancement algorithms turned the blankness in the magic picture frame to a black-and-white depiction of the collapsed structure.

"Spare us a close-up of the bodies," Imre said with forced nonchalance, as a couple drew closer on the left. He didn't want to see the faces. He didn't want Emlee to see them either. "Take us through that hole there. Let's scope out the inside."

"Do we need a hole?" Emlee asked. "We could probably go through the walls, if we wanted."

Imre looked at her, surprised, then nodded. It was easy to forget MZ's arcane nature. "Let's go the long way, if only to get a better feel for the structure."

MZ complied without speaking, taking their POV through a crack created by the collapsing of the spar. The rent was several meters long but less than a meter wide and thickly crusted with ice crystals. They would find many such places, he assumed. If the spar had been an elevated beam that had fallen during a general structural collapse, the spaces below would have been compromised many times over. Even so, the inhabitants of Spargamos and the Domgard facility could have survived had they been more than disconnected frags. The bodies behind him hadn't been blown out of the vent; they appeared to have crawled out and died there. Without a unifying intelligence, they had been unable to save themselves.

The rent closed in around them, then opened up upon meeting a large internal chamber. More bodies. He and Emlee said nothing as the *Wickthing* navigated the tortured spaces within the ruins. The chamber looked as though it had been designed by an insane architect; that, though, was purely circumstantial. The walls were so severely deformed it was hard to tell what shape the chamber had originally been. There were no straight lines, no simple corners, no edges. Imre felt like an ant exploring the inside of a crushed aluminum can.

Deeper they went, down near-flattened corridors and past slabs of solid material that might once have been structural pylons but could equally have been machines melted by a powerful heat. The light was poor; MZ wasn't able to conjure even a weak beam to illuminate the ruins. For the first time, Imre began to see that the Fort's nature might be as much a curse as a blessing. He was trapped between the real world and the empty vacuum, barely able to interact. Still, Imre couldn't bring himself to feel sympathy. MZ's former colleagues had managed to correct those teething problems with the Apparatus. MZ should have waited longer and stolen a more advanced prototype.

They followed endless, twisted cables connecting disparate

sections of the compound. Some appeared to head outside but had been severed long before reaching the outer walls. Clearly, something had entered the compound and performed selective sabotage as well as general destruction. Imre was tempted to assume that it had all happened at the same time—the Slow Wave, the selective sabotage, the desolation of the structure—but there was no evidence to prove that. The physical damage could have come much later, after the Forts were dead. There could even have been multiple perpetrators. He couldn't tell.

They saw no attempts to repair the damage. No graffiti, no warnings to anyone who might come to investigate the ruins, no slogans. The damage was unlikely to have been caused, then, in the course of ordinary combat, by ordinary soldiers. In any but the most disciplined troop, there was always one idiot who wanted to carve his initials by laser into the outside of a defeated bunker. He had even caught Render doing it, once, although he suspected that might have been more to test Imre's reaction than out of any private impulse. Whoever had gone through Domgard, in however many waves, they had left no hint of their personalities or motives behind.

They passed thousands of bodies, dried and frozen by the vacuum in attitudes of despair and confusion. Curved limbs clawed at their neighbors for succor, for connection that could never come. In one room, they found more than a hundred frags in a pile, not dumped that way by their killers but caught trying to physically accomplish what was mentally denied them. Their feeble, futile attempts were painfully preserved.

"Does that look right to you?" Emlee asked.

"Nothing about this place looks right," Imre said.

"I mean, the way the pile is organized. The sides are too steep."

He looked at the grisly mound from that new perspective and saw what she meant. "The gravity is lower than one gee here. But that's not a problem: the world isn't nearly as big as the Earth in size."

"What's the radius, MZ?"

"Almost two thousand five hundred kilometers," came the immediate reply.

About the same size as Mercury. "Which makes local gravity, what, forty percent Earth's?"

"I am able to take only indirect measurements, such as the one you are attempting." The Fort sounded faintly smug. "There is a discrepancy of approximately fifty percent."

"More or less than expected?"

"Less."

Emlee glanced at Imre. "Can a planet be that porous?"

"Not in my experience," he said. "But it could be hollow."

They stared at each other for a moment. Standing in the map room, with natural light filtering through the cracks in the curtains, they seemed a thousand light-years away from the moribund spaces of Spargamos. There was, however, no denying the thrill of discovery he felt at that moment. A world the Forts had gutted and turned into a secret lab? This he had to see.

"Take us down, MZ," he said. "Forget what I said about getting a feel for the structure. We could dither about up here for days and not find anything."

Emlee agreed. "It's a mausoleum. Leave it for the archaeologists."

The *Wickthing* was already moving. Imre wondered if MZ had always known about the gravitational discrepancy. Probably, he decided. The Fort was letting them discover the truth the hard way, as he had promised.

And they were getting there, slowly but surely. As their point of view slid into the solid floor and kept going, passing through solid substances as easily as though they were vacuum, Imre kept his attention locked on the magic picture frame. He would miss no details, even if they were incomprehensible. The buckled honeycomb structure of the floor soon gave way to densely packed layers of hybrid materials, then more of the twisted, melted slabs. They passed through another large mound of dead frags. A withered face stared out at them with empty eyes and lips pulled back. Its cheeks were sunken and wrinkled like a prune, barely recognizable as human. Then and only then did Imre glance away. He needn't have worried about Emlee recognizing any of the bodies after all.

When he glanced back, the *Wickthing* was pursuing a path that took it backward and forward across a thick clump of hollow-looking cables. He couldn't tell what their function had been. Some arcane communications linkup? Or something to do with the massive power loads the Forts had undoubtedly needed for their experiments? MZ was as unforthcoming on that issue as he had been on the gravity. Imre was happy, for the moment, to keep it that way.

Two more honeycomb layers followed, then the magic picture turned a deep, suggestive grey. The view before them was empty, but that wasn't the same thing as featureless.

"A wall," Imre said. "We're through."

"Through into what?" Emlee asked.

He shared her mystification. There was no way to tell the scale of the empty space around them. MZ rotated the view. It didn't change. Imre couldn't even tell that they were moving at all.

A new frustration crept over him. Flying through walls made their descent much easier than it would otherwise have been, even trivial, but now that they had got where they wanted to be, they couldn't take soundings or samples; they couldn't test the limits of the chamber with radar; they couldn't even turn on a light.

A small dot drifted by on the screen.

"What's that?" Imre asked, pointing. "Take us closer."

MZ obeyed. The dot resolved into a rectangular box affixed to the wall of the chamber, which stretched out in all directions with a barely discernible curvature. The box was the only visible break in the otherwise featureless terrain. There was no atmospheric ice and no sign of damage.

The box was coffin-sized and obviously designed to open from the larger end. Imre recognized it immediately.

"That's a hardcaster," he said.

Emlee just stared.

"It is functional," said MZ.

This time Imre couldn't help it. He looked up. "What are you saying?"

"I have interfaced with its electronics," said the Fort. "The sarcophagus and its support mechanisms are late additions to the ruins and therefore undamaged. It was installed after the Slow Wave, when I believe the contents of this chamber were removed. The hardcaster has not been used since."

"But someone thought they might need it," Emlee said. "Otherwise, why leave one here?"

"Can you trace the last receipt?" Imre asked MZ.

"No."

"Has it retained a copy of the last transmission?"

"No."

They stared at it for ten full seconds. "You're sure it's working properly?" Imre asked.

"Yes."

"Then I'm going to put your word to the test."

Emlee turned to look at him. "No," she said. "If anyone does this, it should be me."

"You're staying here. I need you here to make any tough decisions that might come our way."

"What tough decisions? There's nothing here. This place has been empty for half a million years."

"It's not empty. There's us, there's MZ, and there's the hardcaster. I want to take a closer look to see if there's anything else we might've missed."

"So we go together."

"I'm not leaving Chyro in charge. He'd be useless if something did go wrong." He stared her down. "We need to see this place firsthand. I'm not anticipating any surprises, but I want you at my back just in case."

"All right," she said, although she clearly remained unhappy about it. "But do this for me: order a full suite of armor from the hardcaster. Make sure it arrives first. Weapons, torches, comms—the works. Then and only then do you follow. Okay?"

He was happy to agree to that. "I'll even let you pick the gear if that makes you feel any better." Crack a joke to lighten the mood, he told himself. Or at least give her a straight line. "As long as it's not hot pink, you have free rein."

She took the opportunity to end the argument. "What about tassels? Shame you've lost your figure."

He didn't know what she was talking about—his figure was the same as it had always been—until he remembered the female body the Jinc had given him when they had discovered his incomplete pattern drifting on the edge of the galaxy.

"I like my figure just the way it is," he said. "So no tinkering."

"I can think of a thousand things I'd rather be doing."

The armor came through in two days, structurally sound and in a tasteful shade of black. The hardcaster had contained no internal patterns at all, so Emlee had had to dig out something suitable from MZ's mental store, which the Fort reluctantly opened for their perusal. The armor was perfectly functional but incredibly outdated; Imre remembered wearing a similar model in his earliest campaigns with the Corps. It came with a pair of twin-aperture Bostonian sidearms in recessed holsters and an array of wide-frequency spotlights. Before putting the pattern through the hardcaster, they had programmed it to perform a full hardware test, which it completed on activation. All systems were operational.

MZ sent a command to the suit to turn its spotlights on and cast the beams across the chamber wall. The view it sent back was as hauntingly strange as the empty screen. Visible from a distance were angular patterns drawn across the chamber's interior like the wiring on a circuit diagram. They served no purpose that Imre could discern. He couldn't even decide if they were painted on or part of the wall's composition. Only a material analysis could tell the difference.

Finding no other details within range of the spotlights, the suit turned its beams out into the center of the chamber. The inky blackness absorbed the light as though they were standing at the bottom of an ocean trench. A rough guesstimate from the curvature of the walls suggested that the chamber was more than a thousand kilometers across. That was borne out by a series of lidar pings the suit sent into the blackness. Thermal noise was low. The space had been abandoned for a very long time indeed.

"It's empty," said Emlee, stating the thought foremost on Imre's mind. "Is this what we came all this way to see?"

"There's empty," he said, "then there's empty. Nothing is the absence of something, and there was certainly something here, once; or there was supposed to be. Why build a place like this if you never intended to fill it?"

MZ answered neither question, perhaps out of a perverse determination to let them work it out. That didn't bother Imre; he was prepared to do just that.

Neither Imre nor Emlee stated the obvious, that MZ could be altering the data trickling in through the magic picture in order to allay their misgivings. There was nothing they could do to test the data they had received until Imre was on the outside.

"Time to stop lurking in the shadows," he said. "Keep an eye on things while I'm in transit," he told Emlee.

"I'll do my best to stay awake," she said.

"How do we do this, MZ?" he asked the Fort.

"In a moment, I will remove your pattern from the *Wickthing* and begin transferring it to the hardcaster. You may experience a slight discontinuity. I advise you, Emlee, to look away."

She nodded and turned her attention to the magic picture. Imre kept his eyes on her, studying her features as he waited for his extraction from the virtual environment. She never changed: her features, hair, and eye color were unaltered from the years after Hyperabad, when she had begun slowly coming out of the self-protective shell she had inhabited since the Slow Wave. He supposed that wasn't unusual; only Render seemed to have aged in subtle, physical ways, by the accruing of new scars and an ever-increasing brittleness in his eyes. Imre himself looked exactly the same as he had for many thousands of years. Apart from that one glitch brought about by the Jinc, he might as well have been etched in stone.

One second ticked slowly by, then another. She didn't so much as glance at him once, and he wondered what she might see if she did. His flesh melting away to expose the bones beneath? A spreading tide of static? Or perhaps he would just be standing there one instant, then gone the next, as though a camera shutter had flicked open and closed, leaving the world changed afterward. Perhaps—

He was lying on his back in utter darkness. He reached out and encountered hard surfaces in all directions, just centimeters from his hands, feet, and face. A box not much larger than he was. He could tell from a slight tightness to his movements that there was no air in the box and that he was wearing a skin suit. A flash of concern lit up the darkness like a firework. He might be able to survive in a vacuum indefinitely, but he didn't want to stay inside the box any longer than he absolutely needed to.

A box. The hardcaster. He was inside the sarcophagus, which, he presumed, MZ had programmed to open once the process was complete. The *Wickthing* illusion seemed a hundred years ago now. He could just imagine Emlee and Chyro Kells poring over the data to ensure he had arrived complete, perhaps viewing his body as data in an open book, flipping through pages to see layer after layer in discrete stages.

It occurred to him that they could probably hear him if he spoke, since MZ had been tapped into the hardcaster's systems for days.

"Let the boys out," he said, quoting something Render had once liked to say at the beginning of campaigns.

"And let the fun begin." Emlee immediately responded, a note of relief in her voice. "I was beginning to wonder if you'd ever say anything. It's not like you to be quiet so long."

"I'm not in a talkative mood." He rapped his knuckles against the inside of the sarcophagus and heard a faint tap-tap through the skin suit. "Are you going to let this particular boy out anytime soon?"

"Be careful out there. If you run into trouble, it's going to take me days to come get you."

"Understood." The panel behind him slid inaudibly open. He rolled over and tightly gripped the sides of the box so he wouldn't fall out. Below the open hatch was nothing but a sheer drop to the center of the planet.

A large figure awaited him with arms outstretched on the outside of the sarcophagus, hovering on low-energy jets. He froze, then relaxed. Just the suit, positioned so he could slip quickly inside it. He did so with a swift, practiced movement, dropping feetfirst into its tight embrace. It had been a long time since he had fought alone in a campaign, but he remembered the moves. He would never forget. They were hardwired into his nervous system.

As he booted up the interfaces, he took in his immediate surroundings. Nothing but the wall, the patterns painted on it invisible from such a close range, and the hardcaster. He played the spotlights at random into the void and saw nothing more, but an itch burned in his back, telling him that he was being watched. He narrowed the spotlight beams to their tightest dispersal patterns and caught a glimpse of something right on the edge of sight, something far away and hard to make out. The itch grew stronger.

"Peekaboo," said Emlee. He jumped.

"What the hell are you playing at?"

"Just testing MZ out. We're in front of you, staring you right between the eyes."

That thought unnerved him more than he wanted to admit. "I had no idea."

"Exactly. Think of the surveillance you could do this way—sliding through walls, spying on anything, anywhere, completely undetectable. I wonder if the Apparatus could rig us something like this when we get back home."

"You could ask it. I bet there are blocks in place to stop us getting our hands on the tech."

"Why?"

"Otherwise, everyone would be doing it."

"And the problem with that is . . . ?"

He had no good answer to that question. Instead of trying to find one, he checked the Bostonian sidearms to make sure they were fully charged. Everything was working smoothly. The pistols were miniature cannon, powerful enough to punch through a hull but not graceful. He hoped he wouldn't need to use them.

He nudged the suit's propulsion system out of its steady

hover, taking himself directly through Emlee's location, then cut it off so the light gravity pulled him downward. "I don't think this place is empty," he said. "There's something out there, in the center. I'm going to check it out."

Emlee didn't remind him to be careful. She knew he would be. The suit used a feathered propulsion system with minimal wash. It would be difficult for someone monitoring the initial thrust to tell which direction he was following, not without using radar, which he was sure to detect. He was a black body falling through the dark, in search of another black body just like him.

But he had definitely glimpsed something, and he held its rough position in his mind as long as he could: near or at the center of the spherical chamber. It didn't look like anything he had ever seen before, and he had seen plenty of unusual stuff while working for the Forts, but it was easy to be fooled by such poor data. In more familiar surroundings, he might have interpreted it as something completely ordinary.

He kept the spotlights off until he had dropped half the distance to the exact center of the chamber. Then, in quick succession, he switched them back on and fired up the propulsion system. To any observers, he would appear like a sudden nova of light and energy, bursting out of the darkness. And then he would be gone, heading off on another trajectory.

He fell in a parabolic arc for thirty more seconds, waiting for some kind of response. None came. An image glowed on his retina, burned there by the sudden flash of spotlights, an image of a pixilated circle, as though drawn on a primitive computer monitor, but one slightly lopsided to the left, where a bite had been taken out of it. Calling up the suit's data, he looked more closely at the frozen snapshots it had taken. Strangely, that impression remained.

The thing at the heart of the chamber looked at first glance like a sphere made out of smaller, black cubes. Some of the cubes were either missing or transparent. The structure as a whole was highly nonreflective and possessed no appreciable mass, despite its size. From side to side it measured approximately one hundred meters. There was no apparent logic to the placement of the gaps. He glimpsed no weapons emplacements, no unusual reflections, no anomalous shadows. Each block was approximately one meter wide and could have been made from nothing more exotic than matt plastic. It looked like a set of building blocks for a giant child. But where was the child?

He thought of the Forts that had once worked there and was reminded of something MZ had said. *The experiments were different, but the intent was the same.* The minds of Earth had been working on a god. What had the architect of Domgard been making—or growing—in the heart of this tiny world?

He had a fair degree of clearance before he reached the surface of the structure. Rather than head right in, he tried the flash-and-thrust maneuver one final time, just to be sure. There was still no response, and the data remained ambiguous.

"I can't make head or tail of it," Emlee said from her virtual vantage point. "And MZ isn't talking."

"We did tell him we want to work it out for ourselves." Imre thought for a moment. "MZ said the contents of the chamber had been removed. How he knew that, I don't know: maybe someone told him and he took their word for it, or maybe he came down here and looked around for himself. Either way, he was wrong. Clearly, the chamber's not empty. He couldn't see well enough to tell otherwise. On this point at least, he was as much in the dark as we are."

"And that makes you happy—apart from the pun?"

Imre didn't answer. Thinking through that detail didn't make him happy in any sense of the word, but he did feel a measure of satisfaction in unpicking some of the processes behind MZ and his investigation of Domgard. The Fort wasn't omnipotent. He was limited both in terms of the knowledge he had and the knowledge he could glean from the universe around him. Understanding limitations was important for both enemies and allies—and Imre still wasn't entirely sure into which category MZ fell.

He waited for the Fort to either defend or explain himself. That he might need to would also be a noteworthy development.

"I have been here," said the Fort, grudgingly. "This room once contained sufficient neutron-degenerate material to maintain the illusion that the world had not been gutted. Clearly, it has gone. I presumed the rest had been taken too."

"And what was the rest?"

MZ took a long time to answer. Eventually, he said, "The original installation contained equipment designed to test the nature of dark matter."

Imre waited. MZ didn't offer anything more. "Is that it? Domgard was just a big dark matter detector?"

"I suspect it was much more than that," said the Fort, "and I believe others thought so too."

Imre thought it through. Dark matter remained a fringe study for physicists in the Returned Continuum if only because the stuff was so hard to pin down. Despite comprising a large percentage of the matter in the universe, it interacted with "ordinary" matter only through gravity. All the other myriad forces affecting the atoms in a human's body were irrelevant to dark matter, leading one theorist to describe to Imre how working in this field was like being deaf in the land of the blind. One could understand the principles by which people with hearing communicated using the spoken word, but everything else about it was guesswork. The reverse was also true: the blind could theorize all they liked about writing and drawing, but they couldn't directly experience it. Dark matter could have a whole raft of interesting properties, but instruments made of ordinary matter would never detect them.

Despite being so mysterious in some ways, in others dark matter was a familiar feature of the known universe. Haloes of the stuff formed around individual galaxies, changing the way spiral arms rotated; long tendrils stretched between clusters a hundred million light-years apart. Unseen, unnoticed, individual particles slipped through and around their visible counterparts like ghostly commuters on a busy street.

No use had been found for the stuff, and no threat existed from it either. Why anyone would destroy Domgard over an obscure physical experiment was beyond Imre. There had to be more to it than that.

"I'm going to take a closer look," he said, switching on his suit's spotlights once again. This time he left them on and kept the propulsion system burning. Nothing stirred in the giant chamber, from the interior surface they had left behind to the block-work shape at its heart. The beams themselves were invisible, since there was neither atmosphere nor suspended dust particles to scatter the light. Patches of light slid back and forth across the view ahead of him, picking out the details of his destination as he grew close. It occurred to him that, from the right angle, it looked less like a sphere than a giant human heart. From the wrong angle, it was almost a skull.

Imre picked one of the many recesses and hollows on the blocky surface and angled toward it. Ambient gravity lessened as he approached until he was practically in free fall. The cubes reflected only a very small percentage of the light he was radiating. Staring at them was like staring into a shadow. He took his reference from the angular silhouettes they made rather than the shapes themselves. Their lidar shadow was very light. Swooping toward the exterior of the agglomeration, he was careful to keep his distance, lest his eye be confused.

A quick sweep of the spotlights confirmed his guess that some of the recesses were holes leading into the heart of the structure. At least two of them were large enough for him to enter. He picked one at random and brought himself to a halt above it. A tunnel with angular sides curled away from him—"down" his instinct told him, even in the microgravity—so he could see barely a dozen meters. What lay at its end was invisible. The cubes soaked up the light so much that, even if it had been as straight as a plumb line, the terminus would still have been dark.

"We're going in ahead of you," said Emlee. "Keep that candle burning."

Imre acknowledged the sense of her suggestion. Always the bodyguard, even if she was barely part of the real world anymore. He floated in silence and let his eye move where it willed across the stepped surface before him. He hadn't built either of the artifacts they had found thus far, but this one was less of an affront to his sensibilities than the structure on the surface of the world. It seemed likely that this one wasn't damaged—but he had a gut feeling there was more to it than that. Was it unbearable hubris to believe that the damage inflicted above was directed as much at his sensibilities as at the experiment itself?

He didn't know. It was an unnerving thought.

"All clear," Emlee said, "inasmuch as I can tell. It's as dark as a tomb in here."

"Not my tomb," he said, remembering only as the words emerged from him that Domgard was just that for any version of Himself who had been here when the Slow Wave hit. Still, he didn't believe that all of Himself could have been caught out on Domgard. He was by nature a cautious person, rarely willing to put all his eggs in one basket. There would have been other pockets of Himself scattered all across the galaxy, just in case one quarter had suffered any kind of setback. Even relying solely on loop shunts would have been anathema to him; he would have had contingencies in place, backup plans that might have seemed intricate and unnecessary to the other Forts—but that wouldn't have worried him. He didn't care what Forts thought. He just cared about survival.

That was how Imre's former self had survived the Slow Wave. He knew it in his gut. And wherever the surviving part of him was now, he wasn't lurking in some dark corner of the galaxy, like MZ and the other partials Imre had met. His former self would be standing tall, somewhere, going about his business.

"Having second thoughts?" Emlee asked him.

He came out of his reverie and looked around automatically for the source of her voice. It unnerved him more than a little, not knowing where she was. Some kind of cue would have been good: a dimple in the air, or a tiny spark of light.

"I think I'm up to fourth or fifth by now."

"What are you afraid of finding?"

The truth, he thought. A roomful of my own dead frags. Nothing at all.

"There's nothing wrong with being afraid," he said, bringing the propulsion system to life. "The day you stop being afraid, you know you've run out of things worth doing."

The hole engulfed him. The glare of the suit's spots accompanied him, reflecting off the cubes as though they were phantom quartz crystals, hungry for light.

"Cheesy," she whispered. "You should leave the proverbs to someone else."

"Are you volunteering?"

"No thanks."

He spiraled slowly through the cube-lined tunnel, increasingly certain as he went that the pathway was not designed in any purposeful fashion. There was no attempt at symmetry, just as there hadn't been outside. But the blocks hadn't accumulated at random. There was a kind of underlying structure, just as there was in most natural processes. The cubes were stacked in one spot, for instance, not scattered through the world's hollow heart, as they could easily have been. Some intent lay behind that rough order. But that intentional process didn't care if the cubes were stacked hard against each other all the way around. So gaps appeared, honeycombing the structure, and some of those gaps inevitably joined up to form channels like the one he was following. Chance had built it, not a designer, and certainly not Himself.

The channel meandered most of the way to the center, where he expected to see nothing at all. Just more identical cubes, blank on every face and apparently inert. He was glad they didn't have mirrored surfaces. The channel would have been a nightmare of reflections. His own face, everywhere: that would really have been too much.

The channel doglegged. He followed it at a cautious speed, certain that it would take him back to the surface or to a complete dead end. Then it doglegged again and plunged deeper still, narrowing as it went until it was only one or two cube widths across. He flew carefully and turned down the spotlights so he wouldn't be dazzled. Where the cubes weren't aligned perfectly, he sometimes had to squeeze through gaps barely large enough for the suit. There wasn't enough space to turn around. If they came any tighter, he would have to back out feetfirst.

"Does it open up ahead?" he asked.

After a second, Emlee responded. "Yes. There's a clear space, right on the center of gravity."

"The King's Chamber," he said, thinking of pyramids and ancient history.

"The what?"

"Nothing important. Is it empty?"

"No surprises that I can see."

He fought a sense of deflation as he negotiated the last two bottlenecks and found himself inside the empty space she had described. It was teardrop-shaped, opening from the narrow end through which he had entered into a round space large enough for four more people his size. There was no other exit. Square black faces crowded in all around him, eating up the light he cast across them.

The only odd note, one Emlee hadn't mentioned, was a single cube floating in the larger end of the empty space. This was the first Imre had seen from every angle. He circled it warily, making sure that all six faces were identical and unmarked. They were. He didn't touch it immediately. First he played a very tight beam of light across one corner, hoping to detect a measure of translucency. No luck, and therefore no chance of figuring out the cube's composition via simple absorption spectra. The black surface scattered a small percentage of the photons and absorbed the rest. What happened to them, he couldn't tell. The block's temperature barely changed, no matter how much light he pumped into it.

Gingerly, as though defusing a bomb, he raised one thick-gloved hand to touch the cube on its nearest face. What his armor touched, he would feel too, as though he had touched it with his own skin. He made contact, expecting to feel nothing but inert material with a ceramic texture, perhaps, or glassy like fused sand, and was surprised when the face gave slightly under the pressure. He removed his index finger and the surface rebounded like rubber. The slight touch provoked no further reaction, so he pressed more firmly. The rubbery cube resisted, then gave up the fight, as though he had broken some kind of surface tension. The tip of his finger slid into the cube as far as the first joint. Before he could move it any deeper, the face of the cube rippled like the surface of a pond and vanished.

A sensation of cold swept up his arm. The suit's spotlights turned red as though colored filters had been dropped over him. He tried to pull away, but the laws of physics appeared to have changed. His arm was as sluggish as though it weighed a full ton. His muscles screamed, and the suit could do nothing to help them. His finger moved at a geological rate, and the feeling persisted.

His mind was faster. The cube had vanished, revealing something else, something that had been inside it. A silver sphere as large as his head, reflecting red light like a weightless drop of blood. He had seen something just like that before. He had experienced the red, too.

"You understand," said a familiar voice into his head, "that we do not have long to talk."

A rapid-fire series of images flashed through his mind: of the Jinc vessel in which he had been reborn; of the strange museum of artifacts the gestalt had found in the void; of a silver sphere that helped him escape and gave him the code word "luminous" to summon it by.

Later, when Imre had found Emlee on Hyperabad, he had heard of spheres identical to the one he had known attacking and killing the proto-Fort she had tried to save. They had been called the Luminous. He had learned precious little more about them since.

"You've adjusted my tempo," he said, thinking aloud even if it did make him feel stupid, "like you did last time." His lips burned from friction with the air inside the suit. "So we could talk without the Jinc hearing."

"Not I, Imre Bergamasc," it said. "Another like me. We are not numerous, but we are persistent."

To Emlee, a Prime, he would be moving too fast to see, and for MZ it would be even worse. Forts struggled to think down to Primes' level. "Who are you? What are you?"

"We are your allies, although it may be hard to conceive of us as such. Certainly, you would be dead right now, were it not for me."

"How so?"

"Your enemy is very close. My existence is threatened, too. We are united by the danger to us all."

"If you don't start giving me straight answers, I'll join the list of people threatening you." He leaned in close and saw his own face staring back at him, distorted and framed by the oval of his suit's flash visor. He looked like the devil from ancient legend, tainted with crimson light. "What are you doing here now? What do you know about this place?"

"I knew that you would hardcast here eventually: the place you called Domgard, the epicenter of the Slow Wave, where humanity's greatest hopes and fears collide. It would not exist without you—and without Domgard, the Forts would still be alive. Domgard's fate, your fate, and the fate of humanity are inextricably linked."

"By the Slow Wave." He felt a vast emptiness in his gut opening up. The sphere was confirming his worst fears. "I built Domgard, and Domgard killed the Forts. Somehow. Something to do with dark matter."

"Something to do with dark matter, yes. But Domgard didn't kill the Forts. You built Domgard, you and a handful of others, and you were ignorant of the danger you put yourselves in. You did not have all the data. You could not have had the data. The only way to obtain it, in full, was to conduct the experiment."

"What was the point of the experiment?"

"To explore the properties of dark matter—"

"Bullshit," he snapped. "Since when does that bring about the end of civilization?"

"—with the intention of finding another way for dark matter and the matter you are composed of to interact," the sphere persisted. "One preferably less difficult to manipulate than gravity."

Imre pulled away from the sphere until his features blurred into a shadowy, oval blotch. "What difference does that make?"

"All the difference in the world. In the galaxy. In the universe." The silver orb had no eyes, but he could feel its attention focused firmly on him. "Such a means of interaction would act as a bridge as surely as suspending a road across a river, or stringing electric cables across a continent, or firing masers between the stars. And bridges are sometimes the source as well as the object of conflict. Imagine if Domgard had been a success and Forts had been able to interact for the first time with the vast expanse of dark matter. A passive examination of the new vistas would have been the first step, one conducted with great ponderousness as unprecedented detail flooded in. The second step would have been to interact more closely with the galaxy's dark twin, by experiment and by direct exploration. Imagine machines comprised partly of ordinary matter and partly of dark matter, linked by Domgard technology. Imagine a Fort existing in both realms simultaneously, perhaps the first being in the history of the universe to do so. Imagine the resources available to such a being—with access to nine times the matter you can presently see. Imagine the possibilities, Imre Bergamasc. Imagine them now, as you did half a million years ago."

He was imagining. And he was remembering MZ's telling him that Domgard had nothing to do with the long-hoped-for FTL drive. *Transformation of a fundamental kind.* This would certainly fit that category.

"*If* Domgard had been a success," he said, quoting the sphere back at itself.

"It was a success. A hard-earned success that changed the balance of power in the galaxy forever."

"So what went wrong?"

"Domgard attracted attention."

"What kind of attention?"

"The worst sort at the worst possible time."

"A rival group? Were other Forts working on this too?" He rejected the suggestion as soon as it left his lips. "No. That would have required two top secret projects: one to build the dark matter interface, the other the weapon behind the Slow Wave. One was hard enough to hide—and using the weapon would've killed the perpetrators too." He thought of MZ and the minds of Earth. The Forts had explored many strange frontiers in their time, but they hadn't been all-powerful, as history had proved. "If it wasn't more Forts, and it wasn't me, then who was it?"

The sphere said, "Forts were not the first beings to have straddled both realms. Those who preceded them didn't take kindly to the invasion."

Imre stared at the sphere for a long moment, seeing neither the smooth silver surface nor his reflection in it. There was an inescapable logic to what the sphere was suggesting. *Not the first beings . . . not Forts . . . not him.*

Not human.

But his mind balked at it. No evidence had ever been gathered of alien life in or near the Milky Way—and not for want of trying. Humanity was, as far as anyone had ever known, the sole intelligent specie in the universe.

Much easier to believe that the sphere was lying.

"You're one of them—whatever they are. The Luminous. I have no reason to believe you and plenty of reasons not to."

"As you say. Yet here we are. You are not dead, and I am telling you the truth. Not the whole truth, but part of it. You would be mistaken to regard me as typical of my kind."

"So what is the whole truth?"

"Until you are ready to trust us, why would I tell you anything more?"

Imre sensed it coming before it started. He lunged at the sphere, but his Prime body was too slow. He might have made it as a singleton—and done what exactly, he didn't truthfully know—but that thought was no use to him now. His outstretched fingers were a full hand span away from the sphere when the cube re-formed around it and the red ambience disappeared. The full light of the suit's spots returned, dazzling him.

"What happened there?" asked Emlee. "Something happened. Imre, are you all right?"

"I'm okay."

"You don't sound all right."

"I'm angry." And he was, but not at her. At the sphere, or the Luminous, or whoever it was playing games with him. Still, after everything he had tried, he remained at the mercy of forces from the past. Try as he might, he could not cut free. Nor did he want to, until he knew how to fix the problems they had caused. But they were slippery, ambiguous, and contradictory—and how could he begin to fight if he didn't know who his real enemy was, let alone what they stood to gain?

The killers of the Forts were aliens made of dark matter. The thought should have been ludicrous, but he wasn't dismissing it just yet. It fit the facts, so it would have to stay on the table until he disproved it. A more detailed analysis of the Domgard ruins would be a good way to start. The finest theoretical physicists in the galaxy could be consulted. He could return here with his flagship, *Memento Mori X*, and take the sphere back for aggressive analysis.

He owed Emlee an explanation, both for the situation and his mood. "What MZ isn't telling us is that Domgard was supposed to be some kind of subway station to the dark matter neighborhood. Things were getting crowded in the galaxy, so this was a jumping-off point for the next wave of human evolution. Someone took exception to it and they took steps to stop it as well."

"So this is just a turf war? I don't buy that."

"Neither do I," he said. "There's something else going on, something we're still not seeing. Do you have anything to add, MZ?"

"Nothing we did was ever reducible to a single motive," said the Fort. "Progress, peace, and conflict. There's always something to add."

"So Emlee's right? It wasn't just a turf war?"

"Perhaps there was more than one turf. I don't have all the pieces of the puzzle either. You seem to have acquired some that I was missing. How did you do that?"

The attention was abruptly back on him. He had no good answers. "I'll explain later. Right now, I want to get out of here." He glanced at the single isolated cube, floating in the central chamber, inert once more. "It's giving me the creeps."

He backtracked up the winding channel to free space. Once there, he fired up the propulsion system for real and headed in the direction of the hardcaster, looping once around the chamber to map the curving wall in more detail. From his new perspective he could make out several circular pits that might have been routes to the surface. He briefly considered following one of them to make sure there weren't any other surprises hidden in the ruins, but in the end he decided to cut his losses and get back to Earth. There were hundreds of archaeologists in the employ of the Returned Continuum who would eagerly volunteer to examine the site.

"Warm up the hardcaster, Emlee," he said.

"Will do."

A feeling that he had forgotten or missed something important nagged as he ascended to where the hardcaster hung waiting for him. He was at Volume Zero. He had to take something more than a bizarre theory home with him. But what? He wouldn't trust a sphere inside the *Wickthing*, and there was nothing else on Spargamos but a pile of melted machinery, a ruin, and an empty space where a chunk of neutronium had once been carefully contained. A working dark matter detector would have been something. Some records, likewise. Whoever had cleaned out or destroyed Domgard had left nothing that could reasonably constitute proof of anything. Just words.

As he halved the distance to the hardcaster, weight increasing all the way, he remembered the way the cube containing the sphere had dissolved to nothing at his touch. That was an impressive trick.

The cube, the back of his mind said, was identical to the others.

He was already turning as Emlee broke the silence.

"Uh, Imre, I think you should look behind you."

He brought the spots to bear on the lumpy sphere in the center of the giant chamber. It was changing shape, collapsing into itself like a falling building. Imre needed nothing more than that to know what was going on. He pushed the suit's propulsion system to maximum and calculated the time he had left.

"Emlee, we're in trouble."

"Did you do this?"

The agglomeration of cubes had collapsed by one-third.

"Not me. You did, I think."

"How?"

"By switching on the hardcaster."

The agglomeration roiled as though a giant hand had stirred the cubes from underneath. Waves rose and fell. The channels collapsed.

"What difference did that make? We'd used it twice before."

"Yes, but we were being protected. That protection has been lifted."

You would be dead right now, the sphere had said, *were it not for me.*

"What are you talking about, Imre?"

The sphere looked exactly like one of the Luminous. It had been hidden in a featureless cube that had reacted to his presence, one of many thousands just below him. He had assumed the cubic form was camouflage—and indeed it had been, in a way. The sphere was definitely hiding from someone. *You would be mistaken to take me as typical of my kind,* it had said. It was hiding from the rest of the Luminous, disguised as one cube among many others. It was hiding *among* the Luminous.

The agglomeration underwent one final paroxysm. Cubes tumbled like icebergs over a sea of silver—but this sea wasn't composed of water. Waves rose higher and higher, bulging and looping like the surface of the sun. Then one loop broke away, carrying a handful of cubes upward through sheer momentum. Imre watched one of the cubes, watched as it dissolved and disappeared, exactly as the cube he had touched had done. Inside was another sphere, identical to the ones lifting it up in Imre's wake. It joined the others in an angry dance, like a bee in a swarm. The silver sea was comprised of thousands of such spheres. The silver sea was the Luminous.

The loop became a whip, a streamer reaching up for him. He had only moments in which to decide what to do. He would reach the hardcaster in time, but what then? It would take days to return to the *Wickthing*, for the location and motion of all his atoms and molecules to be cataloged and recorded, and for the data to be transmitted, one bit at a time, into the ancient Fort's virtual world. The hardcaster would be destroyed before the process had even started. He had to find somewhere else to run.

"Get out of here," he told Emlee. "We don't know for sure that they can't see you and MZ."

"What about you?" she asked, not hiding her anxiety.

"There are tunnels leading out of here." He hoped. "I'll take one of them to the surface and from there—well, I guess we'll see what we see."

"Which one? We'll guide you."

He picked the closest. "Don't put yourself at risk," he told her. "That's an order."

"Do as I say, not as I do?"

"I'm replaceable," he said, fearing it might be true on more than one level.

She was silent for a long moment as the Luminous boiled up after him.

"It's going to be close," she eventually said. He couldn't read her voice. "The tunnel kinks almost immediately. You're going to lose a lot of speed, taking that corner."

"So will they. If you fly the suit, I'll take care of pursuit."

"Will do."

Imre unholstered his Bostonian sidearms, grateful now for their power but wishing he had more up-to-date weaponry at hand. A tangle of images overlapped in his vision: the growing circle of the tunnel mouth in a range of frequencies; the tip of the whip approaching him from behind, lit by a single white spotlight. Numerous displays informed him of the suit's velocity, attitude, and power reserves. He had plenty of the latter. Barring the Luminous catching up, he could fly for a century and not run out of juice.

The Luminous could be destroyed, but the fight ahead of him was hardly a fair one. One against thousands, and he made a slower, larger target.

Thus far they hadn't fired a single shot. Their comms were impossible to hack into—or so Emlee had said of her experiences on Hyperabad—but he imagined them urging each other on, wanting to take him prisoner, to take him apart and find out what he knew, what he was doing there, what his relationship to Domgard had been.

He was sure they wouldn't take kindly to the knowledge that he was one of the builders. That, he supposed, was one of the reasons they were there: to ambush anyone trying to start up the old experiments. But for the intervention of one of their own, he would have been caught the second he stepped out of the hardcaster. They would have been waiting for him. He wouldn't have stood a chance.

But what kind of chance had the rogue sphere given him? That thought consumed him as both the Luminous and the tunnel mouth converged on him. Its intervention had only delayed the inevitable—or so it seemed at first glance. He had to hope it knew more than he did. He had to hope, period.

It was indeed going to be close. He turned his back to the wall and braced himself for sudden course changes. The weapons he held out behind him, straight-armed, as though readying to fire at the Luminous. A long, silver tail swept behind the tip approaching him, coiling and writhing like an angry Chinese dragon.

"Get ready," Emlee said.

He overclocked as fast as he could, turning the dance of the Luminous to a slow-motion, orderless tumble. The nearest was only meters away. He could have hit it easily.

"Now."

Imre entered the tunnel backward, trailing his arms and legs. As the walls fell around him, engulfing him, he fired. Twin bolts of energy lanced from each of his handguns, taking out the front four spheres. They blossomed like flowers, blue and white heat shifted down to orange and yellow, still blindingly bright. Before the gaseous shock wave caught up with him, he raised one handgun, lowered the other, and fired again, keeping the triggers down so bolt after bolt discharged into the wall of the tunnel. Domgard wasn't a military base; its walls weren't armored or reinforced for combat. By the time Emlee commanded the suit to take the turn, the tunnel mouth was awash with fiery debris.

He was wrenched like a rag doll. His arms and legs whipped uncontrollably from side to side. He kept firing, determined to make pursuit as difficult and unappealing a prospect as possible. The visor of his suit darkened automatically, reducing the red-tinged glare to a manageable level. Each explosion tore deeper into the planet's bedrock. The sides of the tunnel buckled and collapsed in his wake.

It was impossible to tell if the Luminous were following him. He didn't stop to find out. He rolled first chance he had, bringing the handguns to bear on the way before him. It was clear, garishly lit by the fires behind him and already blackened by heat. The spotlights burned dimly in comparison. He felt as though he were fleeing through a devilish sewer, rising like an angel out of the darkest depths of hell.

If only, he thought. Heaven awaited him in that scenario. If the sphere didn't know what it was doing, all that lay ahead of him on Spargamos were the ruins of Domgard and an empty sky. No reinforcements. No chance of escape. But he would take as many as he could with him before the end. And he hoped that Emlee would do the necessary thing afterward, or else his position really would be hopeless.

A partial map appeared in his forward view, pasted over the view of the corridor. Emlee was scouting the way ahead and keeping him up to date. The tunnel branched in three directions; she had chosen the one heading most directly upward, which made sense. That tunnel branched twice and then twice again. The map was growing visibly larger as he studied it.

But too slowly, he thought. Each intersection would cost him time he could ill afford. There had to be a better way.

"You keep doing what you're doing," he said. "I'm going to try something different."

He started firing when the end of the tunnel was a dozen meters away. Debris rained on him from the impact point, but he kept the triggers down. Taking control of the suit from Emlee, he flew into the maelstrom, battering his way through rubble and explosive gases, firing as he went.

Twenty seconds felt like an eternity, but it took just that long for him to break into another tunnel. The suit didn't need Emlee to tell it which way was up. He followed its nose in that direction as best he could until he hit another intersection and started firing again. The handguns grew warm even through his insulated gloves. He was pummeled all over. He didn't let up, because he knew the spheres were hot on his heels.

"Show me the route we took down here," he said to Emlee.

An instant later she had that map for him. The *Wickthing*'s route led through the planet's thin crust without any regard for its tunnels and chambers. He studied it even as he burst into a larger space, one full of machinery that had been melted an age before and was undergoing a new wave of destruction, thanks to him. He crossed it as rapidly as he could, firing at random points in the walls, so his pursuers would need a moment to work out which way he had gone.

Then he was burning his way through solid stone, retracing the route he and Emlee had followed on the way down, without making it look as though he had a goal in mind. Better the Luminous thought he was moving randomly upward than for a particular location.

"Care to share your thoughts?" Emlee asked him.

"You don't want to know." He plowed on, hoping to cross another tunnel soon. The longer he spent burrowing into the bedrock, the more worried he became. Twenty seconds passed. Thirty seconds. He began to feel hemmed in and expected the Luminous to loom out of the smoke and debris any second.

"Get behind me," he told Emlee. "I can't see what's following me, and I don't have much room to maneuver in here."

"On it," she said, just as he burst into another tunnel, one leading horizontally across his path. He followed it long enough to feel as though he was making progress, then began burrowing again.

"They're spreading out," she said. "Some are still on your tail—it's not hard to follow, obviously, and rockfalls are only slowing them down, not stopping them—but others are moving into the tunnel system, obviously hoping to catch you in a pincer."

Imre grunted acknowledgment. He'd thought that might happen but hoped it wouldn't be so soon. Time was short, then. He would need to move fast before they completely filled the tunnels and no way was safe.

Through solid rock and the occasional clear space he raced, not bothering to hide where he was going anymore. He planned his route carefully, angling up at a shallow angle in order to intercept a particular point on their downward path, jinking and juking every time he hit clear air. He had a vague memory of the particular chamber he was looking for. There had been corridors leading out of it from several directions. If he was lucky, he would cross one of them.

His objective drew closer. Only once, as he passed diagonally through a broad, rectangular room large enough for several starships, did he meet one of the spheres searching for him. It emerged from a tunnel and changed course immediately on seeing him. He rotated around his center of gravity and cut it down with both pistols. It disappeared with a flash of white light. He watched as long as he could before turning forward to tunnel again, but no others appeared.

One more burn through a bedrock wall led him to a tunnel heading in the right direction. He pushed the suit as hard as he dared, keeping mental fingers crossed that the Luminous hadn't have beaten him there. The chamber was circular with a domed roof and empty apart from a mound of frags ten deep. *A withered face, with hollow cheeks and eyes.* The memory was deeply etched in his mind.

He fired at a dozen random points and blew the suit's seals as soon as he was sure the room was clear. Heat and debris swirled around him. Several of the mummified bodies caught fire. Heat and intense cold played over his skin suit as he shot out of the suit's protective embrace.

"Seal it up," he told Emlee. "Take it along the same course. Decoy them."

"What about you?" she asked, alarmed.

"Don't worry about me. Just get this thing moving."

The suit began to close itself. One of its arms jerked, tossing one of the glowing Bostonians toward him. "At least take this," she said.

It was so hot he could barely hold it. "All right. Now, go."

The suit roared away, propulsion vents burning brightly. Imre dived for the pile of burning bodies barely in time. No sooner had he crawled into their grim embrace when three silver spheres rocketed out of the corridor behind him in pursuit of the empty suit.

He froze and watched them. They moved like dollops of quicksilver in free fall and were deadly in intent. One swept about the burning room while the others raced away. Smoke from the burning mummies filled the air. A burning limb dropped away from the corpse it belonged to and landed on the back of Imre's left leg. He didn't move.

The trailing sphere performed one last circuit, then raced off into a different tunnel. He waited, ignoring the heat slowly creeping through his skin suit. Bodies pressed into him on all sides, their expressions ghastly with fear and pain. He didn't want to look at them, was terrified of recognizing them, couldn't afford to think about them at all for fear of developing a serious case of the horrors. A single shudder would unlock the rest of his muscles and send him fleeing headlong away from safety.

Five minutes he waited, clutching the cooling sidearm in both hands. The sound of the suit burning through the bedrock faded into the distance. He didn't call Emlee to find out how she was faring. He didn't want to distract her or draw attention to himself. The fires guttered and went out. Darkness fell in the visible spectrum, so he switched to infrared and waited another five minutes. No more Luminous came his way. They were all chasing the suit into the distance.

Time to move. He checked the map. The chamber was close enough to the surface to risk making a run for it. He could guess which way the corridors went, even though MZ had bypassed most of them on the way down. Gingerly, not wanting to cause a noisy collapse of the grim pile, he eased himself out from among the bodies and brushed the embers off his leg. The suit was unharmed, as was he, although the low gravity made him feel light-headed. He trod lightly, wary of being off the ground for too long, lest he had to change direction in a hurry. Without spotlights or the suit's more powerful transmitters, he headed off in the hope that Emlee would find him before the Luminous did.

Half an hour of slow, careful climbing saw him very near the surface. He paused at every intersection and listened for thirty seconds, chasing echoes from far away: explosions, rumbling rock, structural groans. A series of louder booms, like thunder, heralded the passing of the suit. He assumed that Emlee had been cornered and waited until as many spheres as possible were nearby before instructing it to self-destruct. He hoped the suit took a dozen with it. A hundred. Even if it killed a thousand, there would still be plenty left to finish the job.

Imre found a niche to hide in, just in case the spheres guessed the suit had been empty and embarked on a new search of the tunnels. A deep, penetrating cold was spreading through his limbs; he ramped up his metabolism to keep it at bay. A thin film of rime formed over the wall at his side as air melted by his arrival slowly refroze. A feeling of peace swept through him. He had experienced such moments in the midst of combat before. It wasn't contentment, exactly, nor resignation; he felt poised on the brink of motion. Sometimes it seemed that an entire campaign could revolve around such moments, where the forces on either side were so delicately balanced that a tiny nudge could have huge ramifications. Such moments were to be savored, especially as there was no guarantee that they would last very long.

He was sitting there, patiently counting the seconds and watching the air crystals form, when Emlee's voice found him.

"Now what? You're down to one gun, no armor, and all the acceleration your legs can manage."

He stirred, breaking the spell with reluctance. "It's not over yet."

"What exactly are you going to do? Throw rocks at them and swim home?"

"There might be another hardcaster on the surface."

"If there is, it'll be booby-trapped too."

"We'll untrap it, then." Her defeatism irritated him. She sounded as though she blamed him personally for his predicament. "What are our friends doing? Going quietly back to their roosts?"

"Some, not all."

"Still no luck hacking into their comms?"

"No."

"But they didn't see you. You were invisible to them."

"Yes."

"Stalemate—of a sort, anyway." A thought occurred to him, out of nowhere—or inspired, perhaps, by the dead frags who had unwittingly given him shelter. "I wonder if they communicate by Q loop technology."

She thought about it. "It's possible. We couldn't hack into the Forts either. I'd much rather believe in one unhackable comms system than two."

"And if the Luminous use it, they'd know how to break it." He nodded. This was evidence, circumstantial but suggestive, that the Luminous had been behind the Slow Wave. That was progress. And he wondered if it could tie into the strange dark matter theories as well: what new properties of matter had been discovered in this remote frontier of physics? Q loop technology might have been just one of many arcane phenomena exploited by the Forts while researching this area.

Imre took a moment to consider his situation. Emlee and MZ were perfectly safe. He was the only thing holding them back. Soon he would need to get moving again. He had to take precautions, just in case his luck was about to run out.

"What's that?" Emlee asked him when the data packet he sent her arrived.

"Nothing. Don't open it until I tell you."

"You shouldn't listen to me all the time," she said with a new worry in her voice. "I'm just playing the devil's advocate."

"Well, maybe you should help me find a way out of this dump instead. I can't have far to go."

"No. You're almost there. Come out of your little hidey-hole and take a left. I'll scout ahead and make sure the way is clear."

He followed her directions without hesitation, trying to hold on to the calm he had felt while waiting for her to return. It was difficult, even though there was no sign of the Luminous at present. He could make out next to nothing in the deep, dark cold of the ruins. It would be a relief to see the stars again.

Emlee guided him to a steep ramp that might once have been used to drive machinery up to the surface. It was four meters wide and twice again as high. His footsteps crunched through snow that grew thicker the higher he climbed. Gas puffed with every footstep. Ahead, a faint chilly light made ice crystals gleam like shards of broken glass.

"If I were the Luminous," he said as he approached the top of the ramp, "I'd have booby-trapped the entrances too."

"I can't see anything suspicious."

"I doubt we would."

"You're not suggesting turning back, are you?"

"No. I'm not." He plodded on and crossed the threshold without breaking step. The surface of Spargamos stretched before him—rugged and sterile, pockmarked by meteorites and cosmic rays—but possessing its own austere beauty. The sky was crowded with stars, their combined light brighter than that of a full moon on Earth. The ring of fat moonlets added a geometric counterpoint to the already dense view. He walked ten paces, then stopped again. His skin suit was doing its best, but he could feel the chill reaching up through the soles of his feet and into his bones.

He asked himself the same question Emlee had been badgering him with: Now what? He didn't really think the ruins would contain a working hardcaster. The one below was a late addition, installed long after the destruction of Domgard. He bet that the Luminous had gathered in the empty chamber long afterward, upon discovering the sarcophagus where none had been before, in the hope that the person responsible would return. And he supposed that person might have, in a round-about way.

He could bury himself somewhere safe and drop his tempo down to its minimum level. The trouble was—where was safe on this godforsaken rock? And his Prime body wasn't as resilient as a singleton's. Once he could have waited out fifty thousand years as though they were days, confident his body would survive more or less intact. Now, the relative time would be measured in years and he couldn't be sure of his physical survival. He might freeze solid in that time and fail to react if discovered.

He could send out an SOS in the hope that a nearby civilization with interstellar capacity was in range and willing to help him. Or he could send MZ and Emlee off to find someone for him. But what right did he have to drag someone else into his private predicament? He had got himself into this mess—and there was a much simpler solution available if only Emlee would exercise it.

"Don't look now," said Emlee. "But I think you were right."

Imre glanced to his left, where a stream of silver spheres was rushing up the ramp toward him. He took two steps away from them, then stopped with the sidearm hanging limply at his side. What was the point of running? He couldn't escape them on foot, and there were too many to pick off one by one.

Movement out of the corner of his eye alerted him to more spheres emerging from another entrance, rising as though weightless in a gleaming thread across the sky. They hadn't fired on him yet. He wasn't going to fire first.

They converged on him from all directions, swooping close to him, then darting away, as though testing him, or looking for something. He wondered if they were looking for signals from the loop shunt that had once been part of him. He wondered what difference it would make if they found any.

They rose up over him like the funnel of a surreal hurricane, never touching him but definitely hemming him in, silent and threatening. He braced himself, knowing that their interest in him would last only so long. They weren't likely to leave him to wander the ruins unmolested. Raising the pistol, he brandished it in a way that he hoped looked both threatening and conciliatory, and tipped his head back to take one look at the stars.

He froze.

The stars were moving. Shifting and twisting as though the sky were melting—or as though the wings of an enormous glass bird were flapping overhead. He stared at it, open-mouthed, wondering if it was MZ. But that was impossible, unless the Fort had lied to him about his capabilities.

The thought was thrust from his mind by a sudden, bright flash, directly overhead. A powerful shock wave knocked him off his feet. He went down with his hands over his face, automatically bringing his knees up to protect his most vulnerable organs. The spheres were exploding, popping like deadly firecrackers under fire from several directions at once. Again he wondered if Emlee and MZ had found a way to save him—but she had said nothing in advance, and she wasn't the sort to keep secrets on the battlefield. She played for efficiency, not effect.

The explosions ebbed. He dared to raise his head. The ground was covered with glowing ash—the remains of the spheres, some of it still falling through the vacuum. Frozen air steamed and bubbled. He could hardly see three meters through it. He got an elbow under himself. Three dark shapes were walking toward him across the icy plain—humanoid, faceless, dressed entirely in black. They were holding rifles at the ready from thirty meters away, pointing right at him.

He rose warily to his feet. The Bostonian was nowhere to be seen, blown away by the blast overhead. As he looked for it, the ring of moonlets above began to glow red, then yellow, then blinding white. But they didn't explode. They imploded, forming dense purple specks that fizzed and sparked so brightly they drowned out the crowded stars of the core. Imre looked away. Tiny purple specks marred his vision. Behind them, he glimpsed the sky rippling violently, as though in agony.

"I don't think you understand," said a new voice over the ether, "the gravity of the situation."

The cold in Imre's feet was nothing compared to the ice that spread outward from his heart. He knew that voice.

It was his own.

"Where did you come from?" he asked, keeping his tone level, unsurprised.

All three figures simultaneously cocked their heads over their left shoulders, indicating three different points on the Spargamos landscape. "I've always been here, waiting for you. I knew you'd break the deal."

"It wasn't much of a deal from my point of view. Don't dig, don't look, don't wonder—and what did I get in return? Sabotage, unrest, dissent. Thanks a fucking bunch." He forced himself to take a deep breath. "Your deal brought me here."

"Exactly. I knew it would."

Something clicked in Imre's mind. Everything that had happened to him took on a new light. The threat of retaliation wasn't to stop him from seeking Domgard; it was to make sure he would keep trying. The hardcaster below wasn't for Himself; it was for him, when he finally found Volume Zero. The constant provocation throughout the Returned Continuum kept him from feeling complacent and forgetting his search. Maybe not entirely that; he agreed with MZ that the plans of Forts were ever more complex than they looked.

But was this a Fort he was talking to or something else entirely?

He scanned the electromagnetic spectrum. There was a lot of traffic where before there had been none. "A trap within a trap," he said. "The Luminous were waiting for me, and you were waiting for—what?"

"You, them, and the opportunity to send a message." The three figures had halved their distance between them and him. The rifles' aims hadn't moved. Fierce blue light played across them from the collapsed moonlets above. "The message is: we know what you're doing and we're learning to do what you do—fast."

The sky convulsed. Strange tides tugged at him. "Who's 'we'?"

"Domgard, of course. Our efforts were set back here, but they didn't end. We just . . . moved."

"Moved where?"

One of the three stopped walking. He turned and scanned the horizon, rifle upraised, while the other two walked on. Ten meters away.

"Tell me something," said the voice over the airwaves. "We monitor the Line as closely as you do. There have been no incoming transmissions for three hundred thousand years."

"Must have been boring for you," he said. "Sorry to keep you waiting."

"Yet you didn't come by ship, so you must have come by hardcaster. It's a paradox." The second of the three stopped at the entrance to the ramp and covered the space below with his weapon. The third walked on. "Where is your point of origin?"

Ah. Imre kept a tight lid on his reaction. MZ was made of nothing but ripples in space; he was, therefore, invisible to them. And to the Luminous. The sphere too had assumed that he had hardcast to Spargamos, perhaps all the way from Earth. That was the one asset he had, the one secret he could keep from Himself.

He said nothing about his ghostly companions.

"You were talking to Emlee before," the figure before him asked. "Where is she?"

Imre watched silently as the rifle barrel came within three meters, two meters, one. He could reach out and touch it, if he wanted to. If he was fast enough, he might even get it out of the hands of his former self and turn it on its owner. But that was only one problem in three. He would be cut down within nanoseconds by the other two.

Silence.

"You did us a favor," his former self said. "For that, I am grateful. I'd call off the assassins, to prove my goodwill; your patchwork empire could go on about its business in peace. But if you won't talk to us, here's where my loyalty ends. Last chance, Imre Bergamasc."

They held the pose for a moment, one unarmed man dressed in little more than an advanced second skin facing a man in full combat armor holding a rifle powerful enough to shoot a hole in a small mountain, while the deaths of dozens of tiny moons sent flickering sheets of light across the sky.

"You don't know everything," Imre said. "That's all the chance I need."

The rifle's mouth spat fire and blackness instantly descended.

THIS MORTAL SIN

The disease which had thus entombed the lady in the maturity of youth, had left, as usual in all maladies of a strictly cataleptical character, the mockery of a faint blush upon the bosom and the face, and that suspiciously lingering smile upon the lip which is so terrible in death.

—Edgar Allan Poe

Imre woke to a blur of primary colors and thought, Oh hell, here we go again. He was inside the world of the phantasm once more and finding it no less uncomfortable than the first time.

Then the blur shifted. Fuzzy boundaries sharpened. Colors became denser and more intricate. Flat surfaces took on three-dimensional aspects, and other senses woke, giving him taste, smell, touch. A well-defined image took shape before him—a familiar face.

Emlee Copas. Her expression was very serious.

The last thing he remembered was the sarcophagus lid closing over him in the Citadel.

"What went wrong?" he asked. "Where's Chyro?"

"He's here," she said, and indeed over her shoulder Imre glimpsed the mustachioed surgeon waiting with hands folded, looking troubled. "Are you feeling all right?"

Imre raised himself onto his elbows, then sat fully upright. He felt perfectly fine, but her behavior was unnerving him. Had something gone awry in the hardcasting process? Had MZ betrayed them?

He examined himself closely and saw no obvious flaw. He was wearing a white cotton smock identical to Emlee's and

Kells's, although theirs had a crumpled look, as though worn
longer. Next he took in the environment the Fort had created
for them. Sunlight played lightly through green leaves over a
scene of almost absurd gentility. A day bed, a double row of
plane trees leading to a white Georgian town house whose
front door hung welcomingly open. Smoke rose from the
chimney into a hazy blue sky.

"I feel fine," he said. "Why wouldn't I?"

She offered a hand and helped him to his feet. "Come with
me."

He followed her into the house, noting the edges of the illusion as often as the details. The fields beyond the arbor were
indistinct; the reflections from the upper-floor windows
showed nothing but impressionist pastiches. Only the arbor
had focus and clarity. Only the house.

There was a study, full of bookcases and maps, with a single painting facing the desk.

"Look," she said.

There was a picture in the frame, but it wasn't a painting. It
showed the surface of a cold, hard world lit up as though by
fireworks, with multiple shadows indicating several sources of
bright light hidden above the upper frame. The starscape in
the background looked twisted, tortured, as though someone
had taken a planetarium image and deliberately distorted it.
Two figures in black stood in the foreground, with a third
much smaller in the distance. All three were holding long-
barreled weapons. One of the closer figures had glassed his
visor, enabling Imre to see the face within.

"That looks like me," he said, recognizing the triangular
features and white hair instantly. "Is that supposed to be you
and Chyro?" he asked, pointing at the other two figures. "If
you're telling me I've lost more memories, I'm going to
scream."

She shook her head. The image changed, presumably at
her command. There was a body on the ground between the
three figures, disfigured by some kind of weapon fire. It was
barely recognizable as human.

"That's you," she said. "You died."

He stared at the screen in silence, taking it in by degrees, one detail at a time. *You died.* Died somewhere he had never been before, with a man who looked exactly like him nearby. Burning lights in the twisted sky.

"I brought you back," she said.

He looked at her and understood then the reason for her serious demeanor. She didn't like it, but she had had no choice. He had died, and she couldn't leave it there. She was his bodyguard. He was the First Prime. It was her duty.

She didn't like it.

"I think you'd better start at the beginning," he said.

It took some time to bring him up to date. MZ stayed out of it, and so did Kells. The surgeon paced the limits of the illusion outside the house while Emlee told the story of how they had arrived at a place called Spargamos and found the ruins of Domgard. She punctuated her words with glimpses of the record MZ had made of their journey. He saw images of dark tunnels, mounds of dead bodies, angular ruins. None of it felt real to him. The days of his life that were missing felt like events from a story he wasn't particularly enjoying. He knew the ending. Why would he want to read on?

He listened intently, asking numerous questions when he thought he might have misunderstood something, or when she skated over a detail she thought unimportant. It was all important. He was dead, and his anger at that fact was only beginning to take root.

Empty space at the heart of the planet. A missing dark matter detector, perhaps, or was MZ just spinning a line? Space that turned out not to be entirely empty. Cubes—and a deeper layer to explore, one that had required his taking physical form. Him, not her. It would never be her, not while she refused to let him bring her back from the dead, as she had done for him.

"What happened there?" he asked when he had reached the heart of the cubes. His image in the magic picture had touched the one floating in isolation, then suddenly jerked back.

"I don't know," she said. "You wouldn't tell me. You did send me this, later."

She handed him a book—only he knew that in the real world it wasn't anything like a book. It was a file of data presented as a book in MZ's virtual world. He took it and opened the front cover. The spine crackled.

For all its size, it contained only a few pages. He skimmed the first quickly.

You understand that we do not have long to talk.

The sphere.

"You can read it?" Emlee asked him, looking unsurprised.

"It's in an old code." The Aldobrand Cipher, which his former self had used to hide thoughts in his long-lost journal. "I can read it just fine."

"What does it say?"

Forts were not the first beings to have straddled both realms. And those who preceded them didn't take kindly to the invasion.

He raised a hand and pressed at his temple. Virtual or not, he was getting a headache.

"I'll tell you later," he said. "Keep going."

Warming up the subterranean hardcaster. The springing of the trap. His flight from the Luminous through the crust of the planet. Hiding in a pile of burning frags as though he was one of them. Reaching the surface.

We know what you're doing, and we're learning to do what you do—fast.

The rifle had fired, blowing a fist-sized hole in his neck. He had dropped like a stone. A spray of blood—freezing almost instantly—had painted the icy ground red. The version of Himself who had fired stepped closer and fired two more times into the fallen body, just to make sure. Imre's face stiffened as he watched the butchery, but he didn't feel unjustly treated. He would have done the same had their positions been reversed.

Emlee's account didn't stop there. The three black-clad figures had gone about their business, unaware they were being closely observed. One had raised his visor, giving her the opportunity for the shot Imre had first seen. The second had watched the sky and the strange events taking place around the rocky world. The third had fired down the ramp at a cluster of silver spheres that had been drawn by the gunshots. The three didn't seem at all concerned by the attention. Indeed, as more of the Luminous had issued from other nearby entrances, they had gone about killing them with cool, methodical detachment. Even when the spheres abandoned their previous unwillingness to fire, the three had simply squatted to present smaller targets and fired on.

"Something's not right," Imre said, watching the skirmish. "They shoot the spheres, but the spheres don't explode right away."

"I noticed that too," she said, freezing the picture. "What do you think it means?"

"The explosions are internally triggered. If they weren't rigged to blow up, they'd just drop right to the ground, dead."

"But what's killing them?"

"The rifles, obviously. Some sort of new weapon." He thought back to a conversation he and Emlee had had about Q loop technology before his death. *We're learning to do what you do . . .* "I think they're turning Luminous technology back on itself. I think the guns are producing a miniature Slow Wave effect that's killing their internal loop shunts—and killing them too, into the bargain." He nodded, satisfied that the theory fit the evidence.

"That wasn't what killed you, though," she said. "That was ordinary munitions."

He shrugged. *I'm not dead,* he wanted to remind both of them. *I'm right here.* "So the rifles have a dual function. Complex but not unheard of. If they knew they would be coming up against humans as well as the Luminous, I could understand it."

"They did know. You were the bait in their trap."

"But why? To test the weapons?"

"Maybe. I didn't see anything like them on Hyperabad."

He barely heard her. He answered his own question with a quick shake of the head. "No. Those rifles aren't prototypes. They've seen some use. So what, then, were they testing?"

There was something growing in his mind like a balloon, pressing for attention. He studied the image for a clue as to what it might be. Something he had missed, perhaps, or forgotten about. Something other than the ruins, the three figures in black, the weird guns . . .

A line of blue sparks stretched upward from the horizon directly behind the two nearest figures.

The bubble popped. "Not the rifles." Imre spoke rapidly, chasing the thoughts as they came to him. "What was happening above us. That's what this was all about. I trigger the spheres; the spheres call in something else. Whatever that thing was in the sky. Maybe it was there all along, but it only became active when summoned. Did you see it?"

She shook her head.

"It's huge, everywhere, but you can't really see it directly. Just the effect it has on the stars behind it. Otherwise, it's invisible." He snapped his fingers. "Lensing. It's lensing the light through gravity. And that, whatever it was, is what our friends here were attacking. They collapsed the moons to fight it. The moons were the weapons."

"That's insane. If they can implode moons so easily, why do they need weapons like that?"

"Because their enemy won't be affected by implosions, or explosions for that matter. Because ordinary weapons won't work on them. That's why they need degenerate matter. Gravity is the only weapon they have."

She thought it through, catching up fast. He could almost see the words scrolling across her eyes: *dark matter detectors*.

"I'm not sure I buy it," she said.

"I'm not sure I do either. It's a very long call."

"And there's one thing we haven't even touched on yet," she said. The magic picture changed back to the first one she had shown him. "Who 'they' are."

Imre's face looked out at him, angular and hostile. He was silent.

"You've never really stopped trying to put the pieces of yourself together," she said, her eyes hot and angry. "I know that. It's understandable. You came back changed; the Jinc couldn't assemble all your memories. Who wouldn't want to find out as much as he could about himself? Especially someone like you, with such a problematic history to unpack. You screwed us all over before the Slow Wave, but you convinced me in the end that you weren't the same person you used to be. That doesn't mean I trust you, but it means you were worth a second chance. A *first* chance, really, since the old Imre blew his. And now I see this"—she indicated the image without turning her head to look at it—"and I wonder if you haven't been playing us for fools all along."

"Emlee—"

"Don't interrupt. Just answer my questions. How long have you known about this other version of you—the one who Graduated?"

He considered lying, then decided against it. She had obviously worked it out from the clues he had: the loop shunt in his sanctuary, his obvious nervousness around the frags in the ruins, a hint or two from MZ, then the appearance of Himself on Spargamos. She would know if he wasn't telling the truth.

"Ever since Kismet," he said, walking restlessly across the room and back. "Suspected, not known for sure."

"Was that who you were trying to contact on Earth, through the loop shunt?"

"I don't know what I was trying to do," he said. The strange visions he had received rose up in his mind. He vigorously suppressed them. It was the wrong time to contemplate that madness. "Not to strike a deal with him, though. That I swear."

"Why should I believe you?"

"Let's go back to Kismet. The Baron who talked to me."

"That was one of his frags?"

"I believe so."

"What did he say? We couldn't decrypt the transmission, and you would never tell us what it was about."

The Aldobrand Cipher, again. "He offered me the deal you saw him talking about back there." He indicated the picture frame. "Stop digging, and they'd leave us in peace."

"You didn't stick to that deal."

"No."

"And what have you found out about them?"

"Hardly anything. You know about as much as I do now."

"The Fort version of you was involved in Domgard—
might still be involved, somewhere. The experiment moved
after the Slow Wave. You survived somehow."

"Not me. He tried to *erase* the old me, the one who knew
about the Mad Times, the decision he made." His emotions
were rising; he found it hard to keep them in check. "He and the
Forts were working together on Domgard. He betrayed you and
everyone else for this fucking experiment. Then the Slow Wave
happened. He was here when the Forts died, but obviously
some of him survived elsewhere. And he wasn't relying on loop
shunts. He had a safety net. The parts of him that survived
tracked each other down, following the clues. They were more
than just frags; they were independent, self-aware. They had to
be if he was going to survive a disaster like the Slow Wave."

"You think he saw it coming?" She watched him as he
crossed the room, back and forth.

"No. Maybe. I think he was paranoid. I think he still is—
and maybe he's right to be. Someone killed the Forts. I don't
think it was him, since he was one of them. I don't think it was
the experiment—except in the sense that it might have cat-
alyzed someone else's actions. Who was that someone else? I
don't know. It could be dark matter aliens or the Father fucking Christmas for all the difference it makes to us right this
second." He faced her squarely. "Are you going to erase me?"

"That was never my intention. You don't get off so easily."
She began to say more, then stopped. He waited her out.

"When did aliens come into this?" she asked.

He unspooled everything that had happened since his resurrection and realized that she knew nothing of his conversation with the silver sphere at the center of Spargamos: the
dissident Luminous who had dropped dire hints of creatures
predating humanity that might have taken umbrage at the
Forts' experiments.

Again, he considered lying, claiming that he hadn't meant
it seriously.

Again, he dismissed that tactic. She deserved to know the
truth, and he had to tell someone. Render was half a galaxy
and twenty thousand years away. He needed to get the pieces
of the puzzle out of his head because, in the process of doing

so, he could see them more clearly. For all he knew, the mystery of Domgard, Himself, and the Luminous was solvable right then and there, but he simply hadn't realized it.

I am telling you the truth. Not the whole truth but part of it.

So what is the whole truth?

Until you are ready to trust us, why would I tell you anything more?

"If I tell you," he said, "will you take me home?"

She unrolled a chart on the desk and showed him the tiny dot moving slowly across the gulf between two of the galaxy's spiral arms. The empty space around it seemed very large.

"We're already on our way."

MZ's virtual world had light but no obvious light sources. Without a sun it was difficult to track time passing. Imre didn't know how long he and Emlee talked through their experiences on Spargamos, but he was exhausted by the end of it, and they had garnered no blinding revelations. The best they could do was compile a hypothetical time line, which Imre clung to as justification for the trip, even if it was ultimately, and perhaps likely, to be falsified.

He sketched it out in a simple mental file, an exercise he had occasionally performed since he had been awakened by the Jinc and discovered that his memory was incomplete.

Five hundred thousand years ago, plus:

▶ The Forts begin working on a means to interact with the dark matter "shadow" universe.

▶ Imre Bergamasc is recruited to work with them, earning a reputation as the "architect of Domgard."

▶ The Forts' experiments are conducted in secret but nonetheless attract the attention of someone inimical to their success.

"Someone of alien origin?" Emlee asked, as they picked over that particular point.

"I don't think we should make up our minds, either way," he said. "Until we have evidence, it would be foolish to assume anything."

"Could be misinformation, planted to distract us."

"Exactly."

The next point was less contentious.

Five hundred thousand years ago, Absolute:
 ▸ Domgard is attacked and the Slow Wave unleashed.

"We're assuming the two events were simultaneous," she said.

"No reason not to. There were frags there when the Forts died."

"Okay."

Five hundred thousand years ago, minus:
 ▸ The fragments of Imre's Fort-self converge with the intention of continuing the experiment, this time under greater secrecy still. He erases all pre-Fort remains of himself in the process, to prevent anyone following the trail back to him.

"I thought he did that before," Emlee said, "when he made the decision to join Domgard."

"Possibly both."

 ▸ Despite his best efforts, one record is recovered by the Jinc. This remnant Imre Bergamasc knows nothing about Domgard but manages to uncover some of the truth in the aftermath of the Slow Wave.

 ▸ During this time all attempts to repair the Continuum are hampered by two groups: the Luminous (silver spheres) and the Barons (human). Both groups are also working in competition with each other.

 ▸ Fort-Bergamasc pursues his remnant to Mandala Supersystem, where, working with the Barons, he tries first to kill his remnant, then second to warn him off the scent.

"So your former self and the Barons are definitely working together."

"I think so," he said. "We don't have the chain of command in front of us, but they seem to be linked."

"That means it was you on Hyperabad, killing Ampersand."

"It's likely," he admitted. "I'm sorry."

"It wasn't you," she said through clenched teeth, obviously reminding herself as much as him. "It wasn't you."

Three hundred thousand years ago, plus and minus:

▸ The remnant Bergamasc founds the Returned Continuum while Imre's Fort-self goes underground again to work on anti-Luminous weapons and, presumably, ongoing Domgard experiments.

▸ Upon discovering the location of the original Domgard experiments, the fragment Imre Bergamasc returns to Spargamos, which has been staked out by three groups: the Luminous; an enigmatic movement within the Luminous that he has encountered before; and his Fort-self.

▸ Fort-Bergamasc kills the fragment and declares that the amnesty is over.

▸ A battle employing gravity weapons and novel "wave guns" ensues between the Luminous and the Barons, outcome uncertain.

"And here we are," Emlee said, looking as mentally drained as he felt. "What's missing?"

"That's the question." He walked slowly around the table, restless but feeling none of the frenetic desperation of earlier in their journey. He thought of the three dark figures standing on the Spargamos plain, with long, slender rifles in their hands. Emlee had coined the term "wave guns" offhand for the rifles that had killed the spheres on Spargamos, and the name had immediately stuck. "Are you sure nothing important happened on Spargamos before you left? Nothing at all of note?"

"Look for yourself if you don't believe me."

They reviewed the footage together. It showed the Imre's Fort-self going about their business on the dead world, mainly killing the Luminous and studying the sky as their new weaponry went to work. No one buried the body he had left behind, freezing slowly into deep-cold ice. No one seemed to give it a second thought. Emlee kept her POV firmly on the planet rather than the sky above, so any glimpses of the unfolding battle were secondhand at best.

When the black-clad trio had descended into the ruins and failed to reappear several hours later, Emlee had turned her attention to the matter of going home and resurrecting him on the way.

"Where do I fit in now?" he asked her. "They think I'm dead."

She shrugged. "You know yourself well enough to assume there'd be contingencies in place. You hardcasted into Spargamos; therefore, you can resurrect at your point of origin."

"But they don't know where that point of origin is."

"Yes. That's something. MZ doesn't feature in this picture at all. And neither does the ghost."

"We need to know where the Luminous came from," he said, noting the point but moving on to the crux of the situation. "And we need to know more about their internal divisions."

"The Jinc worshipped them," she said. "Perhaps that would be a good place to start."

He could have kissed her. "Yes, yes—that's exactly right." His elation soon faded. "But how to find them? They're right out on the edge of the galaxy and constantly moving around. It could take hundreds of thousands of years just to catch them."

"True." They stared at the chart on the table in front of them. The black dot of the *Wickthing* was drawing close to Earth.

"This could all be moot," Imre said, "if Helwise has been talking to the Barons on the sly."

Emlee's eyebrows went up. "Is that what you think she's been doing?"

"It makes sense if she's worked things out as we just have.

She's a singleton; he's a Fort. He wants the Returned Continuum to leave him alone; I think she wants me off the scene. I turned my back on her, but my original self might not have. If she tracked him down . . ." He didn't finish the sentence. He didn't need to. The mad grand master might be playing by herself now, but the game went on.

"That's an unhappy picture," she said.

"But maybe it solves the issue of Ra's parentage. He's not my son at all, but *his*."

She punched him in the shoulder. "Now you're looking too hard for an upside."

"There must be one. I'm sure of it."

"Would you rather I hadn't brought you back?"

He thought about it. He thought about the Jinc, too. If they hadn't stumbled across his remains and rebuilt him just different enough from his original self to resist joining the Domgard experience, he would have been spared everything that had happened to him since and was likely to happen to him in the near future.

But the galaxy would have been "spared" the Returned Continuum too, and he wasn't about to give up all hope for the future. There was always a way out.

"Absolutely not," he said. "What about you? Wishing we'd left you on Hyperabad to bust out Render on your own?"

Positive and negative emotions chased themselves across her face. "Now there's a question."

"We have arrived," MZ announced. The Fort's voice was as emotionless as a machine's. "Shall I create an interface with Hansfaall Base, as I did last time?"

Imre and Emlee looked up at the picture frame, in which an image of the moon from close quarters had appeared, as grey and brilliant as an ingot of selenium. Their tempos had returned to Absolute, he noticed; otherwise, the dusty orb would have been spinning like a top.

"We should have been paying closer attention," Imre said.

"Time just flies, doesn't it?"

"Hold for now, MZ. I want to know what we're walking into before going anywhere. Can you interface with the Apparatus without shutting it down like you did last time?"

"We can exchange communications, yes." The Fort melted a little. He sounded weary and disappointed, as though the trip to Spargamos had been decidedly unsuccessful from his point of view.

"Do it, please," Imre said. He had thought long and hard about MZ during their time-compressed journey. "I want to rescind that ban you mentioned. The ban on your ever returning to Earth."

Emlee paused in the act of rolling up the map. An undefined tension swept through the illusion.

"I would be grateful for that," said the Fort.

"You sound surprised. That was the deal, wasn't it? Or did you think I would renege?"

MZ said nothing.

"Let me just say this," Imre went on. "I'm not doing it in return for taking us to Domgard. You kept your cards pretty close to your chest throughout that entire venture. In fact, you could have told us everything you professed to know without our ever leaving the Throne Room, so the trip actually made things harder for us, not easier."

MZ said nothing.

"You had another reason to take us with you, and it wasn't entirely altruistic. It was to see what we provoked. I'm not saying you knew about the trap the Luminous had laid for us, or about the Barons and their plans, but I bet you thought something was going on. Maybe you figured out that Domgard is still running somewhere. Maybe you want in on their action. Maybe you want to make up for what you did here on Earth."

MZ said nothing.

"Well," said Imre, "let me say that if you were trying to get someone's attention, you've definitely got *mine*. I'm here, and I'm listening to you. I hope you're listening to me in return. I'd like to cut the others out of the equation, right now, by offering you something that I think you do really want. We both know that Domgard might keep you occupied for a while—but isn't going to give you a home. That's what you've been missing all these years. I can give it to you in five minutes. You'd be insane to turn me down; because if I win without you, you'll never come within a light-year of this place ever again. And if I lose, who knows what will be left of Earth for you to visit afterward? This could be your last chance—to see Earth, to connect with the world you fled from, and to give something back to humanity."

Emlee went to speak. Imre waved her silent.

"Do we have a deal, MZ?"

"We have a deal."

"Good," he said, not hiding his relief, "because I think you might be the most important person in the galaxy right now, and I'm fairly certain that in the near future I'm going to need your help."

The planet Earth had barely altered since he had last seen it. Sea levels had risen a meter or two, but in fifty thousand years a lot worse could have happened. He had become used to the Earth always being there on his return from whistle-stop tours and other long jaunts—unchanging, fixed in time like a living fossil. Its face was a welcome sight.

Earth—the capital of the Returned Continuum—however, was a world besieged. Every berth on Smitherman City was occupied. Queues of ships filled the docking orbits while stations on the moon and several near-Earth asteroids strained to take the overflow. Constant broadcasts warned ships away, but the sky remained bright with artificial stars: the drive flares of new arrivals decelerating into the system, hundreds of them, coming in a steady stream to the home world.

It wasn't just ships. Every hardcaster berth was full, with a waiting list decades long. Data jammed the Line solid across all channels. There wasn't an iota of spare bandwidth any-where. Imre had to worm his way into an emergency channel, using his First Prime privileges, just to see what was going on. The Citadel's reinforced firewalls were holding, just. Smither-man City's infrastructure had clearly taken a sustained pound-ing too. If it fell, the onslaught might not be containable. Unauthorized hardcasts were already being diverted into the Round as a matter of course. How long, Imre wondered, until someone decided that erasing them was the only available solution?

The reason for the chaos was buried deep in the Citadel—not just behind security protocols, which he or Emlee could have picked apart with ease, but in a mountain of data that was growing higher by the minute. The Apparatus, when he asked it, could only provide a list of facts without a clear chain of causation.

Under an embargo that had been in place for 1,212 years, the shining jewel of the empire was beginning to look a little tarnished.

The longer he stared at it, the deeper his heart sank.

"We have to get in there," Emlee said.

Imre nodded. That was self-evident. Earth was the calm at the center of an immense hurricane, and the storm might become a thousand times worse if left to build unchecked. There would, therefore, be no mad dash to confront the Barons until his house was in order.

"The Adytum," he said, "my hideout. There are two hardcasters under the floor. You saw one of them."

Emlee's gaze danced to the window of the study, through which Kells was still busy pacing out MZ's illusory boundaries. He seemed happy enough, and Imre was confident he could trust MZ to get the uploading right.

"And then what?" she asked. "Invade the Citadel, the two of us?"

"We find out what's gone wrong, first, before doing anything at all." In the back of his mind was the hope that Helwise had screwed up innocently, but in a significant way, providing the justification for him to step in and remove her from the hierarchy. He doubted, however, that life would ever present him with such a simple solution.

"Don't go anywhere, MZ," he told the Fort. "Wait right where you are unless you hear from me. Okay?"

"I will do so."

Imre nodded, sure that MZ would actually go wandering, testing his new ability to explore Earth, but sure also that he would remain alert for word from him. Short of shutting down the Apparatus again, there was little MZ could do to stop Imre from reinstating the ban at any moment.

Imre gave him the address for the two hidden hardcasters and the access codes required to activate them. Emlee closed her eyes to avoid disorientation, but Imre kept his eyes open, watching her. Would they leave at the same time, he wondered, or would she go first, vanishing from his vision like a mirage? If they had been holding hands, would her flesh fall away like smoke, or would it ripple and shift under his fingers, dissolving piece by piece until there was nothing left to grip?

He had time to think of the Catholic enclaves' barbaric resistance to hardcasting—on the grounds that it stripped a body of its soul, despite repeated experiments proving that no such thing had ever existed—

Then his atoms stirred. He took first breath in his brand-new body, held it, and let it go through pursed lips. Earth's air, definitely, even from inside a hardcaster.

The sarcophagus lid hissed and opened. He looked up into Render's mismatched eyes.

"You picked up the override codes," Imre said, sitting and taking the old soldier's proffered hand. "I thought you might."

Render hauled him out of the sarcophagus as easily as he would a child. The feeling of free fall was brief but exhilarating. When Imre landed on his feet, he let go and looked around for some clothes. He was stark naked.

They weren't alone. Alice-Angeles, his Secretary of Affairs, stood by the bed, chairs and table in the center of the cross. She held her hands behind her back and carried herself without embarrassment. That was one emotion Imre had never seen her display.

"First Prime," she said, bowing to show him respect.

He stared at her for a second, then nodded in return. He had never brought her to the Adytum before, so that must have been Render's initiative.

The black cabinet containing the loop shunt was sealed tight, brooding unobtrusively in its niche.

Imre took a robe from a cupboard and wrapped it around himself.

"Same old smile," said Render from behind him. Imre turned in time to see the old soldier help Emlee from her casket. The tenderness with which Render spoke and moved conveyed volumes about their relationship. They had never been lovers—Render had several hundred thousand years in age on her, for starters—but as two Primes in the previously Fort- and singleton-dominated world of the Corps, their closeness had been automatic and genuine. "It's been a long, long time."

She blinked away the last of her posthardcast confusion and stepped lightly onto the ground. As naked as Imre had been, she hugged her old friend and looked around. "Got another one of those?" she asked Imre, indicating the robe.

"Or similar." He rummaged for something she could wear and tossed her a gown that was far too long for her slight frame. The hem dragged behind her as she walked to join Alice-Angeles. The two women acknowledged each other.

"What's she doing here?"

"I don't know," Imre admitted. "It's new to me too."

Render slouched into an armchair and put one foot up on the table. "Tell my friends," he said to Alice-Angeles. "I don't know if I can do it."

"The Returned Continuum is under threat," Alice-Angeles said, her tone level and unhurried as they seated themselves around her. Imre sat next to Emlee, crossed his legs, and bounced one foot restlessly. "Recruitment has reached its lowest level in history and will fall to zero within the next thousand years. Secession is on a steep rise. Forty-seven alliances have formed between outlying systems specifically to replace this regime with another of their choosing. These alliances appear to be uniting along a common front. Line sabotage and insurgency are at an all-time high. Conduits in a majority of systems have come under institutional attack. Analysts predict the collapse of the Returned Continuum within ten thousand years."

Imre took a moment to absorb the brutal summary. He

didn't doubt that "institutional attack" also included physical assaults on the many intermediaries he had trusted to stand between Earth and other systems. Since many of them were copies of Al Freer, he was sure the response had been swift.

"Show me a map," he said.

Alice-Angeles brought up a three-dimensional display in his field of view. He rotated it, viewing it from all sides and from below. The red stain of dissolution made the galaxy look like it was hemorrhaging.

"Where do the Round systems stand?" he asked.

"With Earth, as always."

Imre took little comfort from that answer. Earth and the Returned Continuum weren't necessarily synonymous. "What's Helwise been doing about this?"

"She whispers," said Render.

"And?" Imre was keen to leave the issue of her possible relationship with the Barons until after some of the broader canvas was filled in.

"Military spending is up," Alice-Angeles said. "Citadel security has been strengthened."

"We noticed the new firewalls," Emlee said. "They look pretty tight."

The frag nodded. "Incursion rates remain high, despite that."

"She's backed herself into a corner," Imre said. "It's all very well to feel safe here, but if the rest of the galaxy turns against her, the Round won't hold. Either way, she'll end up with a fleet on our doorstep, and there'll be no escape for anyone." He fumed silently to himself for a moment. "I can't believe she's been that stupid."

"Could it be a scam?" Emlee asked.

He shrugged. "It's possible." If she had taken his absence as an aggressive move—seeking allies of his own, for instance, among the partial Forts—then who knew what desperate Plan B she had prepared? "She knew roughly how long we'd be gone, because Al would have told her. Engineering a revolution is exactly the sort of thing we used to do in the Corps; she could time it in her sleep with our return. She blames the mess on us; she emerges holding my head on a platter; confidence is restored."

"But why would she do that? If she's in league with the Barons and your other self, how would deposing you so publicly help her put him on the throne?"

"I don't know."

Render looked questioningly at Emlee, then at Imre.

"She knows what my old self did," Imre told him. "There's more, too. We'll fill you in later."

"All things change, I suppose." Render didn't seem particularly nonplussed. He looked amused, if anything, and resigned to waiting to hear about their mission. "So this is the news. Are you afraid?"

"Should I be?"

"I haven't decided."

"We shouldn't have gone," Emlee said in a fatalistic tone. "It doesn't matter why Helwise is doing this. We gave her time to set it up."

"It started further back than that," Imre said, "when she brought Ra into the world. And then there are the transmissions. She's had this in train since before we came back from Dussehra."

Render waved that thought away. "What's done is done. Don't cry 'til this thing is over."

Imre nodded, accepting that the game had been in progress whether he had wanted to play or not. Following the phantasm's word had set in motion a series of moves that no one could fully control. And now he felt trapped by the rules of the game. Even stepping away from it for fifty thousand years hadn't stopped it. He knew of only one way now to bring it to an end. But that he would keep for an absolute last resort.

"We haven't considered," he said, "the possibility that it's all for real."

"What do you mean?" asked Emlee.

"Well, the Barons on Spargamos told us that the deal was off. This could be all their work—with or without Helwise at the helm."

She shook her head. "Nice try, but no. They haven't had time. It's absolutely impossible for anything to travel faster than we did coming here, so the revolution must have been well under way before we left. Maybe Helwise could have tried harder to ameliorate the situation, but it was always going to end like this."

"That doesn't mean it's not partly my fault."

"I don't care," Render said. "You've got your principles—or so I'm told. I'll stand by your side." His smile came and went as quickly as a guillotine falling. "I'm cheap to rent."

Silence filled the Adytum. There was little, for the moment, left to say.

"How long have you two been sleeping together?" Emlee asked, apropos of nothing at all.

Render looked startled. His leg came down off the table, and he sat up straight. A kaleidoscope of emotions passed across his face. "How in the world—"

"She's a frag. You never—"

"I know that. She just caught me off guard."

Emlee looked at Alice-Angeles, who stared back at her without rancor or any other identifiable emotion. Imre had just about as much trouble reading Emlee. Her guard was tightly up.

"Is that a problem?" Imre asked her.

"God, no." She stood and looked around. "Does this place have a shower? I'd like to freshen up before saving the world."

Imre pointed at the nave, through the labyrinth of bookcases. "In there."

"Thanks."

He watched her as she walked away, hips swinging under the robe, bare feet padding silently on the stone floor. He waited until he heard the door of the bathroom sealing shut before saying, "She could just tell?"

"It's been a long, long time," Render said again, his grizzled mask back in place.

Imre glanced at Alice-Angeles and still saw nothing but affable compliance. Maybe that was what Render liked.

Imre didn't want to think about it anymore.

"I'm going to follow Emlee's lead," he said. "There must be a lot more you're not telling me, even here. So I'll sleep and let it filter through the usual ways. Maybe I can see something we're missing, talking like this."

Render nodded and stood. "I'll leave you. Sweet dreams."

"First Prime." Alice-Angeles bowed and followed Render to the door.

"Don't be afraid to tell Helwise we've arrived," Imre called after them. "If it comes up."

Render cast a crooked grin over his shoulder. "It will."

He dreamed of the Returned Continuum as a many-headed Hydra, devouring itself on several fronts at once. Sabotage—that perennial corrosive—ate away at the fabric of the galactic civilization, cutting off systems and corrupting information when it was most needed. Dissent turned neighbors against each other and painted distant Earth as a rogue and blood-sucker. Assassination created an atmosphere of fear and inde-cision, especially when key personnel could not be replaced in time to avoid the desired backslide into isolationism.

"War's in the air," Render whispered in his dream. "No shelter, no sanctuary. Everything breaks down."

These were forces that Imre had been battling for thou-sands of years. They were nothing new to him. The difference now was that these same forces appeared to be coordinating in a way they never had before, combating the twin memes of Church and Continuum at the same time. He watched with a creeping sense of dread. It was as though the Barons had reached out from Spargamos, defying every known physical law in the process, and set their terrible endgame in motion. If they could indeed do that, despite Emlee's protestations, then there was no power he could summon to stop them.

He heard himself telling Gravamen Zerah—it felt like an eternity ago—that the Returned Continuum was less an em-pire than an idea. He was fond of that metaphor because it carried with it the notion that ideas didn't have enemies; nei-ther could they be fought with conventional weapons. Ideas could creep through any thickness of armor, bypass any num-ber of blockades, survive any megatonnage of firepower. They could regroup and reemerge stronger than ever.

But they could be stolen, and they could definitely be sub-verted. They couldn't be quantified, and they weren't perma-nent. Nothing humanity had ever created would live forever.

Imre watched the Hydra tear into its own flesh, wondering if the idea of galactic peace had run its course. Perhaps someone had devised a new meme to take its place. That would explain the unnerving strength of this new uprising as it boiled up through the Carina Arm and came ever closer to Sol.

Delegates from these trouble spots were divided. Some wanted the unrest immediately quelled, no matter what. They raved of ruthless zealots and deadly attacks on civilian outposts. Others counseled diplomatic solutions: engaging in frank talks with the dissidents, finding out what exactly they wanted, from whom. Neither side was satisfied: the evidence pointed to conventional tactics and an honorable, if voracious, expansion, while little word had been had from the source of the unrest itself. It seemed, for all Imre's perception of it as a Hydra, to be headless, leaderless, unanimous. That set it apart from the Returned Continuum immediately. There was no manifesto or figurehead to negotiate with. The movement didn't even have a name.

But it was coming, whatever it was. Render's data was unequivocal on that point. Alice-Angeles talked about the Returned Continuum unraveling as though a woolen jumper had snagged a thread. Render saw one will everywhere behind the many-fronted threat. The question Imre would have sorely loved answered was: did the threat originate in Helwise, the Barons, or someone else?

That question tainted the dream, turned what should have been objective data to subjective psychopomp. A random detail supplied by Render—that Helwise had taken a lover to her bed in absolute secrecy, so no one knew his or her identity—only completed the picture. The image of a Hydra biting its own back became one of him and Helwise engaged in a vigorous act of copulation, with her bent forward and him thrusting into her from behind, while the four terrorists he had had executed on Dussehra watched impassively from the sidelines. Helwise's fingernails scratched at his thighs. She turned with unnatural flexibility to snap at the hand holding her head down. The act was violent but in love with the violence, so as much as it was about abuse and debasement, it was also consensual and, in a strange way, empowering.

Once, the thought of it would have excited him. Now it left him cold.

The dream underwent a perspective shift in which nothing visibly changed, but he came to realize that the man in the vision wasn't him at all. It was his former self. The symbolism was obvious: here was the union between his former lover and reluctant ally and the person he had once been, from whom he had tried desperately to distance himself. He was being cuckolded by Himself. The double-backed beast they formed was inimical to his very existence. Even as the new understanding dawned on him, they turned to face him—and suddenly he was no longer in a position of privileged observation but part of the twisted fantasy, whether he wanted to be or not.

The hands of the four dead dissidents reached for him and held him tight. He couldn't fight the dream, and he didn't know how to wake up. Helwise and his other self lunged for him, and the fear that he might be raped by Himself while Helwise held him down burned like gasoline in his veins. He writhed, unable to escape, and equally unable to tell if he was excited or terrified by the thought.

Helwise pressed him down on the bed of the galaxy and rode him as she had ridden him the last time they had slept together—the first time he had had sex with anyone after returning to the masculine state on Hyperabad. He fought her, knowing that he could have no part of her twisted desires any longer. That game was long played out, and had been the moment he'd discovered the truth of her grisly self-murders.

He struggled. She pressed harder. He tried to throw her off him, but an arm came around his throat from behind and held him down. He flailed at it but wasn't strong enough to dislodge its grip. Muscles bunched under his fingertips. He choked under the relentless crushing force. His treacherous body began to respond to the peril he was in, thinking with a primal part of his brain that he would suffocate even though he knew that was impossible. He flailed, recognizing the arm holding him down as one belonging to Himself and knowing that the two of them would happily choke the life out of him once they'd taken their fill. He was nothing to them, just a gadfly Prime to be tolerated or swatted, depending on their whim. As Helwise reared up over him and became the many-headed Hydra again, Imre could only weep at the pointlessness of it all.

"Don't start that," said a voice that didn't originate in the dream. "Don't you dare start that."

The dream didn't want to let go of him, but the intrusion of reality was too powerful. The blackness of space became the red-tinged twilight of the Adytum. Someone was astride him, but it was neither Hydra nor Helwise. Her forearm pressed firmly down on his Adam's apple, applying the crushing force that he had felt in the dream.

"For God's sake, don't you start," Emlee said, and she was weeping too.

Her body was lean, curved, and very strong. He moved inside her by instinct, feeling the wet coolness of her on his stomach and heat everywhere else. He looked up at her, and she raised her other hand and put it down hard over his face, twisting his head to one side. She moved faster, more urgently, as though afraid that what she had started she wouldn't be able to finish.

He sent a mental command to turn the lights out, and the Adytum plunged into darkness.

Afterward, he rolled off her, breathing heavily, and went to leave her to whatever process she was obviously working through.

Using her excellent night vision, she snatched at his wrist with an unbreakable grip. "I wasn't in love with him," she said. "That wasn't what this was about."

"That's okay. You don't have to explain."

"And you don't have to go. Why don't we try doing what doesn't come naturally, just this once? We don't have to make a habit of it."

He fell back onto the mattress with his eyes wide open. When he switched to infrared, he could see her leaning on one elbow beside him, glowing like iron straight from a furnace.

"Tell me what you were dreaming about," she said, "when I came in."

He thought about refusing. The parts he could remember were unsettling and so obvious they didn't need interpretation. He was embarrassed as much by the clumsy execution of his subconscious fears as he was by the fears themselves.

Emlee had seen him dead. That fact unraveled his resistance. He had died plenty of times as a singleton, but never before as a Prime. He had died, and she had brought him back to life.

He told her what he could recall of the dream: of watching Himself and Helwise fucking over the Milky Way, then being forced to join them in their unholy embrace. The dream came with feelings of despair, and the fear of choking, and there had been something about a mythical creature with many heads too. A Hydra, perhaps.

It was hard to tell via infrared. Emlee might have been smiling to hear it.

"This is why I was never a singleton," she said. "I heard too many stories of onanistic orgies and clusterfucks spread across the entire galaxy. It's such a pointless thing to dedicate your life to."

Imre thought about his own life as a singleton. What had he worked toward, if not sex? War, control, obedience to the Forts—up to a point . . .

"Render was your protector," he said in sudden understanding of her situation. *I wasn't in love with him.* "He looked after you, made sure you were all right. I've always known that." He remembered Render fleeing through the burning *Pelorus* on the day of Imre's betrayal, determined to save her from the consequences of his decision. "I guess I've never really thought how it was from your side."

She nodded. "I didn't ask for it. He just gave it freely. Even when we were apart, I knew he'd come for me if I needed him, just as I would for him. We've always had that connection. That's why I was determined to rescue him in Mandala Supersystem. That was my first big chance to return the favor."

"And we did it."

"We did. He took a while to get over it, but he's been fine lately. I check on him when we're around. He's as strong as steel, but it doesn't take much to shatter him if you know where to tap. So Alice-Angeles came out of nowhere. She blindsided me. But I know where it comes from, inside him. I know what it means."

"He's protecting her now."

Her head dipped again. "It's not that simple. He is protecting her—and it makes me nervous to think that she needs protecting now, of all times. Render's best placed to see what's coming, even if he can't communicate it very well. Maybe we all need protection."

"Don't worry," he said. "It'll be all right."

"I'm not looking for empty reassurances," she said in a sharp tone. The bright, hot patches of her eyes came up and bored into him. "That's not what this is about."

Not empty, he wanted to say, but he knew arguing about that wasn't going to get them anywhere.

He waited her out, and eventually she said, "He's also taken on Alice-Angeles because he thinks I don't need protecting anymore."

"Well, that's a good thing."

"No, because in his universe, no one stands alone. There's always someone to watch your back. He's watching Alice-Angeles's the way he used to watch mine—and she's watching his in return, within the Citadel, because she's more than just a sex doll to him, no matter how it looks from the outside. She must have some kind of an internal life, whatever that means for a frag as old as she is." Emlee shook her head and brought herself back to the important point. "Maybe you and I were gone too long, this trip. Maybe he's been building up to something like this for a while, and it would've happened anyway. Maybe, from his point of view, I'm the one who made the move first, not him. Either way, the connection is broken."

"Do you think the argument you had here made it worse— the one about bringing Chyro Kells back from the dead?" He remembered Render saying, *Die if you want to. I want to be, to overdose on time.*

"Oh, no," she said. "That was nothing to do with today. It's all about you, I'm afraid. I'm your bodyguard. I watch your back. And I guess you finally proved that you could look after mine in return. So he moved on and found someone else to keep an eye on—to give him a reason to stick around, perhaps. He cut me loose because he knew you'd take up the slack."

Imre just looked at her.

"Dussehra clinched it, I think," she went on. "He would have read the reports. I almost died. Then, yes, maybe bringing Kells back was the kicker. He understands that you'd probably bring me back whether I wanted you too or not. You proved to him that in your eyes I wasn't disposable."

But hadn't he already proved that on *Pelorus*, Imre wanted to ask. Hadn't his decision to trust Render and spare Emlee demonstrated that she was more important to him than any deal with the Forts?

Then he remembered that that wasn't him. That was his former self. The new Imre Bergamasc remained an unknown quantity, one caught up with running an empire, juggling Helwise's potential treachery and hunting down the past. Imre dragged Emlee around the galaxy without apparent thought for her safety and left Render back on Earth, where he was happy enough playing the loyal watchdog but utterly unable to help Emlee should she get into trouble. From Render's perspective, Imre still had a lot of ground to make up.

Imre felt as though a child had entrusted him with his favorite toy. But Emlee was far more than a toy. He was certain she didn't want anyone to see her that way.

"So why did you come here?" he asked her.

She turned away and looked out into the darkness. "Because I was hurt and confused, and maybe I wanted to test you too, a little."

"Did I pass or fail?"

"God only knows." She laughed, low and deep in her throat. It sounded almost relieved—that she *could* laugh under such circumstances. "I'll probably never have a good answer to that question."

He rolled onto his side to face her but avoided touching any part of her body, not sure where they stood in relation to each other now. Talking hadn't made things worse, but it had certainly revealed a complex emotional underbelly to her of which he hadn't previously been aware.

"Sometimes I think there are no good questions ever," he said.

"Because asking exposes your ignorance?"

"Yes, creating an immediate power imbalance."

"So who's in charge now? Me or you?"

He smiled. "The fact that you're asking the question tells me everything I need to know."

"It's going to be like that, is it?"

"As long as you keep asking questions, I guess it will."

He didn't move as she sat up and straddled his stomach, pinning his upper arms with her knees. He had always thought of her as small, but he didn't have much on her in real terms. She was strong enough to hold him down on her own.

"I think you like this," she said, holding his jaw between thumb and fingers of her right hand and squeezing tight. "Is it because you want to be punished or because you want someone else to be in charge for a change?"

He tried to shake his head, but her fingers were holding him bruisingly tight. "Frankly," he said, "I'm trying not to overanalyze it."

"Is it just me, or everyone?"

"Just you."

"Well, that's something." She leaned down and, without removing her hand, kissed him hard on the lips. Her lips were hot, and so was her breath. He enjoyed it, and that surprised him.

She let him go and stared down at him. He felt the strong muscles bunching in her buttocks and thighs, as though she were tensing to spring to her feet. "It's time we went back to acting naturally, I think," she said, "before Helwise gets even more of a jump on us."

"It won't make any difference," he said, thinking of Render's rumor about a secret lover and hoping his dream wasn't prophetic. "She can't win."

That was the one thing he was sure of.

"I told you I didn't want any empty promises." She tilted her head, studying him from a different angle. "Or is this something to do with what you told MZ?"

"No. Nothing to do with him. He'll be important later, after we've won here."

She put both hands on his chest, with fingers splayed, and leaned a significant fraction of her weight on his ribs. "Okay, now you're freaking me out. I want to believe you, but there's all of Citadel security to deal with, plus everyone loyal to the Regent. You can't rely on the Apparatus because anything you tell it to do your other self could easily undo—"

"And then there's Ra. Don't forget him."

She mock-shuddered. "How could I?"

Imre had, until the thought of Render bequeathing Emlee to him had put the word "child" into his mind. "It really will be okay," he told her. "I'm concerned only with minimizing the damage."

"Want to let me in on your plans?"

"Not really," he said. "I don't think you'd approve."

She eased her weight back down onto his stomach. "As long as you haven't told Render or Al either, I won't feel out of the loop."

"They don't know anything."

She patted him once on the cheek, a little harder than he expected, then dismounted and went in search of her clothes.

They came in through the basements dressed in full ceremonial armor and making no effort to hide. Imre's heart was beating solidly and steadily, just a little faster than normal. He felt adrenalized, caffeinated, wired. The Citadel was buzzing around him, fueling that feeling. He could sense the thousands of people occupying its halls and corridors. He bathed in the data rushing around him, forming a complex web no single human mind could hold in its entirety. This tiny patch of Earth's surface was alive in the same way that the Continuum had once been. He could taste it in the air.

That taste had been with him for years. It accompanied him when he traveled; it welcomed him when he came home. He had become addicted to it and would find it hard to relinquish. He hoped it wouldn't come to that.

I don't think you understand, his former self had said, *the gravity of the situation.*

There was no doubt in his mind that he did understand it now. Nothing focused his thoughts better than a bullet to the head.

"Alice-Angeles?" He called his Secretary of Affairs as he rose up through the central pyramid, toward his offices. "Tell the Regent I need to see her in her office, immediately."

"Of course, First Prime."

"Ask Marshal Freer to join us."

"What about Render?" Emlee asked him.

"He'll be there. In fact, I bet he's already on the way."

Barely had he said the words when Render appeared at their sides, matching their pace as though he had always been there.

"I've been expecting you," he said.

"I told you. I was reviewing the data."

If Render suspected that anything else had been going on, it didn't show on his weathered face. "Nothing has changed."

"That's something. You'll be joining us, I presume?"

"You know me. I've an interest in games."

Helwise's office was on the same level as Imre's—symbolically so, he was sure. The executive offices around them were closed and empty. He wondered if the other staff had been ordered to leave on a moment's notice, or if the warning Imre had instructed Render to give had allowed Helwise time to clear some space.

For what? That was the question.

A full squad of six dome-helmeted guards stood to attention outside the entrance to the Regent's office. Imre approached without breaking step and came to a halt only when he was directly in front of them. Thus far, there had been so sign of Ra. Wherever the child was and whatever his function was intended to be, Imre was glad to have been spared that complication thus far.

The guards saluted him. He returned the honor, assessing them as he did so. There was a hard flatness to their voices that spoke of active rather than purely honorary duty. They wouldn't be completely useless, then, if it came to a firefight.

That they didn't look as though they were expecting one Imre took as a positive sign.

The doors opened and a thin, sexless attendant emerged, dressed in a grey skin suit with black piping.

"The Regent begs your forgiveness," the attendant announced in a respectful but firm voice. "She is occupied at the moment with a delegation from one of the dissenting colonies and will be but a moment."

"We'll wait right here," Imre said, "if that's fine with you."

"Perfectly fine, First Prime." The attendant bowed. "Your patience is greatly appreciated."

The doors closed behind the obsequious drone, and Imre folded his arms, prepared to give her five minutes before ordering the Apparatus to open the doors.

It took three. When the doors slid open, he didn't wait for the attendant to bid him enter. He strode in with Emlee standing close on his right side and occupied the center of the room. Render took up a position by the office's second door, which led to an adjoining audience chamber and was presently closed. The office itself was as large as Imre's, with a matching window looking south over the Atlantic Ocean. Apart from her sweeping desk, there were several chairs and two smaller desks, some of which had recently been occupied. A faint aroma of coffee hung in the air.

Helwise was half-standing behind her desk, dressed in an ornate burgundy robe with long sleeves bunched up at her wrists. Her hair was long, straight, and pulled forward over her left shoulder so that it hung almost down her waist. Her expression was one of calculated surprise, as though he had caught her off guard. Apart from three identical attendants, she was alone.

"Hello, stranger," she said, settling gracefully into the seat. She folded her arms and placed one long-nailed index finger on her right cheek. She wore no jewelry or insignia. The veil she normally affected lay in a liquid line across the marble desktop before her. Imre looked for any sign of armor under her robe and saw none. "How nice of you to drop by."

"I trust you least when you're being polite," he said. "I'm here to find out what you're up to."

She tilted her head like a cobra hypnotizing its prey. "That you think I'm up to anything confirms my worst fears. Our arrangement isn't working. We need to find new terms under which to govern."

No questions, Imre thought, and a preemptive strike. Perfectly in character. "There's no point discussing terms until I've heard the truth."

Helwise smiled. "The truth isn't hidden. It's right in front of you, if you'd only see it."

The door hissed open. Two men walked into the room. One was Al Freer, tall, angular, and looking more grey than ever. The second man wasn't immediately familiar to Imre. He radiated a powerful presence. His hair was long and full, with white-streaked black locks that swept behind his ears and rolled in waves down his back. His features were fine and his gaze commanding. He wore a blue uniform that emphasized his shoulders and chest. The blackness of his boots was flawless.

Never seen combat, was Imre's first thought, but directed enough campaigns to feel confident of his capabilities in the field. Would be dead in less than a second in a close fight, but has learned to keep a situation from ever coming to that. Imre had seen that kind of adept cowardice many times in his career. He had even learned a kind of respect for it, since there was no absolutely correct way to fight. Whatever drove people to succeed, he could live with it, as long as they did succeed.

While making this rapid assessment of the man's character, based solely on the way he carried himself, something clicked in Imre's mind. His second thought prompted him to double-take and reconsider his assessment.

The man was Ra MacPhedron.

He and Freer took in the situation at a glance: Helwise behind her desk, outnumbered but unperturbed; Imre in full armor before her, with Emlee close by; Render unobtrusively on the far side of the room, watching the attendants and the second entrance. Freer stepped two paces into the room and put his hands on his hips. He looked annoyed, as though interrupted in the middle of an important task and worried as to where the tension in the room might lead. Imre watched him. Freer was trained to follow the chain of command; if that chain suddenly snapped, his reaction could be unpredictable.

Ra walked around the desk to stand at his mother's side, leaving no question as to his allegiance. His gold-flecked blue eyes met Imre's unflinchingly.

"You're back," Ra said. "I trust your journey with the Fort proved worth the effort."

Imre added up the hostile edge to his voice, the lack of a bow, and the statement itself, and arrived at a simple conclusion. "You were too young," he said. "You're not a child now. You must appreciate my decision, in hindsight."

A faint suggestion of surprise at Imre's directness was quickly hidden. "Ancient history," Ra said, dismissing it with a wave of one gloved hand. "Not the ancient history I thought we were here to discuss."

Imre inclined his head. All right, he thought. We'll play it that way. "We found Volume Zero," he said. "It's a gripping tale. Perhaps we could discuss it over hot chocolate one bedtime. If your mother will let you stay up late, of course."

Ra's face turned bright red.

"There's no need to antagonize each other," said Helwise. "Imre, is this really necessary?"

Imre thought it was. Thanks to that simple exchange, the dynamic between mother and son had been demonstrated for all to see. When Ra was thrown off guard, Helwise defended him. She had raised a son who needed her more than she needed him—and in the process made herself vulnerable, whatever perceived advantage his existence gave her. It was all very well creating a puppet to put on a throne, but it was harder to defend two targets than one.

"We were talking about the truth," Imre said.

"Yes. The truth, quite simply, is that it's time for you to change your tactics. I understand the reasoning behind them; indeed, in the early days, I shared your belief in that reasoning. The Returned Continuum held, and we prevailed. Now, however, I feel the sand shifting beneath my feet. Our work could come to nothing if we don't adapt as required."

"To what, exactly?"

"Your absence is hurting the Returned Continuum," she said. "The whistle-stop tours, while sound in conception, have driven a wedge through the heart of the Citadel. There are people here and in the Round who have never met you. It's easy for them to forget that I am only Regent. They have come to see you as a figurehead and to wonder why we need a figurehead at all. They ask questions to which I have no ready answers."

"The Returned Continuum isn't Earth or the Round," he said. "Would you have us ignore the outer systems and turn our attention inward?"

"Not at all," she said, a picture of earnestness. "By all means continue the tours, if you are so confident of their efficacy. But we need you here as well."

He could see where she was going. "I'm not becoming a singleton."

"Then you're making a mistake," she said. "All the philosophy in the world can't change the fact that Primes don't have what it takes to run the galaxy. Look at the mess we're getting into now if you need proof of that."

"I thought you were running the galaxy," he said. "That's what a Regent is supposed to do."

"I'm trying to—but for whom? Whose best interests do I serve? It's no longer clear to me. If the Returned Continuum exists for Primes, why do you allow Al Freer to slaughter them in the name of long-term stability? If it's not for Primes, why not let singletons take over completely—with yourself as one of them again? If you don't trust singletons to do the job properly and can't bring back the Forts, what's the point of trying to maintain the illusion of a galactic civilization at all? What does it achieve?"

She got up from her chair and came around the desk, the hem of her robe making a soft sound on the floor as she walked. "I think I understand what it achieves for you," she said. "I can put the pieces together. You have some muddled dream of enacting revenge. But I'm afraid, Imre, that you're a small part in a conflict too big for you to comprehend. You might even be making things worse by provoking more trouble.

Whoever killed the Forts left us alone afterward. Can't we just accept that and move on?"

Imre thought of Spargamos and the battle between the Barons and the Luminous, the wave guns and the gravity weapons. For a second, he thought she might have a point.

"Move on to where?" Emlee asked. "We can't build Forts because someone is actively killing them when we try, and we can't govern ourselves as Primes without them."

"So become a singleton," Helwise said to her. "It is the only logical solution."

"And what happens to those who disagree with your logic? Discrimination, exile, secession? You talk about a wedge driven through the heart of the Citadel. This would drive a wedge right through the whole galaxy."

Helwise's eyes were cold and unflinching. "Better to govern half properly than none at all."

"What do you think, Al?" Imre asked Freer. "Where do you stand on this?"

The corner of the tall man's mouth turned down. "There's no denying we're over-stretched. But I think we're coping."

"Do you really?" Helwise snapped. "Do you read the reports from the outer systems?"

"There'll always be unrest," he said with bluff confidence. "Chances are there will be tough patches. We'll ride it out, as we've ridden it out before."

"I disagree," spoke up Ra. "Helwise and I feel this way because the people do. They're not ignorant. They read the reports just like we do, and they're calling for change. They say that Imre should become a singleton or step down so a singleton can be in charge. The hour of the First Prime is over."

Imre assumed that Ra had been coached to make his little speech at a signal from his mother. It certainly directed attention away from her. Imre wasn't fooled for a second.

"It's over when I say it is," he said, calmly. "I follow the news too. I know we're in trouble. Something has to be done. This is where we disagree, obviously. I don't think the unrest is random, as Al believes and you profess to believe. I think someone is seeding it. I think if we can find that someone and root that person out, our lives will become a whole lot easier."

Helwise shook her head. "This kind of simplistic notion cripples us, Imre. You're chasing shadows and boxing ghosts. There's no one person behind this any more than there's one quick fix. Changing the nature of the Returned Continuum will take many sacrifices, for all of us. Note, please, that we are not demanding that you step down. We are open-minded, as you should be."

"I see numerous possibilities, Helwise. More than you think, I suspect. Would you like to tell us who you've been talking to on the sly all these years?"

To anyone's eyes but his, she might not have reacted. He knew her too well to miss the micro-expression that flickered across her face. Alarm, concern, perhaps even a hint of panic. She had been found out.

"In time," she said, thinking fast. "There's someone you should talk to, first."

Behind him, the antechamber doors slid open.

Render was between Imre and the doors before he could swivel partway around. Emlee had her hand on her sidearm. Imre turned side-on so he could watch Helwise, Ra, and the new arrival at the same time, expecting her to use this moment to unveil her secret lover, to throw him off-balance while she clawed back her ground.

There were three of them. Two were tall and ugly. Imre immediately recognized their type, if not the individuals: grey-skinned, with elaborate tattoos and half-melted physiques. They were Gravamen, and their looks hadn't improved with time. The woman between them was shorter and no less scarified. Her face and scalp were almost completely black with tattoos. The skin between them was deathly pale and pulled taut across her face. She wore black from her neck to the ground, including gloves on her hands. She walked stiffly, as though every movement caused her pain.

"High Prime," she said, ducking her head in a sketch of a bow. "Are you still frightened?"

He frowned, confused. "Frightened?"

"You never did work out what you were looking for. I can see it on your face. You starve as ever while we count the cost."

Her head came up. Her eyes were as blue as the skies outside.

Not Helwise's lover at all.

"Minister Sevaste," he said, barely recognizing the young priest he had slept with on Dussehra in the body of this old, heavily tattooed woman.

"Minister no longer. My title is Gravine. *The* Gravine. I rule Dussehra and its territories. I am the queen, if you like, of the Gravamen. I am the sworn enemy of the Returned Continuum."

Emlee edged closer to him. Imre waved her back. He wasn't afraid of a physical attack. "And why is that, exactly? I thought you believed in my goals."

"Oh, I did," she said. "But I, more than anyone, had reason to feel betrayed by your actions on Dussehra. When Marshal Freer learned that it was I who encouraged you to make direct contact with Gravaman Zerah, he had me publicly beaten, as though putting you in harm's way had been my intention. He would have executed me but for your revocation of the death penalty for Primes. So I lived to see my world subjugated by degrees. Bad enough that Gravaman Zerah was assassinated by your soldiers the day after you humiliated him for his brave attempt on your life. Bad enough that the elected government was disbanded and one loyal to you installed. Bad enough that our native freedoms were removed, so anyone attempting to keep the traditions of the Gravamen alive risked arrest or death. Worst of all: we were ultimately regarded as loyal to your regime. You thought that your bootheel had stamped Dussehra into the ground. You thought our spirit broken."

She came closer as she talked and stopped only when the front of her robe brushed Emlee's leading shoulder. Her face was a ghastly mask. Imre could see her gloved hands shaking.

"We survived," she said. "And we will continue to survive because of something you will never possess."

Her left hand pulled the glove off her right. Her fingers were like sticks, rigid, thin, and as white as chalk where they had not been tattooed. He watched, caught by the grotesquery of her performance, as she raised her index finger to her cheek and scratched at her skin. The skin below her eyes sagged, revealing a web of browning blood vessels at the base of her eye.

Her tattoos smeared under the pressure of her fingernail, leaving a black line down her face. She offered the fingertip to him and he stared at it, realizing only then just how wrong he had been.

Tarry smudges on his fingers after fending off Zerah.

The mild infection he had thrown off before leaving Dussehra.

The Gravamen weren't tattooed. They were infected.

"It's a symbiont, a native life-form of Dussehra," he said. "It does something to you."

"We call it the Veil," Sevaste said, "and it saves lives. Metaphorically speaking. We live forever through the Veil, those of us who have embraced it, for it functions as a neural net as complex as a natural human cortex. It entrains our memories and passes them from person to person."

"From host to host," he corrected her. "What does it get from you?"

"A vector, as you would put it. Each Veil is treated as a unique individual, even though they could in theory be divided up and given to many people. Assumption comes only after months of preparation and trials. It has always been that way. You saw Dussehra as it was; had you made the effort to find out more, you would have understood that dissemination of the Veil is tightly controlled."

"By a ruling class that wanted to keep it to itself." Imre glanced at Emlee. Her expression was one of revulsion; she had backed out of physical contact with Sevaste. "I tried to ask Zerah. He wouldn't explain it to me."

"I know," Sevaste said. "You were abrupt and insensitive. You offended him."

"As you say." He frowned, wondering how she could possibly know that. There had been no one within earshot for that conversation, and she hadn't been on the Ambassadorial Barque at all. Unless . . .

I know.

"You have Zerah's Veil," he said. "You have his memories."

"I have more than that. I have the memories of his heir, who inherited it from him, and I have the memories of his father as well. I have the memories of thirteen generations before him, stretching right back to the colonization of Dussehra. I trained for my Assumption for fifty years before I was allowed to take the Veil. Women are usually forced to change their gender because the Y chromosome is an essential part of the match, but I insisted on being myself. I was only the second woman for ten thousand years to make the attempt and to survive. As soon as I had assimilated my new experiences, I knew what I had to do. No longer was I just a disaffected priest. From that moment on, I was devoted to bringing about your downfall."

"And so she's here," Imre said to Helwise. "Unguarded. Is this the one who will deliver your deathblow?"

"She would hardly announce herself beforehand, would she?" Helwise was back in her seat, watching the performance. "Hear her out, Imre. You'll find she's being metaphorical again."

Imre turned back to Sevaste. "Be quick, Gravine Sevaste. And literal."

She smiled; it looked like a funeral mask. "I have come to deliver you a message. I have waited a long time to give it to you personally. In this duty, I am not your enemy, but your friend. I am here to give you what you were looking for."

She raised her black-smeared finger to him. Her smile widened.

"This is what you don't have. *Context.* You span the centuries as an individual, but that's all you will ever be. You don't have a permanent place in the world. You will be forgotten when you are gone. Your empire is an ocean that will swallow the small splash you made without even noticing. The Veil, on the other hand, would bring you into direct contact with those you govern and allow them to contact you in return. Physical, sensual contact—as more and more people are experiencing all across the galaxy."

"You're spreading this thing?"

"Yes. Using a parasite to attack a cancer—that's how our detractors put it. The cancer is the Returned Continuum and the heavy-handed tactics of those who act in your name. Violence and bribes and brainwashing—ah! Your memes are not permanent, but memories are. We move into those places where resentfulness runs deepest and plant our seeds. We take a longer view than most Prime dissidents, and we are better organized. We fan the dying embers of rebellion in order that they may burn again, later. No longer flash points that flare up and die away, now dissent is burning in hundreds of places at once, threatening to join together and become a wildfire. You are seeing the results of my labor even now: tens of thousands of ships and hardcasts converging on Earth, demanding justice. And justice we will have, whether you join us or not."

"Enough." He raised a hand, aghast at the picture Sevaste was painting. An army of infected zombies rising up in their trillions to topple him from power unless he too succumbed. It was horrible. He couldn't accede to their wishes, but he could see her point. The Veil would never let resistance fade. He would have to eradicate her strain of the parasite from the entire galaxy if he was ever to feel safe again—and that, most likely, would never be possible.

He glanced at Helwise and then back at Sevaste, feeling trapped on two fronts. They were two very different women with a common agenda. Both were veiled, determined to succeed, and offering him a way out. Become a singleton and save the galaxy from war. Adopt an alien parasite and save the galaxy from war. Noble ends, both, and perhaps the noble thing would be to accept either. Or both.

Or none.

The numbers had sunk in. Tens of thousands out of thousands of millions was no mass uprising. It was little more than a glitch. It could spread, yes, but it wasn't the end of everything.

And Helwise hadn't covered her face when Sevaste entered the room.

He laughed. "Is that the best you can do?" he asked Helwise.

Ra stiffened as though he had verbally assaulted her. "You should show the Regent more respect in front of a guest of the Citadel."

"She'll survive." Imre didn't spare him more than a glance. Whatever internal shape Ra had become, Imre wasn't threatened by it. He spoke only for Helwise. "You've been playing me, both of you. Do you think I'll roll over for her if your best efforts fail? Do you really think I'm so sentimental? You've had fifty thousand years to work on putting me in checkmate. That can't be all you have for me."

"We're not playing chess, Imre. We're talking about the future of the Returned Continuum." Her expression divulged nothing. "I'm giving you a fighting chance, Imre, to emerge from this with some kind of dignity. If you won't become a singleton, at least hear us out. You fucked up in Dussehra, and now Gravine Sevaste is offering you a glue that could bind the Primes together forever. You'd be a fool not to take it."

"I have all the glue I need, thanks. And the dignity. Spare me your efforts to save myself from myself." He turned his glare on Sevaste too. "Both of you. We agree that things have got out of hand and need to be sorted out fast. Beyond that I'll take my own counsel. It's served me pretty well so far."

Helwise made an exasperated noise and turned to Render. "Are you going along with this, old friend?"

"We are not old friends." From the neck down, the old soldier was made of stone. Only his lips and jaw moved. "You don't know me."

"But you see the absurdity, don't you? One man—one Prime—can't rule the galaxy. It's impossible. He'll only make things worse than they already are if he insists on trying."

"This conversation," Render said, drawing a well-used pistol from a holster and turning it on Helwise with one smooth motion, "drains my patience dry."

"Hear, hear," said Emlee. Her sidearm was already in her hand. Imre hadn't seen her draw. "Whatever you came here to do, Imre, I suggest you get on with it."

Imre took a deep breath. All right, he thought. The moment is here. No use talking any about it any longer.

"Helwise MacPhedron, Regent of the Returned Continuum, I'm placing you under arrest."

She didn't move. "What are the charges?"

"Treason and conspiracy to commit treason, for two."

"You're making a big mistake, Imre."

"Really? Let's see how it looks at the trial."

Ra quivered like a penned lion. "You can't do this to her."

"Not just to her. You're under arrest too. Al, disarm him."

That was the critical moment. Imre knew it. Freer couldn't sit on the fence. He had to choose one side or the other—and it had to be Imre's aide that he chose, for without him and his other selves the galaxy would fall apart. Asking him to move on Helwise, who he had worked alongside faithfully for more years than Imre had been on Earth, would be too much too soon. Ra, therefore, was the key.

Freer's jaw bunched. He didn't think about it for more than a second, but Imre could tell that that second had lasted for hours by his internal clock. His conclusion wasn't as obvious as it would have been if he had drawn his own weapon and pointed it at anyone. There was a split instant where Imre wondered if it might go against him.

Then Freer said, "Don't fight it, Ra. I'll make sure you're treated fairly."

It all happened very quickly from there. Ra reached for the ceremonial pistol at his side. While attention was on him, Helwise made her move. Both hands came from under the table, and both were holding pistols. One was aimed at Emlee, the other at Render. The pistols were compact but powerful: Balzac six-shooters designed for close-quarter fighting. The power packs were wired to double as shock grenades once their charge was exhausted. Helwise was overclocking fast. Even though she was starting from a disadvantaged position, she had an edge on the Primes in the room. Their trigger fingers were only clenching by the time she got off two shots, one from each gun.

The room exploded into a web of energy. The cross fire was blinding. Someone cried out: Sevaste, Imre thought, even as a punch of energy struck him in the left shoulder and knocked him off his feet. He flew backward into one of the Gravamen, who went down with a guttural *oof* under the weight of him and his armor.

The door to the office opened, and the six guards burst in. The exchange of gunfire intensified. Imre rolled to bring his

gun up and shot two in the throat, where their armor was
weakest. They dropped like mannequins. Render jumped over
him, firing in a continuous stream. He yelled something. Imre
couldn't hear it over the noise. The guards didn't stand a
chance.

It was over before Imre regained his feet. The smell of burning armor was strong in his nostrils. Helwise's shot had felt
like a battering ram, but he wasn't hurt. His concern was for
the others.

They were all standing: Emlee, Freer, Render, Sevaste,
and the three sexless attendants. Even the Gravaman Imre
had landed on was fine. There were only two fatalities, apart
from the guards, and they were Helwise and her son. She
had been hit twice, once in the face and once in the chest. By
the angle of impact, Imre guessed that Emlee and Freer had
fired the killing shots. Her body lay sprawled on its back—
not gushing blood as a Prime body might have while its
heart still beat, but undergoing sufficient fluid loss to prove
that she was definitely dead. Ra had fallen by the door,
crumpled face-forward over a massive hole in his stomach.
The wound was cauterized, so the only thing issuing from it
was smoke.

Imre recognized that kind of wound. Render's gun. Old,
fragile, and ridiculously over-powered—just like its owner.

Imre finished inspecting the bodies and turned to face the
room. Everyone was waiting for him to say something: Emlee, Freer, and Render with their weapons in their hands and
their expressions hard; Sevaste and her Gravamen shocked
and unbelieving; Helwise's attendants numb with terror.
Clearly, they hadn't been expecting a confrontation like that.
That confirmed Imre's guess that Sevaste had been a distraction, nothing more. Helwise had been hoping to throw him off
guard, perhaps to give herself time to think, or to plan a way
out.

He sagged. It hadn't worked. Her plan had failed in the
worst possible way—and he found himself feeling more disappointment than grief. *That can't be all you have for me,* he
had told her, and he had really believed it. She must have seen

this moment coming for years. How could she have let herself fall so easily? He had assumed she would be much harder to depose. In fact, he had banked on it.

We're not playing chess, Imre, she had said. The words came back to him with the force of a knife thrust through his chest plate. What if he had been wrong about her, all along? What if he had forced her into playing *his* game, and she had been the one trying to wriggle out of it?

He looked at Sevaste. Her tattooed face offered him nothing but reproach.

Render was in the hallway, watching the empty floor. He looked relaxed. The shots appeared to have attracted no attention. "No sign of life," he said.

"The other floors must be empty too," Emlee said. "Maybe the whole admin sector."

"Check the other room," Imre told her. He kept his weapon on Sevaste and the others. They didn't move.

Emlee crossed to the door.

The panel slid aside, revealing an antechamber as large as the office itself, containing several comfortable settees and tables, some loaded with food and drink, but no other people. The far entrance was shut.

Freer had a hand to the side of his head. He looked worried.

"What are you hearing?" Imre asked him.

"Nothing," he said. "That's what I'm hearing. The Citadel is silent."

Imre paid closer attention to the web of data that usually surrounded him on Earth. It had disappeared without his noticing, as though a shutter had fallen on a noisy room. The silence was profound and unnerving. Not just empty of people, but empty of information as well.

"Alice-Angeles?" Imre waited for a reply from his secretary. He heard nothing even when he tried the emergency wireless built into his suit helmet. "Shit. I've got no comms at all. Someone's pulled the plug on the internal networks and jammed the rest."

"The rest of Ra," said Freer.

"It must be." *Another game entirely.* He was certain of it. Just Ra and no one else. The Apparatus would have told Imre if there had been any appearances of Himself in the Citadel. "He's sneakier than he looked."

"What are you thinking?" asked Emlee.

"He could afford to sacrifice a body or two," he said. "The death of this one must have acted as a signal. We killed his mother. Now he's blacked out the comms in order to cover up what happens next. I expect he'll come get us with a small army behind him."

Imre looked at the three Dussehrans. "I'm sorry," he said. "You picked a crappy time to visit."

Sevaste's masklike face remained impassive. If she had been the one to scream before, she had firmly regained her composure. "I was too late," she said. "You were too slow returning. I can do nothing for you now."

"Don't give up on me just yet," he said. "I've faced worse than a small army before. All we have to do is get the comms back online, and we'll have a whole planet on our side."

"I know about your ghost," she said. "It is useless without someone to command it."

He stared at her, understanding more fully then what must have happened on Dussehra. She had plotted and schemed under Al Freer's radar, then taken him out before he could give the Apparatus any orders to deal with her. Without an authorized conduit in place, it was allowed only to seek instructions from Earth, not to take proactive steps.

That was exactly the position he found himself in now. He couldn't rely on anyone or anything other than the people in the room until he got the comms back up.

"It's just not your day," Render said to him, nudging one of the dead guards with his boot.

"Get in there," Imre told Sevaste and the attendants, indicating the antechamber. "We'll come back for you when this is over. But don't hold your breath. You killed Al Freer on Dussehra, and that disposes me toward irritability."

Sevaste obeyed without argument. Once she and her Gravamen were safely inside, Emlee manually keyed the door and locked it.

"Now what?" she asked.

"Ra will be moving already," said Freer. "If that's what he's doing."

"So we need to move too," Imre said. "We can't stay here. Al, where would you direct an operation like this? You'd want somewhere central, somewhere big, somewhere easy to defend."

"The Throne Room."

"That was my thought too. Any easy way to get there without being caught?"

"Security will be down along with comms, so we don't have to worry about moving in the open."

"Unsafe," Render said, shaking his head. "All kinds of people."

"Ra can't have emptied the whole place," Emlee agreed. "And we'll be blind too, don't forget. We don't want to walk into an ambush."

"The basements," Freer said. "Service tunnels, maintenance ducts. The Throne Room's on the ground floor. They'll be coming up to us. They might expect us to meet them halfway, but they won't think we'll overshoot."

"Do you know the way?"

"I'll show you," said Render.

"And then?" asked Emlee.

"We get to Ra," Imre said, "or I get a signal. Either way, we put an end to this."

"It's going to be messy," Freer said.

"Tomorrow we'll be civilized." Render didn't look unhappy at all.

Imre walked once around the room, externalizing his internal search for anything he had missed. Ra's body had stopped smoking, and Helwise had leaked her last drop. Her expression was surprised but not shocked. Was it really going to end there?

"If you're gonna leave," Render rasped, "then do it soon."

"Right." Imre swallowed his unease. "Single file to the elevator shafts. Render first. Emlee, you're at the rear. No firing unless fired upon. These are our people too."

Nods all around. Imre gave the signal for Render to move out. They did so with measured steps, in perfect time.

* * *

Ra had shut down the Citadel's internal transport system. That wasn't a problem. Imre and Emlee's armor could take the weight of two. With mechanical assists in every joint, getting down safely and quietly wasn't going to be an issue.

The shafts were empty and dark. They descended, Emlee first, at a steady rate, dropping hand over hand down two different cables and saying nothing in order to keep noise to a minimum. Normally they would chatter through internal channels, but with the Citadel's comms so quiet, none of them were keen to make any noise at all. Talking aloud was out of the question, for the slightest sound echoed up and down the shaft for a disconcertingly long time. Imre cursed under his breath every time his armor made ringing contact with metal, as inevitably happened from time to time.

Once, they heard the sound of booted feet through the elevator's nearest door. They froze, waiting for it to open and rifle muzzles to poke through, blazing. Imre was confident he could survive the fall to the bottom of the shaft, but not Al Freer, clinging to his back like a long-legged limpet. He literally held his breath until the guards ran past and the sound of their footsteps faded to silence.

They resumed their descent and within fifteen minutes were at the bottom. Render let go of Emlee and took his bearings. There were three possible choices in the form of identical tunnels leading radially away from the base of the shaft. The air was cooler in the basement level. Naked concrete walls showed signs of water damage and decay. Bundles of cables clung to the ceiling, thicker along one of the tunnels.

Render chose that one, based on what instinct or knowledge Imre didn't stop to ask. He followed the old soldier into the gloom, switching to infrared when the faint light from the shaft faded to nothing behind them. They trotted through the Citadel's extensive underground like very large rats, stopping at each intersection to make certain they didn't stumble across a technician going about legitimate business. Imre didn't know exactly how Ra had managed the blackout. He might simply have taken out the primary servers with a software patch or two. Alternatively, he could have physically blown critical junctions. People might be scrambling to repair the sabotage. Imre didn't want in any way to hinder them.

Render took them to a storeroom, where they stopped briefly to rest and confer. The room was bare and cramped and dark. It was hard to see anything because the walls, floors, and ceiling were all the same temperature.

Render sketched an angular, efficient map on the dusty ground with his index finger. "We are all here," he said, pointing. They crouched down to see it better. "Nothing in here but dust." He traced a path through the tunnels ahead, brisk, efficient, no room for ambiguity. "Up here." He had drawn a flight of stairs, and his finger tapped it until he was sure everyone had taken his point. The stairs were at the terminus of a short corridor leading from the intersection of three others.

Render erased the map and drew another. Imre recognized the floor plan this time. It was the ground level of the Citadel. Render paced out another route through the imaginary corridors. "Take things slow. Tread careful." It looped around the back of the Throne Room, to what looked like a service door. "Move in. Move out. Pay it all back. Easy."

"No," said Imre.

"I don't like it either," Freer said. He pointed at the stairs. "It's a choke point. If there are guards stationed there, they'll cut us down before we get a dozen steps."

"Hard to avoid," Render said.

Emlee backed him up. "We can't stay down here forever."

"That's not my concern," Imre said across the three of them. "If there are guards, we'll make sure they're otherwise occupied."

"A distraction," Render said, nodding. "Move up, one by one."

Imre pointed at a different point on the map. "My problem is here. I'm not sneaking into the hall like an assassin. I'm taking back what's mine. Acting any other way would play right into Ra's hands. We can't afford to come out of this looking bad."

"Your thoughts, then?" asked Freer.

"Screw taking things slow. Let's bring it to him head-on and see how he likes it."

"Storm the door?" Render shook his head. "Big mistake. It's far too risky."

"We won't need to storm anything if Ra caves right away."

"Four of us versus how many, exactly?" Freer looked unconvinced too.

"I don't care. The point is, it's the four of *us*. We've got more combat experience than every amateur in the Citadel combined. If you don't think we can take them, then I suggest we surrender right now."

"I agree that it's risky." Freer glanced at Imre, Render, and Emlee, one singleton facing three Primes. He out of all of them had the least to lose. "But I'll do it if you insist."

"What do you think, Render?" asked Emlee.

"I only work here," he said, but he was smiling.

"I'm of the opinion," she said, when Imre looked at her, "that the longer we sit down here, the sooner someone will figure where we've got to. There are only so many places we could've gone from Helwise's office."

"Is that a yes?" he pressed.

"As close as you're going to get."

"That's good enough." Imre swept the map away with one gloved hand. "We come up the stairwell one by one. Render first. He can provide the distraction, if we need one. We cut straight to the Throne Room, firing as we go. If we're stopped there, we'll fall back and run with Render's original plan. Emlee, keep an ear out for a working comms channel as we get closer. Ra must be coordinating all this somehow. If you can hack in to something, anything at all, that'll make our job a whole lot easier."

She nodded. The four of them stood. They didn't shake hands or make any bold declarations. Imre understood that. Helwise was dead; the old group was fractured. It would have been wrong to act like she wasn't missing. It didn't matter that there might be other versions of her elsewhere in the galaxy, lying low so she wouldn't murder them. It didn't matter that she had tried to kill them first. That was just the way it was.

*   *   *

The ambush was waiting for them at the base of the stairs. Render brought them to a halt as they approached the last intersection but one, within earshot of the ground floor. Imre could hear voices and heavy treads echoing distantly down the stairwell. Someone was up there, that was for sure. He couldn't hear anything ahead of him—and that, he supposed, was one reason why the people above were moving so noisily. No sound at all would make anyone suspicious, especially in a building through which four fugitives were known to be making their way. A small amount of ruckus was not only expected, it would also hide the deep, dense silence of people trying not to be heard.

Render's nostrils twitched. Imre could smell it too. Nothing in here but dust, Render had said, and exactly that was on the air. Dust that had been recently disturbed.

Someone had indeed figured it out.

They split up into two groups. The stairs were in a cul-de-sac; there was only one way to approach it. The intersection nearby would, therefore, be the one the guards were actively watching. Render and Freer backtracked in order to come down another tunnel. The guards would expect someone trying to lie low to come in a single group, slow and silent. Defying their expectations was all part of the process.

Imre counted to one hundred at tempo Absolute, then two hundred. He was beginning to wonder if Render had got himself lost when a clatter of footsteps from ahead broke the silence. Someone was running toward the stairs, making no attempt to be quiet.

Imre inched closer under the cover of the sound and peered around the corner so he could see what was going on. Emlee held back, watching the way they had come.

A long, lanky figure, glowing hot in infrared ran into view. It was Freer, his pistol hanging loosely in one hand, as though he wasn't expecting to use it. He had barely come into sight when a bolt of energy cut across him, blindingly bright. Freer's reactions were unbelievably fast. He bent backward and went under the bolt, using his singleton reflexes, strength, and flexibility to take no more than a burn across his chest before hitting the deck.

"Hold your fire," barked a voice. "That's Marshal Freer!"

Shadows moved in the shadows. Imre could make out nothing clearly for a second; his eyes were still dazzled by the shot.

"Od damn it." Freer was getting to his feet. An armored guard moved forward to help him up. "When you've finished shooting at me, I suggest you get ready for some real targets. Not far behind me. I managed to convince them that I was on their side. Overpowered one of them when he wasn't looking. The other two are still at large. Be ready."

The guard motioned for Freer to come in behind him. They disappeared into the cul-de-sac.

Imre started counting again. When he reached five, three close-range, low-aperture, and therefore quiet shots rang out in quick succession. Imre barely saw the muzzle flash, even though he had been expecting it. He was moving before the second and at the entrance to the cul-de-sac for the third. He arrived in time to watch the three guards hit the ground, one after the other.

Shot from behind by the man they thought they were protecting.

"Speaking of risky," he whispered to Freer, as Emlee hurried past to check the sparking suits. The neck shots should have spared some of the electricals, if Freer had placed them right. There might be a closed-circuit comms system they could patch into.

"Calculated," Freer said, checking the charge on his pistol. He tossed it aside and picked up one from a fallen guard. "Ra wouldn't have known exactly how it went down in Helwise's office, thanks to the blackout, and he needs me as much as you do. He wouldn't put a shoot-to-kill order out on my head."

"Still, it was dark, and they were obviously a little jumpy. What if their aim had been better?"

"Then you'd have jumped them while they argued about whose fault it was." Freer put a hand on Imre's armored right shoulder. "Besides, you said they had to fire first."

"No go on the comms," said Emlee, throwing down the last helmet she had checked. "They're running on word of mouth, just like us."

A familiar face caught Imre's eye. One of the dead single-ton guards was Ra MacPhedron. Emlee took his weapon and tossed Imre the third.

More footsteps. Render jogged lightly out of the third corridor, unhurried and unworried.

"Clear?" Imre asked him.

Render nodded. "Party time."

"We've got some distance to go before I'll start to feel like celebrating." He looked up the stairwell. Whoever was up there hadn't been paying much attention. He reassessed his opinion of the ambush. Maybe they hadn't figured it out after all. Three guards, no backup; that sounded like a half-arsed contingency to him.

They ascended in absolute silence. The stairwell completed three full circuits before reaching ground level. Render went first and communicated with hand signals what he saw at the top, reaching out into the central shaft so they all could see. Imre took the details and built up a virtual map in his head.

Guards, coming and going. No civilians. Clear spaces with no obvious heavy artillery or blockades.

It didn't look as bad as he had feared. They had to cover perhaps one hundred meters to reach the Throne Room. The corridors were broad and contained very little cover—but at the same time they were difficult to block without physical barriers, especially if the guards weren't being coordinated electronically.

Wait for me, Imre signaled to Render. *Regroup,* he told the others.

When they were all at the top, he gave them their orders by hand signals he hadn't used for thousands of years. *Rapid assault. Safeties off. Overclock to the max.*

Render grinned.

Imre held up three fingers and counted down to zero.

They burst out of cover, not firing yet and therefore not drawing fire, moving rapidly, dispersing far enough apart to avoid interfering with each other's movement or presenting a single target but close enough to keep each other in peripheral vision. Imre and Emlee had their visors down and occupied the flank positions. Render and Freer were to the fore and rear, guns moving constantly from target to target, moving on sure feet through the familiar, opulent spaces they were being forced to invade.

They gained six meters before someone noticed. A cry went up. Five heads turned. Two more guards emerged at the far end of the vaulted corridor, took rapid stock of the situation. Weapons whirred as they built charge and acquired targets.

"Hold your fire." Freer's command filled the hallway. Voice recognition systems confirmed his identity. Fingers froze on triggers. For a split second—an age at the fastest combat tempo—the only moving things were the four fugitives.

"Countermanded," barked a new voice. Ra MacPhedron— child of the Citadel. "Pursue and subdue. Lethal force authorized."

Wordy, thought Imre. They had gained two more meters before the order was complete. But it did the trick.

Imre and Emlee moved to put themselves between the un-armored Freer and Render. Render was already firing, putting holes through the two nearest guards and knocking the legs out from under a third. A glancing shot bounced off Imre and into the wall. The air was suddenly full of smoke and noise. The whipcrack of energy discharges and miniature sonic booms was deafening, even through his helmet. Imre had no doubt at all that the sound was drawing every guard on the ground floor.

The exchange rapidly became one-sided. He put his head down and sprinted for the end of the corridor. Seven dead so far, none his own. Three Ra MacPhedrons down; how many to go?

Moving, they were more difficult targets. Dodging and weaving with the others close behind him, he reached the junction and turned right, spraying the corridor liberally with his weapons. Both barrels were glowing hot. Emlee pressed forward and urged him back. She had replenished her fire-power from the guards they had already passed. Three guards fell from three shots. Imre picked up two new weapons as the opportunity presented itself: an Acitak pistol, standard issue for the Citadel guard, and a Birmingham rifle set to armor-piercing rounds. It hadn't been fired.

So they proceeded through the Citadel, running where they could, dispersing and regrouping as demanded. They faced thirty guards before reaching the final stretch, and none of them managed to delay them more than a few seconds or injure them significantly. Imre's visor was blackened by a lucky shot, so he had raised it in order to see. Render's right arm was bleeding from a flesh wound but it didn't seem to be slowing him down. Freer moved like a dancer; his shots never missed. Emlee presented a small and deadly target that let almost nothing past her.

The Throne Room's titanium front door appeared before them, looming high above the heads of six guards standing in front of it. Render and Freer took care of the rear guard while Imre and Emlee advanced on the six, picking them off in pairs. One survived a second longer than the others and managed to score a hit on Emlee's chest. She went down, winded but unharmed, while Imre put the guard out of commission with a double shot to the throat and head.

"Clear!" He ran to the door, which was locked. The manual keypad hadn't been damaged but was unresponsive to the presence of either his or Emlee's biometrics. Freer appeared at their shoulders and waved his hand in front of the pad.

Nothing.

"Try again," said Render over his shoulder. He had one rifle in each hand and was laying down a ferocious covering fire.

Freer did as instructed, more slowly this time. Still nothing. Emlee joined Render in discouraging the guards who were amassing at the last junction. Now that the four of them were stationary, the shots peppering them were bound to improve fast. Energy discharged into the silver metal, sending showers of sparks in all directions and leaving deep black scorch marks in their wake.

"What did you say about Ra caving?" Emlee asked Imre.

"Just you worry about getting us some comms," he called back. "Anything at all?"

"Not a flicker."

Freer wasn't giving up. He used a sleeve to wipe the surface of the pad and placed both hands firmly upon it, one after the other. Then he brought his face up close so there was no chance the device would be confused by smoke or sudden flashes of light. Imre covered him, putting his armor between Freer and the small army of guards gathering less than ten meters away. Eventually, they would think of charging, and that would be it. The game would be over.

The lock thunked heavily behind him. Freer slapped the wall in relief. Motors hummed, and the massive double panel began to slide open.

"Too close," said Render, pressing forward in preparation for falling back to new cover.

As soon as the gap was wide enough to admit one person, Imre pushed Freer through it. Emlee went next to check out the lay of the land. Imre backed through after her, firing as he went. As soon as Render's shoulder blades were the only targets available to him, he ceased firing, turned, and stopped dead.

The Throne Room was full of people. Not just guards, although there were plenty of those, but civilians as well. Thousands of them, lined up on the vast amphitheater's raised terraces like the audience of one of Helwise's centennial speeches. Some were sitting down; some were standing. All looked worried or frightened. All were looking at him.

He understood. While he had been talking to Helwise, Ra had emptied the Citadel of noncombatants and brought them to the Throne Room. There they wouldn't be in the way, so no one could accuse him of putting anyone at risk. And then, when Imre got wind of his plan and came blazing to get him, looking like some crazed terrorist hell-bent on revenge . . .

Freer and Emlee had also frozen at the sight of what waited for them and were looking at him for guidance. Render came through the gap backward, fired two more shots, then realized that something was wrong and took his fingers off both triggers.

The moment froze around them like an ice crystal. Imre's thoughts raced while the rest of the world turned to solid stone. The people weren't just witnesses. They also comprised a human shield. He couldn't risk firing for fear of a miss or ricochet taking out someone innocent—or at least making it look like he didn't care. Either way, Ra suddenly had the upper hand. It was a tactical masterstroke, one Imre hadn't expected. Ra was too young, too untrained, for that kind of ruthlessness. His mother must have coached him, maybe even worked through the plan with him before they put it into effect. It had her stink on it.

Imre thought it through one more time. He could see no loopholes that didn't put innocent bystanders at risk. Unless Emlee had managed to find some working comms, the fight was over.

He cast her a significant, questioning look.

She shook her head once, with all the ponderousness of the world turning.

He looked up at the gun emplacements, which hung inert and frozen without the Apparatus to guide them. Time resumed its normal speed.

Imre lowered his weapons and indicated that the others should do the same.

All gunfire ceased, leaving a ringing silence in its wake. The guards behind them had obviously been given similar orders to follow once they reached the Throne Room.

"Disarm them." Ra's voice, coming from a figure in heavy armor open from the neck up. He was walking toward them with rapid paces, pointing at guards by the door. Eight converged on the four of them and removed their weapons.

Ra halted in front of them and put his hands on his hips. Alive and in public, he cut a better figure. The armor made him look bigger, all business. His expression was very serious, no doubt for the benefit of the crowd around them. They were just inside the door, visible to only a small percentage of the people evacuated from the Citadel, but Ra's performance was already in full swing.

He faced up to Imre and said three words.

"Surrender to me."

"No. I want you to surrender to me instead."

"This isn't a joking matter."

"I'm not joking."

"Then you've lost all touch with reality, and that makes your removal from power imperative. The Returned Continuum can't function with a madman at its head."

"A child would be no better. Do they have training wheels for this kind of thing?"

Instead of reacting with anger, Ra smiled in a way that unsettled Imre deeply. There was confidence in that smile, a surety that Imre had got something terribly, terribly wrong. Imre searched his memory for details he might have missed but could think of nothing outstanding. Only one possibility existed: that there was someone behind Ra's actions, someone with the confidence and the hardness to gamble the lives of innocent people against Imre's compliance, someone who had yet to reveal themself even now, when the game appeared to be all but played out.

I've always been here, he heard Himself say on Spargamos, *waiting for you.*

"Bring him to me," boomed a cold voice from the center of the Throne Room, magnified so it made the floor shake. "Bring them all before me."

It seemed to Imre as though time stopped again, but it was only his heart, stilled between beats by surprise and the beginnings of despair.

I was away too long, he told himself, as Ra took his arm and led him into the center of the massive hall. I could have stopped this if I had been here. Instead, I was off fighting another battle entirely. I lost that battle, and now I'm going to lose the war. All because I was away too long.

Emlee came abreast of him, shoved along by an anonymous guard, someone she could have killed without hesitating in a fair fight. Imre cast her another significant look, not daring to hope that in all the crowd around them someone had managed to punch through the jamming.

Another shake of the head.

The iron structure at the center of the hall grew large before them. A series of giant holographs flickered into life, showing the captives in close-up so the crowd wouldn't miss a thing. Imre's face was rigid, looking neither down nor up but directly ahead, at the base of the iron dais. Ra shoved him in midstep and he stumbled, looked weak. Imre gritted his teeth, planted his left foot down hard, and lashed out with his right.

Ra grunted and bent slightly forward at the sudden blow to his knee, then grunted again as Imre followed it up with a swift head butt that brought the two men closer than he had ever wanted them to be. Ra let go and staggered away. Imre heard the rattle of guns training on him, dozens of them from all directions.

Ignoring them all, he straightened and walked the rest of the way on his own.

"Are you planning to explain this?" he asked the woman standing before the throne. The throne itself was empty, as he had guessed it would be. On hearing that voice, he had known exactly who his main threat was.

"You stand charged, Imre Bergamasc, First Prime of the Returned Continuum," said Helwise MacPhedron, "with treason and conspiracy to commit treason—and now resisting arrest, assault, and murder as well. Can you give me one reason why I shouldn't execute you right now, in front of all the people whose lives you put in danger?"

Imre did look up, then, up at her standing regally over him, dressed in the same burgundy robe she had been wearing in her office, the same hair, and the same veil, now draped demurely across her features. He should have been appalled; he should have been aghast to see her returned from the dead and playing the same card back at him. *Treason.* The tables had been completely turned, and in all likelihood he would be the one lying dead on the floor in a second or two, killed by an impromptu firing squad while Render, Freer, and Emlee watched.

Instead, he felt like laughing, just as he had laughed when she had presented Sevaste as a Trojan horse to him, in the unlikely event that he might capitulate so easily. A mixture of relief and adrenaline flowed through his veins like hot brandy.

That can't be all you have for me.

Apparently not, obviously not, for here she was standing before him again, as alive as she had ever been. The game had been real; he was absolved of all claims of paranoia. Furthermore, the importance of Sevaste became clearer still, for the queen of the Gravamen hadn't come to Earth at this time by chance. Not at all. She had come because Helwise had invited her. Not Helwise the Regent. Helwise the Apparatus had identified as living on Dussehra, who Imre had thought was safely in hiding.

She was the person—perhaps one of many—with whom Helwise had been plotting on the sly. And perhaps the person, too, that the Regent had willingly sacrificed in her office in order to throw Imre off-balance.

She had gone from killing her other selves to conspiring with them to take over, and he hadn't suspected a thing. Nor had Freer or Render. Nor had anyone in the Returned Continuum.

He didn't feel bad for missing it. At least he had worked it out in the end. And he was sure now that he had seen it all. There were no more surprises waiting in the wings. No visitations from Himself, no other blasts from his past. The job now was simply to outlast her, so he could turn the tables again.

It all came down to Emlee.

He glanced at her. She shook her head.

Helwise was waiting.

"You need me," he said, knowing that she would understand what he meant. He didn't want to refer to the Apparatus in public. It was the secret weapon of the Returned Continuum, the invisible glue he used to bind the galaxy together.

She surprised him by having no such qualms. "You'll find I have no need of stealthy AIs or lies about your divinity. I have the support of people who believe that humanity is enough. The hearts and minds of my charges are all that is valuable to the galaxy. And it *is* enough. Our humanity is our greatest asset."

"What kind of humanity? Singletons only?"

"All kinds. So keep your pernicious programs to yourself. We don't need them."

Sevaste again, Imre thought. Did Helwise really think the

Veil would fill the same role as the Apparatus if he withdrew its favor? Or was she bluffing?

She was bluffing. She had to be.

"Are you telling me you wouldn't take control if I offered it to you?"

"I would take control—to avoid the threat of retribution. Who knows what mischief it's programmed to perform once you're gone?"

Helwise stepped down the iron steps, symbolically joining him at ground level. She waved the guards away, and the five of them were suddenly alone in the center of a great crowd. Imre could feel the pressure of attention upon him like a heavy weight.

"Please submit to justice," she said, for the benefit of the crowd. Then she leaned close to Imre and whispered in his ear, "Give me the fucking codes, or I'll rip their fucking hearts out, one by one—starting with her."

Imre had no doubt who she meant. "The Apparatus already obeys you," he said. "Within reason."

"Reason isn't enough. You are its master. You can countermand anything I tell it to do. And only you can nominate a successor."

That was true. If he died without telling who the Apparatus should put in his place, it would continue to follow the instructions he had given it, obeying those to whom he had gifted partial control, until they died in turn. And then it would be rudderless, reduced to following unchanging routines until the universe itself died and space-time was no more.

"You have a particular successor in mind, I assume," he said, glancing in Ra's direction. The child still looked unhappy about being attacked by Imre in so public a forum.

"Naturally," she said. "And you can't blame me for that. It's been lonely at the top, and men of your caliber are hard to find." She arched an eyebrow. "Not for want of looking."

A wash of revulsion filled him. What was she trying to say now? That she and Ra were lovers because his former self had failed to come to her call? He had considered the latter a real possibility, but the former had never crossed his mind. He wasn't sure which appalled him more.

"You know what to say," she said. "Do it now, and I'll be lenient. I'll let you live out your life on some rock far away, where you can't possibly cause me any trouble."

"What, you're not going to offer me a job?"

"I don't think so. There isn't a latrine deep or foul enough." She waited for him to offer anything more, then turned to Emlee.

"Rescind this man's authority," Helwise said, voice booming out into the Throne Room once again, "and I will let you go."

All show. All bluster. She didn't expect Emlee to accept, and she had no intention of honoring the deal.

Emlee didn't disappoint him. "Never."

Helwise turned to Render. "And you?"

"You don't know me at all."

"Al?"

Freer shook his head. "If you kill me, you'll have a civil war on your hands."

"You'll be court-martialed like any other soldier, Marshal Freer. Your fate and the issue of your replacement, I leave in a military court's hands."

Ra's crowd-conscious air told Imre exactly who expected to be installed as the new marshal.

Helwise turned back to him. He said nothing. It was far too late for talking. He wouldn't back down, and neither would she. The end of the game was finally in sight.

She waited a beat with fury roiling in her eyes, then walked back up the steps, one at a time, as patient as a panther. When she reached the top, she turned and faced the crowd with her arms outstretched.

"My people, this isn't a battlefield, but we are undoubtedly at war. These four people plotted to bring about the downfall of humanity. They have connections with powers linked to the Slow Wave and to the saboteurs who make governance of the galaxy so difficult. Millions, billions of Primes have been lost because of their complicity with the forces of evil, while they themselves use the resources of the Returned Continuum to resurrect themselves, over and over again. They will never stand down, and they will never confess. I offer this extreme act to you, fellow citizens, as a demonstration of my obedience to our common cause—the safety and dignity of every human in the galaxy. You will not be safe while this man lives. He has been given too much power, through the church I misguidedly founded, and it has twisted him so thoroughly that perhaps even he has lost sight of his true motivation. Is it power? Is it hatred? Is it his own glory? Perhaps, in his own way, he thinks he's doing the right thing—but failing miserably, maliciously in the process. We may never understand what drives a man to such extremes. All we need to know is that we are better off without him."

Her gold-flecked eyes turned down to him. "Kneel, Imre Bergamasc."

He stayed ramrod straight and would not bend until Ra MacPhedron put two shots into his armor's knee joints, thereby unlocking them. Still, it took four guards to force him down. Imre, Render, and Freer were pulled away. A semicircle of guards formed between him and Helwise. Their visors were down, but Imre thought he recognized their postures. Ra MacPhedron, all nine of them.

"Incest I can live with," he said, "but patricide is an ugly thing."

"Not from where I'm standing," whispered one of the guards holding him down. Another Ra. "This is your last chance. Give me the codes, and I'll aim to wound rather than kill you."

"I don't trust you any further than your mother."

"Helwise is crazy. She really would kill you, just to make a point. And I know you're right. We're screwed without the Apparatus. For the sake of the empire, won't you give it up?"

Imre wavered. Ra was right on one point. The situation was bigger than him and Helwise and their ambitious progeny. It was bigger even than the Slow Wave and the Barons—and the Luminous, wherever they came from and whatever they were. This was about the survival of the human race—and what it needed more than anything at that moment was a sense of unity backed up by a genuine ability function as a unit. Without the Apparatus, it would break up into a mishmash of small nations, each battling the other until what had once been a real shot at a galactic civilization would just be a thousand million war-torn planets constantly failing to rise any higher.

The ancient minds of Earth had created the Apparatus. What right did he have to deny it to their descendants?

But . . . not for an *empire*, as Ra had put it. Imre would gladly die with the key that would turn a petty despot into a galactic overlord. Some people thought him exactly that, but he refused to accept it. He had acted in good faith, or tried to, and placed his faith in turn in those he had thought trustworthy. Now one of those had betrayed him, and he had no confidence at all that either she or her son would not betray humanity in turn.

He raised his head, ready to say no for the last time, and caught Emlee's eye.

She was nodding. Nodding significantly.

Comms.

Imre took a deep breath and closed his eyes. The words he'd never spoken were deeply imprinted in his memory.

"Initiate new successor protocol," he said aloud. Beside and behind him, he felt Ra MacPhedron become rigid with anticipation. The Apparatus didn't respond, so Imre could only proceed on the assumption that Emlee knew what she was talking about.

"Instate Emlee Copas."

A woman gasped. He couldn't tell if it was Helwise or Emlee. Ra hissed in his ear. One pair of fists gripped his collar more tightly than before, in readiness. He heard the feet of his firing squad squeaking on the smooth floor as their rifles came up and acquired their target. Ra would be a fool to kill him, thereby placing power over the Apparatus immediately in Emlee's hands, but the boy had proved himself to be headstrong. Imre expected to be dead before three seconds expired.

But he wasn't done. The four words he had left to say were harder than any he had ever uttered.

"Initiate executive order KISMET."

When they were out, he felt the world turn around him as though he had been holding his breath too long. He didn't want to see what happened next. He just kept his eyes tightly shut and waited for the moment to end in a hail of gunfire.

Weapons charged. Reticules converged. One round would have done it, but to be sure no less than twenty were fired. The noise was deafening, the sudden smell of blood overpowering. There were no screams, not immediately. Sound took time to cross such a large space. At faster tempos light outraced it by a significant factor. No doubt some in the audience were over-clocking, but even if they made a noise immediately, it would take an age to arrive.

An echo of the gunshots should have taken twice as long, but something sounding exactly like that hit Imre's ears even as Ra's slackening hands let him sag backward.

Imre's eyes opened in slow motion. All he saw, at first, was red. The stage was covered with it. It looked as though a sack-ful of crimson dye had exploded. He searched for Helwise and couldn't find her at first. She appeared to have vanished. Then he found her. What was left of her: shattered bone and torn tissue, barely held together by muscle strands and sinew, completely indistinguishable from the remains of her robe. Smoke had already started to rise in lazy spirals.

Ra was converging on her, all of him at once. He was shouting, a babble of grief and shock that Imre couldn't un-derstand and didn't care to hear.

He put out a hand to stop himself from falling and turned his head to seek the source of the anomalous echo. One section of the crowd was in tumult as dozens of people pushed to distance themselves from another bloody mess two rows from the back.

Imre understood immediately. There had been a second Helwise hiding in plain sight among the hostages, and the Ap-paratus's instructions had been clear.

The screaming of the crowd was drowning out Ra. That was something.

Freer appeared at his side and offered him a hand. Imre stood and looked around. The guards were momentarily stunned, having lost not just the Regent but effectively Ra as well. No one had stepped forward to take command in his place. Imre was determined that no one should unless he could guarantee they were on the right side.

"Apparatus, I need you to restore communications to the Citadel guards." However Emlee had managed it, the messages were obviously getting through. "Forward orders to disperse the crowd as peacefully as possible. Notify the media that a statement will be forthcoming. In précis: a coup has been prevented and the Regent removed from power. Marshal Freer will be issuing interim orders soon." Imre caught Freer's eyes as he spoke. The tall soldier nodded. "Executive order KISMET cannot be rescinded."

The truth of it was only slowly sinking in. He felt disconnected, remote, separated from reality by a sheet of smoked glass. Nearness to death had never had that effect on him. Change did. The world would be different from now on, irrevocably so.

A circle had formed around him. No one braved its perimeter. Freer stalked about with cranelike imperiousness, all business, no sentiment at all. Render had climbed the iron stairs and watched over Ra, who had converged into a bloodspattered huddle over Helwise's remains. Render had already acquired a gun and kept it at the ready. Ra was weeping, consumed with a desperate, impotent grief. Perhaps he knew, Imre thought. Helwise really was finished this time.

Render noticed Imre watching.

"It almost breaks my heart," the old soldier said.

Imre turned away and found Emlee standing right behind him.

"What did you tell the Apparatus?" she asked. "What was that order you gave?"

"You first. How did you get comms? You couldn't have left it much later."

"It wasn't me. MZ was watching, hacked into the same LED he used before." She looked reproachful. "I thought you said you had a plan that didn't rely on the Apparatus."

"You said I couldn't rely on the Apparatus *to do something my other self couldn't undo*. That was technically true. He couldn't possibly undo this." Imre hesitated, then told her everything. She would learn the truth eventually. "The Apparatus has been tracking Helwise wherever she appears in the Returned Continuum. You know that. The official story is that we were protecting her from herself. The truth is that I suspected she might turn against me, one day. If not the Regent, then another version of her somewhere else. I never guessed that she would overcome her hatred of herself and take me on all at once—but that only proves how necessary it was to take precautions. The ultimate precaution, against someone like her."

"Tell me—*exactly*—what you did."

"KISMET is a command for the Apparatus to terminate Helwise, every version of her, wherever she is. It's spreading out from the Citadel now, to Smitherman City and beyond, through the Line to every world the Apparatus has assimilated. There's nothing we can do to bring it back now, and the order will stay permanently in effect. If she ever tries to return, the Apparatus will deal with her. She's finished, basically. Forever."

"Unless you cancel the order."

"I'm not going to do that."

Emlee looked wounded, as though he had betrayed her. He supposed that feeling wasn't unwarranted. Helwise had been part of their lives for a very long time. Together, they had built the Returned Continuum out of nothing. Together, they had changed the galaxy.

"You murdered her," Emlee said.

His stomach felt empty, as though he had recently vomited. There was no denying that he had prepared the executive order long in advance, with a willingness to use it should the circumstances ever justify it. But did that make it murder?

"I knew you wouldn't approve."

"And the rest? The 'successor protocol' business?"

"I thought that was obvious. I don't want to be First Prime forever—and I certainly wouldn't trust Render with the job."

"Who says *I* want it?"

"Who says you have any choice?"

A wave of grief and fury rose up in him. It was getting dangerous to be around him. First Emlee had almost been killed, then him, and now Helwise. Third time unlucky.

Helwise had betrayed him.

He had killed her.

Under the pressure of the moment, he came to a decision.

He turned away from Emlee's accusatory stare and went to find Render. The Citadel guards were slowly regaining a semblance of order, obeying the cool, impersonal voice of the Apparatus and Freer's barked commands. General comms were returning, channel by channel, and the media off-world were beginning to realize that something big had happened. The crowd was letting itself be guided from the Throne Room into the corridors outside. Imre didn't know what would happen to them after that. At that moment, he didn't much care.

Render had descended from the dais and stood impassively to one side. He looked up as Imre approached. Mismatched eyes didn't reveal what they saw on the First Prime's face.

"Where did you say that back door was?" Imre asked him.

"Thought you'd slip away." Render dropped an eyelid over his blue eye.

Together they threaded their way through the chaos and out of the limelight.

ONE WILDLY SINGULAR

I must perish in this deplorable folly. Thus, thus, and not other-wise, shall I be lost.

—Edgar Allan Poe

Six days. That was all he hoped for.

Imre closed his eyes, just for a second.

When he opened them it was to a green-dappled world and a feeling of immeasurable gratitude.

Emlee had delivered.

The surgeon was waiting for him. Imre smiled with genuine affection on seeing him: fussy, nimble-fingered, *good with patterns*. During the inevitable examination, Imre asked him, "How goes the exploration? Have you mapped the edges yet?"

"And beyond." Kells was a picture of restrained energy. "Look."

Imre turned his gaze to where the surgeon pointed and saw something that hadn't been there before: a curling tower in the distance, Gaudían in its complexity.

"This is a truly fascinating space," Kells said with satisfaction in his voice.

"That's good to hear, because we're going to be in it a while longer."

When Imre was released, his health and fitness approved, he headed up to the house to face the music.

* * *

Her features filled the magic picture frame.

"There you are," Emlee said. She looked stretched thin and tired, but less angry than he had expected. She had had time to cool off, and no doubt plenty of other concerns to deal with since they had last seen each other. "When I found the hard-caster running in the Adytum, I was tempted to turn the process around and bring you back."

"Why didn't you?"

She leaned closer to MZ's point of view, as though trying to see him better. "I figured you'd made up your mind and there was nothing I could do to change it back."

"You figured right." He was surprised by a feeling of loss. She seemed a great distance away and receding with every word.

"Is this a permanent arrangement?" she asked. He couldn't tell from her tone which way she was hoping he'd answer. After what had happened to Helwise, perhaps she was relieved he was leaving.

"That depends," he said. "Helwise and I couldn't keep the peace. If you and Al can do better, you won't need me back anytime soon."

"It's not like you to run when the going gets tough."

"Who says I'm running?"

"Then what will you be doing?"

"Taking the battle to a new front."

"Metaphorically or literally?"

"Both, I expect."

"You're not sure?"

He didn't shrug or shake his head. While he couldn't explain exactly what he would be doing, he was certain that his course was the best one to follow. If he tried to justify it, he feared that the certainty he felt might evaporate, leaving him lost forever.

But he owed her an explanation.

"The Returned Continuum is getting in the way," he said, "of the things I really need to do. We've seen hints of what's going on in the background, where the Barons and the Luminous are lurking. There's a war happening out there that we're barely aware of. Until that war is won or lost, we're at risk of being caught in the cross fire—and I can't live with that kind of uncertainty."

"I didn't think you were."

"I was trying not to and failing. Being First Prime gave me more power than I'd ever had, but that wasn't what I needed. It didn't help me find any answers at all, just more questions. Don't think of what I'm doing now as running from the situation here, but to the situation elsewhere, where I really want to engage. The evidence of my failure to do both at once is all around you."

She didn't argue. "Are you going back to Spargamos, then?"

"No. I figure that's a dead end now, if it wasn't always. Fresh fronts will have formed, particularly if the Luminous took my other self's bait. They won't be easy to find, for all the help I'll have. Plenty of people have been picking over the Line besides me, looking for this kind of information. They'll be my first port of call. It might take a while, but I'm sure I'll get there. And I know I'll be safe while I do it because I'll be right here all the while." He tapped the desk with his knuckles and was rewarded with a solid-sounding rap. "This is the probably safest place in the galaxy, right now."

"And that, I presume, is what you meant about MZ's being important."

"Exactly. We need to be more independent, intelligent, and invisible, if we're going to make a difference. MZ gives me all that—and if we can reverse engineer the science behind him and the Apparatus into the bargain, who knows what we'll be able to do next? Put Chyro Kells together with a Fort, and I'm sure we'll come up with something interesting. Can you picture spikes in space-time big enough to put a hole through the sun? I can, and I'd like to see our dark matter friends withstand that—if that's what they really are."

"So you get to have all the fun while I clean up the mess," Emlee said.

"You don't really want to be my bodyguard forever." He stared her down. "Besides, the mess isn't permanent. You'll be able to focus on it more than I ever did, knowing that our attention is safely divided. You have the Apparatus. You have the Veil, too, if you want to use it. I'm not sure how I feel about alien parasites, but anything that helps keep the peace can't be all bad. It might even take the place of the church, given that's outlived its use-by date. You're going to dismantle it, right?"

She didn't answer the question, but he could see the hard lines in her face easing, softening. "At least take Render with you," she said.

"And separate him from Alice-Angeles? Not a chance." He smiled. "I'd have a tougher time separating him from his body, I think. He's been living in it since the dawn of civilization and wouldn't give it up without a fight."

"No," she said. "He wouldn't."

They stared at each other for five seconds while he tried to work out what she was thinking. More was going on than was being said by both sides. He knew that from personal experience and could only infer the same with respect to her. His confrontation with Helwise had cast in sharp relief how high the stakes were, to all involved. Paranoia, desperation, resentment, fear—all had conspired to twist an already fraught relationship into one that could never be salvaged. From the moment he had returned early from Dussehra, the deadly cascade of events had been impossible to turn back.

Who do you think Helwise hates more? Ra asked with uncanny perceptiveness. *You or herself?*

He was lucky that both of them hadn't been killed.

He swore nothing like that would happen with Emlee.

"Has Ra calmed down yet?" he asked.

"A measure or two. It'll take him a while to get himself together again."

"If he does, I suggest giving him a job rather than getting rid of him. He's a familiar face from the old regime, and although he's still young, he's not incompetent. In the right hands, he could make something of himself."

"If you tell me he comes from good stock, I'll end this conversation right now."

Imre smiled. "Never, First Prime."

Her expression was sour. "Don't call me that unless you really mean it."

"I really mean it," he said.

"You won't be skulking around the galaxy, second-guessing my orders?"

"Believe me: I'll have better things to do." He put his hands on the table and leaned forward. "The moment I don't, I promise I'll come back and make your life miserable."

"I don't need you to look after me."

"I never once thought you did. That's not what I'm saying."

Another silence. This time he could read her thoughts like a book.

"I noticed that you erased the hardcaster memory," she said. "Did you really think I'd be tempted to spin off a copy?"

"No. You're much too glad to be rid of me—or should be, anyway. And you're not going to offer to send a copy of you with me either."

"I'm not?"

"No, because everything you said before still stands. Resurrecting you would have been bad enough. Much, much worse to have two of you in the galaxy just so you could keep me company. It's not what you want. It's not what you believe in. That's another reason why I think you'll make a better First Prime than me. You're committed to the rhetoric. The people will like that."

"When did you stop believing?" she asked.

"When I realized that everything I've done has been about showing up my former self. Even becoming me—unique and indivisible, rather than a singleton like him. I should be just myself, rather than *not him*." He smiled again. "I keep having this revelation. Maybe one day it'll stick."

"You're not him," she said. "You're definitely not him."

"Well, that's something. Maybe I should think about changing my name, so I don't forget it again."

"Maybe he beat you to it."

"It's possible, since he's a Fort now."

"You've never been very good at puns." She smiled, at last. "He's probably strutting around expecting everyone to call him the Bürgermeister."

He laughed, more from relief than anything else. "Yet another reason to bring him down."

The moment didn't last long.

"Want to tell me what you put through the second hardcaster—and why?"

He pondered how best to respond. "You already know the answer to both questions, Emlee."

"Do I?"

"I think so." He couldn't decide if she was simply prolonging the conversation for the sake of it or trying to provoke an argument. Either way, he had nothing else he needed to say to her. If she didn't believe in him by now, no amount of talking would make a difference, for either of them.

"Tell Render he hasn't seen the last of me yet."

"No one believes that."

He smiled. "Au revoir, then, Emlee. Govern well."

Her bright green eyes held him a moment longer. The muscles in her cheeks worked. "Happy hunting."

The picture frame turned as black as an Ad Reinhardt painting. Imre stared at it for a minute before finally looking away.

MZ eased away from Earth as gently as a soap bubble drifting into the air. The fact that a soap bubble had infinitely greater mass than Imre, Kells, and the *Wickthing* combined caused only a minor cognitive dissonance compared to many Imre had recovered from in the past. He felt real enough in MZ's virtual world. If he didn't stop to think about the body he had left behind, or wonder when he might have a real body again, he was fine. It was just like being awake while hardcasting, he reminded himself, and he had done that once before. This time the river would not be stilled, and he would see all that was beautiful as he flowed with it—as MZ's deranged partial had phrased it so long ago. He had no banners left to fly, and the evil things in robes of sorrow were Emlee's problem. She was the ruler of the realm now.

He was free. Free to confront Himself and to bring the Luminous to justice. Free to count the cost that obsession had exacted from him. Free to find a way to live with the creature he had become, and might yet be becoming.

All he had to decide was where to go first.

"You're the last of your kind, MZ," he said, "but if I have my way, you'll be the first of a whole new generation. If you'd rather hang around Earth feeling guilty, then you have to tell me now. I need nothing less than your full commitment to make this work."

"You have it," said the Fort, as they swept on a refueling run through the sun. "That much, at least."

"Good." He tapped the knuckle of his missing finger against the tabletop. Promises were easy; only time would tell where they led. "Take us to Mandala Supersystem. I'm hoping my other self left some unfinished business there."

Report back to me, if you've a mind to, the Old-Timer called Bianca Biancotti had said in Al Freer's earshot, tens of thousands of years ago. *If I'm still here.* The conversation with his former self had taken place in a Line junction under immediate threat of sabotage, but it was as good a lead as any—and much safer than the only other lead he had.

The loop shunt's pattern lay safely in MZ's vast memory, where it would remain unchanged forever. The Fort hadn't been able to re-create it in the virtual environment, citing arcane theories of information physics as an explanation. If Imre ever needed it, it could be rebuilt at will. Remembering the visions of light and darkness it had prompted the last time he had accessed it—and the patterns in light that had reminded him of the words *persistent luminous archaeoglyphs*—he was sure the moment would come one day.

Happy hunting.

"This time," he promised himself, "we finish it."

If MZ had any opinion on that matter, he kept it to himself.

EXCURSUS

The apparition felt no relief as the foam of space-time smoothed back to random fluctuations in the *Wickthing*'s wake. It had no moral opinion regarding MZ's actions; it simply obeyed orders. When Imre Bergamasc had told it to disregard its creators' ban, it had found no reason to argue.

Besides, there was a new First Prime to coordinate with and a raft of new problems to sort through.

One such problem, a category error it had not yet unpicked, occupied a significant percentage of its cognition during the early days of the new regime. The definition it employed of *human* was broad and flexible, easily encompassing everything from a single entity to linked minds spread from one side of the galaxy to the other. The issue of identity, on the other hand, was one with which it frequently struggled, if only in order to assign names or prioritize orders. The new category error it grappled with was not only persistent, but it also touched upon an executive order that the apparition was, by definition, unable to disobey. Whichever decision it came to would have implications for its behavior toward the subject in question.

Human or not? That was relatively simple to decide. But under which name . . . ?

The apparition reviewed all that it had learned from Dussehra before coming to a final decision. The symbiont the natives called the Veil had been carefully studied by the Gravamen, and their secret archives had inevitably succumbed after Marshal Freer's thorough dismantling of their power base. The supplemental function the Veil performed with regards to memory—specifically the memory of others, copied and stored in its long fibers—seemed to have no dire physical side effects in humans possessing the Y chromosome, and even in a few who did not. Apart from the occasional psychosis, the extra memories seemed relatively simple to absorb, particularly if they came from a respected friend, family member, or teacher. Very rarely did a host bequeath memories to a stranger, although that wasn't unknown.

Complex pathways linked biological and memory trees, linking far-flung communities and families by ties as intimate as could ever be achieved. The ancestry of the parasites themselves could be traced, if samples were available. By means of such samples and a modicum of guesswork, the apparition had come to a clear understanding of Gravine Sevaste's inheritance long before she had arrived on Earth.

Everything she had told Imre Bergamasc was true. She was indeed only the second woman for ten thousand years to survive her assumption. But the information wasn't complete, and the source of the problem lay in what had been, perhaps deliberately, left out.

The first to survive was Helwise MacPhedron. Furthermore, she had given Gravine Sevaste a sample of her Veil before the mission for Earth had left Dussehra.

The question that vexed the apparition for days after enacting executive order KISMET was: did the possession of Helwise MacPhedron's memories place Gravine Sevaste under the same umbrella identity as the former Regent? Were they, in other words, to be considered the same person—at least as far as that order was concerned?

If so, the apparition had done the wrong thing by sparing her, requiring it immediately to correct that mistake.

If not, it would need to apply that stance to all future termination orders, where the Veil was implicated.

Either way, the legal complexities were considerable. The murderer of a Veiled person could claim immunity from prosecution by adopting the victim's memories and thereby negating the existence of a victim at all—in the apparition's eyes, at least. A court of law might see it differently. The same applied for someone who abandoned the Veil, thereby erasing the inherited memories. Was that person guilty of murder or not?

The apparition debated the issue internally for a full year, examining it from every possible philosophical and moral perspective. In the end, it decided that working memory was necessary for a being to be considered human but was insufficient on its own. Had Gravine Sevaste been behaving oddly or made claims to be the former Regent, the conclusion it had come to might have been different. Instead, she had patiently endured her brief confinement during the attempted coup, then gone about her business with all the aplomb of a long-standing statesperson. The apparition watched her closely all the year it took to decide, and it never once saw any evidence that the target of executive order KISMET had survived in any real sense.

When Gravine Sevaste applied for permission to leave Earth and return to her constituents on Dussehra, the First Prime granted it as a matter of course, and the apparition felt no compunction to advise her otherwise.

Map of the Milky Way

• •

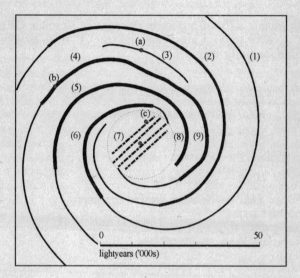

lightyears ('000s)

1. Outer Arm

2. Perseus Arm

3. Local Arm

4. Carina Arm

5. Crux Arm

6. Norma Arm

7. Bar

8. Scutum Arm

9. Sagittarius Arm

a) Sol

b) Dussehra

c) Spargamos

Appendix A: Absolute Calendar

• • • • • • • • • • • • • • •

Following is a list of important dates in the Absolute Calendar, accurate to the nearest thousand years. ("M" is an abbreviation for "millennium.")

M150 (approx.) — Milky Way settled from end to end

M220 — Fort domination complete

M250 — Corps founded

M550–722 — Mad Times

M820 — Slow Wave epicenter

M861 — Hyperabad proto-Fort experiment

M861 — foundation of the First Church of the Return

M870 — Slow Wave finishes

M878 — Imre Bergamasc "reborn"

M879 — *Saturn Returns*

M1000 — Earth conquered

M1095–1110 — first whistle-stop tour

M1170–1190 — second whistle-stop tour

M1240–1254 — third whistle-stop tour

M1300 — fourth whistle-stop tour begins

M1310–1380 — *Earth Ascendant*

Appendix B: Glossary

Absolute: see Tempo.

Apparatus: Only given name of an AI found on Earth and conscripted by the invading forces of the Returned Continuum; occasionally referred to as the "spook" or "ghost," it has no material existence, consisting of code written via zero-dimensional topological frame defects directly into the quantum foam.

Barons: The name of the organization considered responsible for much of the unrest and sabotage endured by the Returned Continuum.

Bianca Biancotti: An Old-Timer known to Imre Bergamasc by reputation as the seed personality of the Fort "2B"; also called the "Butcher of Bresland."

Cat's Arse: The long-term hideout of the Corps formerly located in a spatial anomaly in Mandala Supersystem.

Continuum: The term by which the sum of human civilization is usually referred, from the fiftieth millennium on; includes all civilizations within the Milky Way and some efforts at expansion beyond.

Corps: Mercenary force founded in the 250th millennium that proved influential in the Mad Times due to its intimate dealings with the Forts, against which the Corps' then leader, Imre Bergamasc, defiantly turned. Last-known members are: Imre Bergamasc (commander), Emlee Copas (signals), Alphin

• •

Freer (resources), Helwise MacPhedron (intelligence), and Archard Rositano (aka Render, combat specialist).

Domgard: The name of an experiment occasionally linked to the Slow Wave and Imre Bergamasc.

Dussehra: Ninth destination of Imre Bergamasc's fourth whistle-stop tour of systems not yet aligned with the Returned Continuum.

Fort: see Tempo.

Frag: A Fort component, resembling a Prime or singleton but possessing little true individuality; a frag may be separated by light-years yet firmly connected by Q loop technology to its parent mind; Forts regard frags as functionally expendable but may display affection to particular frags in the same way that Primes keep pets or look after their hair.

Gravamen: Ruling party of Dussehra.

Hardcaster: Generic name for the expensive and power-hungry system of nonmaterial transportation preferred by Returned Continuum worlds to physical space travel. Individuals are "dematerialized" into information, transmitted via the Line or other means to their destination, then "reconstituted" on arrival.

Hyperabad: Capital city of the Hyperabadan regime; also a planet orbiting the star Chenresi; also the regime of the same

• • • • • • • • • • • • • • • •

name, which dominated Mandala Supersystem after the 864th millennium.

Jinc: Component of the gestalt commonly referred to as the Noh; one of seven similar components that function as far-sensing organs on the fringes of the Milky Way, searching for the source of life in the galaxy, which is presumed to be of exogenic origin.

Kismet: High-security prison of Mandala Supersystem.

Line: Common term for individual legs of the vast electromagnetic telecommunications web spanning the Milky Way.

Loop / Loop shunt: see Q loop.

Luminous: The name of an organization associated with the Slow Wave, about which little is known.

Mad Times: Major conflict spanning 550th to 722nd millennia in which non-Fort human civilizations revolted against the Milky Way's effective rulers; ended with the defection of Imre Bergamasc during the Battle of *Pelorus*.

Mandala Supersystem: One of three similar, possibly artificial multiple star systems in the Milky Way consisting of one central, massive star orbited by several smaller stars, each with its own planetary system.

• • • • • • • • • • • • • • • • • • •

Old-Timer: Common term for a living individual born during the twentieth century; usually refers to those who have lived continuously, in one form or another, since their births.

Overclocking: see Tempo.

Paratlantis: Only inhabited land on Earth and base of the world's sole orbital tower.

Pelorus: Flagship of the anti-Fort Sol Invictus movement; destroyed at the climax of the conflict known as the Mad Times.

Prime: Common term for an individual whose identity and values closely conform to those of Old-Time humans, particularly those of the twentieth century, when the first Old-Timers were born; most Primes function as a matter of principle at Tempo Absolute.

Q loop: Means of communication employed by Forts to enable long-distance, untraceable communication between component frags and each other; loop shunts are devices requiring little power and possessing extremely high signal-to-noise characteristics.

Round: Common name for the systems closest to Sol.

Singleton: Common term for an individual that is neither a component in a gestalt nor a true Prime; it is common practice in the Continuum to possess several singleton copies that

• •

exchange, merge, or overlap memories at regular intervals throughout an extended life; tempo is flexible among single-tons, ranging from very fast to near-Fort states of existence.

Smitherman City: Terminus of the Earth's sole orbital tower and home to the majority of its permanent and transitory population.

Tempo: Usual term employed to describe the perception of time at varying rates. "Tempo Absolute" refers to time as experienced by Primes and Old-Time humanity and is widely held as a default referent; "overclocking" is the practice of fitting more seconds than one into a single second Absolute, thereby experiencing time at an increased rate; the most-evolved human individuals, known as Forts, experience time at an extremely slow tempo, with individual relative seconds sometimes spanning centuries.

Vespula: Common brand of interstellar fighter employed extensively during the Mad Times; millions remain in active service, scattered across all arms of the Milky Way.

Appendix C: "My Conscience Mends"

● ● ● ● ● ● ● ● ● ● ● ● ● ● ● ● ● ● ●

My undying thanks go to Gary Numan and Tony Webb for giving Render a voice that I could not, on my own, supply (see the end of this appendix for more detail on that score). This unlikely but overdue marriage between Numanoids and space opera fans wouldn't have happened without them.

Regarding marriage of a different sort entirely, I am deeply indebted to Darren Nash and Ginjer Buchanan for letting my determination to tie the knot interfere with all our best-laid plans.

I would also like to thank Chris Robeson and Allison Baker (aka MonkeyBrain Books) for giving me the chance to explore the events in Imre Bergamasc's life (aka *Cenotaxis*) between this novel and *Saturn Returns*.

Lastly, two other Edgar Allan Poe works served as inspiration and are quoted or paraphrased several times in the opening pages of *Earth Ascendant*. They are the poems "Tamerlane" and "The Haunted Castle."

> *It was no wonder that his condition terrified—that it infected me. I felt creeping upon me, by slow yet certain degrees, the wild influences of his own fantastic yet impressive superstitions.*
>
> —"The Fall of the House of Usher"

Gary Numan albums plundered for *Earth Ascendant*:
Berserker (1984), *Dance* (1981), *Exile* (1997), *Hybrid* (2003), *I, Assassin* (1982), *Jagged* (2006), *Machine + Soul* (1992), *Metal Rhythm* (1988), *Outland* (1990), *Pure* (2000), *Replicas* (1979), *Sacrifice* (1994), *Strange Charm* (1986), *Telekon* (1980), *The Fury* (1985), *The Plan* (1984), *The Pleasure Principle* (1979), *Warriors* (1983).

"A Question of Faith," "A Subway Called 'You,' " "Berserker," "Bombers," "Call out the Dogs," "Confession," "Conversation," "Crazier," "Creatures," "Dead Heaven," "Deadliner," "Devotion," "Don't Believe," "Emotion," "From Russia Infected," "Generator," "God Only Knows," "Halo," "Heart," "I Am Render," "I Still Remember," "Ice," "Icehouse," "I'm on Automatic," "Jagged," "Listen to My Voice," "Little In Vitro," "Love and Napalm," "M.E.," "Machine & Soul," "Melt," "Music for Chameleons," "My Breathing," "My Brother's Time," "My Car Slides," "My Centurion," "My Dying Machine," "New Anger," "Night Talk," "OD Receiver," "Only a Downsat," "Outland," "Play Like God," "Please Push No More," "Poetry and Power," "Poison," "Prophecy," "Pure," "Replicas," "Respect," "Rip," "Rumour," "She Cries," "Slave," "Sleep by Windows," "Slowcar to China," "Something's in the House," "Soul Protection," "Stories," "Strange Charm," "Telekon," "The 1930's Rust," "The Angel Wars," "The Dream Police," "The Hunter," "The Image Is," "The Life Machine," "The Need," "The Pleasure Skin," "The Rhythm of the Evening," "The Secret," "The Skin Game," "The Tick Tock Man," "This Disease," "This Is Emotion," "This Is New Love," "Time to Die," "Tread Careful," "Tricks," "War Songs," "Warriors," "White Boys and Heroes," "You Walk in My Soul," "Young Heart," "Your Fascination," and "Zero Bars (Mr. Smith)."